*USA Today* bestselling author **Naima Simone**'s love of romance was first stirred by Mills & Boon books pilfered from her grandmother. Now she spends her days writing sizzling romances with a touch of humour and snark.

She is wife to her own real-life superhero and mother to two awesome kids. They live in perfect domestically challenged bliss in the southern United States.

**Joss Wood** loves books and travelling—especially to the wild places of southern Africa and, well, anywhere. She's a wife, a mum to two teenagers and slave to two cats. After a career in local economic development, she now writes full-time. Joss is a member of Romance Writers of America and Romance Writers of South Africa.

Discover more at millsandboon.co.uk

# TRUST FUND FIANCÉ

NAIMA SIMONE

# RECKLESS ENVY

JOSS WOOD

MILLS & BOON

First Published in Great Britain 2020
by Mills & Boon, an imprint of HarperCollinsPublishers,
1 London Bridge Street, London, SE1 9GF

*Trust Fund Fiancé* © 2020 Harlequin Books S.A.
*Reckless Envy* © 2020 Harlequin Books S.A.

Special thanks and acknowledgements are given to Naima Simone for her contribution to the *Texas Cattleman's Club: Rags to Riches* series

Special thanks and acknowledgements are given to Joss Wood for her contribution to the *Dynasties: Seven Sins* series

ISBN: 978-0-263-28001-2

0920

**MIX**
Paper from
responsible sources
**FSC**
www.fsc.org
**FSC® C007454**

This book is produced from independently certified FSC™ paper to ensure responsible forest management.

For more information visit: www.harpercollins.co.uk/green

Printed and bound in Spain
by CPI, Barcelona

# TRUST FUND FIANCÉ

## NAIMA SIMONE

To Gary. 143.

# One

A man had a few pleasures in life.

For Ezekiel "Zeke" Holloway, they included kicking back on the black leather couch in the den of the three-bedroom guesthouse that he and his older brother, Luke, shared on the Wingate family estate. He had an ice-cold beer in one hand, a slice of meat lovers pizza in the other and Pittsburgh playing on the mounted eighty-five-inch flat-screen television. Granted, he might've been born and bred in Texas, but his heart belonged to the Steelers.

And then there was this. He lifted the dark brown cigar with its iconic black-and-red label and studied the smoldering red tip before bringing it to his lips and inhaling. A hint of pepper and chocolate, toasted macadamia nuts and, of course, the dark flavor of cognac. It could be addictive…if he allowed it to be. These cigars cost fifteen thousand dollars a box. Which was why he only permitted himself to enjoy one per month. Not because he couldn't afford to buy more. It was about discipline; he mastered his urges, not vice versa.

And in a world that had suddenly become unfamiliar, cold and uncertain, he needed to believe he could control something in his life. Even if it was when he smoked a cigar.

He sighed, bracing a hand on the balcony column and slowly exhaling into the night air. Behind him, the muted hum of chatter filtered through the closed glass doors. Guests gathered in the cavernous parlor behind him. James

Harris, current president of the Texas Cattleman's Club—of which Ezekiel was a member—hosted the "small" dinner party. As a highly successful horse breeder in Royal, Texas, and a businessman, James commanded attention without trying. And when he invited a person to his elegant, palatial home, he or she attended.

Even if they would be rubbing elbows with the newly infamous Wingates.

Bringing the cigar to his lips again, Ezekiel stared out into the darkness. Beneath the blanket of the black, star-studded night, he could barely make out the stables, corrals and long stretch of land that made up James's property. He rolled his shoulders, as if the motion could readjust and shift the cumbersome burden of worry, anger and, yes, fear that seemed to hang around his neck like an albatross. It was ludicrous, but he could practically feel the hushed murmurs crawl over his skin through his black dinner jacket and white shirt like the many legs of a centipede. He could massage his chest and still nothing would alleviate the weight of the censure—the press of the guilty verdicts already cast his and his family's way.

Not even the influence and support of James Harris could lessen that.

Lucky for Ezekiel and his family that the denizens of Royal high society hungered for a party invitation from James more than they wanted to outright ostracize the Wingates.

Ezekiel snorted, his lips twisting around the cigar. Thank God for small favors.

"And here I thought I'd found the perfect escape hatch."

Ezekiel jerked his head to the side at the husky, yet very feminine drawl. His mouth curved into a smile. And not the polite, charming and utterly fake one he'd worn all evening. Instead, true affection wound through him like a slowly unfurling ribbon.

Reagan Sinclair glided forward out of the shadows and into the dim glow radiating from the beveled glass balcony doors. It was enough to glimpse her slender but curvaceous body. The high thrust of her small but firm breasts. The fingertip-itching dip of her waist and intriguing swell of her hips. As she drew nearer to him and a scent that reminded him of honeysuckle and cream teased his nostrils, he castigated himself.

At twenty-six, Reagan was only four years his junior, but she was good friends with his cousin Harley, and he'd known her most of her life. She was as "good girl" as they came, with her flawless pedigree and traditional upbringing. Which meant she had no business being out here with him in his current frame of mind.

Not when the dark, hungry beast he usually hid behind carefree, wide grins and wry jokes clawed closer to the surface.

Not when the only thing that usually satisfied that animal was a willing woman and hot, dirty sex. No...*fucking*.

Ezekiel blew out a frustrated breath. Yes, he'd had sex, but made love to a woman? No, he hadn't done that in eight long years.

If he had any sense or the morals that most believed he didn't possess, he would put out his cigar, gently grasp her by the elbow and escort her back to her parents. Away from him. He should—

Reagan touched him.

Just the feel of her slim, delicate hand on his biceps was like a cooling, healing balm. It calmed the anger, the fear. Leashed the hunger. At least so he could meet her thickly lashed, entirely too-innocent eyes and not imagine seeing them darken with a greedy lust that he placed there.

"I know why I'm hiding," he drawled, injecting a playfulness he was far from feeling into his voice. "What's your excuse?"

Those eyes, the color of the delicious chicory coffee his mother used to have shipped from New Orleans, softened, understanding somehow making them more beautiful. And horrible.

He glanced away.

On the pretense of finishing his smoke, he shifted to the side, inserting space between them. Not that he could escape that damn scent that seemed even headier with her so close. Or the sharp-as-a-razor's-edge cheekbones. Or the lush, downright impropriety of her mouth. The smooth bronze of her skin that damn near gleamed...

*You've known her since she was a girl. You have no business thinking of her naked, sweating and straining beneath you.*

Dammit. He narrowed his gaze on the moon-bleached vista of James's ranch. His dick wasn't having any of that reasoning though. Too bad. He had enough of a shit storm brewing in his life, in his family, in Wingate Enterprises. He refused to add screwing Reagan Sinclair to it.

In a life full of selfish decisions, that might be the cherry on top of his asshole sundae.

And regardless of what some people might think, he possessed lines he didn't cross. A sense of honor that had been drilled into him by his family before he'd even been old enough to understand what the word meant. And as a little dented and battered as the Wingate name might be right now, they were still Wingates.

That meant something here in Royal.

It meant something to him.

"Let's see." She pursed her lips and tapped a fingernail against the full bottom curve. "Should I start alphabetically? A, avoiding my parents introducing me to every single man here between the ages of twenty-two and eighty-two. B, boring small talk about the unseasonably hot summer—it's Texas, mind you—gel versus acrylic nails and, my personal favorite, whether MTV really did need a reboot of *The Hills*. Which, the only answer to that is no. And C, karma—I avoided every one of Tracy Drake's calls last week because the woman is a terrible gossip. And now I find out that I'm seated next to her at dinner."

He snorted. "I'm pretty sure karma starts with a *K*," he said, arching an eyebrow.

"I know." She shrugged a slim shoulder, a smile riding one corner of her mouth. "I couldn't think of anything for *C*."

Their soft laughter rippled on the night air, and for the first time since arriving this evening, the barbed tension inside him loosened.

"And I just needed air that didn't contain politics, innuendo or cigar smoke," she continued. The velvet tone called to mind tangled, sweaty sheets at odds with her perfectly styled hair and immaculately tailored, strapless cocktail dress that spoke of unruffled poise. Even as Ezekiel's rebellious brain conjured up images of just how much he *could* ruffle her poise, she slid him a sidelong glance. "One out of three isn't bad."

Again, the miraculous happened, and he chuckled. *Enjoying* her. "I know it would be the gentlemanly thing to put this out…" he lifted the offending item between them "…but it's one of my few vices—"

"Just a few?" she interrupted, a dimple denting one of her cheeks.

"And I'm going to savor it," he finished, shooting her a mock frown for her cheekiness. Cute cheekiness. "Besides, no one in there would accuse me of being a gentleman."

Dammit. He hadn't meant to let that slip. Not the words and definitely not the bitterness. He was the carefree jokester of the Holloway brothers. He laughed and teased; he *didn't* brood. But these last few months had affected them all. Turned them into people they sometimes didn't recognize.

Talk and accusations of corruption and fraud did that to a person.

So did a headlong tumble from a pedestal, only to discover those you'd known for years were only wearing the masks of friends, hiding their true faces underneath. Vultures. Sharks.

Predators.

He forced a smile, and from the flash of sadness that flickered across her lovely features, the twist of his lips must've appeared as fake as it felt. For a moment, anger that wasn't directed at himself for fucking caring about the opinions of others blazed within him. Now it was presently aimed at her. At her pity that he hated. That he probably deserved.

And he resented that more.

"Gentlemen are highly overrated," she murmured, before he could open his mouth and let something mean and regrettable pour out. Her quiet humor snuffed out the flame of his fury. Once more the utter *calm* of her presence washed over him, and part of him wanted to soak in it until the grime of the past few months disappeared from his skin, his mind, his heart. "Besides, I want to hear more about some of these vices."

"No, you don't," he contradicted.

Unable to resist, he snagged a long, loose wave resting on her shoulder. He pinched it, testing the thickness, the silkiness of it between his thumb and forefinger. It didn't require much imagination to guess how it would feel whispering across his bare chest, his abdomen. His thighs. Soft. Ticklish. And so damn erotic, his cock already hardened in anticipation. As if scalded by both the sensation and the too-hot mental image, he released his grip, tucking the rebellious hand in his pants pocket.

Giving himself time to banish his impure thoughts toward his cousin's friend, he brought the cigar to his mouth. Savoring the flavor of chocolate and cognac. Letting it obscure the illusory taste of honeysuckle, vanilla and female flesh.

"You're too young for that discussion," he added, silently cursing the roughness of his tone.

"Oh really?" She tilted her head to the side. "You do know I'm only four years younger than you, right? Or are you having trouble with remembering things at your advanced old age of thirty?"

He narrowed his eyes on her. "Brat," he rumbled.

"Not the first time I've heard that," she said, something murkier than the shadows they stood in shifting in her eyes. But then she smiled, and the warmth of it almost convinced him that the emotion had been a trick of the dark. "So don't hold back. And start with the good stuff. And by good, I mean very, very bad."

He exhaled, studying her through the plume of fragrant smoke he blew through slightly parted lips. "You think you can handle my bad, Ray?" he taunted, deliberately using the masculine nickname that used to make her roll her eyes in annoyance.

Anything to remind him that he'd once caught her and Harley practicing kissing on his cousin's pillows. That she used to crush on boy bands with more synthesizers than talent. That he'd wiped her tears and offered to pound on the little shit that had bullied her on the playground over something she couldn't change—her skin color.

Anything to reinforce that she wasn't one of the women whose front doors would witness his walks of shame.

With an arch of a brow, she leaned forward so she couldn't help but inhale the evaporating puff. "Try me," she whispered.

A low, insistent throb pulsed low in his gut, and his abs

clenched, as if grasping for that familiar but somehow different grip of desire.

Desire. For Reagan? Wrong. So damn wrong.

*Coward*, a sibilant voice hissed at him. And he mentally flipped it off, shifting backward and leaning a shoulder against a stone column.

"Let's see," he said, valiantly injecting a lazy note of humor into his voice. "I can put away an entire meat lovers pizza by myself *and* not use a coaster for my beer. I'm unreasonably grouchy if I'm awake before the god-awful hour of seven o'clock. Especially if there's no coffee to chase away my pain. And—this one I'm kind of embarrassed to admit—I buy at least five pairs of socks every month. Apparently, my dryer is a portal to a world where mismatched socks are some kind of special currency. And since I can't abide not matching, I'm constantly a spendthrift on new pairs. There. You now know all of my immoralities."

A beat of silence, and then, "Really?"

He smirked. "Really," he replied, then jerked his chin up. "Your turn. Regale me with all of your sins, little Ray."

As he'd expected, irritation glinted in her chocolate eyes. "I have no idea how I can follow that, but here goes." He huffed out a low chuckle at the thick sarcasm coating her words. "Every night, I slip downstairs after everyone has gone to bed and have a scotch by myself. No one to judge me, you see? Since my nightly ritual could be early signs of me becoming an alcoholic like my uncle James. What else?"

She hummed, trailing her fingertips over her collarbone, her lashes lowering in a pretense of deep thought. But Ezekiel knew better. She'd already given this a lot of consideration. Had already catalogued her perceived faults long before this conversation.

Acid swirled in his stomach, creeping a path up his chest. He straightened from his lounge against the pillar, prepared to nip this in the bud, but she forestalled him by speaking again. And though a part of him yearned to tell her to stop, to warn her not to say another word, the other part… Yeah, that section wanted to hear how imperfect she was. Craved it. Because it made him feel less alone.

More human.

God, he was such a selfish prick.

And yet, he listened.

"I hate roses. I mean, *loathe* them. Which is important because my mother loves them. And every morning there are fresh bouquets of them delivered to the house for every room, including the kitchen. And every day I fight the urge to knock one down just to watch them scatter across the floor in a mess of water, petals and thorns. Because I'm petty like that. And finally…"

She inhaled, turning to look at him, those eyes, stark and utterly beautiful in their intensity, pinning him to his spot against the railing. "Once a month, I drive over to Joplin and visit the bars and restaurants to find a man to take to a hotel for a night. We have hot, filthy sex and then I leave and return home to be Royal socialite darling Reagan Sinclair again."

Heat—blistering hot and scalding—blasted through him, punching him in the chest and searing him to the bone. Jesus, did she just…? *Holy fuck.* Lust ate at him. Lust… and horror. Not because she took charge of her own sexuality. It was a twisted and unfair double standard, how men like him could escort woman after woman on his arm, and screw many more, with only an elbow nudge or knowing wink from society. But a woman doing the same thing? Especially one of Reagan's status? Hell no. So for her to take her pleasure into her own hands? He didn't fault her for it.

But the thought of her trolling those establishments filled with drunk men? Some man who wouldn't have an issue with not taking the utmost care with her? Of potentially hurting her? That sent fear spiking through him, slaying him.

And then underneath the horror swirled something else. Something murkier. Edgier. And better off not being unearthed or examined too closely.

"Reagan..." he whispered.

"Relax," she scoffed, flicking a hand toward his face. "I made the last one up. But turnabout is fair play since I'm almost eighty-two percent sure you were lying to me about at least one of yours. Maybe two."

He froze. Stared at her. Stunned...and speechless. Mirror emotions—hilarity and anger—battled it out within him. He didn't know whether to strangle her for taking twenty years off his life... Or double over with laughter loud enough to bring people rushing through those balcony doors.

"That wasn't very nice," he finally muttered, his fingers in danger of snapping his prized cigar in half. "And payback is not only a bitch but a vengeful one."

"I'm shaking in my Jimmy Choos," she purred.

And this time, he couldn't hold back the bark of laughter. Or the *goodness* of it. Surrendering to the need to touch her, even if in a platonic manner, he moved forward and slipped an arm around her shoulders, hugging Reagan into his side like he used to do when she'd worn braces and friendship bracelets.

There was nothing girlish about the body that aligned with his. Nothing pure about the stirrings in his chest and gut...then *lower*. A new strain took up residence in his body. One that had nothing to do with the whispers and gossiping awaiting him inside. This tension had everything to do with her light, teasing scent, the slender hand branding his chest, the firm, beautiful breasts that pressed against him.

Still, he squeezed her close before releasing her.

"Thank you, Reagan," he murmured.

She studied him, nothing coy in that straightforward gaze. "You're welcome," she said, not pretending to misunderstand him. Another thing he'd always liked about her. Reagan Sinclair didn't play games. At least not with him. "That's what friends are for. And regardless how it appears right now, you have friends, Zeke," she said softly, using his nickname.

He stared down at her. At the kindness radiating from her eyes. An admonishment to hide that gentle heart of hers from people—from *him*—hovered on his tongue. The need to contradict her skulked right behind it.

Instead, he set his cigar down on an ashtray some enterprising soul had left outside on a wrought iron table. He wasn't an animal, so he didn't stub it out like a cigarette, but left it there to burn out on its own. In a while, he'd come back to dispose of it.

Turning to Reagan, he crooked his arm and waited. Without hesitation, she slid hers through his, but as they turned, the balcony door swung open and Douglas Sinclair stepped out.

Ezekiel knew the older man, as he was a member of the TCC. Tall, lanky and usually wearing his signature giant Stetson, he could've been an African-American version of the Marlboro Man. He shared the same brown eyes as his daughter, and right now those eyes were trained on them— or rather on Reagan's arm tucked into his.

A moment later, Douglas lifted his gaze and met Ezekiel's. Her father didn't voice his displeasure, but Ezekiel didn't miss the slight narrowing of his eyes or the barely-there flattening of his mouth. No, Douglas Sinclair was too polite to tell Ezekiel to get his hands off his daughter. But he stated it loud and clear just the same. Ezekiel might be a TCC member as well, but that didn't mean the traditional, reserved gentleman would want his precious daughter anywhere near him.

Not when Ezekiel's family had been accused of falsifying inspections on the jets that WinJet, a subsidiary of Wingate Enterprises, manufactured. Not when three of their workers had been injured on the job because of a fire in one of the manufacturing plants due to a faulty sprinkler system. Not when they'd been sued for those injuries because those inspections hadn't been up-to-date as the reports had stated.

Even as VP of marketing for Wingate Enterprises, Ezekiel had found it damn near impossible to spin this smear on their name. No one wanted to do business with a company so corrupt it would place profit above their employees' welfare. Not that his family was guilty of this sin. But public perception was *everything*.

And while most of the club members had stood behind the Wingates, Douglas hadn't been vocal in his belief in their innocence.

So it was no wonder the man didn't look pleased to find his daughter hiding in the dark with Ezekiel.

Not that Ezekiel could blame him. Reagan shouldn't be out here with him. But not for the reasons her father harbored.

"Reagan," Douglas said, one hand remaining on the door and holding it open. "Your mother has been looking for you. It's almost time for dinner, and Devon Granger is eager to escort you into the dining room since you'll be sitting next to him."

Ezekiel caught the soft sigh that escaped her, and felt the tension invade her slender frame. But when she spoke, her tone remained as soft and respectful as any dutiful daughter to a father she loved and revered.

"Thanks, Dad. I'll be there in a moment," she murmured.

"I'll wait for you," came his implacable reply.

If possible, she stiffened even more, but her lovely features didn't reflect her irritation. Still, anger for the other man's high-handedness kindled in Ezekiel's chest. She was a grown woman, for God's sake, not a wayward toddler. His arm tautened, trapping hers in the crook of his elbow. Next to him, Reagan tipped her head up, glancing at him.

*What the hell are you doing?*

Deliberately, he relaxed his body, releasing her and stepping to the side.

"It was nice seeing you again, Reagan," Ezekiel said. Switching his attention to Douglas, he gave the man an abrupt nod. "You, too, Douglas."

"Ezekiel." Then, extending his hand to his daughter, he added, "Reagan."

She glided forward, sliding her hand into her father's. She didn't shoot one last look over her shoulder at him. Didn't toss him another of her gentle, teasing smiles or a final farewell. Instead, she disappeared through the door, leaving him in darkness once more.

And yeah, it was for the best.

No matter her father's reasons for not wanting to leave her alone with Ezekiel, his concerns were valid. If anyone else had noticed that she stood alone with him in the shadows, the rumors would've burned like a brushfire.

And the longer they remained enclosed in the dark, the harder it would've become for him to remember that she was off-limits to him. Because of their history. Because she was too good for him. Because her parents were seeking out a suitable man for her.

And Ezekiel—a man with a slowly crumbling business empire and more emotional baggage than the airplanes WinJet manufactured—wasn't a good bet.

Not a good bet at all.

# Two

Reagan jogged up the four shallow stone steps to her family's Pine Valley mansion. Once she reached the portico that stretched from one end of the front of the house to the other, she stopped, her chest rising and falling on deep, heavy breaths. Turning, she flattened a palm against one of the columns and, reaching for her foot, pulled it toward her butt in a stretch.

God, she detested running. Not even the beautiful scenery of the well-manicured streets and gorgeous multimillion-dollar homes of their upscale, gated community could distract her from the burn in her thighs, the hitch in her chest or the numbing boredom of it. But regardless, she exited her house every morning at 7:00 a.m. to jog past the mansions where Royal high society slept, the clubhouse larger than most people's homes, the Olympic-size pool that called her to take a refreshing dip, and the eighteen-hole golf course. The chore wasn't about pleasure or even staying healthy or retaining a particular dress size.

It was about discipline.

Everyone in this world had to do things they disliked. But likes and dislikes didn't compare to loyalty, sacrifice, love… And though whether or not she jogged every morning had nothing to do with those ideals, the exercise served as a reminder of what happened when a person lost control.

When they allowed their selfish wants to supersede everything else that mattered.

Her reminder.

Her *penance*.

Didn't matter. She would continue to do it. Even if running never became easier. Never ceased to make her feel like she wanted to collapse and call on the Lord to end her suffering.

Moments later, as she finished her stretching, the door behind her opened. Her father stepped out, and once again that familiar and so complicated flood of emotion poured through her as it did whenever she was in Douglas Sinclair's presence.

Awe. Reverence. Guilt. Shame. Anger. Resentment.

*Love.*

She was a murky, tangled hodgepodge of feelings when it came to her father.

"Good morning, Dad," she greeted, straightening from a deep lunge.

"Reagan." He peered down at her, his customary Stetson not hiding the frown wrinkling his brow. "Out running again, I see." He tsked, shaking his head. "We have a perfectly good gym downstairs with top-of-the-line equipment, and yet you insist on gallivanting around the neighborhood."

*Gallivanting.* If his obvious disapproval didn't grate on her nerves like a cheese grinder, she would've snorted at the old-fashioned word. But that was her father. Old-fashioned. Traditional. Conservative. All nice words to say he liked things done a certain way. Including not having his daughter jog around their posh neighborhood in athletic leggings and a sports tank top. Modest women didn't show their bodies in that fashion.

Unfortunately for him, she couldn't run in a high-waisted gown with a starched collar.

Forcing a smile to her lips, she said, "I'm hardly parading around, Dad. I'm exercising." Before he could respond to that, she pressed on. "Headed into the office?" she asked, already knowing the answer.

She could set her watch by him. Breakfast at 7:00 a.m. Leave for the law office at 7:45. To Douglas Sinclair, integrity was a religion. And that included being accountable to his time and his clients.

"Yes." He glanced down at his watch. "I left a message with your mother, but now that I'm seeing you, please don't forget that we have dinner plans tonight. The Grangers are coming over, and you need to be here. On time," he emphasized. More like commanded. "I understand your committee work is important, but not more so than honoring your commitments. I expect you to be here and dressed at six sharp."

*He doesn't mean to be condescending. Or controlling. Or patronizing. He loves you.*

Silently, she ran the refrain through her head. Over and over until the words melded together. He didn't know about her work at the girls' home in Colonial County. It wasn't his fault he saw her through the lens of another era—outdated traditions, unobtainable expectations…

A disappointed father.

"Devon is attending with his parents. So you need to be at your best tonight," he continued. "You seemed to show interest in him at James Harris's get-together last week. You two talked quite a bit at dinner. With his family, his position in his father's real estate development company and business connections, he would make an ideal husband."

*Jesus.* This again. Reagan just managed not to pinch the bridge of her nose and utter profanity that would have her father gasping.

He just didn't stop. Didn't give her a chance to breathe. To make a single decision for herself.

Since she'd turned twenty-six five months ago, he'd been on this relentless campaign to see her married. Just as her brother had. As her sister had only a year ago.

It was all so ridiculous. So damn antiquated. And stifling. She could find her own goddamn husband, *if* she wanted one.

Which she didn't.

She loved her parents; they'd always provided a more-than-comfortable home, the best schools, a good, solid family life. But her father was definitely the head of the household, and Henrietta Sinclair, though the mediator and often the voice of reason, very rarely went against him. While the relationship might work well for them, Reagan couldn't imagine allowing a man to have that much control over her.

Besides, she'd done that once. Let a man consume her world—*be* her world. And that had ended in a spectacularly disastrous display.

No, she didn't want a husband who'd give her a home and his shadow to live in.

"Dad, I appreciate your concern, but I wish you and Mom would stop…with the matchmaking attempts. I've told both of you that marriage isn't a priority for me right now." If ever. "I'll show up for dinner tonight, but don't expect a love match. While Devon Granger may be nice and husband material, he's not *my* husband material."

Poor Devon. His most interesting quality had been providing a distraction from Tracy Drake, seated on her other side. And since the notorious gossip had spotted Ezekiel Holloway following Reagan and her father back into the house within moments, she'd been chock-full of questions and assumptions. The woman had missed her calling as a CIA agent.

Her father scoffed. "A love match." He shook his head, exasperation clearly etched into his expression. "Don't be ridiculous. I'm not anticipating a proposal at the end of the evening. I just want you to at least give him a chance." He glanced at his watch again, impatience vibrating off him. "As your father, I want to see you happy, settled. With a husband who can provide for you." He flicked the hand not holding his briefcase. "Don't be naive, Reagan. Do you think people aren't talking about the fact that your sister, who is three years younger than you, is already married? That maybe there's something—"

"I'm not Christina," she interrupted him, voice quiet and steady in spite of how *hurt* trembled through her like a wind-battered leaf. She knew what lay on the other side of that *something*. And she didn't need to hear him state how their friends and associates whispered if she was faulty in some way. Or to hear the unspoken concern in her father's voice that he wondered the same thing. Except swap out *faulty* for *broken*.

"I'm not Doug either," she added, mentioning her older brother. "I have my own aspirations, and marriage isn't even at the top of that list."

"God, not that again—"

"And if you would just release the money Gran left me, I could further those goals. And a life of my choosing. Filled with *my* decisions," she finished, tracing the faint child-hood scar on her collarbone. Trying—and failing—not to let his annoyed dismissal of her wants puncture her pride and self-esteem. By now, both resembled a barroom cork-board, riddled with holes from so many well-meaning but painful darts.

"We've been over this, and the answer is still no," he ground out. "Your grandmother loved you so much she left that inheritance to you, but she also added the stipulation for a reason. And we both know why, Reagan."

*We both know why... We both know why...*

The words rang between them in the already warm morning air.

A warning.

An indictment.

Oh yes, how could she forget why her beloved grandmother, who had left her enough money to make her an instant millionaire, had added one provision in her will? Reagan couldn't access the inheritance until she either married a suitable man or turned thirty years old.

In order to be fully independent, to manage her own life, she had to chain herself to a man and hand over that independence or wait four more years before she could... *live.*

It was her punishment, her penance. For rebelling. For not following the Sinclair script. For daring to be less than perfect.

At sixteen, she'd done what most teenage girls did— she'd fallen in love. But she'd fallen hard. Had been consumed by the blaze of first love with this nineteen-year-old boy that her parents hadn't approved of. So when they'd forbidden her to see him, she'd sneaked around behind their backs. She'd offered everything to him—her loyalty, her heart, her virginity.

And had ended up pregnant.

Understandably, her parents had been horrified and disappointed. They'd wanted to send her away, have the baby and give it up for adoption. And Reagan had been determined to keep her unborn daughter or son. But neither of them had their wish. She'd miscarried. And the boy she'd been so certain she'd spend the rest of her life with had disappeared.

The price for her stubborn foolishness had been her utter devastation and her family's trust.

And sometimes...when she couldn't sleep, when her guard was down and she was unable to stop the buffeting of her thoughts and memories, she believed she'd lost some of their love, too.

Over the years, she'd tried to make up for that time by being the obedient, loyal, *perfect* daughter they deserved. It was why she still remained in her childhood home even though, at her age, she should have her own place.

But ten years later, she still caught her mother studying her a little too close when Reagan decided to do something as small as not attend one of her father's events for his law firm. Still glimpsed the concern in Henrietta's eyes when Reagan disagreed with them. At one time Reagan had made her mother physically ill from the worry she'd caused, the pain she'd inflicted with her bad decisions. So to remain under the same roof where Henrietta could keep tabs on her, could assure herself that her daughter wasn't once again self-destructing... It was a small cost. She owed her parents that much.

Because in her family's eyes, she would never be more than that misguided, impetuous teen. She was her family's well-kept, dirty little secret, a cautionary tale for her sister.

The weight of the knowledge bore down on her so hard, her shoulders momentarily bowed. But she'd become the poster child for *fake it until you make it*. Sucking in an inaudible deep breath, she tilted her chin up and met her father's dark scrutiny.

"I guess we're at an impasse, then. Again," she tacked on. "Have a great day, Dad."

Turning on her heel, she headed inside the house before he could say something that would unknowingly tear another strip from her heart. She quietly shut the door behind her, leaning against it. Taking a moment to recover from another verbal and emotional battle with her father.

Sighing, she straightened and strode toward the rear of the house and the kitchen for a cold bottle of water. The thickly sweet scent of flowers hit her seconds before she spied the vase of lush flowers with their dark red petals.

*I hate roses. I mean, loathe them... Every morning there are fresh bouquets of them delivered to the house... And every day I fight the urge to knock one down just to watch them scatter across the floor in a mess of water, petals and thorns. Because I'm petty like that.*

The murmured admission whispered through her mind, dragging her from the here-and-now back to that shadowed balcony a little over a week ago.

Back to Ezekiel Holloway.

She drew to a halt in the middle of the hallway, her eyes drifting shut. The memories slammed into her. Not that they had a great distance to travel. He and their interlude hadn't been far from her mind since that night.

Zeke.

She'd once called him that before she'd fallen in love, then fallen out of favor with her family. Before her childhood had ended in a crash-and-burn that she still bore the scars from.

Before she'd erected this imaginary wall of plexiglass between her and people that protected her. But she'd slipped up at the dinner party. The pseudo-intimacy of the dark coaxing her into falling into old, familiar patterns.

An image of Zeke wavered, then solidified on the black screen of her eyelids.

Lovely.

Such an odd word to describe a man. Especially one who stood nearly a foot taller than her and possessed a lean but powerful, wide-shouldered body that stirred both desire and envy. Regardless, her description was still accurate. He'd been beautiful as a teen, but the years had honed that masculine beauty, experience had added an edge to it. The dark hair cut close to his head only emphasized the stunning bone structure that reminded her of cliffs sculpted to razor sharpness by wind and rain. A formidable face prettied by a firm mouth almost indecent in its fullness and a silken, neatly cropped beard framing his sinful lips.

Then there were those eyes.

The color of new spring grass warmed by the sun. Light green and striking against skin the color of brown sugar.

Yes, he was a lovely man. An intimidating man. A powerful, *desirable* man.

Zeke was a temptation that lured her to step closer. To stroke her fingers over that dark facial hair that would abrade her skin like rug burn. To pet him like the sleek but lethal panther he reminded her of. To taste that brown sugar skin and see if it was as sweet as it looked.

But he was also a warning sign that blinked *Danger!* in neon red. Not since Gavin, her teenage love who'd abandoned her and broken her young heart, had she been the least bit tempted to lose control again. None had poked that curious shifting inside her, stirred the dormant need to be... wild. To act without thought of consequence. To throw herself into an ocean of feeling and willingly go under.

Ten minutes with Ezekiel and that tingle deep inside her crackled, already singeing the tight ropes tying down that part of her. The last time she'd loosened those bindings, she'd hurt her family terribly.

No, she couldn't allow that to happen again.

So, though part of her had railed at her father's autocratic behavior that night, the other half had been relieved as she'd walked back into the house and away from him. Okay, maybe Zeke had infiltrated her dreams since then. And in those dreams, she'd remained on the shadowed balcony. He also hadn't stopped with touching her hair. And maybe when she woke, her body trembled from unfulfilled pleasure. A pleasure that left her empty and aching.

It was okay. Because they were only dreams relegated to the darkest part of night where secret desires resided.

Didn't matter. Not when her mind and heart agreed on one indelible truth.

Ezekiel Holloway spelled trouble with a capital *T*.

Best she remembered that.

And the possible consequences if she dared to forget.

# Three

Ezekiel hunkered down on the still green grass, balancing on the balls of his feet. The late-afternoon sun didn't penetrate this corner of the cemetery where the Southern live oak's branches spread wide and reached toward the clear, blue sky. The tree provided shade over the marble headstone. And as he traced the etched lettering that hadn't yet faded after eight years, the stone was cool to the touch. If he closed his eyes and lost himself like he did in those nebulous, gray moments just before fully wakening, he could imagine another name inscribed on the marker.

Not Melissa Evangeline Drake.

Heaving a sigh that sounded weary to his own ears, he rose, shoving his hands into his pants pockets, never tearing his gaze from the monument that failed to encapsulate the woman who had once held his heart in her petite hands.

A name. Dates of her birth and way-too-soon death. Daughter, sister, friend.

Not *fiancée*. Not *the other half of Ezekiel Holloway's soul*.

And he didn't blame them. After all, he'd only had her in his life four short years, while they'd had twenty-two. She belonged to them more than she ever did to him. But for a while, she'd been solely his. His joy. His life. His *everything*. And she'd been snatched away by a man who'd decided getting behind a wheel while drunk off his ass had been a good idea.

One moment, they'd been happy, planning their future together. The next, he'd received a devastating phone call from her father that she was gone. The only merciful blessing had been that she'd died on impact when the drunk had plowed into the driver's side of her car.

And a part of him had died with her that night. The part that had belonged to her and only her.

"I can't believe it's been eight years to the day since I lost you," he said to the tombstone, pausing as if it could answer.

Most days, he struggled to remember what her voice sounded like. Time might not heal all wounds, but it damn sure dimmed the details he tried to clutch close and hoard like a miser hiding his precious gold.

"I have to tell you this is not the anniversary I imagined we'd have." He huffed out a humorless chuckle. "I tried to call your parents yesterday and this morning, but they didn't answer. I understand," he quickly added, careful not to malign the parents they'd both adored. "Losing you devastated them. And I'm a reminder of that pain. Still…" He paused, his jaw locking, trying to trap in the words he could only admit here, to his dead fiancée. "I miss them. I had Aunt Ava and Uncle Trent after Mom and Dad died, but your folks… They were good to me. And I hated losing them so soon after you. But yeah, I don't blame them."

They all had to do what they needed to move on, to return to the world of the living.

He'd thrown himself into work and any kind of activity that had taunted fate to come for him again—skydiving, rock climbing, rappelling.

And the women. The daredevil adventures might burn off the restlessness, but they couldn't touch the loneliness. The emptiness. Only sex did that. Even if it was only for those few blessed hours when he was inside a woman and pleasure provided that sweet oblivion. Adrenaline and sex. They were his sometime drugs of choice. Temporary highs.

When those were his ways of coping with the past, the loss, how could he hold it against the Drakes that they'd chosen to cauterize him from their lives?

"I know it's been several months since I've visited, and so damn much has happened since then—"

"Zeke?"

He jerked his head up and, spying the woman standing on the other side of the grave, blinked. Surely his brain had conjured the image to taunt him. How else could he explain Reagan Sinclair here in this cemetery?

Unbidden and against his will, his gaze traveled down her slender frame clothed in a pale-yellow dress that bared her shoulders and arms and crisscrossed over her breasts. For a second, he lingered over the V that offered him a hint of smooth, rounded flesh before continuing his perusal over the long, flowing skirt that brushed the tips of her toes and the grass. She resembled a goddess, golden, lustrous brown skin and long hair twisted into a braid that rested over one shoulder. And when he lifted his scrutiny to her face, he couldn't help but skim the vulnerable, sensual curves of her mouth, the almost haughty tilt of her cheekbones and the coffee-brown eyes.

Silently, he swore, yanking his regard back to the head-stone. And hating himself for detecting details about this woman he had no business, no *right* to notice. Especially standing over the grave of the woman he'd loved.

"Hey," she softly greeted him, blissfully unaware of the equal parts resentment and need that clawed at him.

"What are you doing here?" he asked, tone harsher than he'd intended. Than she deserved.

But if the question or the delivery offended her, she didn't show it. Instead, she moved closer, and even though he'd thoroughly scrutinized her only moments ago, he just noted the bouquet of vibrant blue-and-white flowers she held. She knelt, her skirt billowing around her, and laid the flowers in front of the gravestone. Straightening, she paused, resting a hand on top of the marble before stepping back. Only then did she meet his gaze.

And in that instant, he was transported back eight years. A lot about the day of Melissa's funeral had been a blur, but how could he have forgotten that it'd been Reagan who'd found him at this very same, freshly covered grave after everyone else had left for the repast at the Drakes'? Reagan who had slipped her hand into his and silently stood next to him, not rushing him to leave, not talking, just… refusing to leave him alone. She might've been his cousin's friend back then, but that day, in those long, dark moments, she'd been his.

He smothered a sigh and dragged a hand down his face, his beard scratching his palm.

"I'm sorry," he murmured. "This day—"

She shook her head, holding up her hand to forestall the rest of his apology. "I understand." She paused. "Does it get any easier?" she asked, voice whisper soft.

Did it? Any other place on any other day, he might've offered his canned and packaged reply of *yes, time is the great healer*. But the words stumbled on his tongue. Then died a defeated death. "Most days, yes. The pain dulls so it doesn't feel as if every breath is like a knife in the chest. But then there are other days when…"

His gaze drifted toward the other side of the cemetery. What his eyes couldn't see, his mind supplied. Two matching headstones, side by side. The people buried there together in death as they'd been determined to be in life.

*I feel empty*, he silently completed the thought. *Unanchored. Alone. Abandoned.*

He would've denied those words, those feelings if anyone vocalized them to him. Especially his older brother,

Luke. But in his head where he couldn't run from his denial?

Well…even if he had the speed of Usain Bolt, he couldn't sprint fast enough to escape himself.

"I forgot your parents were buried here," Reagan said, her voice closer. Her scent nearer, more potent. "I always wondered why they weren't with the rest of the Wingates in their mausoleum."

"Because they weren't Wingates," he replied, still staring off into the distance, squelching the clench of his gut at his explanation. Smothering the unruly and insidious thought that he wasn't one either. That in a family mixed with Wingates and Holloways, he and Luke were still… different.

"My father was a Holloway, Aunt Ava's older brother. He created a bit of a scandal in the family and society when he married my mother, a black woman. But in spite of the derision and ostracization they faced—sometimes within his own family—my parents had a happy marriage. Even if they remained somewhat distant from the rest of the Holloways."

"They were protecting their world," Reagan murmured. "I don't think there's anything wrong with that."

"They were very careful, sheltering. But they still taught us the value of family. When they died in that car crash eleven years ago, Aunt Ava and Uncle Trent took Luke and me in…even though by then, we were both in college and technically adults. They gave us a place to call home when ours had been irrevocably broken."

He turned back to her. "They might have taken us in, and we now work for the family company, but my parents didn't consider themselves Wingates, so Luke and I didn't bury them as ones."

She slowly nodded. Studied him in that calm-as-lake-waters way of hers that still perceived too much. Unlike most people, she didn't seem content with just seeing the charmer, the thrill seeker.

He didn't like it.

But damn if a small part of him didn't hate it either.

"Where will you choose to be buried? The Wingate side or the Holloways?" she mused. But there was nothing casual or easy about the question...or the answer. "God, that's a morbid question. I heard it as soon as I asked it. Still... can't be easy feeling as if you're split in two. Trying to figure out if love or obligation, a debt unpaid, holds you here."

His pulse thudded, echoing in his ears. And inside his chest, the arrow that had struck quivered in agitation.

"What are you doing here?" he asked, abruptly changing the subject away from his family. From his own discomfort and inner demons. "Can't be just to visit Melissa's grave."

That clear inspection didn't waver, but after several seconds, she released him from it, glancing over her shoulder. And he exhaled on a low, deep breath.

"No, my grandmother rests just over there. I come by every other week. It's only been a couple of months since we lost her, so being here..." She shrugged a shoulder. "It brings me more comfort than it does her, I'm sure. But I try to bring enough flowers for her and Melissa."

"Thank you," he said, his palm itching to stroke down the length of her dark brown braid. He slid his hand in his pocket instead. "And I'm sorry about your grandmother." The troubles with WinJet and the fire in the manufacturing plant had consumed him, and he'd been working like a madman since, so he hadn't heard about her death. "I didn't know her, but she must've been very special."

The brief hesitation might not have been caught by most people. But most people weren't paying attention to every breath that passed through Reagan's lips.

"We shared a close bond," she said.

"But?" Ezekiel prodded. "There's definitely a *but* there."

His light teasing didn't produce the effect he'd sought—
the lightening of the shadows that had crowded into her
gaze.

"But it's difficult to discover the one person you believed
loved you unconditionally didn't trust you."

The tone—quiet, almost tranquil—didn't match the
words. So one of them was a deception. From personal
experience, he'd bet on the tone.

And against his better judgment but to his dick's delight, when he reached out, grasped her chin between his
thumb and forefinger and tipped her head back, he had
confirmation.

Her eyes. Those magnificent, beautiful eyes couldn't
lie. If windows were eyes to the soul, Reagan's were fucking floor-to-ceiling bay windows thrown wide open to the
world.

A man could lose himself in them. Step inside and never
leave.

With a barely concealed snarl directed at himself, he
dropped his arm and just managed not to step back. In retreat. Because that's what it would be. Flight from the need
to fall into the pool of those eyes.

He'd had that sensation of drowning before. And he'd
willingly dived in. And now the person who was supposed
to be there to always keep him afloat lay in the ground at
both of their feet.

Fuck it. He took that step back.

"Why do you think she didn't trust you?" he asked,
focusing on Reagan and not the fear that scratched at his
breastbone.

She released a short, brittle huff. "Think? I know."

Shifting, she gave him her profile, but he caught the
slight firming of her lips, the drag of her fingertips across
the left side of her collarbone. He narrowed his eyes on the
small movement. She'd done that the night of the party. Was

it a subconscious tell on her part? He catalogued the detail to take out and analyze later.

"Well, tell me why she didn't trust you, then," he pushed. Gently, but it was still a push. Something inside him—something ephemeral but insatiable—hungered to know more about this woman who had grown up right under his nose but remained this familiar, sexy-as-hell stranger.

"Did you know that I'm a millionaire?" she asked, dodging his question—no, his demand.

Ezekiel nodded. "I'm not surprised. Your father is a very successful—"

"No." She waved a hand, cutting him off. "Not through my father. In my own right, I'm a millionaire. When my grandmother died, she left each of her three grandchildren enough money to never have to worry about being taken care of. But that's the thing. She *did* worry. About me anyway." No breeze kicked up over the quiet cemetery, yet she crossed her arms, clutching her elbows. "She added a stipulation to her will. I can only receive my inheritance when I turn thirty—or marry. And not just any man. A *suitable* man."

Her lips twisted on *suitable*, and he resisted the urge to smooth his thumb over the curve, needing to eradicate the bitterness encapsulated in it. That emotion didn't belong on her—didn't sit right with him.

"The condition doesn't mean she didn't trust you. Maybe she just wanted to make sure you were fully mature before taking on the responsibility and burden that comes with money."

Not that he believed that bullshit. Age didn't matter as much as experience. Hell, there were days he looked in the mirror and expected to glimpse a bent, wizened old man instead of his thirty-year-old self.

"I could accept that if I weren't the only grandchild hit with that proviso. Doug and Christina might both be married, but neither of them had that particular restriction on their inheritance. Just me."

"Why?" he demanded.

Confusion and anger sparked inside him. He was familiar with Reagan's older brother and younger sister, and both were normal, nice people. Maybe a little too nice and, well, boring. But Reagan? She was the perfect image of a Royal socialite—composed, well-mannered and well-spoken, serving on several committees, free of the taint of scandal, reputation beyond reproach. So what the hell?

She didn't immediately reply but stared at him for several long moments. "Most people would've asked what I did to earn that censure."

"I'm not most people, Ray," he growled.

"No, you're not," she murmured, scanning his face, and then, she shook her head. "The why doesn't really matter, does it? What does matter is that at twenty-six, I'm in this holding pattern. Where I can see everyone else enjoying the lives they've carved out for themselves—and I can't move. Either I chain myself to a man I barely know and don't love to access my inheritance. Or I stay here, static for another four years while my own dreams, my own needs and wants wither and die on the vine."

Once more, she'd adopted that placid tone, but this time, Ezekiel caught the bright slashes of hurt, the red tinge of anger underneath it.

"I'm more than just the daughter of Douglas Sinclair. I'm more than just the member of this and that charity committee. Not that I'm denigrating their work. It's just… I want to…be free," she whispered, and he sensed that she hadn't meant for that to slip. For him to hear it.

What did she mean by *free*? Not for the first time, he sensed Reagan's easygoing, friendly mask hid deeper waters. Secrets. He didn't trust secrets. They had a way of turning around and biting a person in the ass. Or knocking a person on it.

"Surely your father can find a way around the will. Especially if it seems to penalize you but not your brother or sister," he argued, his mind already contemplating obtaining a copy of the document and submitting it to Wingate Enterprises's legal department to determine what, if anything, could be done. Some loophole.

"My father doesn't want to find a way around it," she admitted softly, but the confession damn near rocked him back on his heels. "My grandmother did add a codicil. She left it up to my father's discretion to enforce the stipulation. He could release the money to me now or respect her wishes. He's decided he'd rather see me married and settled. *Taken care of*, are his words. As if I'm a child to be passed from one guardian to another like luggage. Or a very fragile package." She chuckled, and the heaviness of it, the *sadness* of it, was a fist pressed against Ezekiel's chest. "That's not far off, actually."

Understanding dawned, and with it came the longing to grab Douglas Sinclair by his throat.

"So that's what the introductions to man after man were about?" he asked.

"The night of James Harris's party?" She nodded. "Yes. And the not-so-subtle invites to our home for dinner. In the last week, there have been three. I feel like a prized car on an auction block. God, it's *humiliating*." For the first time, fire flashed under that calm, and he didn't know whether he wanted to applaud the emotion or draw her into his arms to bank it. He did neither, retaining that careful distance away from her. "I just want to yell *screw it all* and walk away completely. No money, no husband I don't want. But…"

"But family loyalty is a bitch."

A smile ghosted over her lips. "God, yes. And a mean, greedy one to boot."

"Ray." That smile. The awful resignation in it… He couldn't *not* touch her any longer. Crossing the small distance he'd placed between them, he cupped the back of her neck, drawing her close. Placing a kiss to the side of her head, he murmured, "I'm sorry, sweetheart. Family can be our biggest blessing and our heaviest burden."

Brushing his lips over her hair one last time, he dropped his arm and shifted backward again. Ignoring how soft her hair had been against his mouth. Or how his palm itched with the need to reshape itself around her nape again. How he resisted the urge to rub his hand against his leg to somehow erase the feel of her against his skin. "Whatever you decide, make sure it's the best decision for you. This life is entirely too short to deal with regrets."

Her lashes lowered, but not before he caught a glint of emotion in her eyes.

Oh yes. Secrets definitely dwelled there.

"Regrets," she repeated in her low, husky tone. "Yes. Wouldn't want those." Shaking her head, she smiled, but it didn't reach the gaze he stared down into. "I need to go. A meeting. Take care of yourself, Zeke," she said.

With a small wave, she turned and strode down the cemented path, her hips a gentle sway beneath the flowing material of her dress. Tearing his regard from her slender, curvaceous form, he returned it to the grave in front of him. But his mind remained with the woman who'd just walked away from him and not the one lying in the ground at his feet.

*I chain myself to a man I barely know and don't love to access my inheritance.*

*I stay here, static for another four years while my own dreams, my own needs and wants wither and die on the vine.*

Her words whirled in his head like a raging storm, its

winds refusing to die down. And in the midst of it was his own advice.

*This life is entirely too short to deal with regrets.*

He should know; he had so many of them. Not calling his parents and telling them he loved them more often. Not being more insistent that Melissa spend the night at his house instead of driving home that night. Not letting his uncle Trent know how much he appreciated all that he'd done for Luke and Ezekiel before he died.

Not being able to turn this WinJet disaster around for the company.

Yeah, he had many regrets.

But… The thoughts in his head spun harder, faster.

Reagan didn't want to shackle herself to a man she barely knew and didn't love.

Well, she knew him. Love wasn't an option. The only woman to own his heart had been taken from him. Now, he didn't have one to give. Love… He'd been down that road before and it was pitted with heartbreak, pain and loss. But Reagan wouldn't expect that from him. They had a friendship. And that was a solid foundation that a good many marriages lacked.

The idea—it was crazy. It bordered on rash. And his family would probably call it another one of his harebrained adventures.

None of them understood why he pursued those exploits. He'd been in control of precious little in his life. Not his parents' untimely demise. Not where he and Luke landed afterward. Not Melissa's death. And even though he enjoyed his job at Wingate Enterprises, that family loyalty, the debt he felt he owed Ava and Trent, had compelled him to enter into the family business.

And now he had to bear witness to the slow crumbling of that business.

He didn't need a psychologist to explain to him why he had control issues. He got it.

When he climbed a mountain or dived from a plane, his safety and success were in his own hands. It all depended on his skill, his preparation and will. He determined his fate.

And while his chaotic and uncertain life was beyond his power, he could help Reagan wrest control of hers. As he remembered the girl who had stood with him during one of his loneliest and most desolate moments, it was the least he could do to repay her kindness.

Yes, it could work.

He just had to get Reagan to agree with him first.

# Four

It'd been some years since Reagan had been to the Wingate estate.

Five to be exact.

The gorgeous rolling hills and the large mansion sitting on the highest point brought back so many memories of a happier, much less complicated time.

Though Reagan was a couple of years older, she'd been good friends with Harley Wingate when they'd been younger. Some would say the best of friends, who stayed in each other's homes, wrote in diaries and then shared their secrets and gossiped about boys. Reagan smiled, wistful. Those had definitely been simpler times.

Before her miscarriage and Harley leaving the United States for Thailand. Reagan had never revealed her pregnancy to her friend, and then Harley had left with her own secrets—including who had fathered her own baby.

Sadness whispered through Reagan as she drove past the home where she'd spent so many hours. A mix of Southwestern and California ranch architectural style, it boasted cream stone and stucco with a clay tile roof and a wraparound porch that reached across the entire second story. Memory filled in the rest. Wide spacious rooms, a library and dining areas, an outdoor kitchen that was a throwback to the ranch it resembled. Several porches and patios stretched out from the main structure and a gorgeous pool that she and Harley used to while away hours beside. Expensive, tasteful and luxurious. That summed up the home and, in many ways, the family.

Reagan's father had been proud his daughter was friends with a Wingate daughter.

She'd ruined that pride.

*Not going there today.* Not when she'd received a mysterious and, she freely admitted, enticing voice mail from Ezekiel Holloway asking her to meet him at the guesthouse on the estate. What could he possibly have to discuss with her? Why couldn't they have met at his office in the Wingate Enterprises building just outside of Royal?

And why had her belly performed a triple-double that would've had Simone Biles envious just hearing that deep, silk-over-gravel voice?

She shook her head, as if the action could somehow mitigate the utter foolishness of any part of her flipping and tumbling over Ezekiel. If the other reasons why he was off-limits—playboy, friend-zoned, he'd seen her with braces and acne—didn't exist, there remained the fact that he clearly still pined over his dead fiancée.

Eight years.

God, what must it be like to love someone like that? In her teenage folly, she'd believed she and Gavin had shared that kind of commitment and depth of feeling. Since he'd ghosted her right after the miscarriage, obviously not. And her heart had been broken, but she'd recovered. The scarred-over wound of losing her unborn child ached more than the one for Gavin.

Unlike Ezekiel.

It'd been a couple of days since she'd walked out of the cemetery leaving him behind, but she could still recall the solemn, grim slash of his full mouth. The darkness in his eyes. The stark lines of his face. No, he'd *loved* Melissa. And Reagan pitied the woman who would one day come along and try to compete for a heart that had been buried in a sun-dappled grave almost a decade ago.

Pulling up behind a sleek, black Jaguar XJ, Reagan shut off the engine and climbed from her own dark gray Lexus. Like a magnet, she glided toward the beautiful machine. Her fingers hovered above the gleaming aluminum and chrome, hesitant to touch and leave prints. Still those same fingertips itched to stroke and more. Grip the steering wheel and command the power under the hood.

"Am I going to need to get you and my car a room?"

*So busted.* Reagan winced, glancing toward the porch where Ezekiel leaned a shoulder against one of the columns. Unless he lounged around the house in business clothes, he must've left the office to meet her here. A white dress shirt lovingly slid over his broad shoulders, muscular chest and flat abdomen, while dark gray slacks emphasized his trim waist and long, powerful legs.

"You might," she said, heading toward him but jerking her all-too-fascinated gaze away to give the Jaguar one last covetous glance. "V8 engine?"

He nodded. "And supercharged." She groaned, and he broke out into a wide grin. "I didn't know you were into cars," he remarked, straightening as she approached.

Reagan climbed the stairs to the porch, shrugging a shoulder. "My brother's fault. He started my obsession by sharing his Hot Wheels with me when we were kids, and it's been full-blown since then. We make at least two car shows a year together."

"What else are you hiding from me, Reagan?" Ezekiel murmured, those mesmerizing green eyes scanning her face.

Heat bloomed in her chest, searing a path up her throat, and dammit, into her face. Ducking her head to hide the telltale reaction to his incisive perusal, she huffed out a small laugh. "Hiding? Please. Nothing that dramatic. I'm an open book."

He didn't reply, and unable to help herself, she lifted her head. Only to be ensnared by his gaze. Her breath stuttered, and for a slice of time, they stood there on the edge of his porch, staring. Drowning. At least on her part.

God. Did the man have to be so damn hot?

Objectively, she understood why so many women in Royal competed to have him in their arms, their beds. Even if it were just for hours. Oh yes, his reputation as a serial one-night monogamist was well-known. Was the rumor about him never actually sleeping with a woman true as well? Part of her wanted to know.

And the other?

Well, the other would rather not picture him tangled, sweaty and naked with another woman, period. Why just the thought had her stomach twisting, she'd rather not examine.

"C'mon in," he invited, turning and opening the screen door for her to enter his home.

Nodding, she slipped past him and stepped into the guesthouse he and his brother shared. *Guesthouse*. That brought an image of a garage apartment. Not this place. A towering two-story home with a tiled roof, wraparound porch, airy rooms with high ceilings and a rustic feel that managed to be welcoming, relaxing and expensive—it provided more than enough room for two bachelors.

It wasn't the first time she'd walked the wood floors here. After Luke and Ezekiel's parents died, they'd moved here, and she'd visited with Harley. But then, she hadn't been personally invited by Ezekiel. And they'd never been alone.

Like now.

"I have to admit, I've been dying to find out what all the cloak-and-dagger mystery is about," she teased as he closed the front door behind them. "I've narrowed it down to plans for world domination or spoilers for the next superhero movie. Either way, I'm in."

A smile flashed across his face, elevating him from beautiful to breathtaking. *That's it*, she grumbled to herself, following him into the living room. She was only looking at his neck from now on. That face elicited silly and unrealistic thoughts. Like what would that lush, sensual mouth feel like against hers? Did he kiss a woman as if she were a sweet to be savored? Or a full-course meal to be devoured?

God, she had to stop this. The man might as well be her big brother. No, scratch that. There were moral and legal rules against lusting after your brother like she did Ezekiel. Still, it was all shades of inappropriate and wrong. Mainly because while she didn't see him as a sibling, he definitely viewed her as one.

The reminder snuffed out the embers of desire like a dousing of frigid water.

Ezekiel snorted, gesturing toward the couch. "As if I would ever share spoilers. Now world domination..." He shrugged a shoulder. "I can be persuaded."

"I'm not even touching that," she drawled. "But your questionable values don't deter my curiosity one bit." She lowered to one end of the sofa. "So dish."

Rather than taking a chair or joining her on the couch, Ezekiel sat on the mahogany coffee table in front of her. His white dress shirt stretched across the width of his broad shoulders as he leaned forward, propping his elbows on his muscular thighs. All the teasing light dimmed in his eyes as he met hers.

Unease slid inside her, setting beneath her breastbone. Unease and a niggling worry.

"What's wrong?" she whispered. "What's happened?"

Harley? Her parents? Something else with Wingate Enterprises? She, like everyone else in Royal—hell, the nation—had heard of the trouble at their jet manufacturing plant. Unlike the gossip swirling around the Wingates proclaimed, she didn't believe the allegations of corruption. They didn't coincide with the people she'd known for years. And she absolutely didn't believe that Ezekiel would've gone along with something so nefarious. They might not have been close, but the boy and man she'd called a friend had a core of integrity and honesty in him that wouldn't have abided any fraudulence or deception. Especially any that could potentially cost people their lives.

"Reagan," he said, pausing for a long moment. A moment during which she braced herself. "Marry me."

The breath she'd been holding whooshed out of her. She blinked. Blinked again. Surely, he… No, he couldn't have possibly…

"E-excuse me?" she stuttered, shock slowing her mind and tongue.

"Marry me," he repeated, his jade gaze steady, his expression solemn. Determined. "Be my wife."

*Oh God.* His determination slowly thawed the ice that surprise had encased her in, permitting panic to creep through. He'd lost it. He'd finally cracked under the pressure from the trouble at Wingate. What other explanation could there be?

"Ezekiel…"

"I'm not crazy," he assured her, apparently having developed the talent of reading minds. Or maybe he'd interpreted her half rising from the couch as a sign of her need to escape. He held out a hand, stalling the motion. "Reagan, hear me out. Please."

He sounded sane. Calm, even. But that meant nothing. The man had just proposed to her—if she could actually call his demand a proposal. Who just commanded a woman to marry him? As if she were chattel—hold up. Now *she* was the one losing *her* mind. Demand, ask, send a freaking telegram… Nothing could change the fact that she'd suddenly plummeted into an alternate universe where Ezekiel damn Wingate had ordered her to become his wife.

All manners flew out the window in extreme circumstances like this.

"What the hell, Zeke?" she breathed.

The man nodded, still cool. Still composed. "I understand your reaction. I do. But just let me explain. And if you say no and want to leave, I won't try to stop you. And no hard feelings, okay?" She couldn't force her lips to move, and he evidently took her silence as acquiescence. "I've been thinking about our conversation at the cemetery for the last couple of days. Your situation with the will and not wanting to give in to your father's matchmaking campaign."

"Siege is more like it," she grumbled.

A corner of Ezekiel's mouth quirked. "Yes, we'll go with that. *Siege.*" Once more, his face grew serious, and she barely smothered the urge to wrap her arms around herself. To protect herself from the words to come out of his mouth. "The stipulation in your grandmother's will is you have to marry a suitable man in order to receive your inheritance. You also said you didn't want to marry a man you didn't know. A man who would try to control you." He released a rough, ragged breath. "We've been acquainted, been friends for years. And I have no interest in overseeing you or your money. As a matter of fact, I'm willing to sign a contract stating that your inheritance would remain in your name alone, without any interference from me."

"Wait, wait." She held up a hand, palm out, silently asking him to stop. To let his words sink in. To allow her the time to make sense of them. "Are you telling me you want to marry me just so I can access my grandmother's money?"

"Yes."

"But why?" she blurted out.

Unable to sit any longer, she shot to her feet and paced away from him. Away from the intensity he radiated that further scrambled her thoughts. Striding to the huge picture windows on one wall, she stared out, not really seeing the large stables or the horses in the corral in the distance. This time, she surrendered to the need to cross her arms over her chest. Not caring if the gesture betrayed her vulnerability, her confusion.

"Why?" she repeated, softer but no less bemused. In her experience, no one in this world did something for nothing. What did Ezekiel want from her? How did he benefit from this seemingly altruistic offer? "I've had no indication you were even interested in marriage." Only forty-eight hours earlier he'd been holding a vigil over the woman he'd wanted to pledge himself to for life. "Why would you voluntarily tie yourself to a woman you don't love?"

"I'm not looking for love, Reagan." She sensed his presence behind her at the same time his words reached her.

The quiet finality in that statement shouldn't have rocked through her like a quake, but it did. She wasn't looking either; that often deceptive emotion required too much from a person and gave too little back. But hearing him say it…

"I don't want it," he went on. "Love isn't included in the bargain, and you should know that upfront. Because if you need that from me, then I'll rescind the offer. I can't lie or mislead you. And I don't want to hurt you."

"I don't need it," she whispered. "But that still doesn't answer my question. Why?"

His sigh ruffled her hair, and as he shifted behind her, his chest brushed her shoulder blade. But rather than feel cornered or smothered, she had to battle the impulse to press back into him, to bask in the warmth and strength he emanated.

So she stiffened and leaned forward.

"Would it be advantageous for the world to believe that

you, a member of the upright Sinclair family, are in my corner during this WinJet shit storm? Yes. Do I find the thought of companionship appealing? Yes. Is it hard admitting that not only am I sometimes lonely, but that it's an ache? Yes. They're all true, but not the biggest reasons for my proposition," he said.

Proposition, she noted, not proposal. Yet, she didn't latch onto that as much as him being lonely. God, she knew about the hole loneliness could carve. And how you might be willing to do anything to alleviate it.

"Freedom," he said. "That's what you whispered. Maybe you didn't mean for me to hear it, but I did. You long to be free. I don't know of what, and I won't pry and ask if you don't want to enlighten me. But it doesn't matter. I can give it to you. If you accept me, you'll have access to your inheritance and all those dreams and goals you mentioned won't remain stagnant for four more years."

She closed her eyes, a tremble working its way through her body before she could prevent it. He'd listened to her. That was a bit of a lark. Having someone pay attention, consider and not dismiss her needs, her desires. *Her.*

"I still don't think it's fair to expect you to legally commit yourself to me. Marriage isn't something to be taken lightly," she maintained, although, dammit, her arguments against this idea were weaker.

"It won't be forever," he countered. "A year, eighteen months at the most. Just long enough for you to receive the money. Then we can obtain an amicable divorce and go our separate ways, back to being friends. Ray." He cupped her shoulders and gently but firmly turned her around to face him. He waited until she tipped her head back and met his unwavering but shadowed gaze. "Besides the obvious reasons, I understand why you might be hesitant to agree. I might be related to the Wingates, but with the fire and the bad press, our reputation isn't as clean as it used to be. And you might very well be dirtied by association—"

She cut him off with a slice of her hand between them. "As if I care about that," she scoffed. "No, my concern stems from this smacking of something out of an over-the-top TV drama. And that no one will believe it since we've never even been seen together as a couple. Or that all of this will seem like a stunt and only have more aspersions thrown your way."

"You let me worry about appearances and spinning this. I'm a VP of marketing, after all," he said, a vein of steel threading through his voice. "The only person we need to convince and impress is your father since he holds the reins to your inheritance. If he approves, we can have a quick wedding ceremony and start the ball rolling toward him releasing your money."

Reagan studied his beard-covered jaw. Jesus, she was really considering this propo—no, *proposition*. This was more akin to a business arrangement. Complete with a contract. Except with a ring. And a wedding.

And a commitment. A commitment without…

She lifted her gaze to his and found herself locked in his almost too intense stare. Which was going to make this all the more difficult to vocalize.

"I know you, uh…" Fire blazed up her neck and poured into her face, and she briefly squeezed her eyes shut. "I know you enjoy female company. Won't marrying me, um, interfere with…" She trailed off.

"Are you trying to ask me if I'm going to be able to endure going without sex?" he asked bluntly.

Damn. "Yes," she pushed forward. Because although she threatened to be consumed in mortification, she needed this point to be clear. "If I agree to this—and that's a big *if*—we have to appear as if we're in love even though it's not true. And that includes not going out on," she paused, "*dates* with other women while we're married."

She didn't even consider suggesting sex as part of their bargain. Ezekiel saw her as his cousin's best friend, not a desirable woman. Offering him the option would only embarrass both of them, and she'd tasted rejection and humiliation enough to last her a lifetime. There were only so many times a woman could be told she was unwanted in words and action before she sympathized with the turtle, afraid to stick out her head from her shell in fear of it being lobbed off.

"Ray, look at me." She did as he demanded, a little surprised to realize her gaze had dipped to his chin again. "I control my dick, not the other way around."

*Oookay.* Hearing him utter *that* shouldn't have been sexy. It should've offended her. But it was, and it didn't. If the flesh between her legs had a vote, she should have a mix tape made with him saying dick over and over again.

Proposition. Platonic. Friend. No sex.

She wasn't sure, but her vagina might have whispered, *Spoilsport.*

"I'm taking that as a yes, that other women would be out of the picture for the duration of our…arrangement," she said, arching an eyebrow.

"Yes, Ray." A smile curved his mouth, and she cursed herself for again wondering how he would feel, taste. Good thing sex was off the table. She probably wouldn't survive it with this man. "Now, your answer. Or do you need more time to consider it? Will you be my trust fund fiancée?"

In spite of the thoughts whirling through her head, she almost smiled at his phrasing. Did she need more time? His arguments were solid. His reasons for sacrificing himself to her cause still remained nebulous, but if he was willing…

She allowed herself to imagine a future where she was independent. Where her work at the girls' home in Colonial County would no longer have to be a secret she kept to herself out of fear of hurting her parents. A future where she could build a similar home here in Royal that supported teenage pregnant mothers who didn't have the family support, health care or resources they so desperately needed.

She should know. She had been one.

And this would solve her dilemma with honoring her grandmother's request even if the stipulation continued to hurt Reagan. She feared estrangement from her father, her family, and marrying Ezekiel would prevent that as well. Once, her father had been delighted about her friendship with a Wingate. Now she had the opportunity to marry into the family. Maybe he might even be…proud of her again?

Blowing out a breath, she pinched the bridge of her nose. Then lowered her arm and opened her eyes to meet the pale green scrutiny that managed to see too much and conceal even more.

"Yes, I'll marry you."

# Five

"Are you sure about this?" Reagan questioned Ezekiel for, oh, probably the seventeenth time since she'd agreed to his…bargain. "It's not too late to back out," she said as he cut the engine in his car. Even riding in the Jaguar hadn't been able to banish the nerves tightening inside her. Which was a shame. The car rode and handled like a dream.

Long, elegant fingers wrapped around the fist she clenched in her lap, gently squeezing. He didn't speak until she tugged her scrutiny from their joined hands to his face.

"I'm sure, Reagan. Just like I was sure the last time you asked. And the time before that. And the time before that." Chuckling, he gave her hand one last squeeze before releasing her and popping open his car door. In seconds, he'd rounded the hood and had her own door open. He extended a hand toward her, and with a resigned sigh, she covered his palm with hers.

And ignored the sizzle that crackled from their clasped hands, up her arm and traveled down to tingle in her breasts. She'd better get used to doing nothing about her reaction to him. It was inconvenient and irritating.

Not to mention unwelcome.

He kept their hands clasped together as they walked up the steps to her home. Ezekiel had advised that they shouldn't waste any time getting the ball rolling on their plan. So she'd called the administrator of the girls' home and let them know she wouldn't be in today. Though she hated missing even one shift, Reagan agreed with Ezekiel. The sooner the hard part of telling her family was over with, the better.

Next, she'd called her parents to ensure they would both be home this evening for an announcement. Forcing a cheer she didn't feel into her voice as she talked to her mother had careened too close to lying for Reagan's comfort, and even now, her belly dipped, hollowed out by the upcoming deception. Necessary, but still, a deception all the same.

"Sweetheart, look at me."

Reagan halted on the top step, her chest rising and falling on abrupt, serrated breaths. But she tipped her head back, obeying Ezekiel's soft demand.

She didn't flinch as he cupped her jaw. And she forced herself not to lean into his touch like a frostbite victim seeking warmth. His thumb swept over her cheek, and she locked down the sigh that crept up her throat.

"Everything's going to be fine, Reagan," he assured her, that thumb grazing the corner of her mouth. "I'll be right by your side, and I promise not to leave you hanging."

She just managed not to snap, *Don't make promises you can't keep*, trapping the sharp words behind her clenched teeth. Of course he would leave. Whether it was at the end of this evening if it didn't go well or at the termination of their "marriage." All men left, at some point. Gavin had. The affectionate, warm father she remembered from her childhood had, replaced by a colder, less forgiving and intolerant version.

As long as she remembered that and shielded herself against it, she wouldn't be hurt when Ezekiel eventually disappeared from her life.

"We should go in. They're expecting us." Stepping back and away from his touch, she strode toward the front door of her family home. A moment later, the solid, heated pressure of his big hand settled on the small of her back. "So it begins."

"Did you just quote *Lord of the Rings*?" he asked, arching a dark brow. Amusement glinted in pale green eyes.

"The fact that you know I did means we might actually be able to pull this 'soul mate' thing off," she shot back.

He gave an exaggerated gasp. "What kind of animal doesn't know Tolkien?"

"Exactly."

They were grinning at each other when the front door opened, and her father appeared in the entrance.

"Reagan." He paused, studying Ezekiel, his scrutiny inscrutable. "Ezekiel." He stretched a hand toward him. "This is a nice surprise."

As the two men shook hands and greeted one another, Reagan inhaled a slow, deep breath. *I can do this. I have to do this.*

Because the alternatives—a parade of men, more disappointment as she turned them down, trapping her in this half life—were hard for her to stomach.

"Well, come on in. We've held up dinner to wait on you." Her father shifted backward and waved them inside. "I'll have Marina add an extra setting for our guest."

"Thank you, Douglas. I appreciate you accommodating me on such short notice," Ezekiel said, his hand never leaving Reagan's back, his big frame a reassuring presence at her side.

"Of course."

Douglas led the way to the smaller living room where her mother waited. As soon as they entered, she rose from the chair flanking the large fireplace. At fifty-five, Henrietta Sinclair possessed an elegance and beauty that defied time. Short, dark hair that held a sweep of gray down the side framed her lovely face in a classic bob. Petite and slender, she might appear on the fragile side, but to play mediator and peacemaker between Reagan and her father for all these years, she contained a quiet strength that was often underrated. Admittedly, by Reagan herself.

"Well, you said you had a surprise, and this is definitely one," Henrietta said, crossing the room toward them. "Welcome, Ezekiel." She held both her arms out toward him, clasping his hands in hers. He lowered his head and kissed each cheek. "It's so good to see you."

"You, too, Ms. Henrietta," Ezekiel said. "Thank you for having me here." He gently extricated his hands from hers and returned one back to the base of Reagan's spine.

And her mother's shrewd gaze didn't miss it.

"None of this 'Ms. Henrietta' stuff. Please, just Henrietta," she admonished with a smile. "And you look beautiful this evening, Reagan." She scanned her daughter's purple sheath dress and the nude heels. "Any special reason?"

"Very subtle, Mom," Reagan drawled, shaking her head. Relief tiptoed inside her chest, easing some of the anxiety that had resided there since she and Ezekiel had left his home. Maybe this wouldn't be as difficult as she'd imagined. "Actually, Zeke and I would like to talk with you and Dad before dinner."

Her father moved to stand beside her mother, and his impenetrable expression would've made the Sphinx cry in envy. Reagan's nerves returned in a flood, streaming through her so they drowned out the words that hovered on her tongue.

Jesus, she was a grown woman. Why did her father's approval still mean so much to her?

*Because it's been so long since you experienced it.*

So true. In ten years, she'd tasted disappointment, glimpsed censure, felt his frustration. But it'd been so very long since his eyes had lit up with pride. A part of her—that sixteen-year-old who'd once been a daddy's girl—still hungered for it.

Maybe Ezekiel sensed the torrent of emotion swirling inside her. Or maybe he was just a supreme actor. Either way, he shifted his hand from her back and wrapped an arm around her shoulders, gently pulling her farther into his side, tucking her against his larger frame. Like a shelter.

One she accepted.

If only for a few moments.

"Douglas, Henrietta, as you know, Reagan and I have been friends for years. Since we were younger," Ezekiel said, his deep voice vibrating through her, setting off sparks that were wholly inappropriate. "In the last couple of months, we've rekindled that friendship and have become even closer. I've spoken to her, because it is ultimately her decision, but I also wanted to obtain your blessing to marry your daughter."

Silence reigned in the room, deafening and thick. Reagan forced herself not to fidget under the weight of her father's stare and her mother's wide-eyed astonishment.

"Well, I—" Henrietta glanced from the both of them to her father, then back to them. "I have to admit, I was expecting you to tell us you two were dating, not…" She trailed off. Blinked.

"I know it seems quick, Mom," Reagan said, stunned at the evenness of her tone. When inside her chest twisted a jumble of emotion—trepidation, fear…uncertainty. "But considering how long Zeke and I have known each other, not really. We just fell for one another, and it felt right."

Good God, how the lies just rolled off her tongue. She was going to hell with a scarlet *L* for *Liar* emblazoned across her breasts.

"Is that so?" her father asked, finally speaking. "Then why is this the first time we've heard of this…*relationship*?"

Reagan hiked her chin up, straightening her shoulders and shifting out from under Ezekiel's arm to meet her father's narrowed gaze. This was their vicious cycle. His censure. Her hurt. Her defiance. Next, their mother would step in to soothe and arbitrate.

"Because we decided to keep it to ourselves until we were ready to share our personal business with everyone else. The only thing faster than Royal's gossip grapevine is the speed of light. We wanted to make sure what we had was solid and real before opening ourselves up for the scrutiny that comes from just being a member of the Wingate family and a Sinclair. There's nothing wrong with that."

"Speaking of that," Douglas added, his attention swinging to Ezekiel. His expression hardened. "With all that Wingate Enterprises is embroiled in right now, you didn't consider how that might affect Reagan?"

"Dad—"

"Of course I did, Douglas," Ezekiel cut in, his tone like flint. "I would never want to expose her to any backlash or disrespect. Believe me, I've suffered enough, and I don't want to subject her to that. Protecting her is my priority. But if my own past and this situation has taught me anything, it's that life is too short and love too precious to allow things such as opinions and unfavorable press to determine how we live. Then there's the fact that we are innocent, even if the court of public opinion has judged us. Family, our true friends and members of the Cattleman's Club believe in and support us. And they will support and protect Reagan as well. As a member yourself, you understand the power and strength of that influence."

Her father didn't immediately reply, but he continued to silently study Ezekiel.

"And I believe the Wingates are innocent as well, Dad," Reagan said. "We've known them for years, and they've always proven themselves to be upstanding, good people. The incidents of the last few weeks shouldn't change that." She inhaled a breath, reaching for Ezekiel's hand, but before she could wrap her fingers around his, he was already entwining them together. "*He's* a good man. An honorable one. I wouldn't choose a man who didn't deserve my heart and your trust."

As soon as the words left her mouth, she flinched. Wished she could snatch them back. But they were already out there, and from the twist of her father's lips, and the lowering of her mother's lashes, hiding her gaze, she could read their thoughts.

*The last one you chose was a real winner, wasn't he? Got you pregnant, then abandoned you.*

*We don't trust your judgment, much less your capability of picking a worthy man.*

Fury flared bright and hot inside her. And underneath? Underneath lurked the aged but still pulsing wounds of hurt and humiliation. *I'm not that girl anymore. When will you stop penalizing me for my mistakes? When will you love me again?*

"And this sudden decision to marry wouldn't have anything to do with your grandmother's will?" her father retorted with a bite of sarcasm.

*Hypocrite.* Her fingers involuntarily tightened around Ezekiel's. How did he dare to ask her that when he'd been throwing random man after man in front of her to marry her off? The only difference now was that she'd found Ezekiel instead of her father cherry-picking him.

"Dad, I don't need—"

"Excuse me, Douglas," Ezekiel interjected, his grip on her gentle but firm. "I'm sure I don't have to tell you about your daughter. She's not just beautiful, but kind, selfless, sensitive, whip smart, so sensitive that at times I want to wrap her up and hide her away so more unscrupulous people can't take advantage of her tender heart. That's who I want to be for her. A protector. Her champion. *And* her husband."

*It's fake. It's all for the pretense*, she reminded herself as she stared up at Ezekiel, blinking. And yet...no one had ever spoken up for her, much less about her, so eloquently and beautifully. In this small instant, she almost believed him.

Almost believed those things of herself.

"I don't appreciate you cutting me off, but for that, I'll make an exception and like it," she whispered.

Again, that half smile lifted a corner of his mouth, and when he shifted that gaze down to her, she tingled. Her skin. The blood in her veins.

The sex between her legs.

No. *Nononono*. Her brain sent a Mayday signal to her flesh.

"I don't know if I deserve Reagan, but I will do everything in my power to try," Ezekiel said, squeezing her fingers.

Affection brightened his eyes, and it wasn't feigned for her parents' benefit; she knew that. He *did* like her. "I know you have doubts, and I can't blame you for them. But not about how I will care for your daughter."

Her father stared at Ezekiel in silence, and he met Douglas's stare without flinching or lowering his gaze. Not many men could do that. And she caught the glint of begrudging respect in her father's eyes.

"You have our blessing," Douglas finally said. He extended his hand toward Ezekiel.

And as the two men clasped hands, her mother beamed.

"Well, thank God that's out of the way. Goodness, Douglas, that was so dramatic," Henrietta tsked, moving forward to envelop Reagan in her arms. The familiar scent of Yves Saint Laurent Black Opium embraced her as well, and for a moment, Reagan closed her eyes and breathed in the hints of vanilla, jasmine and orange blossom. Pulling back, Henrietta smiled at Reagan. "Congratulations, honey."

"Thanks, Mom," she murmured, guilt a hard kernel lodged behind her breastbone.

"Have you two thought about a date yet?" her mother asked, and Reagan swore she could glimpse the swirl of wedding dresses, flowers and invitations floating above her head. "What about next spring? The clubhouse is usually reserved months in advance, but your father has donated enough money to this community that they would definitely fit you in. And we should probably send invitations out now…"

"Mom." Reagan gently interrupted her mother's full steam ahead plans with a glance at Ezekiel. "We were actually thinking of just a small affair in a couple of weeks."

*"What?"* Henrietta gasped, and her horrified expression might have been comical under different circumstances. "No, no, that just won't do. What would everyone say? Your sister had a big wedding, and so did your brother. So many people will want to attend, and they need advance notice. I won't have my daughter involved in some shotgun wedding as if she's—" Her voice snapped off like a broken twig, her eyes widening as suspicion and shock darkened them. "Reagan, are you… You can't be…"

*"No,"* Reagan breathed. "No, Mom, I'm not pregnant."

And as relief lightened Henrietta's eyes, anger washed through Reagan. Despair swept under it like an undertow. When would she stop being the sum of her mistakes with her parents?

"Well, then, what's the rush?" her father asked, his head tilting to the side, studying her. There was a shrewdness there that she refused to fidget under as if he'd just caught her sneaking in after curfew.

"We want to begin our lives together," she replied. "There's nothing wrong with that."

"A wedding in two weeks is…unseemly," her mother complained, shaking her head, her mouth pursed in a distasteful moue. "Six months. That's not too much time to ask. It's still short notice, but we can plan a beautiful winter wedding befitting my oldest daughter and have it right here on the estate. It'll be perfect." She clapped in delight.

God, this wasn't going how she'd expected at all. If it were up to Reagan, she would hightail it to the Royal courthouse, sign the marriage license and have a bored judge legally tie them together. It seemed more fitting to this situation. Definitely more honest.

Weddings with arches made of roses and the finest crystal and favors in the shapes of rings and a towering cake— those were for couples who were truly in love. Who looked forward to a life together filled with devotion, family and golden years together.

Weddings weren't for people who had based their temporary union on desperation, pity and money. Who looked forward to a year from now when they could be free of obligation and each other.

Besides, this wasn't fair to Ezekiel. He hadn't signed up for all of this. Hell, she wasn't even his wife yet, and her parents were acting like interfering in-laws. Waiting six months to marry would only extend their agreed-upon timeline. He'd only counted on auctioning away a year of his life, not a year and a half, possibly two.

She shook her head. No, she wouldn't do this to him. It was one thing to allow her parents to pressure her, but another to subject Ezekiel to it.

But before she could tell them that the modest, small ceremony was their final decision, Ezekiel released her hand and looped an arm around her waist, pressing a kiss to her temple. Her belly clenched. Hard. Just a simple touch of his lips and desire curled inside her, knotting into something needy, achy. Stunned by her body's reaction, she froze, a deer with its hoof suspended over the steel teeth of a trap.

"I don't want to rob Reagan of having this experience

with you, so if it's okay with her, we can wait six months," Ezekiel said. "I don't want her to look back years from now and regret anything. Her wedding day should be special."

How many times could a woman be struck speechless in the matter of minutes? Countless, it seemed.

"Zeke," she finally murmured, tilting her head back. "You don't have to do that..."

"It's no trouble," he replied softly. "Not for you."

She heard his gentle assertion, but she read the truth in his eyes. *Don't rock the boat.* Don't cause—what had been his word?—trouble. *Go along to get along.* That had been her mantra since she was sixteen. While before it had worked for her, now? Now it felt...wrong.

"Stop worrying, sweetheart. It's fine. *I'm* fine." The low, barely-there whisper reached her ears, and with a jolt, she opened her eyes, only then realizing that she'd closed them.

She searched his face, seeking out any signs of his frustration, his disappointment, his *pity*. God, which would be more like a dagger sliding into her chest? Each would hurt for different reasons. No matter how many times she glimpsed them in her family's eyes, they still pierced her.

But only understanding gleamed in his gaze. Understanding and a resolve that both confused and assured her.

For now, she'd concentrate on the assurance. Because if she permitted herself to become any more curious about Ezekiel Holloway—or worse, give in to the urge to figure him out—she might never be able to back away from that crumbling, precarious ledge.

"Okay," she whispered back.

"Wonderful," her mother crowed with another delighted clap of her hands. "We'll start planning right away. And we'll start with a date. How about..."

Her mother continued chatting as they all headed toward the formal dining room for dinner, but Reagan only listened with half an ear.

Most of her focus centered on the palm settled at the base of her spine and currently burning a hole through her dress.

The rest of it? It'd been hijacked by all the thoughts spinning through her head like a cyclone. And foremost in those thoughts loomed one prominent question...

*What the hell have you just done?*

# Six

Ezekiel glanced at his dashboard as he shifted into Park.
9:21 p.m.

Late, but as he pushed open his car door and stepped
out into Wingate Enterprises's parking lot, he knew Luke
would still be in his office. Ever since the shit had hit the fan
with the fire at WinJet, the resulting lawsuits, bad press and
plunge in business, his older brother had been damn near
killing himself to create new areas of investment, including new hotels and the best corporate jet. As vice president
of new product development, he seemed to view saving the
company and jobs of their over two hundred employees as
his white whale.

Ezekiel worried about him.

Usually, the roles were reversed. When their parents
died, Luke had been the one to look out for Ezekiel, to
care for him even though he'd only been twenty-one and
grieving himself. And when Ezekiel had lost Melissa, Luke
hadn't left his side, even moving a small couch into his
younger brother's room to make sure if Ezekiel needed
him, Luke would be right there.

So yes, Ezekiel was used to being the one on the receiving end of the concern. But now, every time he passed
by his brother's room at the house and his bed remained
unslept in, that apprehension dug deeper, sprouting roots.
Being a creative genius had its pros and cons. Luke could

come up with amazing ideas and projects. But he could also become obsessive over them, everything else—including his welfare—relegated to the it'll-take-care-of-itself class.

Ezekiel trekked across the lot, approaching the six-story building that sat right outside of Royal in a large industrial park. The unassuming, almost bland exterior of the structure didn't scream family empire, but inside... He pulled free his wallet and waved his badge across the sensor beside the door, then entered. Inside, the modern, sleek and masterfully designed interior projected wealth, professionalism and power. Aunt Ava had chosen every painting, every piece of furniture and fixture herself. Anyone walking into this building could never doubt the success of those inside its glass walls.

Striding across the empty lobby, he took the elevator to the sixth floor. As soon as the doors slid open, he headed directly for his brother's office. Unsurprisingly, he noted that Kelly Prentiss, Luke's executive assistant of five years, sat at her desk, even at this late hour. Dedicated to his brother, she ensured he ate and took at least minimal care of himself when no one else could.

"Hey, Zeke," she greeted, smiling at him, warmth brightening her green eyes. The redheaded beauty still looked composed and fresh as if it were after nine in the morning instead of at night. "You know where he's at." She nodded her head toward the partially closed door adjacent to her desk.

"How's he doing?" he murmured, aware his brother had the hearing of a bat and wouldn't appreciate them talking about him behind his back. But if he asked Luke the same question, the inevitable "Fine," would tell him exactly zero.

"He's..." She paused, narrowing her eyes in the direction of his office. "Luke. Still trying to shoulder all of this. But I'm watching over him. And I'll make sure he gets home tonight instead of pulling another all-nighter."

"Thanks, Kelly. I'm going in. If you hear yelling, just ignore it. That'll just be me, wrestling him to the floor and trying to knock some sense into him. Y'know, business as usual."

She laughed, turning back to her computer. "I hear nothing and know even less. I'm practicing my speech just in case I'm called as a witness for the defense."

He grinned and forged ahead into the lion's den.

Luke perched on the couch in the sitting area, papers strewn all over the glass table. A disposable coffee cup teetered too close to the edge, a takeout container next to it. He glanced up from his study of the documents long enough to pin Ezekiel with a glare.

"You have never, nor will you ever be able to take me," he grumbled.

Ezekiel snorted. They'd both wrestled in high school and college, and though it pained him to admit it, he'd never been able to pin his brother. Of course, Luke had been in the 182 weight class, and Ezekiel had been in 170. But Luke had never let him forget his undefeated status.

Ass.

"What are you doing here?" Luke muttered, his focus returning to the work spread out before him.

Knowing he possessed a short window before he lost his brother's attention completely, Ezekiel dropped to the armchair flanking the couch.

"Since going home and talking to you wasn't an option, I had to come here. I mean, telling your big brother you're getting married isn't something you should do over the phone."

Luke froze, his hand stilling over a paper. Slowly, his head lifted, and astonishment darkened his eyes, his usually intense expression blank. He didn't move except to blink. A couple of times.

Ezekiel should've felt even a sliver of satisfaction at

shocking his brother—a remnant of the younger sibling syndrome. But only weariness slid through him, and he sank farther into the cushion, his legs sprawled out in front of him.

"What?" Luke finally blurted.

"I said, I'm getting married." Sighing, Ezekiel laced his fingers over his stomach. "It's a long story."

"Start at the beginning," Luke ordered. "And don't skip a damn thing."

Instead of bristling at the curt demand, Ezekiel sighed and filled his brother in on his very brief "courtship" of Reagan Sinclair. When he finished, ending with the tense dinner at his future in-laws' house, Luke just stared at him.

Jesus, what if he'd broken his brain with this too-unbe-lievable-for-a-TV-sitcom story?

"So, wait," Luke said, leaning back against the couch as if Ezekiel's tale had exhausted him. "You mean to tell me, you're willingly entering an arranged marriage—arranged by yourself, I might add—so a woman you barely know can receive her inheritance? And that woman happens to be the daughter of Douglas Stick Up His Ass Sinclair? My apologies for offending your future father-in-law, but not really, considering you're the one who gave him that par-ticular moniker."

"Reagan is hardly a stranger. She and Harley are best friends—"

"How many years ago?" Luke interrupted.

"*And* we have always been acquainted," Ezekiel contin-ued despite his brother's interruption.

"Right," Luke drawled, his shock having apparently faded as that familiar intensity entered his gaze again. "But there's 'hey, great to see you at this nice soiree' ac-quainted, and then there's 'hey, be my wife and let's get biblical' acquainted."

"First, *soiree*? How the fuck old are you? Eighty-three?"

Ezekiel snorted. "And second, I don't plan on getting 'biblical' with her. This is a purely platonic arrangement. I'm helping her out."

Purely platonic arrangement. Even as he uttered the words, *liar* blared in his head like an indictment. Yes, he didn't plan on having a sexual relationship with Reagan. But the images of her that had tormented his nights—images of her under him, dark eyes glazed with passion, slim body arching into him, her breasts crushed to his chest, her legs spread wide for him as he sank into her over and over… None of those were platonic.

In his case, not only was the flesh weak, but the spirit was looking kind of shaky, too.

But he hadn't popped the question to land himself a convenient bed partner. When it came down to it, his dick didn't rule him. He could keep his hands—and everything-damn-else—to himself. Sex just muddied the already dirty waters.

Reagan had claimed to understand that he wasn't looking for love, couldn't give that to anyone else. But she couldn't. Not really. It wasn't as if he longed to climb into that grave with Melissa anymore; he didn't pine for her. But her death—it'd marked him in a way even his parents' hadn't. At some point all children have to face the inevitability of losing a parent. And they even think about how that time will be. His mom and dad's death had been devastating and painful, and to this day he mourned them. But he'd known it would come, just not so soon.

Losing a young woman who not only had her whole future ahead of her, but he'd imagined would be part of his future, had, in ways, been more tragic. More shattering. Because she shouldn't have died. According to statistics, she should've outlived him. But she hadn't. And part of her legacy had been a deeply embedded fear that nothing lasted forever. Anything important, anything he held onto too tightly could be ripped from him. Oh, there existed the possibility that it might not. But he'd played those odds once and his heart had been ripped out of his chest, and he didn't believe he would survive the pain. Not again.

Melissa had taught him that he was no longer a betting man.

So while Reagan might claim to understand why she shouldn't expect love and some happily-ever-after with him, sex would potentially change that. Women like her... She wouldn't be able to separate satisfying a base, raw need from a more emotional connection. And he loathed to hurt her, even unintentionally. Though he'd never caught wind of her being seriously involved with anyone, something in those soft brown eyes hinted that she'd experienced pain before. And he didn't want to add to it.

So for the length of their "marriage," his dick would remain on hiatus.

"And what do you get out of it?" Luke asked, dragging him from his thoughts and back into the present. "Other than canonization for sainthood?"

Ezekiel shrugged. "Companionship. The knowledge that I'm helping a woman I respect and like achieve her goals. Plus, you can't deny that news of a Wingate family engagement and wedding would definitely detract from the gossip and bad publicity surrounding us and the company at the moment. Who doesn't love a whirlwind romance, right?" He sighed, leaning forward and propping his elbows on his thighs. "I know this doesn't make sense—"

"No, to the contrary, it makes perfect sense," Luke cut him off. "At least to me. I'm just wondering if it isn't as clear to you."

Ezekiel frowned. "What the hell is that supposed to mean?"

Luke leaned forward, mimicking his pose. "It means you couldn't save Melissa, so you're trying to rescue Reagan."

"That's bullshit," Ezekiel snapped, anger sparking hot and furious in his chest. "One has absolutely nothing to do with the other." He shot to his feet, agitated. Too fucking...exposed.

He paced away from his brother, stalking across the office to the windows that looked out over Royal. Seconds later, he retraced his path, halting in front of Luke, the coffee table separating them like a tumbleweed blowing across a dirt street. "You accuse me of having a savior complex, but I'm not the one who's basically moved into his office, assuming the responsibility of saving this company all on his own. Analyze yourself before you decide to play armchair psychiatrist with me."

The silence between them vibrated with tension and anger. *His* anger. Because instead of getting in Ezekiel's face and firing a response back at him, Luke reclined back against the couch and stretched an arm across the top of it.

"Hit a nerve, did I?" he murmured, arching an eyebrow.

"Shut the hell up," Ezekiel snapped.

That shit his brother had spouted wasn't true. After Melissa, Ezekiel went out of his way to avoid becoming deeply involved with people outside of his family. He wasn't arrogant enough to think he could rescue people like a superhero in a suit instead of in a cape and tights.

"Zeke." Luke's sigh reached him moments before he stood and circled the coffee table. "What you're doing for Reagan? It's a good thing. I didn't mean to imply it wasn't or that you shouldn't do it. I'm just...concerned." He set a hand on Ezekiel's shoulder, forcing him to look into the face that was as familiar to him as his own. "I need you to be careful, okay? I don't want you to get hurt again."

Ezekiel shook his head. "This is more of a business arrangement than a relationship. We both understand that. You don't have to worry about me. Everything is going to be fine."

Luke nodded, but the skepticism darkening his eyes didn't dissipate. And for the moment, Ezekiel chose to ignore it. Just as he'd chosen to disregard the unexpected urge to protect Reagan from her father's censure tonight. To put her happiness before his own preferences when he'd agreed with her mother's wishes to extend their engagement from two weeks to six months.

Reagan had never come across as fragile to him; though slim and petite in stature, she possessed a confidence and self-assuredness that made her seem unbreakable...untouchable. But tonight? There'd been moments when he could've sworn her bones had been traded for glass. And he'd fought the insane urge to wrap her up and cushion her from the strange tension that had sprung up at moments between her and her parents.

Luke squeezed his shoulder. "Telling me not to worry is like telling the Cowboys not to pass Amari Cooper the football. Ain't going to happen."

Ezekiel snorted, and Luke returned to the couch and his spread of papers. Before he lost Luke's attention completely to work, Ezekiel followed and swept up the empty coffee cup and takeout container. He crossed the room and tossed them in the trash can.

"Thanks, Luke," he said, heading for the office door.

"For what?" his brother muttered absently.

"For being there."

Luke's head snapped up, his light brown eyes focused and sharp.

"Always."

He was right about that, Ezekiel mused, letting himself out and closing the door shut behind him. Through everything, Luke had always been there for him. Had never failed him.

Even when Ezekiel failed himself.

# Seven

Reagan stepped off the elevator onto the executive floor of the Wingate Enterprises building. She barely noticed the tasteful, expensive furnishings or exquisite decor that prevented the office from feeling *corporate* but instead exuded welcome and competence.

She did notice the silence.

And not like the peaceful stillness of the cemetery where she and Ezekiel had encountered each other weeks ago.

No, tension reverberated in this quiet. It stretched so tight, screamed so loud she curled her fingers into her palms to prohibit her from reverting to her six-year-old self and slapping her hands over her ears.

She strode past the desks with people bent over them, hard at work, and the office doors shutting out the world. The anxiety that seemed to permeate the air like a rancid perfume twisted her stomach into knots.

She'd seen the news this morning. Had blankly stared at the screen as words like *DEA*, *drugs* and *smuggling* were thrown at her by solemn-faced news anchors who were unable to hide the inappropriate glee in their eyes over a juicy story. Her first thought had been to get to Ezekiel. To see if he was okay. To…*protect him*.

Reagan shook her head as she approached the circular, gleaming wood desk that sat outside his shut office doors. There was no protecting him or his family from this latest development in what had become a perpetual shit storm that circled the Wingate clan and their company. And he didn't need or want that from her anyway. No, she was here to make sure her friend/fiancé wasn't reeling.

Pausing in front of the desk, she met the curious gaze of the pretty woman behind it. Recognition dawned in her brown eyes seconds later, and she smiled.

"Good morning, Ms. Sinclair. How can I help you?"

Glancing down at the gold nameplate on the desk, Reagan returned the woman's smile. "I'm well, Ms. Reynolds. I don't have an appointment, but is Ezekiel free for a few minutes? I need to speak with him."

"Of course. I'm sure he would love a visit from his fiancée this morning. It also happens he's in between meetings, so it should be fine." She lifted the phone from its cradle and punched a button. "Mr. Holloway, Ms. Sinclair is here to see you." She paused. "I'll send her right in." Replacing the phone, she nodded. "He's waiting on you, and belated congratulations on your engagement."

"Thank you," Reagan murmured, heading for Ezekiel's office.

Would she ever get used to being called someone's fiancée? No, not someone. Ezekiel Holloway's. She doubted it. Three weeks had passed since they'd announced their intent to marry to her parents, and sometimes it still felt like a dream. Or a nightmare. There were days she couldn't decide which.

Even though he expected her, she still rapped the door, then turned the knob. She entered and scanned the office, finding Ezekiel perched behind his desk, dark brows furrowed as he studied the computer monitor in front of him. For a moment, she entertained spinning around and exiting as quickly—and impulsively—as she'd made the decision to come here.

But Ezekiel glanced up, and she halted midstep, her heels sinking into the plush carpet.

God, he looked…exhausted. His brown skin pulled taut over the sharp slashes of his cheekbones, lending his already angular face more severity. Stark lines only enhanced the almost decadent fullness of his mouth, and guilt coiled inside her for noticing. Faint, dark circles bruised the flesh under his eyes as if it'd been some time since the last time he and sleep had been acquainted.

The news about the DEA investigation had apparently dropped sometime yesterday even though she'd just seen it this morning. That had probably been the last time he'd visited a bed. Weariness dulled his usually bright green eyes, and her fingertips tingled with the need to cross the room, kneel beside him and stroke the tender skin under his eyes, to brush her lips across his eyelids. Anything to remove the worry, anger and fear from those mesmerizing depths.

Instead, she remained where she stood. First, Ezekiel wouldn't appreciate her noticing those emotions in his gaze—would most likely deny their existence. And second, that wasn't what they were to each other. Business partners and friends, yes. But lovers kissed and comforted each other to ease pain. And they were most definitely not, nor ever would be, lovers.

Still… God, she wanted to touch him.

Inhaling a deep breath and cursing the madness that had brought her here, she moved forward until reaching the visitor's chair in front of his desk. She didn't sit but curled her fingers around the back of it and studied him some more.

"You look terrible," she said without preamble. Blunt, but preferable to *do you need a hug?*

A faint smirk tilted the corner of his mouth before it disappeared. "Thank you for that. But I doubt you drove all the way out here just to critique my personal appearance. What's going on?"

"I—" Damn. Now that she was here, awkwardness coursed through her. She smothered a sigh. "I saw the news this morning. I wanted to make sure you were…okay."

"Am I okay?" he repeated, loosing a harsh bark of laughter. She tried not to flinch at the sound but didn't quite succeed. "Drugs were found at the WinJet plant. Now, on top of falsifying inspection reports and causing injury to our employees, we're being accused of drug trafficking. The DEA has been called in. And we're the subject of a drug smuggling investigation. No, Reagan, I'm far from *okay*."

He shoved his chair back and shot to his feet.

"Dammit." He cupped the back of his neck, roughly massaging it. He stalked to the floor-to-ceiling window that offered a view of the Wingate Enterprises property and the town of Royal. It was picturesque, but she doubted he saw anything but his own demons. "I'm sorry," he rasped several seconds later. "I didn't mean to snap at you. It's been a rough couple of days."

"I can only imagine," she murmured. After a brief hesitation where she silently ordered herself to stay put, she disobeyed her better judgment and crossed the floor to stand next to him. "No, actually, I can't imagine. And I'm sorry. The last few weeks must have been hell for you and your family."

"The workers who were injured in the fire sued, and we decided to settle the lawsuit. Just when we believed the worst had started to blow over, *this* happens. I can't—" He broke off, his jaw clenching so hard, a muscle ticked along its hewn edge. "It's like we're cursed. Like one of those bedtime stories where the family lives this golden, blessed life and then an evil witch decides to strike them with trouble from every turn." Emitting another of those razor-sharp laughs, he shook his head. "Goddamn, now I'm talking in fairy tales."

Her chest squeezed so hard, she could barely push out a

breath. Ezekiel's big frame nearly vibrated with the strength of his tightly leashed emotions. His frustration, his confusion, his…helplessness reached out to her, and she employed every ounce of self-control to stop herself from reaching back out in return.

"I'm sorry," he breathed, rubbing his palm down his face, the bristle of his trimmed beard scraping in the silence. "Thank you for coming by. That was sweet of you, and though I didn't act like it, I appreciate it."

"It's what friends do," she replied, reminding herself out loud why she couldn't touch him.

"And fiancées?" Ezekiel asked, a hint of teasing underneath the weariness in his voice.

"Of course," she added with a casual shrug of her shoulder. "A real one would offer sex to comfort you, but the way our arrangement is set up…" *Oh hell.* Had she really said that? She'd been joking, but… Oh. *Hell.* "I was just kidding…"

She trailed off as he stared at her, the fatigue in his green gaze momentarily replaced by an intensity that vaporized the air in her lungs. The tension in the room switched to a thickness that seemed close to suffocating. She should say something, try to explain again that she was kidding. But was she? If he asked her for it, would she give her body to him? Let him lose himself for just a little while with her?

No.

*Yes.*

Images crowded into her mind. Images of them. Of him surrounding her, his thick, muscled arms encircling her and grasping her close as his large body surged inside her. Her thighs trembled, and her suddenly aching sex clenched. Hard. She swallowed a gasp at the phantom sensation of being possessed by him, stretched by him. Branded by him.

"But you're not my real fiancée, are you, Ray?" he finally said, and if his tone sounded rougher, well, she ignored it. She had to.

"No," she whispered. "I'm not."

"Because we're friends and you don't want me like that, right?" he asked, that dark gaze boring into her. As if he could see the truth behind her careful lies.

"Yes, we're friends," she agreed, raising a hand to her collarbone and rubbing the scar there through her thin blouse.

"And you don't think of me like that. Do you?" he pressed in that same deep, silken voice.

"No," she lied. Even as her subconscious shamed her for breaking a commandment.

He didn't say anything to that, but something inside her made her suspect he agreed with her subconscious. Did he *want* her to desire him? Or was he just making sure she understood where their boundary lines were drawn?

The latter. Definitely the latter.

"What's next for you? For Wingate Enterprises?" she asked, desperately turning the conversation back to the reason she'd come here.

He shifted his gaze from her and back to the window. "I don't know," he admitted on a gruff whisper. Again, he rubbed the nape of his neck. "Once the DEA gets involved that could mean anything. They could freeze our assets. Confiscate anything they believe is related to the accusations. Lock the doors of the building. Arrest anyone they consider involved... *Fuck*," he snarled. "How did we get here?"

"It's just been a couple of days, Zeke. They'll find out who planted the drugs, and Wingate will be cleared."

He shot her a sharp glance. *"Planted?"* he demanded. He shook his head. "You would be the first person who suggested they were, and that we're not responsible for smuggling or trafficking."

She sliced a hand through the air. "That's nonsense. Your family would never be involved in something like that. There's an explanation, but you being a drug kingpin isn't it." She snorted. Because yes, the idea of it was just that ridiculous.

"God, Ray," he said. And for the first time, his chuckle wasn't a humorless, jagged thing that scraped her raw. "Thank you," he whispered. "Thank you for the first real laugh I've had in days." He lifted his arm, and it hovered between them for a couple of seconds before he brushed the backs of his fingers across her cheek. "Thank you for not turning and hightailing it at my bark and braving my bite."

"Yes, well, I don't appreciate being snapped at. But for that apology, I'll make an exception and like it," she mumbled, echoing the same thing she'd said to him at her parents' home.

He obviously remembered because he smiled. But then his hand dropped away, and he sobered. "Ray," he said, his voice lowering. "If you're having second thoughts about marrying me, I understand. You don't have to be afraid to tell me."

"What?" Surprise rocked through her, and she frowned. "Why would I have second thoughts?"

He sighed, and the exhaustion crept back into his face. "The terms of your grandmother's will state you need to marry a suitable man. And when your father gave us his blessing, he didn't know that my family would soon be accused of being a criminal enterprise. There's no way he can be pleased with this turn of events. Or with his daughter becoming involved with it merely by association."

"I'm not tainted by you, Zeke," she snapped, offended. And yes, her father could be old-fashioned and stuck in his ways, but even he drew the line at convicting a man until he'd been proven guilty. "And I resent the implication that my being connected to you would. I'll handle my father. I'm not calling off the engagement. Are you?"

He hesitated, that springtime gaze roaming her face as if searching for the truth behind her words. Finally, he said, "No, I'm not calling it off."

"Good," she said, tone brisk. "Now, I need you to do something for me." She didn't wait for his acquiescence but strode across the room and settled down on the chocolate leather couch in his sitting area. "Come here. Please," she belatedly tacked on.

He slowly walked toward her, his forehead creased in a frown. "What's going on? Why?"

She patted the cushion next to her. "I meant what I said," she said, plucking up one of the brown-and-red-patterned throw pillows and placing it on her lap. "You look terrible. Like you haven't slept. Or eaten. I can't do anything about the food part, but I can make you take a nap. Here." She tapped the pillow. "Just for a little while."

"Ray…" he protested, halting at the foot of the couch. "I'm not a kindergartner. I can't just take a time-out. I—"

"Will fall down in exhaustion if you don't take care of yourself. This situation is only going to get worse before it's cleared up. If you're not going to watch out for yourself, as your friend, I will. So get over here. Now." She injected a steely firmness into her tone that she didn't quite feel. And part of her burned with pent-up desire. But God, she couldn't touch him. Definitely couldn't sex the worry away. But she had to do something. Had to give him…something.

"Seriously, Ray. I have a ton of work to do and fires to put out. And, dammit, I feel ridiculous," he grumbled.

"Can you just shut up and humor me? I did abandon a beautification committee meeting and poked the wrath of Henrietta Sinclair to drive all the way over here and see you. The very least you can do is give me a couple of min-

utes," she insisted, throwing a glare in just for good measure so he knew she meant business.

"For God's sake…" he muttered, lowering to the couch
and reclining back, setting his head on the pillow across
her lap. "One day you're going to make an excellent mother,
seeing how well you have the guilt trip down."

His words punched her in the chest, and she couldn't
control the spasm that crossed her face. With his eyes closed
and his arms crossed over his chest, he didn't glimpse it,
and for that, she was grateful.

Reagan pushed through the hollowness his innocent
words left behind and pressed her fingertips to his temples. Slowly, she massaged the tender areas, applying just
enough pressure to soothe. Over the years, when her father
had come home tense from a hard day at work, her mother
had sat him down and done the same. And he would release
a rumble of pleasure just as Ezekiel did.

Gradually, his big body relaxed, and his arms loosened,
dropping to his sides. His beautiful lips parted on a heavy
sigh, and he turned his head toward her. It didn't skip her
attention, that if not for the pillow, his face would hover
dangerously close to the part of her that harbored no confusion about what it wanted from this man.

Even now, tenderness mixed with longing. With a lan-
guorous desire that wound its way through her like her
veins were tributaries for this need. His wind-and-earth
scent drifted up to her, and she just gave up and soaked in
it. Here, under the guise of friendship and offering the little
bit of comfort she could allow and he would take, she could
lower her self-imposed barriers and just…bask in him. Soon
enough she would have to raise them again.

For both of their sakes.

"Ray?" came his drowsy mumble.

"Yes?"

His thick, black lashes lifted, and she stared down into his eyes.

"Thank you," he murmured.

"You already said that," she reminded him.

"I haven't thanked you for being my friend."

"Oh," she said. "You're welcome, Zeke."

And damn if that reality check didn't sting.

# Eight

"I'd have to say your engagement party is a success," Luke observed.

Ezekiel had to agree. Tuxedoed and gowned guests crowded into the great room of the Texas Cattleman's Clubhouse. Their chatter and laughter filled the air, and yes, by all appearances, his and Reagan's engagement party was going off without a hitch.

When he'd asked his cousin Beth to help him organize the party three weeks ago, she'd taken over, arranging to have it in the clubhouse where several people in the family were members. Several years ago, the club had undergone a major renovation, and now it was lighter and airier with brighter colors, bigger windows and higher ceilings. Tonight, floor-to-ceiling French doors had been thrown open to the July night, and the warm, flower-scented air filtered into the room, making the already cavernous area seem larger.

Flowers, white, tiny fairy lights and even a beautiful arch decorated the space, and the dark wood floors seemed to gleam. Tall lamps had been placed on the patio beyond the French doors and more of the lights had been entwined around the columns and balustrades. Linen-covered tables, with elegant hurricane lamps and more flowers adorning them, dotted the room and bordered a wide area for dancing.

Everything was sophisticated, luxurious and gorgeous. His cousin had managed to pull off the impossible in a matter of weeks.

Yet, Ezekiel hadn't taken a single easy breath all evening. Like that other shoe just hovered above his head, ready to plunge into the room at any moment.

"Even Aunt Ava seems to be pleased with your choice of fiancée," Luke continued. "Considering her higher-than-God standards, that's a minor miracle."

Ezekiel snorted, sipping from his tumbler of whiskey. Luke wasn't wrong. His aunt might be a thin, somewhat fragile-looking woman, with her dark blond hair brushed with the lightest of gray, but one look into those shrewd gray-green eyes, and all thoughts of frailty vanished. She was a strong, driven woman who had been a wife, was a businesswoman and mother. And if you asked her children, they might tell you in that order. The death of Uncle Trent had been a severe blow to her. But she'd begun to return to her old, exacting, often domineering self just before the issues with WinJet hit.

"I'm glad she came tonight," Ezekiel said, studying his aunt and the man next to her. "I see she brought Keith."

"Since when is Keith Cooper going to let her go anywhere without him?" Luke muttered, the dislike Ezekiel harbored for the man evident in his brother's voice. "I swear, it would be almost laughable how obvious he is if it weren't so pathetic."

As his uncle's best friend, Keith Cooper had been in their lives for years. On the surface, the man with the thinning brown hair, dark eyes and athletic build that had softened from one too many bourbons was an affable, laid-back man with an easy laugh. Married and divorced three times and with no children, he'd adopted the Wingates as his family. Or rather he'd inserted himself into their family.

And maybe that was what rubbed Ezekiel the wrong

way. Keith was always there. Like a snake. The big, toothy smile didn't hide how he watched Aunt Ava with an avarice that made Ezekiel's skin crawl. No, Keith hadn't done anything overt to earn his dislike, but Ezekiel didn't trust him.

Not at all.

"So you know, I have my speech prepared," Luke drawled, tugging Ezekiel's attention from his aunt.

He frowned. "What speech?"

"The best man's speech. Beth set aside a time for toasts after dinner. With everything that's going on, I figured you just hadn't gotten around to asking me yet." Luke slid him a sidelong glance. "But I knew you would ask so I came ready."

"Well, that was subtle as hell." Ezekiel laughed. "Of course you're my best man. Besides, Sebastian said no." At Luke's scowl, he barked out another laugh. "Kidding. Damn. I'm going to need to ask Kelly to schedule an enema to get that stick out of your ass."

"Hilarious. You're so fucking hilarious," Luke grumbled, but a grin tugged at the corner of his mouth. "It must be that pretty-boy face that Reagan is enamored with because it sure as hell isn't your sense of humor."

"Oh, I disagree. I'm quite fond of both," Reagan interjected, appearing at Ezekiel's side and sliding an arm around his waist.

She tipped her head so it rested on his shoulder, and the casual observer would believe this woman, with her radiant beauty and equally bright smile was blissfully in love. Hell, he almost believed it. But apparently one of Reagan's many talents included acting. She didn't flinch or stiffen when he stroked her arm or held her close to his side. Instead, she'd flirted with him, gifting him with affectionate glances and warm smiles.

Reagan was an enigma.

A gorgeous, sensual enigma that he wanted to cautiously

step away from before the obsession of figuring out her many pieces consumed him.

The same woman who appeared to be the perfect daughter bravely entered into a business arrangement of a marriage so she could quietly defy her family and claim her own future. The same woman who lived her life on the center stage of Royal society, but whose eyes glimmered with sadness when she didn't think anyone noticed. The same woman who went rigid when he just brushed a tender caress over her cheek but invited him to lay his head in her lap to offer comfort.

Who was the real Reagan Sinclair? And why did desperation to discover the truth rip and claw at him?

This curiosity, this need to… To what? He knew what. And it—she—was forbidden to him.

Yet…when she'd drawn his head to her lap, had rubbed his temples with such care, he'd inhaled her delicious, intoxicating scent. Had locked down every muscle in his body to prevent himself from tearing away that pillow and burying his face between her slim, toned thighs to find out if her delectable perfume would be more condensed there. He'd closed his eyes against staring at the beautiful, firm breasts that had thrust against her blouse, fearful of seeing her nipples bead under the white silk. If he had, he might not have been able to stop until he had them clasped between his teeth, tugging, pinching…

Jesus Christ.

He lifted the whiskey to his mouth once more and took a healthy sip. Even now, with her hip pressed to his thigh, he wanted to hike her in his arms and show her and everyone else in the room how well they would fit together.

In truth, Reagan deserved a man who could give her all of his heart. A man who didn't view love as a trap with razor-tipped jaws. A man who could offer her security and a name that was above reproach.

He wasn't that man.

And yet, here he stood beside her, claiming her in front of family, friends and all of Royal.

When had he become so fucking selfish?

Luke cleared his throat, his eyebrows arching high. Laughter lit his brown eyes. And something told Ezekiel that Luke's humor was at his expense.

"What?" He frowned.

"Your fiancée asked you a question. But you seemed so engrossed in your drink, I think you missed it," Luke drawled.

A growl rumbled at the back of Ezekiel's throat, but he swallowed down the curse he itched to throw at his brother. He harbored zero doubts Luke at least had a clue where Ezekiel's thoughts had been.

"I'm sorry, sweetheart," Ezekiel apologized, glancing down at her. "What did you say?"

"I asked you to go ahead and confess the truth," she said, shooting him a chiding glance. "You hired a battalion of party planners to carry all of this off. And they worked all day and through the night like shoemaking elves."

He smiled, cocking his head to the side. "I help run a hugely successful, national conglomerate. You think I can't handle the planning and execution of one party?"

She mimicked his gesture, crossing her arms for good measure. His smile widened. Since that day in his office a couple of weeks ago, they'd become a little closer. Friendlier.

And that was both heaven and hell for him.

"Okay, fine. I begged my cousin Beth for help. She and Gracie Diaz attacked it with a competency that frankly scares the hell out of me. And all I had to promise in return was that you'd help with this year's TCC charity masquerade ball. See? I'm a problem solver."

"So in other words, you pimped me out for a party.

You're lucky I'm marrying you," she muttered, but ruined her mock-annoyance with a soft chuckle. "With Dad being a TCC member, I've assisted with past charity balls, so I'd be happy to help."

"I'm glad to hear that," he drawled. "Especially since Beth told me if I don't learn to ask my future wife for her opinion instead of just arbitrarily volunteering her for things, I might need to start Googling for a large doghouse now."

"Beth always was brilliant." Reagan laughed. "Oh, I met your cousins Sebastian and Sutton. And I have no idea how you can tell them apart. They're identical twins, but wow."

"Oh I know. I've known them all my life, and it's sometimes still hard for me to tell them apart if I'm not looking close enough."

Luke snorted. "They used to get into all kinds of shi—I mean, trouble—when they were younger, playing tricks on people."

"I can only imagine. And it's okay, Luke." She grinned. "I've heard the word *shit* before. You won't offend my sensibilities."

Luke chuckled, holding his hands up in the age-old sign of surrender. "Yes, but even though my mother is no longer here, I think she would come down and smack the back of my head for saying it in front of you."

"He's not wrong," Ezekiel added with a laugh. Nina Holloway had been a stickler for manners. "As far as telling my cousins apart, Sebastian has a scar on his lower back from when we were kids. Whenever they tried to play jokes on us and switch places, I would always grab one of them and look for the scar. I wouldn't advise doing that here though."

"I'll save that for the wedding reception then," she promised, and both he and Luke chuckled. God, she was sweet. And in ways, too damn innocent for him. "Are you about ready to head into dinner?"

"Yes." Because this piece of theater allowed him to, he stroked a hand down her long, lustrous waves. Then because he'd already admitted his selfishness, he tangled his fingers in the thick strands and tipped her head back. He noted the flash of wariness in the chicory depths, but she didn't turn from him, didn't playfully admonish him and pull away.

Granting her time to do either, he lowered his head and brushed his lips across her forehead. And because the feel of her under his mouth proved to be more of a temptation than he could resist, he repeated the caress over the gentle slope of her nose. Her soft but swift intake of breath echoed between them. "Lead the way," he murmured.

Slowly, she nodded and as he loosened his hold on her hair, she stepped back. The smile she flashed him trembled before firming. An apology for crossing boundaries lurched to his tongue.

But then he caught the heat swirling beneath the shadows in her eyes seconds before her lashes lowered.

That unintended glimpse arrowed straight to his dick.

Now it was his control that he clenched instead of her hair.

And when she reached back and entwined his fingers with hers as they headed across the room, he clung to the reasons why he couldn't escort her out of this party to the nearest dark room and fuck her senseless.

"Can you believe their arrogance? Being investigated by the DEA and throwing this party as if nothing is happening. Their gall is astounding. Even for Wingates."

Ezekiel's steps faltered and he nearly stumbled as the not-nearly-so-low whispers reached his ears. In front of him, Reagan stopped, her slim shoulders stiffening.

But another ugly voice piped up just behind them.

A disgusted snort. "I wonder if drug money is paying for all of this. Or blood money, as I like to call it."

"Goddammit," Luke quietly spat beside him.

Rage, pain, powerlessness and shame. They eddied and churned inside him, whipping and stinging. A howl scraped at his throat, but he trapped it, unwilling to give anyone more to gossip and cackle over.

"If you'll excuse me for a moment," Reagan said, her voice hard in a way he'd never heard from her. Not until she firmly disentangled her hand from his did he realize how tightly he gripped her.

Unmoving, he and Luke watched as she turned and crossed the short distance to the two older women who had been maligning them. Reagan smiled at them, and as if they hadn't just been ripping his family apart with their tongues, they returned the warm gesture. Hooking her arms through theirs, she led them through the crowd and toward the great room exit. She tipped her head to the club's security who unobtrusively stood vigil at the door, and in moments, the two men escorted the women out.

Ezekiel gaped at her as she retraced her path toward him and Luke.

"Holy shit," Luke marveled. "That might've been the hottest thing I've ever witnessed in my life."

"Watch your mouth," Ezekiel muttered. "That's my future wife you're talking about." But damn if Luke wasn't right. That take-no-shit act had been hot.

"Now," Reagan said, returning to his side, "we were headed into dinner." She clasped his hand again and moved forward as if nothing had interrupted them.

"I need to know, darlin'," Luke said, falling into step on her other side. Whether Reagan was his fake fiancée or not, she'd won his brother's admiration and probably his loyalty with her actions tonight. "What did you say to them?"

"Oh, I just thanked them for coming to celebrate our upcoming nuptials. But that I refused to feed mouths that could congratulate us out of one side and denigrate us from the other. Then I wished them a good night and asked security to escort them out."

Luke threw back his head on a loud bark of laughter that drew several curious glances. "Remind me never to cross you, Reagan Sinclair."

Pride, fierce and bright, glowed within Ezekiel, and even if their relationship was only pretense, he was delighted he could claim this woman as his.

And that scared the hell out of him.

# Nine

"Reagan, I need a word with you, please."

Reagan paused midstep as she crossed her home's foyer toward the staircase, glancing at her father, who stood in the entrance to the living room.

Checking her thin, gold watch, she frowned. Just five fifteen. Douglas Sinclair routinely didn't arrive home until almost six o'clock from his law office. Had he been waiting on her?

"Sure, Dad. But will this take long? I have plans for this evening."

She'd agreed to accompany Ezekiel to a dinner at his family's estate at six tonight. But she'd lost track of time at the girls' home and was now running late. That had been happening more and more lately as her responsibilities at the home had expanded from administrative to more interaction with the girls.

Ezekiel didn't seem to mind when she called to apologize or reschedule dates. She should've told him by now where she spent the majority of her time, because after the engagement party three weeks ago, they'd grown even more comfortable with each other. Yet that kernel of fear that he would dismiss her efforts—or maybe worse, ask why she volunteered there—prevented her from confiding in him. As it did from admitting the truth to her parents.

But he wasn't her father. So maybe she would tell him

tonight after dinner. Not…everything. Still, she could share this. *Maybe*.

Her father didn't reply to her but turned and entered the living room, leaving her to follow. Her frown deepened. What was going on? Douglas's grim expression and the tensing of her stomach didn't bode well for this conversation.

"Sit, please," he said, waving toward the couch as he lowered to the adjacent chair.

Though she would've preferred to stand—easier to make a quick exit—she sank to the furniture. "What's wrong, Dad?"

He crossed one leg over the other and propped his elbows on the chair's arms, templing his fingers under his chin. That sense of foreboding increased. She and her siblings deemed this position his Thinking Man pose. Which usually meant he was about to lecture one of them or deliver an edict they probably wouldn't like.

"Reagan, I initially went along with this sudden relationship with Ezekiel Holloway and gave you my blessing for the engagement, but now I have concerns," her father said.

"About?" she pressed when he didn't immediately continue.

Her heart thudded against her chest, and she forced herself to remain composed. Douglas Sinclair despised theatrics. And the last thing she could afford was for him to accuse her of being too emotional to make an informed decision.

"The Wingate name used to be spotless and above reproach in not just Royal, but Texas. But now, with this scandal about dirty dealings at the jet plants, employee lawsuits and now drugs, for God's sake, I believe it's been dirtied beyond repair."

"Miles Wingate proved that the family wasn't responsible for the falsified inspection reports. Which makes me doubt everything else about the drugs," she argued. "You've known the Wingate family longer than I have, Dad. You have to know they couldn't be capable of trafficking or anything as reprehensible as that."

"I don't know anything of the sort," he disagreed. "People are not always who they appear to be. And while Trent Wingate might've been a trustworthy man, I cannot vouch for his family. Not personally." He lowered his arms and leaned forward, pinning her with a steady stare. "Besides, in the eyes of the public, they are guilty. Their reputation sullied. I don't believe it is wise to connect your name—or this family's name—with theirs at this time."

Her stomach bottomed out. She'd suspected this was where he'd been heading. But hearing him state it...

"James Harris, the president of the Cattleman's Club, as well as other TCC members all support the Wingates. They're not worried about their reputations being 'sullied,'" she said, imbuing her tone with her dislike over his elitist word choice. Hadn't she assured Ezekiel weeks ago that her father might be conservative but not arrogant or self-important? She shook her head.

"Maybe you're too blinded by your...*affection* for Ezekiel," Douglas continued. "But I think the right decision for not just you, but this family would be to break off this engagement. After all, how would it look if my firm was associated with people being investigated by the DEA for criminal behavior?" His mouth curled in distaste, eyes narrowing on her. "This doesn't only affect you. Your mother is also receiving the cold shoulder from some members of this community because her daughter is marrying into that family."

"That family?" she repeated, giving a short, harsh chuckle. Although she found nothing humorous about this conversation. "God, Dad, *that family* has been here in Royal for generations. They've done an immense amount of good for not just this community but outside the city with their philanthropic efforts. They're good people. And because of an accusation, of a rough period they're suffering through, you would abandon them?"

She huffed out a breath. "Before Ezekiel was my fiancé, he was my friend. Harley was my best friend. I refuse to just throw them away because people who indulge in rampant speculation rather than fact have nothing better to do than sit in judgment. I won't be one of them."

"You have no choice," he announced, tone flat and brooking no argument. "Your grandmother's will stipulates that you will receive your inheritance if you marry a suitable man. I determine the definition of suitable. And Ezekiel Holloway is not it. If you go through with this marriage, I won't release one penny to you until you're thirty. And don't try to convince me that the inheritance isn't the reason for this shotgun marriage. I went along wit 't at first, but no longer."

Fury blazed through her, and as she rose, her body trembled with it. Only respect bridled her tongue when she wanted to lash out at the father she loved. Since she didn't trust herself to speak, she pivoted and strode out of the room.

"You will end the engagement, Reagan," her father declared from behind her.

She didn't bother to turn around or glance over her shoulder at him as she pulled the front door open and walked out of her home.

Ezekiel buttoned the cuff of his shirt, frowning as he crossed the foyer of his guesthouse to answer the knock at the door. That had to be Reagan. He'd received her terse text about being on her way, but not only was she fifteen minutes early, they'd agreed yesterday that he was supposed to pick her up from her house. He hadn't needed to hear her voice to guess that something was wrong.

In seconds, he opened the door and his suspicions were confirmed. Though she was as lovely as ever in a pair of light green, wide-legged trousers and a white camisole, her customary smile didn't light up her face. Instead, her lush mouth formed a straight, serious line and shadows dimmed her pretty eyes. Unease slicked a path through him, and he stepped back, silently inviting her inside.

"What's wrong, Reagan?" he asked, closing the door behind her.

She whirled around, facing him, and thankfully didn't make him wait. "My father ambushed me when I arrived home." Her lips twisted into a bitter smile. "He's rescinded his approval of our marriage. Apparently, it wouldn't be good for his reputation or business. *God.*" She thrust her fingers through her dark waves and paced across the foyer, her strides fairly vibrating with her anger. Pausing in front of a painting depicting the Wingate estate, she stared at it for several long moments. But he doubted she was really seeing it. "I'm sorry, Zeke," she whispered. "I'm so angry. And ashamed."

"Ray, look at me," he quietly ordered. When she slowly spun around, he studied her gorgeous features, noting the conflict in her eyes, the sad downturn of her mouth. The slight slump of her shoulders. "Your father's not wrong."

Fire flashed in her gaze, replacing the distress. The breath snagged in his chest at the sight. Dammit, she was beautiful, and that passion only enhanced it.

Still… He couldn't blame Douglas. In the weeks since he'd visited the older man's home asking for his blessing, Wingate Enterprises had started to free-fall. In the wake of this latest scandal, stocks had plummeted, most of their jet contracts had been canceled and there had even been some boycotting of their hotels. They'd had to start laying off staff. With company assets frozen by the DEA, they couldn't even liquidate their holdings to plug up the worst of the bleeding.

So no, Douglas had the right to be concerned about his daughter marrying a man who might not even be able to provide for her. Whose name could bring her more harm than good.

"Of course he's wrong," she snapped. "And I would never abandon you just because of gossip and innuendo. What kind of person would that make me? What kind of friend would that make me?"

*A smart one.* Instead of voicing that opinion, he slid his hands into the front pockets of his pants and murmured, "You never did tell me what you needed your inheritance for, Ray. To go to such extreme measures like agreeing to marry me, you must have a reason, a purpose for the money."

Her expression smoothed, becoming the loveliest of masks. "I already told you. I want my freedom."

"I remember," he agreed, moving closer to her and not stopping until they stood only bare inches apart. "But over the course of the weeks we've spent together, I've also come to know a woman who wouldn't allow something like money to keep her from grabbing that freedom. No, there's something else."

He paused, cocking his head to the side. "Do you think I haven't noticed that you disappear during the day several times a week? As much as I remember the girl you used to be, the woman is still sometimes a mystery. You're keeping secrets, Ray. And your reason for needing this money is one of them." He slid a hand free and pinched a lock of her hair between his thumb and finger, rubbing the rough silk of it. "You can trust me with your secrets, sweetheart."

Indecision flared in her eyes before her lashes lowered,

hiding her emotion from him. But he caught the slight quiver of her lips before they firmed.

"Trust me," he damn near pleaded. His desperation for her to do just that shook him. But he didn't rescind the words.

The thick fringe of lashes lifted, and she stared at him. Weighing him. And relief flowed through Ezekiel when her lips parted because she'd obviously found him worthy.

"I plan to open a fully staffed and independent home for pregnant teen mothers here in Royal."

Shock quaked through him, pleasure rippling in its wake. Jesus. Of all the things he'd expected her to say, a haven for unwed mothers hadn't even been in the top ten. Admiration for her lit him up from within. Outside of his family, most of the socialites he knew served on boards or committees for charities, but very few desired to get their hands dirty.

Why *this* cause? Did she know someone who'd been pregnant, abandoned and homeless? The questions crowded onto his tongue, but rather than ask them, he cupped her face between his hands, stepping closer to her. "This is important to you, isn't it?"

Reagan nodded, and her lips parted as if to offer him an explanation, but after a hesitation, she closed them again, shifting her gaze over his shoulder.

"No, sweetheart, please don't look away from me." When she returned her regard to him, he swept his thumb over her cheek, and for a moment, he wished it was his mouth tracing the curve, tasting that soft, beautiful skin. "Thank you."

"For what?" she breathed.

"For trusting me with that information. I'm assuming your parents don't know about your plans?"

She shook her head, her hair caressing the backs of his hands and wrists. "No. They…wouldn't approve."

"Your secret is safe with me. And, Ray?" He settled a thumb under her chin, tilting her head back so she had no choice but to meet his gaze. His heart thumped against his sternum, and he viciously cursed himself for what he had to do. "Your project is also safe with me. Which is why I'm breaking off this engagement."

Hurt and anger flashed across her face. Her brows drew down into a frown as she settled her palms on his chest. She pushed at him, but he braced himself, refusing to be budged. Instead, he tightened his hold on her.

"Let me go, Ezekiel," she demanded. "If you don't want—"

"Want what, Ray?" he snarled. "Want you to have your freedom, your dreams sooner rather than four years from now? Want you to not damage your relationship with your family over me? Want you to have everything you deserve?" *Want you?* He ground his teeth together, trapping that last question. "I want all of that for you. And whether you admit it or not, your father, your mother—they're important to you. And I'm not going to let you risk that."

*Not for me.*

She sighed and the soft gust of air brushed over his skin. Like a kiss.

"It's not right. None of it," she whispered, the fingers that were trying to push him away seconds ago curling into his shirt. "I wish…"

Her voice trailed off, and he was grateful. Because a part of him hungered to know what she wished, what she desired. Maybe it was for the best—for both of them—that they were making a clean break. Before they crossed a line that neither of them could come back from.

That they would ultimately regret.

Giving in to a need that he refused to acknowledge, he lowered his head and pressed his mouth to her forehead. He inhaled her honeysuckle-and-cream scent, capturing it like a photograph. Her breath tickled his neck, and he stood still for a long moment, enjoying the sensation on his skin.

Lifting his head, he met her gaze. His gut tightened to the point of pain. Sadness swirled in those chicory depths. But so did a touch of heat, of desire. *Fuck.* It wouldn't require more than the barest of movements to take her mouth. To possess it. To find out if his dirtiest midnight fantasies about her texture, her taste came close to reality. With one tiny shift, he could satisfy his curiosity and just *know…*

He stepped back, dropping his arms to his sides. "You'd better go before your family starts to wonder where you are," he said, forcing a neutrality into his voice that didn't exist.

"Right," she agreed softly. "Take care of yourself, Zeke."

"You, too, Ray."

He turned to watch her leave, and though she paused on the threshold of the front entrance after opening the door, she didn't turn around or glance over her shoulder at him.

Only when she left and he stared at a closed door did he exhale and shut his eyes.

He should be grateful. Relieved. And he was. But damn if he could decide if he'd dodged a bullet or lost the one thing that had given him purpose these last few weeks.

Given him peace.

He shook his head and pivoted on his heel, heading for the staircase.

It didn't matter. She was gone.

And in the end, it was for the best.

For both of them.

# Ten

Reagan stepped into the cool interior of the restaurant with a sigh, thankful to be out of the early September heat. It was only about three weeks from the official start of fall, but Texas didn't know it. Fixing a polite smile on her face, she strode to the maître d's stand.

"Hello," she greeted. "I'm meeting Douglas Sinclair. He should have already arrived."

"Of course," the young man said, nodding. "Please follow me."

She was ten minutes late for lunch with her father, but considering he'd sprung the "invitation" on her an hour ago, it couldn't be helped. He should be thankful she'd rearranged her plans to meet him anyway.

The only reason she had acquiesced to this impromptu lunch date was because he'd made it seem important, urgent even. It'd been two weeks since her father had demanded she end her engagement with Ezekiel, and a part of her still resented him for that. But maybe this lunch could be the start of healing that rift. Her father loved her; in her heart, she acknowledged he only wanted the best for her. Even if he could be overbearing and stubborn, she'd never doubted that...

"Reagan." Douglas stood from a table next to the large picture window that looked over downtown Royal. "We've been waiting on you. You look lovely."

She barely registered the kiss he pressed to her hair, focusing on the *we*. This was supposed to be a lunch for just the two of them. But as her attention snagged on the man also rising from his chair, a cold sliver of hurt and anger settled between her ribs.

Of course her father hadn't just wanted to spend quality time with her. He had his own agenda, and that trumped everything.

"Reagan, I'd like to introduce you to Justin McCoy. Justin…" he smiled broadly at the other man "…my beautiful daughter Reagan Sinclair."

*Justin McCoy.* The tall, handsome man with light blond hair smiled at her, his blue eyes quickly roaming over her before meeting her gaze again.

God, she needed a shower. She cut her father a sharp side glance.

"It's an absolute pleasure to meet you, Reagan," Justin said, grasping her hand although she hadn't offered it. He lifted it toward his lips, and her stomach lurched. If not for her father's eagle-eyed gaze, she would've snatched her arm back. Especially since she hadn't given Justin permission to touch her.

On second thought…

She tugged her hand back before Justin could touch her, ignoring her father's frown and Justin's shock. She didn't believe in the *ask forgiveness rather than permission* school of thought. And if neither this man nor her father respected her boundaries, then she didn't have to allow a man who was at best a gold digger to put his hands or mouth on her to spare their egos.

That simmering anger stirred to a boil, and she dragged in a breath before forcing a politeness to her tone that required Herculean effort on her part.

"Mr. McCoy, if you would excuse us for a moment. I need to have a quick, private word with my father."

Not waiting for either man's agreement, she whirled on the heel of her nude stiletto and stalked toward the exit. She pushed through the door and waited for her father on the sidewalk outside the restaurant.

She didn't have long to wait before he appeared.

"How dare you embarrass me like that, Reagan," he fumed, fury glittering in his narrowed glare. "You go back in there right now and apologize for your rude behavior."

"I will not."

His chin jerked up as if her words had delivered a physical slap, and his lips slackened. She'd shocked him. Hell, she'd shocked herself. Her heart drummed against her rib cage, and the tiniest sliver of fear slid through her veins. Since she'd returned to Royal and her family from that home without her baby, empty and ashamed, she hadn't once defied either of her parents. Especially her father. And she would be lying to herself if she didn't admit it scared her now. But no.

Just. No. Apparently, she had her limits, and she'd reached them.

"Reagan—"

"I'm not an idiot, Dad," she interrupted, slicing her hand through the air for emphasis. "I clearly see what this is. An ambush. Another setup. Well, I refuse to go along with it. Not this time. And definitely not with *him*."

"Yes, you will, Reagan," he hissed, his attention shooting over her shoulder. Most likely ensuring no one stood witness to her insolence, as he no doubt saw it. "I won't stand for this blatant disrespect. And I don't know what you think you know about Justin McCoy—"

"It isn't what I *think* I know," she shot back. "That man in there intentionally seduced an innocent girl and got her pregnant just so he could worm his way into a wealthy family. Considering our family history, you would think impregnating a girl would be at the top of your unworthy traits list," she sneered.

"Lower your voice this instant," he ordered, once more glancing around them. And that tore through her like a red-hot sword. Of course. They couldn't chance anyone over-hearing about their shameful family secret. "Wasn't it you who told me I shouldn't listen to rumors and conjecture?"

"Rumors?" She released a jagged bark of laughter. "It's not an opinion that he used Julie Wheeler only to abandon her. It's not opinion that he tried to do the exact same thing with Beth Wingate. Ask Camden Guthrie or Bruce Wheeler. I promise you they will confirm that Justin McCoy's complete lack of a moral compass is a fact. After all, it was Cam's dead wife and Bruce's daughter he betrayed."

"It is my job as your father to decide what is best for you, Reagan. And I might have failed once but never again," he ground out.

Had she thought he'd hurt her before? No, this…this was pain. Having him affirm that he believed he'd failed—that she'd been a failure.

Her breath shuddered out of her, and she blinked back the sting of hot tears.

She loved her father, but at this moment, he disappointed her just as she surely disappointed him. Douglas thought the purse strings controlled her, had kept her obedient and quiet for all these years. But he couldn't have been more wrong. Longing for his approval had. For her mother's, too, but more so his. There was no turning back the hands of time to that innocent period when she'd been a daddy's girl. She might never have what she desperately craved from him. The only difference between now and an hour ago was that she no longer cared.

"And the fact that you would believe he is a better man, a more *suitable* man than Ezekiel Holloway stuns and dis-heartens me." She shook her head. "I love you, Dad, but

I'm not going along with this anymore. I know you want what's best for me, but you've never asked me what that is. You don't care. And that saddens me even more."

She turned and walked away from him. And even when he called her name, she didn't stop.

She was through answering to him.

From now on, she would only answer to herself.

"Mr. Holloway, Reagan Sinclair is here to see you."

Ezekiel jerked his head up from studying a report at his executive assistant's announcement through the telephone's intercom. Alarm blared inside him, and he shot up from his chair, already rounding the desk and stalking toward the office door. There had been no communication between them since he and Reagan had broken off their engagement. What had happened to make her end the radio silence now?

Before he reached the door, it swung open and Reagan stepped in. The impact of her after weeks of not seeing her halted him midstride. Jesus, had he really somehow forgotten how beautiful she was? Or had he just tried to convince himself she wasn't so he could stop thinking about her? Either way, the attempt had been an epic fail.

He'd missed everything about her—her laugh, her quiet way of listening, the cultured yet sensual husky tone of her voice, her scent...her friendship. And hell yes, he'd missed just looking at her. Today, her sleeveless wrap dress molded to her slim but curvaceous figure like a secret admirer, and damn him, but he was jealous of the material that cupped her lovely breasts, slid over the flare of her hips and glided down those slender, perfect thighs. His fingers itched to follow the same paths, to explore that uncharted territory for himself. And to stake his claim.

But she wasn't his anymore. Not even for pretend.

What had been unattainable before had become even more of an impossibility.

Forcing his unruly thoughts and wayward body under control, he demanded, "Reagan, what're you doing here?" The worry at the obvious distress in her eyes and the slightly jerky movement in her normally smooth gait roughened his voice. "What's wrong?"

"Marry me."

He stared at her, struck speechless. Dozens of questions bombarded him, and he mentally waded through them, finally settling on the most important one. "What?"

"Marry me," she repeated, closing the short distance between them, not stopping until her hands fisted the lapels of his suit jacket, her thighs braced against his and that honeysuckle scent embraced him like a long-lost lover.

He swallowed a groan at her nearness, at the feel of her body pressed to his. Lust, hot and hungry, punched him in the gut, then streamed through him in a swollen flood. Desperate to place distance between them so he could fucking *think*, he gripped her hips to set her away from him. But touching her backfired. Instead of pushing her back, he held her close, his body rebelling and taking control. Two weeks. It'd been two *long* weeks.

"Reagan," he rumbled.

"No, Zeke. Don't give me all the reasons why we shouldn't. I don't care. Do you know where I just came from?" she asked, switching topics with a lightning speed that left him floundering. Between that and his dick finding cushion against her stomach, he couldn't keep up. "I just left a restaurant where my father arranged for me to have lunch with Justin McCoy."

"The *hell*?" His grip on her tightened. Douglas had set her up with that asshole?

"Yes." Reagan nodded as if reading his mind. "Apparently my father considered him a more suitable match than you. A man who uses and throws away women for his own gain rather than you, a man who has been nothing but honorable and unfailingly kind and respectful. I had enough. I walked away from him and his machinations. I'm through allowing him to run my life, to make choices for me out of guilt and loyalty."

Guilt? What the hell did that mean?

Shoving the questions aside for the moment, he refocused on her. "I understand your anger, believe me, I do, but take a moment and think this through before you make a mistake you can't take back. This decision will cost you your inheritance. It could damage your relationship with your parents. Is this rebellion worth that? Because you're not in..." He couldn't finish that sentence. Couldn't fathom it.

"No, Zeke, I'm not in love with you," she assured him, and he exhaled a heavy breath. Even as an unidentifiable emotion twisted in his chest. "And maybe this is a little bit of rebellion on my part, but it's so much more. I'm taking control—of my choices, my mind, my life. I respect you, Zeke. But this isn't about you. It's about me. About finally becoming the woman I've been too afraid to own. So, from now on, I'm making my own decisions," she continued. "And that includes you. I choose you, Zeke. And I want you to marry me."

Jesus, did she know what a delicious temptation she was? How he'd fought following after her that evening he'd let her walk out of his house? That had required strength he hadn't realized he possessed. Doing it a second time...

No, she might feel certain here in this office, but she was still upset. Could feel very differently in the morning, hell, hours from now. Maybe after they talked this out, she would see—

She rose on her toes and crushed her mouth to his.

Oh fuck.

His control snapped.

Like a flash fire, the press of her lips to his poured gasoline over the lust that had been steadily simmering. He took possession of that sweet siren's mouth, claiming it with a thrust of his tongue. Possessing it with a long, wet lick. Corrupting it with an erotic tangle and suck that left little to the imagination about what he wanted from her.

And he wanted it all. In this moment where the lines between platonic friendship and desire incinerated beneath his greedy mouth and her needy whimpers, he wanted everything she had to give him.

With an almost feral growl, he reached between them and grasped her wrists, tugging her arms behind her. He cuffed them with one hand and thrust the other into her hair, fisting the strands and jerking her head back for a deeper, dirtier kiss even as he pressed her curves flush against him. Her breasts, so soft, so full, pillowed against his chest and her belly welcomed his erection. His legs bracketed hers, and he shamelessly used the position to grind against her, letting her know without any question how much she affected him. How hard she made him.

Though he dominated her body, she wasn't submissive to him. God no. Her mouth moved over his as if he were her first or last meal. Her teeth nipped at his lips, and he knew when this feasting ended, his lips would be as swollen as hers. She met him thrust for thrust, lick for lick, sweep for sweep. She was his equal.

No. He shuddered as she drew on his tongue, sucking. He was her supplicant. And he would do any goddamn thing for her as long as she didn't stop.

The loud buzz of his intercom blared in the room like the blast of a horn, seconds before his assistant's voice intruded. "Mr. Holloway, I'm sorry to interrupt. But you asked me to remind you about your two-o'clock meeting with the marketing team."

Ezekiel stared down at Reagan, his chest heaving, his breath like a chain saw. Equal parts shock and grinding lust tore at him, and *fuck*, where had this need come from? How had it burned out of control so fast?

Anything that uncontrollable, that hot, that addictive wasn't good. Not for him. Not when he needed to maintain that careful emotional distance. Not when she would possibly want more from him then he was able to give.

Yet…she'd come to him; she needed him. Maybe he couldn't help her obtain her inheritance, but he could unconditionally support her, be that person she could finally lean on. *Still rescuing her*, a voice that sounded suspiciously like his brother whispered through his head. Possibly. Probably. But, she'd assured him she didn't desire more than he was capable of offering, that she didn't love him. Obviously, she craved him as much as he did her—that combustible kiss confirmed that. And, as she'd just stormed in here and told him, she made her own decisions, knew her own mind.

If she did, then they could go through with this marriage, maybe, once Douglas calmed down, still have a chance to obtain her inheritance and have scorching-hot sex, too. He could have her and when the time came, walk away.

Because there were no ifs about that. He *would* walk away. As she would.

Slowly releasing her, he returned to his desk. Planting a hand on the desk, he looked at Reagan again. She hadn't moved, but gazed at him, mouth wet and puffy from his kisses.

Ezekiel pressed a button on his phone.

"Laura," he said to his executive assistant, "please cancel the meeting as well as clear and reschedule my calendar for the next week. I'm going to be out of the office. If anyone asks, I'm getting married."

# Eleven

Good God, they'd done it.

As of two hours ago, she was Mrs. Reagan Holloway, Ezekiel Holloway's wife. She stared out the floor-to-ceiling window of the luxury suite into the bright, dazzling lights of the Las Vegas strip. Ezekiel hadn't spared any expense for the place they would spend their honeymoon.

*Honeymoon.* She wrestled with the emotions twisting and tumbling inside her. Jesus. This was unreal. As unreal as the whirlwind trip to Las Vegas after leaving his office twenty-four hours ago. As unreal as the unexpectedly lovely and private ceremony under a candlelit and crystal-encrusted gazebo in the back of a chapel made of glass. As unreal as this elegant and richly appointed penthouse with its Italian marble foyer, sunken living room and lavish master bedroom.

Was it how she'd imagined her wedding and honeymoon to be?

No.

It was better because it was all *her* choice.

Somehow, it didn't seem possible that just yesterday she'd rushed into Ezekiel's office and demanded he marry her. She winced, her fingers tightening around the stem of her wineglass. Thinking back on her uncharacteristically rash act, she still couldn't believe she'd done it.

Or that she'd kissed him.

Her belly executed a perfect swan dive as she lifted trembling fingers to her lips. A day later, and the imprint of his mouth was still on hers. He'd branded her. Years from now, she would no doubt still feel the pressure, the slight sting, the hungry possession of that kiss. What a sad commentary on her love life that it'd been better than the best sex she'd ever had. Ezekiel Holloway could own a woman's soul with his mouth. No wonder he'd never lacked for company. No wonder women vied for a chance to spend just hours in his bed. Or out of it, for that matter.

She needed to stop thinking about him and other women.

Or that before this evening ended, she and Ezekiel would be swept up in the throes of passion.

Whispers of nerves and curls of heat tangled together inside her belly, and she exhaled, trying to calm both. If that kiss was any indication, Ezekiel was well versed in sex. She, on the other hand, not so much. There had only been a couple of men she'd been with in the last ten years. And while the experiences had been nice—God, how anemic *nice* sounded—the encounters hadn't melted her bones or numbed her brain as just a mating of mouths with Ezekiel had. What would actual sex be like between them? Would he find her lacking? What if she—

"Stop it."

She whipped around at the softly uttered command, a bit of the wine in her glass sloshing over the rim to dot the back of her hand. Silently cursing herself for her jumpiness, she lifted her hand to her mouth and sucked the alcohol from her skin.

Her heart thumped against her rib cage as Ezekiel's gaze dipped to her lips and hand. That green, hooded gaze damn near smoldered, and it seized the breath from her lungs.

Clearing her throat, she snatched her attention from him and returned it to the almost overwhelming sight of Vegas. Not that the view could abolish him from her mind's eye.

He'd ditched the black suit jacket he'd worn to their wedding, and the white shirt stretched over his wide shoulders, emphasizing their breadth. The sky blue tie had also been removed and the first few buttons undone, granting her a glimpse of the smooth brown skin at his throat and over his collarbone. The shirt clung to his hard, deep chest and flat, tapered waist. The black slacks embraced his muscled, long legs and couldn't hide their strength.

She would know that strength tonight. Intimately.

Her lashes lowered, and she blindly lifted the glass to her lips again as her fingertips rose to her own collarbone and found the small scar there, rubbing over the raised flesh.

"Stop what?" she belatedly replied, her voice no louder than a whisper.

He didn't immediately answer, but a stir of the air telegraphed his movement. A moment later, another touch from a larger, rougher finger replaced hers. She opened her eyes to meet his, even as he lightly caressed the mark marring her skin. She gasped, unable to hold it in.

Heat blasted from that one spot, spiraling through her like a blowtorch to her insides. It battled with the ice that tried to encase her. The ice of memories. Of pain beyond imagining.

His gaze lifted from just below her neck to meet her eyes, the intensity there so piercing, she wondered if patients going under the knife encountered the same trepidation. The same sense of overwhelming exposure and vulnerability.

"I've noticed you touch this place here…" He stroked the scar, and she couldn't prevent the small shiver from working its way through her frame. Fire and ice. Arousal and shame. They intertwined like lovers inside her stomach, mating in a dirty dance. "You did it that night on the balcony and at the cemetery. At your parents' home. And again in my office the day you came to see me. It's your tell, Ray. Whenever you're uncomfortable. Or nervous. Possibly even scared."

He swept one more caress over her skin before dropping his arm. But he didn't move back out of her personal space, didn't grant her breathing room. Every inhale carried his earthy but fresh scent—like a cool, brisk wind through a lush forest. She wanted to wrap herself in it. But his too perceptive observation froze her to the spot.

"So whatever you're thinking that has you feeling any of those emotions, stop it. Or tell me so I can take the fear away."

Her attempt at diversion hadn't worked last time, so she stuck to a believable half-truth. At least he hadn't asked her how she got the scar. That, she could never admit to him. Because it would involve telling him her most carefully guarded secret.

"Why?" she murmured.

"Why what?" he asked. "Why do I want to take away your fear?"

She nodded.

"Because I've seen it one too many times in your eyes in the last few weeks, and I don't like it," he said.

She stiffened, taken aback by his words. But he cocked his head to the side, his gaze narrowing on her.

"Are you offended because I said it or because I noticed?" He hummed in his throat, lifting a hand to her again. This time he traced the arc of her eyebrow, then stroked a teasing path down the bridge of her nose before sweeping a caress underneath her eye. "These gorgeous brown eyes? They tell everything you're feeling. Whether you're amused, irritated, frustrated, thoughtful or angry. In a world where people deceive and hide, you're a refreshing gift of an anomaly. Except..." He exhaled roughly, still brushing the tender skin above her cheekbone. "You have secrets, Reagan. Your eyes even betray that. I don't need to know what they are to know they hurt you, make you guard this beautiful heart."

He pressed two fingertips to her chest, directly over the pounding organ. The organ he called beautiful but one that had caused her so much pain and disillusionment.

The organ that even now beat harder for him.

Taking several moments, she studied the dark, slashing eyebrows, the vibrant, light green eyes that seemed to miss nothing, the sensual fullness of his mouth, the silky facial hair that framed his lips and covered his rock-hard jaw. Beautiful. Such a beautiful man.

And hers. At least for the next year.

Hers to touch. To take into her body. To lie next to.

But not to love. His heart belonged to a dead woman, and he had no intention of trying to reclaim it. He'd warned her of that early in their bargain. And this heat between them—this heat that threatened to incinerate rational thought and sense—it warned her that if she wasn't careful, she could once again be that reckless sixteen-year-old willing to throw caution to the wind for love.

She'd vowed never to be that girl again.

Once more she skimmed a finger over the scar at her collarbone. The one she'd earned just before she miscarried and lost her baby.

She courted danger now, with this arrangement with Ezekiel. But if she held tightly to the reminder that pain and love were two sides of the same coin, she wouldn't cross that line into heartbreak. Because she refused to give him her heart.

But her body? Oh, that he could have.

Meeting his unwavering gaze, she slowly set the glass of wine on the glass table behind her. She moved forward, circling around him and heading out of the room toward the luxurious master suite. A huge king-size bed dominated the middle of the room while a wall of windows granted a sprawling view of Vegas and the desert beyond. The small sitting area with two ornate chairs and a small glass table occupied one corner, and a dainty vanity filled the other. A closed door hid the cavernous and opulent bathroom with its double sinks, Jacuzzi tub and glass shower big enough to accommodate an entire sorority.

Yet, as she spun around to face the door, nothing in the bedroom captured her attention like the man in the entrance. With one shoulder propped against the frame and his hands in his suit pants pockets, he silently watched her. Waited.

They hadn't discussed consummating their marriage; she'd avoided the conversation, unsure if it would be wise to go there with him. No, it wasn't wise. But God, she wanted it.

Even though she trembled with nerves and foolish excitement, she stared at him as she slowly dragged down the side zipper on her simple but elegant sleeveless gown. The white satin loosened, and she slid the skinny strap down one arm, then removed the other. Heart thudding almost painfully in her chest and her breath so loud it echoed in her head, she pushed the material down until it bunched at her hips. A small shimmy, and the dress flowed down her legs to pool around her feet.

The urge to dive for the bed and hide beneath the covers rose strong and hard inside her, but she forced herself to stay still, clad only in a nude strapless bra, matching thong and sheer, lace-topped thigh-high stockings. Then, notching her chin up, she silently ordered her arms to remain by her side, her fingers to remain unclenched.

She couldn't do anything about the shiver that worked its way through her body though. Or the throbbing of her pulse at her neck. Or the gooseflesh that popped up along her arms.

Or the moisture that even now gathered in her sex, no

doubt drenching her barely-there panties. All he would have to do was lower that penetrating gaze down her torso and center it between her thighs to see the evidence of his affect on her.

That knowledge both thrilled and unnerved her.

She lifted her gaze from the solid width of his chest, where she'd focused all of her attention while she'd performed her impromptu striptease. And, *oh God*, what she spied there.

Raw, animalistic lust. Those green eyes burned bright with it. An answering coil tightened low in her belly, and she pressed a palm to the ache. His gaze dropped, and when it flicked back up to hers, she couldn't contain the whimper that escaped her. So much heat. So much hunger.

Had anyone ever looked at her as if she were their sustenance, sanity and survival?

No. No one had. Not the few lovers she'd had.

Not even Gavin.

What did it say about her that Ezekiel owned her with that look? That if she'd harbored even the tiniest of doubts about giving herself to him, that needy, ravenous, *necessary* stare undid every snarled tangle of doubt?

Slowly, he straightened, removing his hands from his pockets, and stalked forward, eliminating the distance between them. He didn't stop until not even a breath could've slid between them.

The wall of his solid chest brushed her nipples, sending arcs of sizzling pleasure from the tips to the clenching, empty flesh between her damp thighs. His muscular thighs pressed to hers, and against her belly... She shuddered, desire striking her middle like a lightning bolt. His thick, hard cock burrowed against her belly, and before she could think better of tempting the beast, she ground herself against his mouthwatering length. More than anything, she wanted him to possess every part of her.

"Playing with fire, Ray?" One of his big hands gripped her hip. But not to control her. To jerk her closer. To roll those lean hips and give her more of what she'd just taken.

Her teeth sank into her bottom lip, her lashes fluttering. But when his fingers dived into her hair, clenching the strands and tugging so pinpricks scattered across her scalp, she opened her eyes, meeting his. He didn't handle her with kid gloves, didn't treat her like this demure, sheltered socialite or a fragile girl. And God, *she loved it.* Wanted more.

"I'm not playing," she breathed, stroking her hands up his strong back and digging her nails into the dense muscle there. "No games between us."

"No games," he repeated in that same grit-and-granite voice. "How novel an idea." He lowered his head and nipped at her bottom lip. Then soothed the minute sting with a sweep of his tongue.

She groaned, leaning her head back into his grasp.

"You've showed me this pretty little body, almost making me come with just the sight of you. But I want the words, sweetheart. Tell me you want this—*me*—in your bed. In your body. Tell me..." He bent his head, pressing his forehead to hers. His breath pulsed against her lips, and she could almost taste the dark delight of his kiss. "Tell me you won't regret this in the morning."

Rising on her toes, she grazed her mouth over his. Returned for a harder, wetter taste. His lips parted over hers, and their tongues tangled, curled, took. When she pulled free, their heated pants punctuated the air, resounded in her ears.

"I want you. In my bed. Beside me. Over me. Inside me. This is my decision, Zeke. Eyes wide open. I'll have no regrets about giving myself to you." *My body, but not my heart.* She silently added that vow as a promise to herself and to him. He wanted no strings attached with their union, so when they divorced in a year, no emotional entanglements existed.

Well, she wanted the same. She *needed* the same.

His groan rolled out of him, and his fingers fisted in her hair again, tugging her head back. He slid his mouth over her jaw, down her neck and gently bit the tendon that ran along its length. She clawed at his back, arching into him. Craving more of that primal touch. As if reading her mind, he raked his teeth along her shoulder, retracing the path with the smooth glide of his lips.

Desperation invaded her, and she slid her hands around his torso, attacking his shirt buttons. She'd released the top four when his mouth passed over the scar on her collarbone.

Stiffening, she curled her fingers around the sides of his shirt, the air snagged in her throat. Every instinct in her screamed to jerk away from both his caress and the memories. But when the tip of his tongue traced the raised flesh, she closed her eyes and a half cry, half sigh escaped her throat. He didn't pause in his ministrations, but his hold on her tightened, as if lending her his strength.

The urge to recoil evaporated, replaced by the need to lean into him, press her cheek to his chest. Let him all the way in, past her heavily guarded secrets and into her heart. She ruthlessly squelched that longing under the bootheel of reality, but she did withdraw just a bit and dip her head to seek his mouth. Lose herself in the wildness of him.

His palms cradled her face, taking while she gave and gave. A new urgency roiled within her, and she hurriedly finished unbuttoning his shirt and removing the offensive material from his shoulders and arms. Offensive because it barred her from touching all that glorious, taut skin.

Once more she tore her mouth away from his, this time so she could watch her hands smooth over his broad shoulders and wide chest with something close to wonder. So much strength, so much power. And vulnerability, she mused, scraping her nails over his small, dark brown nipples. He shivered, his clasp on her face shifting to her hips.

"Again," he ordered, grinding his erection into her belly. "And use your teeth this time."

The echo of dominance in that order had flames licking at her. She could do nothing else but obey. Not because he'd demanded it...but because she wanted it.

Lowering her head, she opened her mouth wide over the small, beaded tip, swirled a warm, wet caress around it, then raked her teeth on him. Gently biting and teasing. His rumbled curse pierced the air as a big hand cupped the back of her head and pressed her closer. Emboldened, she sucked and nipped, torturing both of them. She switched to the other tip, delivering the same caresses. By the time she drew on him one last time, fine tremors quaked through his big frame.

"Payback, sweetheart." He strode forward, forcing her to backpedal.

When the backs of her knees hit the edge of the mattress, she sank to the bed, and he immediately dropped to his knees in front of her, wedging himself between her legs.

Embarrassment flashed through her for a quick instant. In this vulnerable position, he had a clear shot of what he did to her. Her thong would hide nothing from him, and even now the cool air in the room kissed the dampness on her sex and high inside her thighs.

But all thoughts of modesty shattered into dust as he scattered hard, burning kisses to her stomach, the tops of her sensitive breasts and the shadowed valley between. He cupped her flesh with both hands, squeezing and molding, and pleasure howled through her. Tilting her head back, Reagan closed her eyes, savoring his sure touch. She curled her fingers into the covers beneath her hips, seeking purchase in this lust-whipped storm.

Peeling away the cups of her bra, he wasted no time tasting her just as she'd done him. His diabolical tongue curled around her nipple, stroking, sucking. Was it possible to be driven insane with pleasure? If so, the trip was more than halfway over for her.

Unable to *not* touch him any longer, she gripped his head in her hands, pressing him to her, staring down at him as he tormented her with that beautiful, wicked mouth. It was erotic—almost too sexual to behold. But she couldn't drag her gaze away.

As he shifted to her neglected breast, he whisked the pad of his thumb over the aching, wet nipple, teasing it. His attention shifted from her quivering flesh up to her face, and their gazes locked. He didn't release her from the visual entrapment as he pursed his lips and pulled her into his mouth. Kept her enthralled as he lapped at her before drawing so hard the tug reverberated in her sex.

*Too much. Too much.*

She closed her eyes, but that was a mistake, because the lack of sight only enhanced the sizzling sensations crackling along her nerve endings.

With one last suck on her tip, he abandoned her breasts and trailed a blazing path down her stomach, briefly pausing to dip into her navel with a heated stroke, then continuing down, down, *oh God*, down.

His breath bathed her soaked flesh, and she tumbled back on the mattress, pressing the heels of her hands to her eyes. Instinct had her squeezing her thighs, but his palms prevented the motion. He spread her wider, and though she didn't look down, she swore she could *feel* his gaze on her. The heat of it. The intensity of it.

Pushing herself up, she balanced her weight on her elbows. Stared down her body as he hooked his fingers in the thin band of her panties and drew the scrap of material down her legs. Leaving her bare, exposed and completely vulnerable. But the fierce, undiluted hunger darkening his face banished those emotions. How could she feel vulnerable when he focused on her as if she were his sole purpose of existing in this moment? No, no. She didn't feel weak, she felt...empowered.

He wanted her just as much as she wanted him.

His thumb stroked between her folds, and she glimpsed how it glistened with the proof of her desire. Lifting his gaze to hers, Ezekiel brought his thumb to his mouth and licked it clean. If possible, his magnificent features tightened further, and an almost animalistic sound rumbled from him. Then he put his mouth on her.

A keening wail tore free from her throat as he dived into her sex. His tongue licked the same path his thumb had taken. Again and again, lapping at her. Devouring her. Destroying her. His hum of pleasure vibrated against her sensitive, swollen flesh, and she writhed beneath him. He left no part of her undiscovered, staking his claim on her as thoroughly as if he'd branded her. His lips closed around the bundle of nerves at the top of her sex, and he carefully drew on her, his tongue swirling, rubbing and teasing.

Desperate and coming undone, she settled her heels on the edge of the bed, widening her thighs and grinding into his relentless mouth. Electrical currents danced up and down her spine, and for a moment, she feared the power of this looming orgasm. Even as the pleasure swelled, she mentally scrambled back from it. Both wanting it to break and fearing the breaking.

But Ezekiel didn't grant her any quarter. He slid a finger and then another through her folds, then slowly pushed them inside her. Her sex immediately clamped down on them, and she cried out, arching hard, her hips twisting, bearing down. Pleading for more of that invasion. That fulfillment. Again, her mind whispered *too much*, but this time she didn't run from it but embraced it. She worked her hips, sexing his fingers even as she pushed into his mouth.

*More. More. More.*

"Take it then, sweetheart," Ezekiel encouraged her, and she realized she'd chanted the demand aloud. "Give it to me."

His urging and the stroking of his fingertips over a place high and deep inside her catapulted her into orgasm. She exploded, her cries bouncing off the walls, and he didn't stop, not until she weakly pushed at his head, her flesh too sensitive.

Lethargy rolled over her in a wave, and she sprawled on the mattress, unable to move. She could only stare as Ezekiel surged to his feet and quickly stripped himself of his remaining clothes.

Her breath stuttered as he bared that big, hard, gorgeous body. She'd already caressed and kissed his wide chest. But his lean hips, that V above them designed to drive women wild with lust, his powerful, muscular thighs, and God, his dick. Long, thick and wide, the swollen tip reached to just under his navel. Maybe she should feel some kind of trepidation at taking him inside her. But no, with the renewed rush of desire flooding her veins, she craved having him fill her. She ached for it. Maybe then this emptiness would dissipate.

Ezekiel paused to grab his wallet from his pants before tossing them aside. From the depths of the black leather billfold, he withdrew a couple of small square foils and tossed one on the bed before ripping open the other.

She waited for him, equal parts eagerness and nerves. There was no turning back—not that she wanted to. She didn't fool herself into believing there wouldn't be consequences for this decision. For both of them.

Yet, as he sheathed himself and climbed on the bed, crawling over her body, she didn't care about the costs. Not when his gaze burned into hers. Not when he settled between her thighs. Not when he cradled her face between his large palms.

Not when his cock nudged her entrance and slowly penetrated her.

She gasped at the welcome, coveted intrusion. Whimpered at the low-level fire of the stretching. Clutched his shoulders at the unmistakable sense of being claimed.

"Zeke," she whispered, burrowing her face into the nook between his throat and shoulder. "Please."

She shifted restlessly beneath him, unsure how to alleviate the pressure that contained both pleasure and the barest bite of pain. It'd been so long for her, that as he pushed, steadily burying himself inside her, she couldn't remain still. Had to find the position, the place that would relieve the ache…or agitate it more.

"Shh," he soothed, tilting her head up and brushing his mouth across hers. "Relax for me, Ray." Another stroke of his lips even as he continued to gain more access to her body, drive farther inside her. "Relax and take me. That's it," he praised, momentarily closing his eyes as she lifted her legs around his waist, locking her ankles at the small of his back. Allowing him to surge deeper. "Fuck, that's good, sweetheart. So good," he ground out.

He held himself still above her, only his mouth moving over hers, his tongue mimicking his possession of her body. She returned every kiss, losing herself in him. Gradually, the hint of pain subsided, and only pleasure remained. Pure, mind-bending pleasure.

On a gasp, she arched her neck, pressing her head back into the mattress. Savoring him buried so deep inside her. Impatience rippled through her, and she rocked her hips, demanding he move. Demanding he take her.

Levering off her chest, he stared down at her, green eyes bright, expression dark.

"Ready?" he growled.

"Yes," she murmured, curling her hands around his strong upper arms. "Please."

With his attention pinned on her face, he withdrew his length, the weightiness of it dragging over newly awakened nerves. She groaned, twisting beneath him. Needing more. Hating how empty she felt when she'd just been so full. But a jerk of his hips granted her wish. He plunged back inside her with a force that stole the air from her lungs, the thoughts from her head.

Over and over, he took her, thrusting, driving, riding. On the end of each stroke, he ground his hips against her so he massaged that swollen bundle of nerves cresting the top of her sex. She'd become a sexual creature void of rational thought, only craving the ecstasy each plunge inside her promised. She raced after it, writhing and bucking beneath him, demanding he give her everything, hold nothing back from her.

And he didn't.

Crushing his mouth to hers, he reached between their straining, sweat-slicked bodies and circled her clitoris, once, twice, and before he could finish the third stroke, she shattered.

She came with a scream, throwing her head back, body quaking with wave after wave of release. For a second, she fought the power of it. But as he continued to thrust into her, riding out the orgasm so she received every measure of it, she submitted to the pleasure, to the loss of control.

And as she dived into the black abyss, she didn't hesitate or worry.

Because she knew, at least for the moment, she wasn't alone.

# Twelve

As Ezekiel steered his Jaguar up the quiet Pine Valley street, he glanced at his wife. *His wife.* He rubbed a hand over his beard before returning it to the steering wheel. Part of him still couldn't believe he could call Reagan Sinclair— no, Reagan Holloway—by that title. Not just bride. That ship had sailed when she led him to their master bedroom and stripped for him in a private show that had him nearly begging to put his hands on that pretty body. Stroke all that smooth, beautiful skin. Taste her mouth and the sweet flesh between her thighs.

He probably shouldn't be thinking about sex with his wife while driving down the road to his in-laws' house to drop some unwelcome news.

Especially when just the thought of Reagan naked beneath him, eyes glazed over with pleasure, her sensual demands for *more* pouring from her kiss-swollen lips, had him shifting uncomfortably in his seat.

Two days. He should've been back to Royal and Wingate Enterprises two days ago. They were supposed to fly to Vegas, tie the knot, then fly back. But after that first night with Reagan, drowning in an unprecedented lust that had seared him from the inside out, he'd extended their "honeymoon." They'd spent it in the suite. Talking. Laughing. Eating. Fucking.

And sleeping.

For the first time since Melissa, he'd slept beside a woman instead of leaving her bed or guiding her from his. And the guilt he'd expected to flay him alive had been absent. Which had only stirred the flood of conscience and shame that had been missing.

But not enough to drag him from his wife's bed or make him uncurl himself from around her warm, naked body to sleep on the couch. Because then she wouldn't be within easy reach when he woke up throbbing and hard for her.

It appeared he couldn't get enough of his new wife. In and out of bed. Although to be fair, they hadn't gone very far from the bed.

He smothered a sigh. Okay, so they'd crossed the platonic bridge and burned it in a blaze of glory behind them. But he hadn't lost complete control over this situation. They could carry on with their plan of living separate lives without emotional entanglements. Sex did blur the line a little, but it didn't obliterate it.

He and Reagan had set those boundaries for very good reasons.

And neither of them could afford to forget those reasons.

A kernel of unease wiggled into his chest. She'd already made him forget his priorities—saving Wingate Enterprises. He couldn't allow this kind of slip to become a habit.

Beside him, Reagan fidgeted. And not for the first or fifth time. Glancing down, he noticed her clenched fists on her lap. Before he could question the wisdom of it, he covered her hands with one of his and squeezed.

"It's going to be okay," he murmured.

She shook her head, a faint, wry smile tipping the corner of her mouth. "I ran off to Vegas with a man my parents disapprove of. I don't know which will send my mother into a coronary faster—the elopement or Vegas. And my father…" She shook her head, releasing a humorless chuckle. "I don't even want to imagine his reaction right now. I started all of this to take my inheritance and keep my family. But it might turn out that I lose both."

"You're borrowing trouble, Ray," Ezekiel said softly. "Your father might be stern and overbearing, but he loves you. He'll stand by you."

She huffed out a breath. "You don't know Douglas Sinclair. Not like I do. If there's one thing experience has taught me it's that he doesn't handle disappointment well. And he never, *ever* forgets."

He jerked his gaze from the road to throw her a sharp look. Something in her voice—bitterness, sorrow, pain... It wasn't the first time he'd detected that particular note, just as he'd noted her habitual stroking of that scar just below her neck.

*Secrets.* And if he was staring into her eyes, he would see the shadows of them there.

Moments later, her parents' home loomed into view and he steered the car up the driveway, pulling to a stop in front of the mansion.

"Reagan." He waited until she switched her gaze from the side window to him. "Whatever you face in there, I will be right beside you. I won't leave you."

Her lips twisted into a smile that in no way reached her eyes. They remained dark. Sad. The urge to demand she pour out her pain onto him, to insist she let him in swelled within him, shoving against his chest and throat. But before he could speak, she nodded and reached for the door handle.

"We should go in," she murmured, pushing the door open and stepping out.

Silent, he met her in front of the car and took hold of her hand. The warning to not muddy the boundaries rebounded against his skull as he raised her hand to his lips and brushed a kiss across the back of it. She glanced at him, and a glint of desire flickered in her eyes. Good. Anything to chase away the shadows.

Just as they cleared the top step, the front door opened, and Douglas Sinclair stood in the entrance. He stared at them, his scrutiny briefly dropping to their clasped hands before shifting back to his daughter.

He didn't greet them but moved backward and held the door open wider. Yet, nothing about his grim expression was welcoming. More likely he didn't want the neighbors to have a free show.

Settling a hand on Reagan's lower back, Ezekiel walked inside, lending her his strength. He valued family loyalty and acceptance. Understood the drive to give one and crave the other. Yet he hated how even while Reagan strode ahead, shoulders soldier-straight, head tilted at a proud angle, she did so with a fine tremor that echoed through her and into his palm.

"Reagan." Henrietta rose from the couch as soon as they entered the small salon. She crossed the room and cupped her daughter's shoulders, pressing a kiss to her cheek. "Where have you been? We've been calling you for days now. Honey, we were all so worried."

"I'm sorry, Mom," Reagan said, covering one of her mother's hands and patting it. "I had my phone turned off. I didn't mean to scare you."

Henrietta studied her daughter for a long moment before shifting her scrutiny to Ezekiel. "Ezekiel," she greeted with a nod. "It's good to see you again."

"You, too, Henrietta," he replied, slipping his hand up Reagan's spine to cup the nape of her neck.

"Mom, Dad, I have news," Reagan announced. "Zeke and I—" She broke off, and he squeezed the back of her neck, silently reassuring her. "Zeke and I are married. We eloped to Las Vegas. I'm sorry that you're finding out after the fact, but we—"

"I asked her to come away with me, and she did," he

interjected, but she shook her head, giving him a small but sad smile.

"No, he didn't. I asked him, and I know you're probably disappointed in my decision to elope, but it was my decision." She squared her shoulders. "*He* is my decision."

Surprise and no small amount of hurt flashed across her mother's face, but the older woman quickly composed her features. She shifted backward until she stood next to Douglas, who hadn't spoken. But his stern, forbidding frown might as well as have been a lecture.

Every protective instinct buried inside Ezekiel clawed its way to the surface, and he faced the other man, moving closer to Reagan. Letting it be known that she was his. And dammit, whether that claim had an expiration date or not, he would protect what was his.

"You deliberately went against my wishes, and now you show up here for, what?" Douglas demanded, his voice quiet thunder. "For our blessing? Our forgiveness? Acceptance? Well, you have none of them."

"No, not your blessing," Ezekiel said evenly, but he didn't bother hiding the steel or the warning in it. "And she nor I require forgiveness for a choice we made together as two consenting adults. Would your acceptance of our marriage be important to your daughter? Yes. But it's not necessary."

"It is if she—or you—want access to her inheritance," Douglas snapped. "Which isn't going to happen. Her grandmother gave me final say over who I deem suitable, and you are not it. Reagan knew that and yet she still defied my wishes, regardless that it would bring hurt and shame onto her family."

"Douglas," Henrietta whispered, laying a hand on her husband's arm.

"No, Henrietta, this needs to be said," he said. "I—"

"No, it doesn't," Reagan quietly interrupted. "It doesn't

need to be said, Dad, because I already know. You've made it very clear over the years—ten to be exact—that I have only brought disappointment, embarrassment and pain to this family. God knows I've tried to make up for it by being the respectable, obedient daughter, by following every rule you've laid down, by placing your needs and opinions above my own. But nothing I've done or will do will ever make up for me being less than worthy of the Sinclair name. For being less than perfect."

"Honey," Henrietta breathed, reaching a hand toward her daughter. "That's just not true."

That sense of foreboding spread inside Ezekiel, triggering the need to gather Reagan into his arms and shield her from the very people who were supposed to love her unconditionally. Because this was about more than an elopement or an inheritance. This—whatever it was that vibrated with pain and ugliness between these three—was older, burrowed deeper. And it still bled like a fresh wound.

"It's true, Mom," Reagan continued in that almost eerily calm voice. "We've just been so careful not to voice it aloud."

Ezekiel looked at Douglas, silently roaring at the man to say something, to comfort his obviously hurting daughter. To climb down off that high horse and tell her she was loved and accepted. Valued.

"If you think this 'woe is me' speech is going to change my mind about the inheritance, you're wrong." The same deep freeze in Douglas's voice hardened his face. "I hope your new *husband*..." he sneered the word "...with his own financial and legal troubles can provide for you. Although, that future is looking doubtful."

Fury blazed through Ezekiel, momentarily transforming his world into a crimson veil.

"Watch it, Douglas," he warned. "No one smears my family name. And since your daughter now wears it, she's included. I care for mine... I protect them above all else. And before you throw that recklessly aimed stone, you might want to ask yourself if you can claim the same."

"Don't you dare question me about how I protect my family," Douglas snapped. "All I have ever done, every decision, is for them. You, who has had everything handed to you merely because of your last name, know nothing about sacrifice. About the hard work it takes to ensure your family not only survives but thrives. About rising above what people see in order to be more than they ever believed you are possible of. You don't know any of that, Ezekiel *Holloway*. So don't you ever question my love for them. Because it's that love that convinces me that my daughter marrying you is the worst decision she could've ever made."

Anger seethed beneath Ezekiel's skin, a fiercely burning flame that licked and singed, leaving behind scorch marks across his heart and soul.

"I may be a Holloway, but I'm still a black man in Royal, Texas. You don't corner the market on that. When the world looks at me, they don't see my white father. They see a black man who should be grateful about being born into a powerful, white family. When they find out where I work and my position, they assume I'm only there because I'm Ava Holloway Wingate's nephew, not because I earned it by busting my ass working my way up in the company while attending college and receiving my bachelor's and master's." He huffed out a breath. "So don't talk to me about hard work or sacrifice, because I've had to surrender my voice and my choice at times so others can feel comfortable about sitting down at a table with me. I've had to work ten times harder just to be in the same place and receive the respect that others are given just because of the color of their skin."

He forced his fingers to straighten from the fist they'd curled into down by his thigh. "And I never questioned your love for your family. I just have reservations about the way you show it."

"Zeke," Reagan whispered, leaning into him. Offering support or comfort, he didn't know. Maybe both.

"Please, if we can all just calm down for a moment," Henrietta pleaded, glancing from her husband and back to Ezekiel and Reagan. "Before we all say something we can't take back."

"Mom, I'm afraid it's too late for that," Reagan said, a weariness that Ezekiel detested weighing down every word. "And I'm sorry for hurting you. Again." Inhaling a deep breath, she dipped her chin in her father's direction. "You, too, Dad."

She turned and walked out of the room, and Ezekiel followed, not giving her parents a backward glance. His loyalty belonged to the woman they'd just selfishly, foolishly rejected.

Fuck it. He would be her family now.

She had him. And no matter that their union was temporary, he would give her a family to belong to.

# Thirteen

Funny how a person could have pain pouring from every cell of their body and still walk, breathe, *live*. Since arriving at her parents' house, she'd become the embodiment of agony, grief and rage. Yet, she managed to grab an overnight bag, descend the front steps, climb into Ezekiel's car, buckle up and not break down as he drove away from a house that had been her home all her life.

Like a horror-movie reel, the scene in the informal parlor played out across her mind. Only to rewind when it finished and start again.

Reagan squeezed her eyes shut and balled her hands in her lap. But all that did was twist the volume up in her head. She'd known deep down that her father blamed her for her past mistakes, had never forgiven her for them. And his accusations as well as his stony silence confirmed it. But still, oh God, did that *hurt*. It hurt so badly she longed to curl up in a ball on the passenger's seat and just disappear.

*Be strong.*

*Never show weakness or emotion.*

*Be above reproach and avoid the very appearance of impropriety.*

Those had been rules, creeds she'd lived by as a Sinclair. And except for when she'd fallen so far from grace at sixteen, she'd striven to live up to that hefty responsibility. But now, after living with so many cracks and fissures because of the pressure placed on her, she just wanted to break. Break into so many pieces until Reagan Sinclair could never be formed again.

Then who would be left? Who would she be?

God, she didn't know. And how pathetic was that?

"Reagan." Ezekiel's voice penetrated the thick, dark morass of her thoughts, and she jerked her head up. He stood in the opening of her car door. A car she hadn't realized he'd stopped and pulled over, and a door she hadn't heard him open. "Come on out."

He extended his hand toward her, his green eyes, so full of concern, roaming over her face. Slowly, she slid her palm over his and allowed him to guide her from the vehicle. Only then did she notice he'd parked on the side of a quiet, deserted road.

She recognized it. Several country roads twisted through Royal, some leading to the ranches that dotted the town and others leading to rolling fields filled with wildflowers. This one lay several miles outside her parents' gated community. A bend in the road and a thick copse of trees shielded them from anyone who might travel past the end of it. As Ezekiel closed the door behind her, turned her so he rested against the Jaguar and pulled her into his arms, she was thankful for the semi-privacy.

"Go ahead, sweetheart," he murmured against her head as he wrapped his arms around her, one big hand tunneling through her hair and pressing her to his chest. "Let it go. No one can see you here. Let it go because I have you."

The emotional knot inside her chest tightened, as if her body rebelled against the loosening storm inside of her. But in the next moment, the dam splintered, and the torrent spilled out. A terrible, jagged sob wracked her frame, and she buried her face against Ezekiel's chest as the first flood of tears broke through.

Once she started, she couldn't stop. How long she wept for that sixteen-year-old girl who'd been abandoned by the boy she'd loved and her family, Reagan couldn't say. It seemed endless, and yet, seconds. Fists twisted in his shirt, she clung to him, because at this moment, he was her port in a storm that had been brewing for years.

Eventually, she calmed, her harsh cries quieting to silent tears that continued to track down her cheeks. And even they stopped. Ezekiel cupped one of her hands and pressed a handkerchief into it.

"Thank you," she rasped, the words sore against her raw throat.

He stroked her back as she cleaned up the ravages of her weeping jag.

"I'm here if you want to talk. Or if you don't want to talk. Your choice, Reagan," he murmured.

The self-preservation of her family's demand for secrecy—as well as her own guilt—battled the urge to unload. But God, she was tired. So tired. Yes, she struggled with trusting people, in trusting herself. Maybe, just maybe, she could try to take a little leap of faith and trust him...

"When I was sixteen, I was involved with a boy—well, he was nineteen years old. My parents didn't approve of him. And in hindsight, I understand why. But back then, I was just so hopelessly in love with him and would've done anything for him. And I did. I rebelled against Dad and Mom. I saw him behind their backs, sneaked out at night to see him. He consumed my world as a first love usually does. But..." she swallowed, closing her eyes "...I ended up pregnant."

Ezekiel stiffened against her, and she braced herself for his reaction. Shock. Disbelief. Pity. Any or all of them would be like a punch to her chest.

He shifted, settling more against his car and drawing her between his spread thighs. Pulling her deeper into his big, hard body. Gentle but implacable fingers gripped her chin and tilted her head back.

"Open your eyes, sweetheart. Look at me."

She forced herself to comply, and her breath snagged in her lungs. Compassion. Tenderness. Sorrow. But no pity. No disappointment.

"You have nothing to be ashamed of, so don't look down while you give me your truth."

She stared at him. *Nothing to be ashamed of.* No one—not her parents, not her brother or sister—had ever said those words to her. But this man did. Against his wishes, she briefly closed her eyes. That or allow him to glimpse the impact of his assurance. He'd said her eyes reflected 'feelings, and she didn't even want to identify the emotion that had her mentally backpedaling. Had fear rattling her ribs and clenching her stomach.

Shoving everything into a lockbox deep inside her, she drew in a breath and lifted her lashes, meeting that piercing green gaze.

"As you can expect, my parents didn't react well to the news. And yes, I was terrified. Yet I also believed my boyfriend when he said he would never leave me. What I hadn't counted on was that dedication not measuring up against the check my father waved in front of his face. Dad paid him off, and he disappeared. And my parents… They sent me away. To a girls' home in Georgia."

"I remember," Ezekiel said. "It was just before the school year ended, and Harley was upset because you wouldn't be with her for the summer. She never mentioned—"

"She didn't know," Reagan interrupted, shaking her head. "No one except my family did. My parents didn't want anyone to find out. I was supposed to go to the home, have the baby and adopt him or her out. I didn't want to give my baby up, but they were adamant. They were embarrassed and ashamed." The words tasted like ash on her tongue. "Especially my father. Before, we'd been close. I was a self-admitted daddy's girl, and there was no man greater than my father in my eyes. But afterward... He couldn't even look at me," she whispered.

"And this?" He gently pushed her fingers aside—the fingers that had been absently rubbing the scar on her collarbone.

"When I was about fourteen weeks, I started cramping. I didn't tell anyone for the first couple of days. But the third morning, pain seized my lower back so hard I doubled over and almost fainted. I did fall, and on the way down I clipped myself on the dresser." She again stroked the mark that would forever remind her of the worst day of her life. "I lay there on the floor, curled up, bleeding from the wound when I felt a—a wetness between my legs. I was miscarrying."

"Oh, Ray," Ezekiel whispered, lowering his forehead to hers, and his breath whispered across her lips. "I'm sorry."

"Spontaneous miscarriage, they called it," she continued, needing to purge herself of the whole truth. To cleanse herself of the stain of secrecy. "They told me there was nothing I could've done to prevent it, but I still felt responsible. That it was my punishment for disobeying my parents, for not being the daughter they deserved, for having unprotected sex, for not being good enough for my boyfriend to stay around, to love me—"

"Sweetheart, no," he objected fiercely, his brows drawing down in a dark frown as his head jerked back. "None of that is true. It happens. My mother suffered two miscarriages. One before me and one after me. It happens to good people, to women who would've made wonderful, loving mothers. It was biological, not penal." Worry flashed in his eyes. "Were you hurt more than you're telling me?"

"Do you mean can I still have children? Yes." Relief swept away the concern from his expression, but she shook her head. "But do I want to? I—I don't know." It was a truth she'd never admitted aloud. "It may have happened ten years ago, but the pain, the fear, the grief, the terrible emptiness..." She pressed a palm to her stomach. "I'll never forget it. And I'm terrified of suffering that again. I don't want to. Losing another child..." She turned her head away from his penetrating stare. "I don't know if I can."

"Reagan. Sweetheart. Will you look at me?"

Several heartbeats passed, but she returned her gaze to him.

He circled a hand around her nape, a thumb stroking the side of her neck while the other hand continued to cup her face. "You don't have to explain or justify anything to me. I get it. After my parents and then Melissa died, the thought of loving another person only to lose them to illness, fate or death paralyzes me. They don't give out handbooks explaining that one day that person might be snatched unfairly from us. No one prepared me for that, just as no one prepared you for the fact that you might lose your baby before you had the chance to hold him or her. And because no one did, we only get to dictate how we deal."

He stroked the pad of his thumb over her cheekbone, his gaze softening.

"Do I think you would one day make a beautiful, caring and attentive mother who would love your child as fiercely as the most protective mama bear? Yes. Do I believe you deserve to know the feeling of cradling a child in your arms, smelling their scent, hearing him calling you Mom? Yes, sweetheart. You deserve all of that and more. But I'm the last person to tell you you're wrong for being afraid of it. And Reagan...?"

He paused, his scrutiny roaming her face, alighting on her mouth, nose and finally eyes. She *felt* his tender survey like caresses on her skin. "If no one else has ever told you, I'm sorry. I'm sorry for the loss of your baby. I'm sorry the boy—because he's not worthy of the title of man—you believed would stand by you abandoned you instead. I'm sorry that you felt deserted by your family. And I'm sorry no one told you that in spite of—no, *because* of—your life lessons, you are even more precious."

The need to reassure him that he, too, deserved more trembled on her tongue. Ezekiel deserved a woman who adored him beyond reason. Who would be his soft place to land as well as the rock he leaned on in times of trouble. The thought of him alone, with the heart he so zealously guarded as his only companion, saddened her more than she could vocalize without betraying emotion either of them would be comfortable with.

So instead, she rose on her toes and pressed her mouth to his. Tried to convey her gratitude for his compassion and kindness. Attempted to relay everything she was too confused to say aloud.

Immediately, his lips parted under hers. His hold on her cheek slid into her hair, and his fingernails scraped her scalp, arrowing shivers of heat directly to her breasts, belly and lower, between her thighs.

Sorrow and hurt morphed to heat, kindling the desire inside her that never extinguished. Not for him. For Ezekiel Holloway, she was a pilot light that never went out.

His groan vibrated against her chest, then rolled into her mouth. She greedily swallowed it, the emotional turmoil of the last hour spurring her on to drown in him and this overwhelming pleasure that bore his personal stamp of ownership.

"Ray." He moaned her name, but his hands dropped to her shoulders as if to push her away. "Sweetheart."

"No," she objected. Stroking her hands over his hips and up his back, she curled her fingers into his shirt. Held on and pulled him tighter against her. "I want you. I want this. Don't deny me, Zeke," she said.

Demanded.

Pleaded.

His gaze narrowed on her, studying her. After the longest of moments, he shifted, spinning them around so she perched on the hood of the Jaguar and he stood between her spread thighs.

He flattened his palms on the metal beside her, leaning forward until she placed her hands next to his and arched her head back.

"I won't deny you anything," he growled.

Then his mouth crushed hers.

He hated the words as soon as he let them slip. Wanted to snatch them back. They revealed too much, when he should've been protecting his tender underbelly from exposure.

But with lust a ravenous beast clawing at his insides, he couldn't care right now. Not when her tongue dueled with his, sucking at him as if she couldn't get enough of him. Nipping at him as if she wanted to mark him. Licking him as if he were a flavor that both teased and never satisfied.

He should know.

Because as he sucked, nipped and licked her, all three were true for him.

This woman... *Goddamn.* She was ruining him with her sinful mouth, wicked tongue and hungry moans. Even now, he couldn't remember another's kiss, another's scent. Another's touch. And that traitorous thought should anger him, fill him with guilt. And maybe later it would. But now? Now, all he could do was dig his fingers through her hair, fist the thick strands and hold her steady for a tongue-fucking that had his dick throbbing for relief.

Nothing else mattered but her and getting inside her.

With fingers that were miraculously steady, he swept them over her jaw, down her throat, lingered on the scar that carried such traumatic memories for her and lower to the simple bow at her waist that held the top of her wrap dress together. He tugged on the knot, loosening it, and didn't hesitate to smooth his palms inside the slackened sides to push the material off her shoulders and down her arms to pool around her wrists.

Reagan started to lift her arms, but he stilled the movement. Instead, he gripped her wrists and pulled them behind her back. Trapped by her dress and his firm fingers, back arched, she was a gorgeous, vulnerable sacrifice for him. Only, as he lowered his head to drag his tongue down the middle of her chest to the shadowed, sweetly scented valley between her breasts, he was the one eager and willing to throw himself on the altar of his need for her.

God, he couldn't get enough of her taste. That honeysuckle scent seemed entrenched in her smooth, beautiful brown skin, and he was a treasure hunter, constantly returning for more.

Tracing the inner curve of her breast, he couldn't resist raking his teeth over it and satisfaction roared through him at the shiver that worked through her body. He'd earned a PhD in the shape and map of her body in the last few days, and yet, every time he discovered a new area that caused her to quake or whimper, he wanted to throw back his head and whoop in victory. He'd never get tired of eliciting new reactions from her, of giving her new things to shatter over.

And that was a problem since he was letting her go in a year.

Smothering the thought that tried to intrude on the desire riding him, he refocused all of his attention on the flesh swelling above the midnight blue lace of her bra. And the hard tip beneath it. Bringing his free hand into play, he tugged down the cup, baring her breast to him. Then, pinching and teasing the silk-and-lace-covered nipple, he drew its twin into his mouth.

He couldn't contain his rumble of pleasure as he stroked, lapped and sucked on her. Part of him believed he was obsessed with her—the last four days pointed toward this. His preoccupation now further emphasized it. How he took his time circling the beaded nub, relearning her although he'd just had her before they left their suite that morning to board the plane home.

The other part of him wanted to get down on his knees and beg her to push him away, ban him from her bed so he could wean himself off an addiction that could only destroy them both in the end.

"Zeke," Reagan gasped, twisting and arching up to him, thrusting her flesh into his mouth. Demanding her pleasure. "I need you," she said on the tail end of a whimper.

Fuck if he didn't love that sound from her. Every needy, insatiable sound that telegraphed her hunger for him.

As he'd said before, he couldn't deny her anything.

Shifting his head, he freed the other breast and reintroduced it to his mouth. Over and over he tongued the tip, swirling and teasing, pulling and worshipping.

Because she *deserved* to be worshipped.

And not just because of this body that could make a grown man find religion. But because she had a strength of spirit and character as well as a spine of steel underneath the genteel socialite demeanor. Because she'd taken her own tragedy and now planned to offer a safe haven to girls who faced the same difficulties.

Because she was just *good*.

Inexplicably, desperation surged through him, and he reached around her to unhook her bra and then rid her of both it and the top still trapping her wrists. He didn't question the need to feel her arms wrapped around him; he just surrendered to it.

He didn't even know how to begin to articulate the request—but simply grasped her hands and drew them forward, clasping them behind his neck. Then he buried his face in the crook between her throat and shoulder, inhaling her scent, opening his mouth over that sensitive spot, savoring the crush of her chest to his.

Yes, he'd been with more women than he could place names and faces to, but none had *held* him. He hadn't allowed it. And now, with Reagan, he craved it as much as he needed to be buried balls-deep inside her. And that need had him backing away from her mentally and physically, his ingrained self-protective instinct kicking him in the chest.

"Zeke?" she murmured, but he stopped the question with his mouth, and anything she would've asked translated into a groan.

As their mouths engaged in a hot, dirty battle, she gripped the front of his shirt and tackled his buttons. Within seconds, she tossed his shirt onto the hood behind him and raked her nails down his bare chest. Over his nipples. Down his abs. To the waistband of his pants.

The air in his lungs sawed in and out as she tugged at his leather belt, loosening it, then opened the closure tab. He didn't stop her—could barely drag in a damn full breath, much less move—when she lowered his zipper and dipped her hand inside his black boxer briefs.

He hissed as her fingers closed around his length, bowing his head so his cheek pressed to hers and he fisted the skirt of her dress. Pleasure spiked up his spine, locking his body. Gritting his teeth, he dipped his head lower, staring at the erotic sight of her slender, elegant fingers curled around his dick. The tips nearly-but-not-quite met around his width, and the brutish, swollen head peeked above her hand. As both of them watched, his seed pearled, and he damn near choked as she spread the drop over his flesh.

Ezekiel almost came on the spot when she lifted her thumb and slid it between her lips.

"What are you trying to do to me, Reagan?" he grunted,

taking her mouth and licking deep. "You want this to end before I even get inside you?" He nipped her full bottom lip in punishment. "You want to see me lose it?"

The question sounded close to an accusation, and a small, utterly wicked smile teased her lips. "Yes. I want you to come *undone* for me."

And then she took him in her hand again, stroking him from tip to base. Squeezing. Up and down, her fist rode him, dragging him to the edge. Undoing him just as she'd claimed.

His stomach caved with each tight caress, each twist of her fist. Bolt after hot bolt of lust attacked him, sizzling through his veins and gathered in his sac. So close. So fucking close.

But he didn't want to spill on her hand. When that happened, there was only one place he wanted to be.

Deep inside her.

Grabbing his wallet from his back pocket, he removed a condom and, in record time, sheathed himself, gritting his teeth against the pressure rapidly building inside him. With hands that should've been rough and hurried but were instead reverent and gentle, he swept higher and higher up her thighs until he reached her lace-covered sex.

For a moment, the lust almost overwhelmed him, drove him to grab, tug and claim. *Possess.* But his affection for her tempered the urge, and he eased her underwear from her with exquisite care. His concern for her had him slip his discarded shirt under her back to protect her skin from the warm metal of the car. His longing for her had him palming her thighs, holding her wide for his ravenous gaze and hard flesh as he pushed inside her. Watching her open for him, welcome him.

He glanced up her torso, over her trembling breasts to her face. And had to grab ahold of his frayed control with a desperate grip when he found her gaze trained on them joined between her legs, too.

"You see how you're taking me, sweetheart?" he whispered. Her eyes flicked to his and the heat there set a match to the already blazing conflagration in his body. "Perfect. You were made to do it. And I was created to fill you."

He didn't speak anymore…couldn't. Everything in him—every muscle, tendon, cell—focused on burying himself in the tightest, sweetest flesh. Tremors quivered through him, and he fought the need to thrust like a wild animal.

"Don't hold back from me, Zeke," she breathed, lying back on the hood and smoothing her palms down her body to cover his hands over her toned thighs. "Come. *Undone.*"

Her wish, her order snapped the cord tethering his control. He fell over her, pulling a taut nipple into his mouth as he thrust inside her over and over. Her legs and arms cradled him, her hips rising and bucking to meet each stroke. And her hoarse, primal cries for *more* spurred him on as he rode her.

Thank God.

He hoped if she'd asked him to stop, he would be able to. He prayed he would've managed it. But with her nails digging into his bare shoulders, the heels of her shoes pressed into his ass, he was so goddamn glad that fortitude wouldn't be tested. Not when sweat dotted his skin, lust strung him tighter than a drum, and pleasure barreled down on him like a train with greased tracks and no brakes.

"Let go, sweetheart," he rumbled, levering off her to reach between them and rub the swollen little nub at the top of her clenching sex.

She bowed hard, and seconds later, her core clamped down on him, nearly bruising him in her erotic embrace. She milked him, coaxing his release, and with several short, hard thrusts, he gave it to her.

Gave it to *them*.

A bone-deep lethargy swept through him, and right under it hummed a satisfaction that burrowed even deeper. Easing off Reagan, he took care of the condom, helped her dress and then righted himself. They didn't speak, but they did communicate. She clasped his hands in hers, brushing her lips over his chin and jaw. And he took her mouth, relaying how beautiful and desirable he found her.

Long moments later, he held the car door open and guided her inside before closing it behind her and rounding the hood. Jesus, he would never be able to drive the Jaguar again and not think of what happened on top of it today. And the fact that a smile eased onto his face at the thought should've alarmed him. Maybe when his body wasn't loose and relaxed after the best sex he ever had, it would.

His cell phone rang as he slid behind the steering wheel. Silently groaning, he reached for it. Damn. He'd forgotten that he'd powered his phone back on a couple of hours ago for the first time since leaving for Vegas. Yes, he'd been out of the office and unavailable for longer than, well, ever, but he wasn't ready to face everything head-on yet. He glanced at the screen, intending to note the caller ID and then send the call to voice mail. But when his brother's name popped up, he hesitated.

It was Luke. And he was most likely worried.

Shit.

Swiping the answer bar, Ezekiel lifted the phone to his ear. "Hey, Luke."

"Where the hell have you been?" his brother roared.

Pinching the bridge of his nose, he glanced over at Reagan to find her studying him, eyebrows arched.

"Vegas. I instructed Laura to let everyone know I would be out of town and to reschedule anything that came up," he said calmly. "I'm a married man, by the way."

"Congratulations," Luke said, even if it seemed to

emerge through gritted teeth. "But Laura said a couple of days, not four."

"Yes, I took two more days," Ezekiel ground out, trying not to snap. "What's the big damn deal, Luke? Yes, we're in trouble, but the company isn't going to collapse while I take some vacation time."

Silence greeted his outburst.

An ominous silence that sent dread crawling down his spine. "Luke?" His grip on his cell tightened until the case bit into his palm. "What's going on? What's wrong?"

A heavy sigh echoed down the line. "I'm sorry, Zeke. Sorry for coming at you like I did." Luke paused, and because they were so in tune with each other, Ezekiel could easily imagine his brother scrubbing a hand over his head in frustration. "And wish I could've called you with better news when you just returned from your honeymoon, but… Zeke, the shit has hit the fan."

"What?" Ezekiel snarled, his heart pounding so loud against his chest he could barely hear his brother above the din. "Dammit, tell me, Luke."

"With our assets frozen, the company hasn't been able to cover debts. One of them being the estate." Luke's voice thickened, and Ezekiel's throat closed in response. "Zeke, the bank foreclosed on our home. Everyone's been forced to move out. Harley is living with Grant until their move back to Thailand. Beth's gone to live with Camden. Sebastian and Sutton are renting a house together, and I'm crashing with a friend for now. But Aunt Ava…" Again Luke paused, and his dark rumble of anger reverberated in Ezekiel's ear. "She's moved in with Keith."

*"Goddammit,"* Ezekiel snarled. Out of his peripheral vision, he caught Reagan's head snapping toward him. Her arm stretched across the console and she clasped his free hand in hers. "He's taking advantage of her, Luke, and using the situation to get her under his thumb. Just when

we were starting to get her back to her old self after Uncle Trent's death. Now she's…" He trailed off, squeezing his eyes closed. "How is this all happening?" he whispered. "Why is this…"

"I don't know, Zeke," came his brother's solemn answer. "I really don't."

# Fourteen

"Reagan, can I just say again how much I appreciate you agreeing to help with the masquerade ball?" Her pretty green eyes shining, Beth Wingate reached across the table in the small meeting room in the Texas Cattleman's Club-house and squeezed Reagan's hand. "Especially since Zeke volunteered you without asking first. I hope you know I warned my cousin against making that a habit in your marriage," she drawled.

Reagan laughed, waving away the other woman's concern. "It's no problem at all, really. With Dad being a member of the club for so long, I'm no stranger to helping out with the events they've sponsored. Honestly, I'm happy to help out in any way I can."

"Good, I'm glad." Beth gave Reagan's hand one last squeeze. "And since I haven't yet had the opportunity to congratulate you on your new marriage, congratulations." Her smile dimmed a little, shadows entering her eyes. "I know this wasn't the homecoming you were expecting though. And I'm sorry you had to return to this…mess."

Reagan didn't have to ask to what *mess* Beth referred. Until two weeks ago, the oldest Wingate daughter had been living on the estate with her family. But now she resided with her fiancé, Camden Guthrie, due to the foreclosure on the family properties.

Beth, lovely and elegant with a slim build and dark blond

hair, had always been the epitome of composure and grace. But even she appeared a little tired and strained despite reuniting months ago with her first love. The trials the family faced obviously weighed on her. And having to continue to organize the TCC's charity masquerade must be one more added pressure.

"The masquerade ball is next month, in October, and even though a few people have regrettably returned their tickets because of our…association with the event, ticket sales are still steady. At least most folks are more interested in attending the social event of the year than in shunning the Wingates." Beth's mouth straightened into a grim line before she shook her head. "Anyway, I really hate that our family issues are overshadowing your marriage, Reagan."

"Please don't apologize, Beth. Our vows included 'for better or worse.' We're just experiencing a bit of the worse right now." Reagan shrugged a shoulder, the relaxed gesture belying the tangle of knots in her stomach. "Besides, it's not like we have the most conventional of marriages."

"Do any of us?" Harley chimed in from next to her. Her childhood friend tipped her head to the side, her long, straight brown hair falling over her shoulder as she studied Reagan. "I mean, Beth reunited with her long-lost love after a ton of lies and secrets. I had a whole secret baby scandal. But the point is we ended up with the men we love and who love us in return."

"Isn't that just like happy couples? You're in love so you see it everywhere." Reagan huffed a chuckle. As delighted as she was to have her old friend back in Royal after five years—even if it was only until after her upcoming wedding—she'd forgotten about Harley's stubbornness. "I adore you like a sister, Harley, but I don't want you to start making Zeke and me into the next fairy tale. We married so I could receive my inheritance, that's all." Even though that goal didn't look obtainable at the moment.

Harley waved away Reagan's objection. "I know, I know, that's the party line between you and Zeke. Regardless of the hows and whys, I'm just glad my best friend and my cousin are together. You make a great couple. And I believe you're good for each other."

Before Reagan could reply, Gracie Diaz swept into the meeting room. "Hey, everyone. I'm so sorry I'm late," she said, the apology slightly breathless.

Reagan remembered Gracie Diaz from her time spent at the Wingate estate. Only a couple of years older than her, Gracie had been the daughter of a family ranch hand, and later, hired by Beth as an assistant for the various charities she managed. Even though there'd been a difference in their statuses, she and Beth were very good friends. But more recently, Gracie had become a national celebrity for winning the sixty-million-dollar Powerball lottery. She was Royal's own rags-to-riches story.

As the stunning brunette pulled out one of the chairs and sat—no, collapsed—onto it, Reagan narrowed her eyes, studying her. Nothing could detract from the beauty of Gracie's thick, dark hair and lovely brown eyes, but Reagan still couldn't help but notice the faint circles under slightly puffy eyes, as if she'd recently been crying.

"No problem, Gracie." Beth frowned, scooting to the edge of her seat and wrapping an arm around her friend's shoulders. Pulling her close for a quick hug, she said, "Now don't take this the wrong way, hon, but you look terrible." Gracie snorted, and Beth grinned at the other woman. "The masquerade plans can wait. What's going on?"

Gracie propped her elbows on the table and pressed her palms to her forehead. "I swear, since winning the lottery and all that money, I've vacillated between being eternally thankful and cursing the day my numbers pulled up." She sighed, and the sound contained so much exhaustion, Reagan winced in sympathy. "Growing up, I never did understand the saying *more money, more problems*, because we never had money. But now…"

"Gracie, what's happened?" Harley pressed, leaning forward and clasping her upper arm.

"You must not have seen the news today," Gracie said, tunneling her fingers through her hair, then dragging the thick strands away from her face. "Apparently my cousin is claiming he bought the lottery ticket, and I stole it from him. Now he's insisting I turn more than half the winnings over to him. Which is ridiculous. I haven't seen my uncle's son in years, but now suddenly I'm a thief who steals from family."

Reagan snatched her phone from her purse, and in moments, brought up the local news' website and viewed the clip posted at the top of the home page. Apparently Gracie's family drama had temporarily replaced the Wingates as the newest scandal. Silently, she watched as a reporter interviewed Alberto Diaz outside Royal's town hall. He claimed that he was devastated and angry that his own cousin could betray him. Convincing sorrow etched his features as he gave his forgiveness to Gracie, but still demanded half of the money.

The sound bite skipped to the same reporter racing to reach Gracie as she opened her car door. Understandably, Gracie was angry at the accusation and refuted the lie before ducking into her car and driving off.

"He's lying," Reagan declared, dropping her phone onto the table.

"Of course he is," Harley agreed fiercely, her eyes blazing. "I can't believe they even gave him airtime for that. They're no better than a tabloid spreading that garbage."

"Yes, well, unfortunately, people thrive on that kind of trash. And it's easier for them to believe the salacious things than the truth." Gracie lifted her hands, palms up. "I'm sorry. I didn't mean to unload this on all of you. There's nothing I can do about it right now."

"You're going to fight him, aren't you?" Beth demanded.

"Oh, you're damn right," Gracie seethed. "I don't mind helping family out. I'm buying Mom a new home in Florida so she can be closer to her sister, and I'm paying for my brother to attend a private school so he can achieve every one of his dreams. So, if Alberto would've asked me for help, for money, I would've gladly given it to him. But this? Accusing me of a crime and trying to extort half of my winnings? That's blackmail, and I'm not giving in to it."

"Good for you!" Reagan praised, admiring this woman's grit and backbone. "And if there's anything we can do, just let us know. You got us in your corner ready to fight."

For the first time since she entered the room, Gracie smiled. "Thank you, Reagan. All of you." She pressed her palms to the tabletop. "Okay, enough about my unscrupulous family woes. Where are we with the masquerade ball?"

Beth covered her friend's hand and squeezed before picking up a paper and passing it to Harley. "I was just about to tell Harley and Reagan about the Cinderella Sweepstakes."

"Anything with Cinderella in it, I'm for it," Reagan teased, accepting the sheet Harley held out to her.

"I know, right?" Beth grinned. "You have the details there, but the gist of it is the local radio station offered a free makeover and ticket to one lucky winner. And considering each ticket is a thousand dollars, this is a wonderful opportunity. The station came up with the name Cinderella Sweepstakes. Isn't that perfect? The contest should bring more publicity and money to the ball. Fingers crossed. With all of us working together, it's going to be a wonderful success this year."

The meeting continued for the next couple of hours, and by the time Reagan left the clubhouse and pulled up outside the small town house rental she and Ezekiel had moved into, satisfaction was a warm glow inside of her. Satisfaction and excitement.

Working with the Wingate women and Gracie had stirred ideas about a possible fundraiser for the girls' home where she volunteered. With her father withholding her inheritance, Reagan might not be able to build her own home anytime soon, but that didn't mean she couldn't come up with an alternative to support the unwed and pregnant girls who needed help. And that included investing her time.

But with Ezekiel and his family feverishly working to salvage what was left of Wingate Enterprises, that time might be reduced as she needed to look for a job. She refused to just stand by while her husband exhausted himself to support her.

An agenda other than love might've been behind their marriage, but she meant what she'd told Beth earlier. For better or worse. And though their union had a time limit, she would stand beside him for however long she wore his last name.

Longer.

Climbing from the car, she shut the door behind her and strode up the short walk to the front door.

"Reagan," someone called behind her.

Lowering the key she'd been about to slide into the door, Reagan turned and smiled as Piper Holloway, Ezekiel's aunt, approached her, carrying a large brown-paper-covered parcel.

"Here, let me get that for you," Reagan said, hurrying toward the other woman.

But Piper laughed. "No need. I'm fine. Believe me, running an art gallery as many years as I have has given me muscles you probably can't see." Reaching Reagan, she leaned over and brushed an airy kiss over her cheek. "I have a little housewarming gift for you and my sneaky nephew." She tsked, shaking her head. "Running off to get married without a word to any of us. If I wasn't so happy for both of you, I'd be more than a little upset I didn't get to stand beside you two on your wedding day."

"It was a little spur-of-the-moment, otherwise I know he would've wanted you there," Reagan murmured. It was true. While Ava Wingate could be a little standoffish, her younger sister Piper was incredibly open and warm. Harley, at least, had preferred her aunt's company and easy affection to her mother's frequent criticism. "And thank you for the gift. You didn't have to travel all the way from Dallas to bring it."

"My pleasure. I wanted to congratulate you two in person anyway."

"Well, I know Zeke will be pleased to see you," Reagan said, turning back to the door and unlocking it. "Come on in."

She stepped back and allowed Piper to enter first. "Hey, Zeke, I'm back," Reagan announced, shutting the door behind her. "Look who I found outside—" She drew to a halt, spying that Ezekiel wasn't alone. "Oh, I'm sorry. I didn't know you had company."

"Hey, sweetheart," Ezekiel greeted, striding forward. He pressed a quick kiss to her lips, then, removing the package from his aunt's grasp, drew her in for a one-armed hug. Reagan's lips tingled, and she forced herself not to touch them. *Part of the show*, she reminded herself. *It's all for show.* "Aunt Piper, I didn't know you were coming over."

"I'm that impolite guest that just drops by unannounced," she joked, wrapping an arm around her nephew's waist and squeezing.

Ezekiel chuckled. "Never impolite or unwelcome. Have you met Brian Cooper?" He turned toward the tall, dark-haired man standing next to the living room couch. "Reagan, Aunt Piper, this is Brian Cooper, an attorney from the Dallas area. His uncle is Keith Cooper."

Surprise winged through Reagan at that bit of news. Why would Keith's nephew be here at their home? Especially considering how Ezekiel felt about the man his aunt Ava had moved in with.

"Brian," Ezekiel went on, "I'd like to introduce you to my wife, Reagan, and my aunt, Piper Holloway."

"It's nice to meet you both." Brian crossed the small room and shook hands with both of them.

Although, his gaze lingered on Piper.

*O-kay.*

With sharpened interest, Reagan studied the other man and woman. Piper, slim, tall, with her edgy, short cut and dark green eyes, was an older, beautiful, sophisticated woman. And apparently Brian, who couldn't look away from her, seemed to agree. They did make a striking couple. And from the way Piper tried—and failed—not to study the younger man from under her dark lashes, she had to notice how handsome the attorney with the athletic build was.

As if he could sense her thoughts, Brian glanced at her, and Reagan arched an eyebrow, a smile tugging at the corner of her mouth. "So you're from Dallas, too?" she asked. "Piper owns one of the most influential and prestigious art galleries there."

"Holloway Gallery downtown?" Brian asked Piper.

"Yes, that's me," Piper acknowledged. "Have you been in before?"

"Yes, I've been to a couple of shows there." He slid his hands into the front pockets of his pants. "The gallery isn't far from my office. Maybe we could get together for a cup of coffee soon."

"We'll see," she murmured, then switched her attention to her nephew. "Since I didn't get an invite to the wedding—and don't think I'm letting you off the hook for that anytime soon—I brought by a painting for your new home."

The next half hour flew by, and when Piper and Brian

left, Reagan closed the door behind them, then whipped around to face Ezekiel.

"I think your friend has a crush on your aunt," she teased.

He snorted. "I hate it for him if he does, because even I felt that brush-off."

"Yeah, it was kind of obvious. Why do you think she did? Piper tried to hide it, but she kept peeking at him." Reagan frowned. "You think maybe she's self-conscious about the age difference? Which is silly. He is younger, but she's a gorgeous, vivacious and successful woman. Any man, regardless of age, would be lucky to have her look their way."

"Sweetheart, are you really asking me to think about my aunt's dating habits? As far as I'm concerned, she's a virgin," Ezekiel drawled.

Laughing, Reagan strode across the floor to him. After a brief hesitation, she pressed against him and circled her arms around his neck. Rising to her toes, she kissed him, and the desire that never banked for him flickered into higher, hotter flames.

They hadn't drawn up rules dictating this new turn in their relationship. Part of her was okay with it—no rules meant she couldn't break them when she just wanted to casually touch him like this. But the other part of her needed to know what they were doing. Because every time she kissed him, touched him, woke up next to him, she couldn't stop craving more. Even if her mind warned her against that greed, that it could only end in heartache, her heart didn't seem to be heeding the memo.

Because somewhere along the line, her heart had chosen him. Maybe when she'd come upon him visiting his ex-fiancée's grave. Maybe when he'd laid his head in her lap and allowed her to help ease some of his burden. Maybe when he hadn't judged her after she'd revealed her past.

Did it really matter when? Her stupid, never-learn-its-damn-lesson heart had thrown itself at him, and he was Teflon. At sixteen, her reckless, headfirst dive into love could be chalked up to immaturity. But this dizzying, terrifying leap? She was going in knowing Ezekiel didn't want her future, her affection outside of the bedroom, and most certainly not her love.

And yet...

Yet he had it. All of her.

"How was your day?" Ezekiel asked, planting one last kiss against her mouth.

"Good." She forced a smile to her lips even though it trembled. "I spent time at the girls' home, then headed over to the clubhouse for a meeting with Beth, Harley and Gracie about the masquerade ball. I bought tickets for us, by the way. I wanted to get ours before they were sold out—what? What's wrong?"

"Nothing. Go ahead with what you were saying." Ezekiel shrugged, stepping back and heading out of the small foyer toward the living room.

No, she hadn't imagined that flicker of unease in his eyes or the tightening of his mouth. Something had triggered his reaction. Running her words through her head, she stared at his back and the tense set of his wide shoulders.

"Zeke, if it's about the tickets... If you'd prefer not to attend the ball because of everything that's going on, I fully understand. It's just that the rest of your family is going, and I thought you'd want to be there as well. But I can—"

"Ray," he said, voice soft but firm. "We're going to the ball. Please drop it. Everything's fine."

No. Everything *wasn't* fine, but he wouldn't share with her. Since returning from Vegas, Ezekiel had grown increasingly distant. Not physically—he was as passionate and insatiable with her as ever. Even more so in some ways. As if an element of desperation had crept into the sex. But a wall had sprung up around his emotions. Like now. He stood mere feet away from her, but he might as well as be on the other side of Royal. Or at the office, where he spent hours and hours into the night trying to salvage his family's business.

Speaking of...

"What are you doing home so early?" she asked. "It's only six, and usually you're still at the office. Did something happen?"

He shook his head, a faint smile playing at the corner of his sensual lips. "No, sweetheart. Everything's fine. I just asked Brian to meet me here instead of at the office. I wanted to talk with him about the legal issues with your inheritance. And I didn't want to do that at the office."

"I wondered about that. Are you sure you can trust him? I know how you feel about his uncle."

Ezekiel rubbed his bearded jaw. "I really like him in spite of who he's related to. I've met him before, and he's always struck me as a good guy. And a damn good attorney. He promised to look into your grandmother's will and see if there's a way to get around your father's hold on your inheritance."

"That's good," she said. "Do you think maybe you could ask him to look into something else as well?" She relayed the circumstances around Gracie and her cousin. "Maybe knowing what legal claim her cousin actually has will give her some ammunition going into this battle."

"Damn, I hate that for Gracie. This money should be a blessing, not a curse." Ezekiel pulled his cell phone from his pants pocket, then tapped out something on the screen. "I have something even better. I'll ask Miles if he can find out anything on this cousin. If he isn't able to, then it can't be found."

Miles Wingate, Ezekiel's cousin, owned Steel Security, a company that protected high-powered clients both physically and online. No doubt he could unearth any information on Alberto Diaz.

"Thanks, Zeke. I'm sure Gracie would appreciate it."

"She's family," he said simply, and for him, that was it. Family took care of family.

"Oh, I have some potentially good news," Reagan announced, circling around Ezekiel and picking up the coffee cups and saucers on the table in front of the couch. "I let the supervisor over at the home know that I would be cutting back on my volunteer time since I would be looking for employment. And she said an administrative position might be opening with the organization, and she would put my name in for it. With my experience there, she thinks I would be a good fit. So not only would I have a job but at a place I love."

"That's wonderful, sweetheart," he murmured. "I hope it works out."

There it was again. That note in his voice. That flash of emotion across his face and in his eyes.

"Zeke," she said, the cups and plates suddenly weighing down her arms.

"Reagan." He stepped closer, cradling her face and tilting his head down. He placed a tender kiss on her forehead, then nudged her chin up to look into her eyes. "Seriously, with your passion for their project, they would be fools not to snatch you up." He took the cups and saucers from her. "How about going out for dinner tonight?"

With a kiss to her temple, he left the living room for the kitchen, leaving her to stare behind him.

He couldn't fool her. Something *was* bothering him.

But why didn't he share it with her? What was he *not* telling her?

And why did the thought of it have unease curdling in her stomach?

# Fifteen

Ezekiel sipped from his glass of whiskey as he stared out the dark window of his new living room. This late at night, he couldn't see much, but he knew what lay beyond the glass. And the view of the tiny, fenced-in backyard with its postage-stamp-size patio couldn't be more different than the rolling, green hills of the ranch where he'd lived for so many years.

*I would be cutting back on my volunteer time since I would be looking for employment.*

*I bought tickets for us, by the way.*

He lifted an arm, pressed a palm to the wall and bowed his head. But that did nothing but amplify the words ricocheting in his head. *Dammit.* Straightening, he tipped his glass back and downed the rest of the alcohol. As it blazed a path down his throat, he welcomed the burn when it hit his chest. Anything was better than the dread and hated sense of inevitability that usually resided there these days.

God knows, he wasn't one of those men who preferred that their women not work. They needed to feel fulfilled and purposeful, too. But that wasn't why Reagan was seeking a job. *He* was the reason. The scandal and the resulting fallout that threatened his family's company and reputation and his own investments. They were living off his savings right now, and they weren't anywhere near the poorhouse, but to Reagan…

He huffed out a hard, ragged breath.

Her father had been right. Ezekiel might be able to provide for her, but he couldn't protect her from the whispers, the condemnation, the scorn. He'd married her so she could have freedom and all he'd given her was a prison sentence to a man and family scarred by scandal. He'd failed her in every way that counted. At least to him as a man, a husband. Hell, he'd had to call another man and ask him for help to solve his wife's problem. Because he couldn't do it himself.

Just today, they'd had to lay off more employees from Wingate. Employees who depended on him, on his family, for their livelihoods. And all he could do was sit in his office with his thumb up his ass futilely trying to figure out a way to help. To do fucking *something*.

If he couldn't save his family's company, how could he possibly help Reagan save her inheritance, help her achieve her dream of a home for unwed, pregnant teens here in Royal? Help her have the life, the future she wanted?

The answer was simple.

He couldn't.

He'd failed Melissa so many years ago. He'd failed the Wingates.

He'd failed Reagan.

And with her beautiful, wounded heart, her indomitable spirit and strength, she deserved better. So much better.

Better was a man who could protect her from the ugliness of life and follow through on his promises.

Better was a man who was brave enough to love her without fear.

Better was not him.

"Zeke?"

Lowering his arm, he pivoted to find Reagan standing in the hall entrance, a black nightgown molding to her sensual curves. The sucker punch of desire to his gut wasn't a surprise. By now, he accepted that he wouldn't be able to look at her, to be in the same damn state as her, and not want her.

He turned back to the window.

"What're you doing up, Reagan?" He'd waited until she'd fallen asleep, their skin still damp from sex, before he'd left their bed.

"I should ask you that same question. And I am. What's wrong, Zeke?" Moments later, her fingers curled around the hand still holding the empty tumbler. She gently took it from him, setting it on the table behind them. "And don't tell me nothing again. I can see how stressed you are. How tired. It's Wingate, isn't it?"

He didn't immediately reply, mentally corralling and organizing his words. But when he parted his lips, nothing of the pat, simple reply emerged.

"When I told Luke about our engagement, he accused me of trying to save you. Because I failed with Melissa."

"Failed with Melissa?" she repeated. "Zeke, she died in a car accident."

"Yes." He nodded, images of that night so long ago flashing across the screen of his mind. "But what you don't know is I was supposed to be in the car that night. I was supposed to be driving. If I had been, maybe…" He didn't finish the thought, but he didn't need to. He'd repeated the words so often over the years, they were engraved on his soul.

"Then maybe you would both be dead," Reagan said, grasping his upper arm and tugging until he turned from the window and looked down at her.

Dammit. He hadn't wanted to do that. Would've avoided staring down into her beautiful face if he had his way. Because those espresso eyes, elegant cheekbones and lush mouth unraveled his already frayed resolve.

"There is no guarantee that you would've been able to save her. The only person responsible for her death is the drunk driver who crashed into her. This isn't your burden to bear, Zeke."

He heard her—had heard the same from Luke, Harley and Piper over the years. But the guilt remained. It burrowed down deep below bone and marrow.

"You know, when I first told Luke I asked you to marry me, he accused me of having a savior complex—of trying to rescue you, because I couldn't do the same with Melissa. I told Luke that wasn't true," he continued, not addressing her assertion of his innocence. "And at the time, I believed it. Melissa had nothing to do with you, and I wasn't trying to save you. But now…" He gently removed her hand from his arm. "Now, I think he had a point, and I was fooling myself into believing I could help you. Provide for you. *Protect* you. I can't, Reagan. Your father was right, and we both know it."

Shock blanked her eyes and parted her lips. Her soft gasp echoed in the room, and he locked his arms at his sides to keep from wrapping her in them. When he'd suggested this arrangement those months ago, his goal had been to avoid the pain that gleamed in her gaze. But now, to be the cause of it… He closed his eyes, yet seconds later reopened them. He did this; it would be a coward's move not to face it.

"When I asked you to marry me—when you agreed—this wasn't the life you envisioned, and it wasn't the one I promised you. Your father said I couldn't take care of you, that I would only bring you hardship and scandal, and he was right. I took away the life you've known, the one you deserve. Because of me, you're estranged from your family and still don't have access to your inheritance."

"You don't know what you're saying, Zeke."

"Yes… I do," he ground out. "I failed you, Reagan, and all I can offer you now to make it right is a divorce. Then you can have your relationship back with your parents and a chance at the money your grandmother wanted you to have.

You can have your dreams and the girls' home you were meant to build. I refuse to take all that away from you."

"Am I so easy to toss aside, Zeke?" she whispered, her fingers lifting to that scar on her collarbone.

"Ray, no," he murmured. Nothing about this was easy. It was ripping him to shreds inside. "That's not true." He reached for her, to draw her hand away from that mark that represented so much tragedy for her, but she stumbled back, away from his touch.

"My ex. My parents. You. What is it about me that's so easy for people to walk away from?" She paced away from him, dragging fingers through her hair. Her hollow burst of laughter reverberated in the room. "No, I take that back. This isn't on me. It wasn't ever on me," she said softly, almost as if to herself.

Spinning around, she faced him again, and he was almost rocked back on his heels by her beauty and the fury in her eyes. "For too long I've blamed myself for whatever deficit in me permitted people to abandon me. I'm through with that. And you don't get to use me as an excuse for running scared and not owning your own shit."

"What do you think I'm doing now, dammit?" He took a step toward her before drawing to an abrupt halt. "Do you think it's easy for me to admit that I've failed you? That I couldn't give you everything I promised? That I wasn't—"

He bit off the rest of that statement, hating to think it much less state it aloud. But she didn't have that problem.

"*Enough?* You weren't enough to save Melissa. You aren't enough to save Wingate. And you aren't enough to save me?" For a moment, her expression softened, but then it hardened into an icy mask. One he hadn't seen on her before tonight. "News flash, Zeke. I didn't ask you to. It isn't me you're so concerned with protecting—it's yourself. I threaten that pain and guilt that you've become so comfortable carrying around it's now a part of you. Because to admit that I'm more than a charity case to you means you would have to deal with the reality that you stand in your own way of finding acceptance and love. You'll have to face the truth that you've been lonely and alone out of choice, not cruel fate."

Anger sparked inside him, flicking high and hot. As did fear. But he fanned the flames of his anger, smoking out that other, weaker emotion. He wasn't *afraid*. She didn't know him. Didn't know all he'd suffered, lost. How could he not throw up shields around his heart? To protect himself from that kind of devastation? Even now, knowing he was letting her go, damn near pushing her out the door, had pain pumping through his veins instead of blood. But the thought of how much worse it would be if something happened to her...

No. Fuck it. Call him a coward. Selfish.

He couldn't do it. Not again.

"Zeke."

He dragged his gaze from the floor and returned it to her face.

The fury that saturated her features thawed, leaving behind a sadness that cut just as deep as her hurt. She sighed, shaking her head. "You *are* enough. You're more than enough. But I can't make you believe or accept it, so I'm leaving. Not because of some perceived stink of association with you. I'm leaving because the first time you 'released' me for my own good, I let you. Then I returned and begged you to marry me. I won't do it again, and I won't stay with a man who doesn't want me enough to fight for me. For us. And I damn sure won't beg him to let me stay."

She strode forward and past him. He lifted an arm in a belated attempt to reach for her, to try to make her understand why he was a bad bet. Why he was putting her before his wants and needs. Because she was wrong—he did want her. Too much.

But either she didn't see his hand or she didn't want his touch, because she blew past him and headed toward the hall leading to their bedroom. He parted his lips to call after her, but then she stopped in the opening without turning around, her slim back straight, her shoulders drawn back.

"I didn't need you to be my superhero. I am fully capable of saving myself. I needed you to be my friend, my lover, my husband. I needed you to love me more than your fear of opening your heart up again. Just like I love you more than my fear of being abandoned again. And for the record, you were—you *are*—worth the risk. But this time? I'm walking away. Because I'm worth the risk, too."

Then she walked away. Just like she'd promised.

# Sixteen

Reagan climbed the steps to her parents' home and, twisting the knob, pushed the front door open. Since her mother was expecting her for lunch, there was no need to knock.

Standing in the quiet foyer, she surveyed it as if she hadn't been there in years instead of weeks. Since that confrontation with her father, she hadn't stepped foot in the home that had been hers since birth. The only reason she did so now was because of a phone call from her mother, asking her to please come over so they could talk. The *I miss you* at the end had sealed Reagan's fate. It was difficult to tell Henrietta Sinclair no on the best of terms. But when she tacked on the emotional warfare? Impossible.

The familiar scent of lemon and roses enveloped her, as comforting as a hug. Funny to think there'd been a time when she'd hated the scent of roses. But now? Now she missed it as much as she missed her family.

Especially now, when she didn't have anyone.

Well, that wasn't exactly true. She had Harley, who was graciously letting her stay with her and Grant until her new apartment came available next week. She had Beth and Gracie, who had been so saddened when she'd told them a week ago about the breakup with Zeke. But had quickly assured her she was still family to them.

And of course, and most important, she had herself.

That night with Ezekiel had been a revelation of sorts.

A revelation that though her past might have shaped the woman she'd become, she was not the sum of her mistakes. Just as she'd told Zeke, she didn't need saving; she wasn't some damsel in distress. And her dream of a girls' home here in Royal wouldn't crumble to dust just because her father held her inheritance hostage. Her dream hadn't been birthed by either her father or Ezekiel, so neither one could—or would—be the death of it.

She loved him… *God*, did she love him. That love was rooted in friendship, admiration, respect and a desire that even now her soul-deep hurt hadn't banished. But she valued who she was and what she brought to the table of their marriage more. That he couldn't see how she possessed the strength to carry him just as he did her… She shook her head. Maybe it was good their relationship ended when it did. That lack of regard for her would've surely poisoned them long before he decided the expiration date on their arrangement had come due.

Inhaling a breath, she shoved away those thoughts and the pain they resonated through her body for the time being.

"Mom?" she called, walking toward the rear of the house and the smaller salon her mother usually occupied this time of day, working on her numerous charitable events and committee responsibilities.

"In here, Reagan."

That was *not* her mother. Shock ricocheted through her like a Ping-Pong ball, and she skidded to a stop on her heels, frozen. After several moments, she unglued her feet and reversed course toward the formal living room. She'd heard her father's voice but seeing him standing there in the middle of the room pelted her with more icy shards of surprise.

"Dad," she said, amazed her voice remained calm when inside she was the exact opposite. "What are you doing here? I was supposed to meet Mom for lunch."

He cleared his throat and locked his hands behind his

back. And oh, how she'd missed him. Reserved, domineering and often stern to the point of being implacable. But he was also protective, loving in his own way and willing to lay down his life for his family. They were all what defined Douglas Sinclair, and the distance between them had left a hollow, empty place in her heart.

"I apologize for the deception, but I asked her to arrange this…" he waved a hand between them "…meeting. Otherwise, I didn't know if you would agree to come."

It was on the tip of her tongue to say she would've, but at the last moment, she swallowed the words. Because she might not have, given that it might've meant subjecting herself to another blistering lecture.

"Well, I'm here now," she said, moving farther into the room. "What's going on, Dad?"

Instead of answering, he reached inside his suit jacket and removed an envelope. He crossed the short distance separating them and handed it to her. She tore her gaze away from him and glanced down at the piece of mail.

"Please," he insisted. "Open it."

With a frown, she acquiesced. And minutes later, the paper trembled in her shaking hand. Unsure that she could've read the single sheet correctly, she scanned it again. But no, the terms remained the same. Her grandmother's inheritance had been released to her.

*He'd* released it to her.

"Dad," she breathed, stunned at the enormity of this. But then an ugly idea crept into her mind, and she lowered the paper to her side. "Is this because I left Zeke?" she demanded. "Because I don't want to be 'rewarded' for that. It had nothing to do with—"

"No, Reagan," Douglas interrupted her. "It has nothing to do with that. I'd decided to give you the inheritance a couple of weeks ago. It's just taken me this long to get past my pride to speak to you." He sighed, and once again, astonishment paralyzed her. Outward displays of emotion—sadness, pain, regret, which he usually kept so sternly in check—softened his eyes and turned his mouth down at the corners. Her heart thudded against her sternum. "The love a parent has for their child…" He shook his head. "It's so hard to explain, but I want to try."

He paced to the large fireplace and silently studied its dark depths before turning back to her. And though his familiar, serious expression was firmly in place once more, his voice shook with the feelings she'd spied only seconds ago.

"Being black in Texas was…rough for your mother and me. Especially in the time we came of age in. And infiltrating the business world carried its own set of hindrances and injustices. But for you, your brother and sister and mother, I would endure it all again. You all are worth every ugly name, every snub, every racist hurdle I had to climb or break through. Still, I swore to myself my children would never have to suffer that kind of pain, struggle and discrimination. I wanted better for you…because I love you so much.

"I guess you could call it an obsession of mine—making sure you were all right. Especially after the pregnancy when you were sixteen. I felt so…helpless. My baby girl was hurting, had been taken advantage of, and I felt like I'd failed in protecting you. And I know I didn't handle the situation right. I don't regret paying off that boy because he was no good for you, but I do regret that in the middle of my pain and powerlessness I made you feel like I didn't love you anymore. That somehow you were less in my eyes. When in truth, I wanted to wrap you up and shield you more."

He paused, then shifted, his profile facing her as he stared out the huge picture window. The view of Pine Valley was lovely, but she doubted he saw it. And she couldn't focus on anything but her father and the words that both hurt and healed.

"Since I failed in protecting you—"

"Dad, that's just not true," Reagan objected fiercely.

He shook his head, holding up a hand. "To me, I didn't do my job as your father. All I wanted for you was a life where you didn't experience that ever again. If something should happen to me tomorrow, I wouldn't have to worry because I'd know you were taken of. Which, for me, meant a husband who could provide for you, care for you, insulate you with his name, his wealth and connections so you wouldn't ever know being poor, disdained or abandoned. Never know mistreatment or mishandling of your precious heart again.

"But nearly losing you because of my own agenda and shortsightedness revealed to me that I took it too far. I was so concerned with you being hurt by society, by this world, that I ended up being the one who hurt you. In my drive to protect you out of love, I forgot compassion. Understanding. Forgiveness. Mercy. All of those are elements of the love I touted. I also forgot that struggle often shapes a person, makes them stronger. It helps us be better. And while I detest what you went through, it did make you into a better, stronger person, and…" He shifted back to her and tears glistened in his eyes. "I love you. And I'm proud of you."

He lifted his arms, slowly opening them to her, and without hesitation she flew into them.

And in that moment, as her arms wrapped around his waist, her cheek pressed to his chest, the sixteen-year-old girl and the adult woman converged into one. "I love you, too, Dad."

# Seventeen

"What the hell?" Ezekiel stared at the email from his personal accountant. More specifically, the numbers inside the email. There were a shit ton of zeroes in that number. "This can't be…"

But even as he murmured the objection, he reread the message again, and there it was in black and white.

He was a millionaire.

For the first time since Reagan walked away from him and out of his house, he felt something other than a pain-infused grief. Like a death. Only difference, there wasn't a tombstone to visit.

*You did the right thing. The only thing you could do.*

He repeated the reminder that had become a refrain in his head over the last week. Whenever he teetered on the edge of giving in, yelling, "Fuck this," and going after her, he remembered that he was doing what was best for her.

*Best for you.*

The taunt whispered across his mind, and he flipped that voice a mental bird.

"What can't be?" a familiar and unexpected voice asked.

Ezekiel jerked his head up and watched Luke close Ezekiel's office door behind him and cross the floor to his desk. Even though the workday was only a couple of hours old, Luke had rolled the sleeves of his dress shirt to his elbows, undone the top button, and his tie knot was loosened.

Concern momentarily overshadowed Ezekiel's shock. No one in this company was working harder than Luke to save it. And it showed in the faint bruises under his brother's eyes denoting lack of sleep, the hollowed cheekbones and firm lines bracketing his mouth.

"When was the last time you went home and had a decent night's sleep?" Ezekiel demanded.

Luke dismissed his question with a flick of his hand. "What can't be?" he repeated. "You receive some good news?"

"Yes," Ezekiel said, struggling against badgering Luke into answering his question. Shaking his head, he shifted his attention from his brother's weary features to the computer screen and the open email. "I just received a message from my accountant." He huffed out a breath, disbelief coursing through him once more. "I have a few personal investments outside of Wingate and apparently, one of the companies I invested in just sold for billions. Billions, Luke. And I'm a millionaire because of it."

Joy lit up his brother's light brown eyes, eclipsing the exhaustion there.

"Holy shit, Zeke!" Luke grinned, rounding the desk to pull Ezekiel up out of his chair and jerk him into a back-pounding hug. "That's wonderful. Damn, I'm glad we finally have some good news around here."

"I'm still in shock. I don't even know what to do right now," Ezekiel murmured.

"I do. Go get Reagan back."

Ezekiel's chin jerked up and back from Luke's verbal sucker punch. "What?" Just hearing her name… It scored him, leaving red-hot slashes of pain behind. "What the hell are you talking about?"

"I'm talking about going to find your wife, get down on your knees if need be and beg her to come back to you," Luke stated flatly. "I love you, Zeke, but you fucked up."

A growl vibrated in his chest, rolling up into his throat, but at the last moment, he didn't let his angry retort fly. Luke loved him and meant well. But still… Ezekiel didn't want to hear this. "Luke, I appreciate—"

"No," Luke interjected with a hard shake of his head. "You're my brother and the most important person in the world to me. Which is why I can tell you the brutal truth even though you don't want to hear it. And I can do it knowing it won't hurt our relationship."

Ezekiel almost turned away, but only his love for his brother kept him from walking away. Well, that, and he harbored zero doubts Luke would drag him back to make him listen.

Luke sighed, rubbing a hand over the back of his neck. "I know I warned you against marrying Reagan when you first told me about the engagement. I was worried for both of you. But when I saw you two at the engagement party, I changed my mind. You belong together… You belong *to* her. And I say this remembering how you were with Melissa. I loved her—she was sweet, kind and loved you. But Melissa is gone, and you have the chance for a future with a woman who not only fiercely defended you like a lioness but who challenges you. Who makes you better. Who loves you. And you, whether you want to admit it to yourself or not, love her."

"Love?" Ezekiel laughed, and the serrated edge of it scraped his throat. "You say that when we have so many examples around us of people who have been gutted by love. Like when you love someone, they don't leave," he snarled.

He snapped his lips shut, hating that he'd let that last part escape. But now that it had, he couldn't stop the images of those he'd lost and the people they'd left behind from careening through his head.

Uncle Trent. His parents. Melissa.

"Besides," he ground out, "my reasons for divorcing

Reagan stand. I'm doing her more harm than good remaining married to her. This way she won't be ostracized by *polite* Royal society or separated from her family. She'll have the chance to obtain her inheritance."

"Bullshit."

Ezekiel glared at his brother, who aimed one right back at him.

"I call bullshit," Luke repeated through clenched teeth. "You're running scared. Like you have for the last eight years. You speak of Melissa and Mom and Dad like they were cautionary tales. Mom and Dad's marriage is a goal, not a warning. Their love was the epitome of courage, of sacrifice and love. And you shit all over that when you use them to justify your fears. Zeke." Luke clapped a hand over Ezekiel's shoulder and squeezed. "You're about to throw your future away over something that you have no control over. You're so worried about what could possibly happen. Yes, God forbid, Reagan could *possibly* die in a tragic accident like Melissa and Mom and Dad. But you could also possibly have a wife and family and be complete in a way you've never known or could dream of. She's worth the risk. *You're* worth the risk."

Ezekiel stared at his brother, but it was Reagan's words echoing in his ears.

*You don't get to use me as an excuse for running scared and not owning your own shit.*

*I threaten that pain and guilt that you've become so comfortable carrying around it's now a part of you. Because to admit that I'm more than a charity case to you means you would have to deal with the reality that you stand in your own way of finding acceptance and love.*

*Jesus.* Ezekiel closed his eyes, and Luke gripped his other shoulder, holding him steady.

He loved her.

He loved Reagan Sinclair Holloway with his heart. His whole being.

Because if he didn't, he wouldn't be so damn terrified of being with her. She was right. She threatened his resolve, his beliefs about himself, his determination to forbid anyone from getting too close. From loving too hard.

Yes, he'd failed.

But not by marrying Reagan.

He'd failed in keeping her out of his carefully guarded heart.

At some point, she'd infiltrated his soul so completely that she owned it. He couldn't evict her. And…he didn't want to.

Did he suddenly believe he was worthy of her? No, but her strength, her warrior spirit made him want to strive to be worthy.

Was he suddenly not afraid? No. He'd believed a man should be brave enough to love her without fear, and that man wasn't him. But he'd been wrong. A man should just be brave enough to love. The fear of losing her might not ever go away, but he couldn't let it rule his life.

*That* man, he could be.

Starting now.

"You're going after her, aren't you?" Luke asked, a smile spreading across his face.

"Yes," Ezekiel said, as a weight he hadn't even been aware of bearing lifted from his chest. "And if she'll have me, I'm bringing her home."

# Eighteen

Reagan stood in the back of the long line that bellied up to the funky but trendy food truck Street Eats. Of all the trucks hawking their fare, this one had a constant stream of people, ready and eager to grab the upscale street food. The sign next to the menu proudly declared the owner Lauren Roberts's focus on organic and farm-to-table produce.

Lauren herself helped serve the food, and even through the serving window, Reagan could easily see the business-woman's loveliness. The Cinderella Sweepstakes included a makeover for the charity ball along with the free ticket, but she didn't need one. Smooth, glowing skin, pretty brown eyes, dark hair that was pulled back into a ponytail at the moment, and curves that Reagan envied completed the picture of a beautiful, confident and successful woman.

Reagan waited until the line had dwindled to a couple of people before joining it. Once she reached the window, Lauren smiled at her.

"Hey there. How can I help you?"

Reagan returned the smile. "Actually, I was wondering if I could have a couple of minutes, Lauren? My name is Reagan Sinclair," she introduced herself. "I'm on the planning committee for this year's Texas Cattleman's Club masquerade ball. And it's my pleasure to tell you that you're the winner of the Cinderella Sweepstakes radio contest."

Surprise widened Lauren's eyes. "You're kidding?"

"No, all true. You've won a ticket and a free makeover," Reagan assured her.

"Hold on a second. I'll be right out."

True to her word, Lauren emerged from around the truck moments later holding two cups.

"Sweet tea on the house," she said, offering Reagan one of the drinks. Sipping from her own tea, Lauren shook her head. "I still can't believe I won! Can I be honest?"

"Of course." Reagan tasted her beverage and savored the cool, refreshing tea with a hint of mint. Good Lord, it was delicious. "Wow, this is good."

"Thanks." Lauren grinned. But the wattage of it dimmed a little as she led Reagan to a nearby bench. Sitting, she curled a leg under the other and twisted to face Reagan. "I'm a little embarrassed to admit this, but I didn't even enter. A friend did it for me." She huffed out a chuckle. "Still, I'm excited to win. I never expected to. And I can't really pass up this opportunity to network with potential customers and investors. And shoot." She held up her hands, that grin tugging at the corner of her mouth again. "What woman doesn't enjoy a makeover?"

"A free one at that," Reagan teased. "Not that I think you need one. You're lovely just as you are."

"That's nice of you to say, but no." Lauren nodded, her eyes gleaming. "I'm looking forward to some changes."

"Well, then I'm glad I'm the one who could bring you the good news. And I'm looking forward to seeing you at the ball."

"Thanks, Ms. Sinclair," Lauren said, rising from the bench.

"Reagan." She stood as well, smiling. "Please call me Reagan. And thank you again for the tea."

"You're more than welcome." Lauren glanced over at the food truck where the line of customers had lengthened again. "I should get back. Thanks again, Reagan." Waving, she retreated back to her truck.

Reagan paused to finish her beverage, then headed toward her car across the street. A sense of accomplishment filled her. It was always awesome when good things happened to good people. And though she'd just met the other woman, Lauren seemed honest, hardworking and nice. Reagan looked forward to seeing her at the ball—

She stumbled to a halt. Shock swelled and crashed over her, momentarily numbing her.

Too bad she couldn't stay that way.

Already, the hurt and anger started to zigzag across that sheet of ice, the fissures growing and cracking. All at the sight of Ezekiel leaning against her car.

God, it wasn't fair. Not at all.

After the way he'd basically cast her aside, the only emotions bubbling inside her should be fury and disdain. She might have walked away, but he'd let her. Without the slightest fight. That, more than anything, relayed how he felt about her.

Yet beneath the fury, there was also gut-churning pain and grief, for how not just their marriage but their friendship had ended.

And the ever-present need... Just one look at his tall, powerful body wrapped in one of his perfectly tailored suits—this one dark blue—and that handsome, strong face with those smoldering green eyes... Just one look, and she couldn't stem the desire or the memories that bombarded her, both decadent and cruel.

Slowly, he straightened, and she forced her feet to move and carry her across the street. Over the short distance, the anger capsized all the other emotions roiling inside her like a late-summer Texas storm. If he'd come to see if she was all right after he'd broken her heart, he could go straight to hell. She didn't need his pity. And she refused to be a balm that he could smooth over his self-imposed guilt.

No, thank you.

She'd wanted to be his wife, not an act of reparation.

"What are you doing here, Zeke?" she asked, voice purposefully bland, even though it belied the knots twisting in her belly or the constriction of her heart.

"Looking for you," he said simply, his gaze roaming over her face. Almost as if he were soaking in every detail.

Mentally, she slapped down that line of thinking. It could only lead to the seed of hope she'd desperately tried to dig up sprouting roots.

"After handing my ass to me in a sling, Harley told me where you were."

Okay, so Reagan and Harley needed to have a serious *come to Jesus* talk about consorting with the enemy. Or since the enemy was Harley's cousin, at least giving the enemy classified information.

"Well, you've seen me." Reagan sidestepped him and reached for the door handle. "Now if you don't mind, I have a meeting." Not a lie, she had an appointment with a realtor to find land for the girls' home she planned on building.

"Reagan," Zeke murmured, lifting a hand toward her. But when she arched a brow, daring him to complete the action, he lowered it and slid it into his pocket.

Self-preservation demanded he not touch her in any way. Her mind asserted she could withstand the contact, but her heart and her body? No, they were decidedly weaker when it came to feeling those magnificent hands on her.

"Reagan," he said again. "I know I don't have the right to ask you for it, but can I have just a couple of minutes? I want—"

"Let me guess. You want to apologize. You never meant to hurt me. And you would like to find a way to be friends again." She inhaled, bracing herself against that wash of fresh pain. But damn if she would let him see it. "Apology accepted. I know. And no. Not right now."

She went for the door handle again. But his fingers covered hers, and she stilled, the *don't touch me* dying a quick and humiliating death on her tongue. She couldn't speak, couldn't move when her nerve endings sizzled as if they were on fire.

He shouldn't affect her like this. Shouldn't ignite this insatiable, damn near desperate need for him. How many years before it abated? Before her body forgot what it felt like to be possessed by him?

She feared the answer to that.

"Please, sweetheart," he murmured, removing his hand, then taking a step back. "Hear me out, then I'll leave you alone."

"Fine," she bit out, conceding. Only because she suspected he wouldn't budge before having his say. And the sooner they got this done, the sooner she could drive away and pretend she didn't ache for him. Both her heart and her body. Just to be on the safe side though... She took another step back. "Just...don't touch me again."

"I won't," he promised.

She pretended not to see the flash of pain in his eyes.

"Reagan." He shifted his gaze away from her, squinting in the distance before refocusing on her. "I wanted you to know that Miles contacted Gracie. He was able to track her cousin's credit card purchases, and he found one at a convenience store for the same time the winning ticket was sold. That transaction was made out of state, not here in Royal. Miles managed to recover the store's video footage, and Alberto was there, on camera, paying for his purchase. Since it's scientifically impossible for him to be in two places at one time, he quickly dropped the claim against Gracie when Miles presented the evidence to him. So she's good."

"That's wonderful, Zeke. Thank you for having Miles look into it. I know Gracie has to be so delighted." Relief for her friend flowed through her, and she made a mental note to call her. But fast on the heels of that thought nipped another. "Is that what you wanted to tell me?"

It was *not* disappointment that crashed against her sternum. It wasn't.

"No," he said. "That was me stalling while I tried to gather my courage and ask you, no, beg you, to forgive me."

*Beg.* She blinked. No matter how hard she tried to conjure the image, she couldn't envision Ezekiel Holloway begging for anything.

"And though I'm asking for your forgiveness, I'm having a hard time extending it to myself. I was so wrapped up in my own pain, my own fear and guilt that I convinced myself I was doing what was best for you. When really, I was doing what was best for me. Well, what I believed was best for me. I couldn't have been more wrong."

Reagan sighed. "I've had twenty-six years of people making decisions based on what they think is best for me. And yet no one bothered asking my opinion on my life. Granted, I accept some of the blame for that, because I was afraid of rocking the boat, of not being loved. But I can't and won't allow that anymore, Zeke. From anyone. And I can't be with someone who respects me so little they think me incapable of making choices for myself."

"And you shouldn't settle for that, Reagan. Anyone who underestimates you is a fool. Like I was," he added softly. "Not that I ever underestimated your strength, your intelligence or drive. No, I misjudged your affect on me, my life…my heart."

"I… I don't understand."

"I didn't either. Until today. I thought I could put you in this box and compartmentalize you in my life. But you…" He breathed a chuckle. "You can't be contained. You're this force that's fierce and powerful but one people usually don't see coming because it's wrapped in beauty, grace and compassion. I didn't stand a chance against you, Ray. And

that's what had me running scared. I fought against the hold
you had on me with everything in me because, sweetheart,
you scare me. Loving you, having everything that is you,
then possibly losing you? I couldn't bear it."

*Loving you.* Those two words echoed in her head, gain-
ing strength like a twister. Wrecking every possible thought
in its path except one. *Loving you.*

Oh God, no. Hope, that reckless, so-damn-stubborn
emotion, dug in deep, entrenched itself inside her. She
closed her eyes, blocking out his face. But she couldn't shut
her ears. And they listened with a need that terrified her.

"I took the coward's way out before," he continued, shifting forward and erasing some of the space between them.
"But now, I'm here, telling you that I'm no longer living in
the past. Not when you're my future."

"Zeke, stop," she whispered, opening her eyes. Because she couldn't take any more. Love for this man
pressed against her chest, threatening to burst through.
No fear. That had no place between them anymore. She
just wanted…him. He'd taken a risk by coming to find her
and lay his heart out for her. And she could do no less but
the same. Life, love—they required risk. Because the reward… God, the reward stared her in the face.

"Okay, sweetheart," he murmured, dragging a hand over
his head. "I'll go, but one more thing. Some investments
paid off for me, and they were substantial. Enough to no
longer put your dream of a girls' home here in Royal on
hold. Half of those earnings are yours. It's not a settlement.
If we're going to divorce, you'll have to file the papers.
I'll respect whatever you decide, but I can't let you go not
knowing what I want. You. A real marriage. A family."

"I don't want your money, Zeke," she said. Pain flickered
in his gaze, but he nodded. "No, you don't understand. I
don't need it. All I need—all I want—is you. Us."

"What?" he rasped. "You mean…"

"Yes, I love you. With everything in me, I love you," she whispered.

"Sweetheart." He stared at her, his breath harsh and jagged. "Please give me permission to touch you."

"Yes. God, yes."

Before she finished speaking, he was on her, his hands cupping her face, tipping her head back. A heady wave of pleasure coursed through her as his mouth crushed hers, seeking, tasting…confirming.

"I thought…" He groaned, rolling his forehead against hers. "I thought I'd lost you. I love you, Reagan Holloway. You're mine, and I'm never letting you walk away from me again."

"Promise?"

"Promise," he swore, pressing a hard, passionate kiss to her lips.

"Then take me home and prove it," she said, laughing, unable to contain the joy bubbling inside her. And she didn't even try to contain it. "But we have to make a stop first. I'd love to have you with me for it." She couldn't imagine beginning this project of love without the love of her life.

"Fine," he agreed, grasping her hand and tugging her away from her car. "We'll take my car, then come back for yours." When they stopped next to the Jaguar, he tossed her the keys.

She gaped at him. Then at the metal she'd reflexively caught. Then back at him.

"Oh my God. You must really love me," she gasped.

Laughing, he rounded the hood of the car. The hood that he'd made love to her on.

"Forever, Ray."

\* \* \* \* \*

# RECKLESS ENVY

JOSS WOOD

# Prologue

*Six years ago...*

Emily Arnott tossed a glass of champagne down her throat and scowled at the massive glitter ball hanging from the ceiling of the overly decorated ballroom of the Falling Brook Country Club.

Three, two, one...

*Happy damn New Year to me.*

Lodged in the corner of the room, Emily blinked back tears and wished she was anywhere but here. It had been Gina's idea to attend this party at the exclusive country club situated on the outskirts of her hometown of Falling Brook as the club was the gathering place for the wealthy residents of the area.

Emily's father had purchased tickets for the much-anticipated ball but, because he hated crowds and people, he'd passed the tickets on to her. As far as Emily could tell, her best friend and college roommate was having a blast. Gina was slow dancing with someone she vaguely recognized, Drew something, and they'd just exchanged a kiss hot enough to strip the expensive paper from the walls of the ballroom.

Gina was going to score tonight while Emily was... not.

Emily closed her eyes and banged the back of her head against the wall, feeling heat creeping up her neck and flowing into her cheeks. Unlike Gina, the move she'd made had not resulted in starting the new year off with a bang or even, sadly, with a mild grope or even a kiss.

No, she'd just been swatted away like an annoying fly.

Emily felt feminine hands on her shoulders and she opened her eyes as Gina drew her into a hug. "Happy New Year, Em. Isn't this the most fantastic party?"

Uh, that would be a no.

Emily, not wanting to spoil Gina's evening, just handed her a pained smile and took a sip from her glass of champagne.

Gina took one look at her face and grimaced. "What happened?"

Emily gestured to Gina's date. "I'll tell you about it tomorrow. Drew is looking for you."

Gina tossed her hair. "He'll wait," she stated with all the confidence of an Italian starlet with more curves than an S-bend. "Why are you standing in the corner looking like you just swallowed a bucket of fire ants?"

As well as being gorgeous, Gina was also persistent. "I swung and struck out," Emily reluctantly admitted.

"It happens," Gina philosophically replied.

Emily knew that it rarely, if ever, happened to her sexy friend.

"What happened, honey?" Gina gently asked her.

Emily sighed and raised her champagne glass. "Aided by a couple of glasses of Dutch courage, I thought I'd have a one-night stand, a little fling."

"It's your twenty-first in a couple of days—it's allowed. And God knows, you deserve some fun."

Gina was the most nonjudgmental person Emily knew and that was only one of the reasons she loved her. "Well, admittedly, I aimed a bit high and made a move on Matt Velez—"

Gina looked around, a tiny frown between her dramatic dark brows. "Who?"

Emily glanced around but didn't spot Falling Brook's ex–bad boy and MJR Investing's wunderkind and their youngest-appointed CEO. If she was really lucky, he would've left the party and she could stop skulking in the corner. No, she couldn't spot him and she was glad because every time she laid eyes on the olive-skinned, dark-eyed, square-jawed and ripped-as-hell Antonio Banderas look-alike, her IQ dropped a hundred points.

With his slightly crooked nose, Matt wasn't pretty per se. But something about his rough angles-and-planes face and enigmatic dark eyes made her breath hitch and her stomach swirl. She was tired of college boys and Matteo Velez was very much a *man*, masculine from the top of his wavy dark hair to his big feet, radiating vitality and complete confidence as he moved through the well-dressed, sophisticated and moneyed crowd.

Every woman in the room, from eighty down, gave him a second, or third, look. Emily knew he just had to crook his finger and any one of them would come running. No wonder he hadn't reacted when, having found herself standing next to him at the bar, she had asked whether she could buy him a drink.

*Drinks are included in the price of the ticket, honey,* he'd told her, sounding disinterested.

*Ah, yeah, right. Um, I'm Em... Emily.*

*Matt.* He'd taken the hand she'd held out, given it a quick shake and quickly dropped it like she'd had a particularly contagious disease.

Gina was always telling her to be up-front, that men liked straightforward women, so she'd searched for something to say that fell between *God, you're hot* and *Please kiss me.*

He'd been about to walk away so Emily had racked her brain for something intelligent, or witty, to say in order to hold his attention.

*Kiss me if I'm wrong, but dinosaurs still exist, right?* Emily had mentally slapped her hand against her forehead, not quite able to believe that she'd said something so cheesy. Matt had looked as astonished as she'd felt.

*Are you hitting on me?* he'd demanded, cocoa-colored eyes flashing. And not with lust. Annoyance, maybe.

*Um...yeah?*

*You're really bad at it.* He'd glanced at the glass of champagne in her hand. *Are you drunk?*

*Tipsy maybe,* Emily had reluctantly admitted. She hadn't been, not really, but admitting to being drunk was better than saying he was making her feel nervous and very much out of her depth.

Matt had caught the attention of the barman, ordered a glass of water and shoved it into her hand. *Drink this and go home. You're a guppy in a room full of sharks and you're going to get eaten up.*

Normally, she would have been halfway across the room by then, but something about Matt had kept her feet glued to the floor. She was striking out but she'd thought she'd give it one last shot. *I'm not looking for anything more than a fun way to see in the New Year.*

Matt's sensual mouth had thinned. *Emily, it is Emily, right?* When she'd nodded, he'd sighed and stepped back. *Apart from being too young for me, you're drunk.*

*Tipsy maybe and I'll be twenty-one in a few days,* Emily had babbled, knowing soil was flying over her shoulder from the ridiculously deep hole she was digging.

Just like she wasn't enough for her mother, she wasn't enough for Matt Velez either. When would she ever learn? And why weren't her feet taking orders from her brain and walking her away?

Matt had groaned and dug his fingers into his eye sockets. *Why do they let infants into parties like these?* He'd dropped his hand and his eyes had slammed into hers. *Okay, let me put this another way...you're most definitely not my type.*

Emily finished telling Gina her story and watched as sympathy replaced horror on Gina's face. She knew her friend was holding back an enormous wince. "Oh, God, Em, you are so bad at picking up guys."

She couldn't argue with her statement. "Tell me about it. I need lessons—"

Emily's words drifted off as she caught a glimpse of Matt Velez slow dancing across the room, his arms around a woman with pale blond hair and wearing a black dress.

Emily picked up a curl off her breast—yep, still blond—and looked down at her tight-fitting cocktail dress. It hadn't changed color either; it was still black.

Not his type, huh? So why was he dancing with someone—his lips against her temple, his hand low on her butt—who looked a lot like her? Emily reached back and placed her hand against the cool wall, looking for something to steady her. There was a close resemblance between her and the woman in Matt's arms but, yet again, she'd been rejected for some strange reason she couldn't comprehend.

Gina gave her a commiserating smile, squeezed her arm and joined Drew on the dance floor. Standing against the wall, Emily glared at Matt's back and raked her hands through her long hair. She saw the worried look Gina sent her and returned a reassuring smile. She was fine, and even if she wasn't, there was nothing Gina could do to change the situation.

Unlike her, Gina grew up with two parents who thought the sun rose and set with her and told her, with great enthusiasm and conviction, that she could be and do anything and that she was loved beyond measure. Emily was a stranger to that sort of love and support: her dad, she supposed, loved her but lived, mostly, in his own world, and her mom bailed on her marriage and motherhood when Emily was fourteen. Few people understood, Gina included, that when the person who is supposed to love and care for you the most in this world leaves you—*by choice*—it's difficult to believe anyone and everyone who becomes important to you will not do the same.

Despite being on intimate terms with that truth, Emily'd spent the past seven years chasing validation and acceptance, her need for connection greater than her fear of being rejected. Despite knowing it would never happen, she was still waiting for her mom to reach out and acknowledge her, for her dad to step out of his solitary world and recognize that she needed him to be, well, her dad.

Three years into college and she still looked for praise from her professors, threw herself at any boy who gave her the littlest bit of attention, and she was overly invested and frequently clingy in her relationships with her girlfriends.

She was, Emily ruefully admitted, a basket case.

And worse than that, she was humiliating herself and she was done. It was time to stop looking for the good opinion and validation of others. As the old year rolled into the new, Emily vowed to become as emotionally independent as possible.

She wasn't going to seek validation and acceptance anymore, and from this moment on, her opinion was the only one that counted. From now on she intended to live her life carefully, thoughtfully, being fully on guard for the possibility of being rejected and abandoned again.

New year, new Emily. It was time for her to grow up.

And, by the way, screw you, Matt Velez.

The woman in his arms—God, he couldn't remember her name—was a poor substitute for whom he really wanted to be his dance partner. Her hair, falling over his hand resting between her shoulder blades, was coarse from repeated highlighting, and her scent was spicy and heavy, clogging his nose and throat.

Matt Velez looked over her shoulder to the corner of the room where Emily stood with her back against the wall, and he wished she was in his arms, her slim, toned body pressed up against his, her scent light and fresh, hair soft.

When he'd turned at her softly spoken offer to buy him a drink and looked into her eyes—a deep, dark blue just a shade off violet—his normally unexcitable heart jumped into his throat. With her high cheekbones and creamy skin, she looked like the poster child for Christmas angels, innocent and pure.

Everything Matt wasn't.

He'd almost said yes to her offer, had been on the point of dragging her out of the room and bundling her into his car when he remembered that she was too young, too innocent, too...

Too desirable. *Far* too desirable.

Matt didn't mess with innocents, and even if Emily didn't have a reputation for being Falling Brook's golden girl, any fool could see that she was as wide-eyed and innocent as they came. She was sweet and soft and ridiculously naive and he was pretty sure she'd never had sex before, never mind a one-night stand.

Matt had never been innocent, had more street smarts at ten than she did now and was an expert at one-night stands, brief affairs and flings.

He used to be Falling Brook's bad boy, their best-known rebel, once hated but now feted because he was the CEO of MJR Investing in nearby Manhattan. It always amused Matt that his handful of Falling Brook clients, born with silver spoons in their mouths, blithely pretended he'd never egged their or their friends' houses, taken their expensive cars on unauthorized joyrides and spent hours steaming up said cars with their indulged and pretty daughters.

Their precious princesses had been eager to walk on the wild side and Matt had been happy to be their guide.

But certain girls, even back then, had been off-limits to the likes of him, and Emily Arnott, had she been closer to his age, would've been one of those girls. The Arnotts were, possibly, one of the most respected families in Falling Brook, and the town was super protective of the single father with a special-needs son and angelic-looking daughter. Not only had Leonard's wife left him when he lost the bulk of his fortune in the Black Crescent embezzlement scandal, but she'd—as the gossip went—also cut all ties with her ex and her kids.

Leonard was left to rebuild his company and raise two kids on his own. But soon—the hot gossip even reached Matt's less salubrious side of the tracks—Leonard's main focus became his company and his work and Emily was left to not only raise herself but to look after her brother, as well.

She'd had a rough time and, according to the rumor mill—and yes, his ears perked up every time her name was mentioned—life for the gorgeous blonde was, finally, evening out. Her brother was now a resident of Brook Village, a home for adults with intellectual special needs, and Emily was about to graduate college and was going to join her father's wealth-management firm.

She was a town favorite and she did not need the town's biggest rebel and player—no matter how much he wanted her—messing with her head.

And Matt didn't need her tap-dancing her way through his.

Because something about Emily Arnott intrigued him, fascinated him, and his fascination went beyond some bed-based fun. He had the insane need to find out what was going on behind those luminous eyes, what thoughts were tumbling around her pretty head. Sure, he wanted to know how she tasted, whether her skin was as smooth and creamy as he suspected, her hair as soft, but images of her being in his life kept bombarding him. Rolling over and seeing her in his bed, early-morning cups of coffee at the breakfast table, curling up on the sofa at night, watching a movie. The normal and the mundane… he instinctively wanted that with her.

But Matt didn't allow himself to want, wouldn't allow

himself to dream. Because when he wanted too much, dreamed too hard, life—and his parents—never delivered.

It was easier not to wish or want; that way, he could avoid disappointment.

The woman in his arms pulled away, tipped her head back and handed him a sensual smile. "Do you want to get out of here?"

Matt, his thoughts on Emily, almost said no but caught the words behind his teeth. "A couple of hours, no commitments and no promises?"

She nodded, her hand stroking the lapels of his tuxedo jacket. "If that's the way you want to play it, lover."

With her—and every other woman he met—it was.

Matt, without allowing himself to look at Emily Arnott again, followed her out of the room and into the chilly night air, desperately trying to ignore his raging disappointment that he was leaving with the wrong blonde.

But dreams were for fools, reality was what mattered, and hey, at least he wasn't seeing in the new year alone.

# One

Matteo Velez sped up the winding tree-lined road to Falling Brook's country club, enjoying the leashed power of his new, eye-wateringly expensive AMG Roadster. Resisting the temptation to keep driving, he gently touched the brakes. The car instantly responded and he pulled to a smooth stop in front of the valet station. Matt considered parking his brand-new baby himself—he loved this car—but eventually, and reluctantly, dropped the keys and a tip into the open palm of the valet.

"Thank you, sir. I'll take good care of it."

Matt winced, remembering that those were the same words he'd often used when he'd parked cars at this same venue more than twelve, fifteen years ago. He'd been fired after two weeks because he hadn't been able to resist the urge to take a guest's Porsche 911 for a spin. He'd nearly lost control of the car and was grateful he'd only lost his job, not his life. The thought of having a teenager in control of his state-of-the-art, furiously powerful car sent chills up and down his spine.

"Can you drive a stick?"

"Yes, sir."

Matt cocked his head and narrowed his eyes at the young man. Matt watched as he carefully slid into the driver's seat and pulled on his seat belt to make the fifty-yard drive to the parking area. He studied the controls before gently easing the gearshift into gear. He pulled off without grinding the gears and kept his speed just above a fast walking pace. Matt relaxed; this kid was, unlike him, a Boy Scout and wouldn't dream of taking a wild ride in his fast car.

Matt watched his car until it was out of sight before buttoning the jacket on his dark gray designer suit, perfectly content to walk into a swanky fundraiser alone. He was used to operating solo; he'd been doing it most of his life, and this was just another cocktail party and silent auction to raise funds for Falling Brook's independent K-through-12 school. He was pretty sure that the well-funded school wasn't short of money, but flaunt-my-designer-threads fundraisers were an important part of the town's social calendar, somewhere to be seen and to show off how wealthy and generous you were.

It was also a great place to mine the town for gossip, for anything Matt could use to his advantage. MJR Investing only had a few clients from Falling Brook, but he was always on the lookout for more. It was at functions like these where Matt heard whispers of infidelities, of divorces, of inheritances and of business losses, all of which could influence MJR's clients', or potential clients', stock portfolios. Forewarned was, as the cliché went, forearmed.

Matt stepped into the luxurious lobby of the country

club, idly noting that nothing had changed. It was what it was, a place for the great and good of Falling Brook to gather, and membership of the club was harder to obtain than a jaunt around the moon.

To his parents, the Falling Brook Country Club was the height of sophistication and the pinnacle of acceptance, and they'd been over the moon when his brother—the academically brilliant Juan—had been admitted into its hallowed halls just a few months before. They didn't know, or care, that their younger son had been a member for years. Then again, Mama and Papa Velez were all about Juan and his achievements; they hadn't shown much interest in the life of their second son, the family "mistake."

When perfection was handed to you the first time around, why waste time, energy and money on your unwanted second son?

He rarely thought of his estranged parents these days and Matt pushed the memories, and the hurt, away. He glanced at the mirror in front of him and caught the reflection of a woman walking into the lobby, blond hair pulled back, highlighting those magnificent cheekbones and wide, purple-blue eyes. It would be easy to say that Emily Arnott still looked like an angel, and with her blond hair and big, round eyes, and fine features, it was an apt comparison to make.

And others often had. But to Matt, older now, the oft-repeated words showed a distinct lack of creativity…

There was no denying that she was beautiful; she was. Tall, slim, composed. Her dress was floor-length, a skin-hugging fabric the color of steel, with a slit parting to display a slim, toned thigh with every step she took. It was a sexy dress, but Matt knew that Emily Arnott could wear a garbage bag and he'd still find her enchanting.

He'd never forgotten her clumsy pass at him so many years ago and the memory was still farm fresh. Six years had passed since he'd turned her down and it was still one of his biggest regrets.

Sure, she'd been too young and a little drunk—and he'd been rocked to his toes by desire—but he could've been kinder when he rejected her, or here's a thought, not rejected her at all. But she'd knocked him, metaphorically, off his feet—something that never happened to him—and he'd been so tempted to take her up on her no-strings offer. But, because his heart had been jumping out of his chest, his blood had been rushing south and his world had been shifting and sliding away, he'd slammed on the brakes, terrified.

A dozen images had flashed through his mind during that brief conversation: her in a simple wedding dress, his ring on her finger. Blond-haired, dark-eyed children, those extraordinary eyes dominating a face lined by age and experience. He'd known he'd find her as beautiful at seventy as he did now.

He'd never known love, had never felt like a part of the family he'd been born into and had decided at an early age that he was better off alone, and not before or since had any woman threatened his lone-wolf status. Emily Arnott, in the space of an ultrabrief conversation, had him thinking of weddings and babies and forever.

*Jesus.*

Nobody but she had ever managed to knock him so badly off-balance and he hadn't cared for the sensation. He'd craved her with a ferocity he'd never felt before. There had been so much he'd wanted as a child, from toys to affection to attention, and slowly, he came to realize that the more he longed for something, the less chance he had of receiving his heart's desire. He didn't *want*. Even as a kid, he'd never allowed passion to sweep him away; he'd made distancing himself into an art form.

If you didn't wish for or expect anything, you never found yourself disenchanted and disillusioned.

But, young and stupid, Emily Arnott had knocked him off his feet. And, because he felt a little—no, a lot—out of control, unhinged and off-kilter, he'd acted like a jerk in his attempt to put as much distance between them as possible. Because, he reluctantly admitted, he'd recognized her as being dangerous...

But he was older now and even more committed to his career and his single life. He wasn't a monk, far from it, but a relationship didn't feature on his list of priorities. And it never would. He didn't allow situations, and definitely not women, to knock him off his stride.

Sure, Emily was still fire hot, and it helped that she, on the very few times she'd acknowledged him since then—either by an arched eyebrow or an I'll-drop-you-where-you-stand look—made it very clear that she had no intention of forgiving his clumsy, jerkish "thanks but no thanks."

Matt moved toward the bank of elevators, conscious of her long-legged stride across the lobby. He pushed the nearest elevator button and inhaled her light, fresh perfume. Three steps, two steps, one...

"Are you going up to the ballroom?" Emily asked, her voice holding a sexy rasp causing the fabric over his crotch area to tighten. He still, dammit, wanted to hear her sexy voice in the dead of night, when they were alone and naked, painting dirty words in the darkness.

Yep, the chemistry and attraction hadn't faded. *Great.*

Matt slowly turned and looked into her purple-blue eyes, noticing the shock and the annoyance. Distaste slid into her eyes but underneath that emotion, something else flashed. "Oh, it's you."

Matt gestured her into the open elevator, followed her inside and pushed the button to take them to the ballroom. When he turned around to face her, her eyes jerked up and Matt arched his eyebrows, pretty sure she'd been checking out his ass.

He gripped the railing behind his back and smiled at her. "Like what you see?"

Emily's cool expression didn't change. "It's a nice package." She shrugged. "But I've grown up—I now like a bit of substance underneath the pretty wrapping paper."

*Ouch.*

Matt, not the type to back down, opened his mouth to retaliate but quickly swallowed down his hot response. And the urge to kiss her senseless. He hauled in some air and tightened his fingers around the railing, words that normally came easily deserting him.

He needed to break the tense silence but had no idea what to say. He didn't socialize much when he was in Falling Brook, preferring to use his house here as an escape from people and the pressures of working in Manhattan, that intense, fast-moving environment. He'd only encountered Emily three times in six years and he didn't know when he'd next have a chance to get her alone.

He might as well bite the bullet and address the elephant in the room. If they dealt with what happened six years ago, then maybe the tension between them would dissipate, hopefully taking his desire for her with it. He really needed to stop thinking about Emily Arnott and all the wonderful and wicked things he'd like to do to, and with, her.

"Let's talk about that night," Matt suggested, hitting the button to get the elevator to stop.

The car shuddered to a halt and Emily scowled at him. "Let's not. And restart the elevator, Velez."

Matt wasn't the type to take orders from anyone. "I'm sorry I hurt your feelings but you were drunk and I don't take advantage of drunk young girls."

It was the truth but only a fraction of it.

Emily's eyes contained chips of ice. "You also told me I wasn't your type."

Did he say that? Man, he was an even bigger idiot than he thought.

"And ten minutes after you swatted me away, you had your hand on the ass of another blonde in a black dress."

Matt winced, now remembering. He'd been so tempted to go back and find Emily but, knowing he shouldn't and couldn't, found a very inadequate substitute. And he'd obviously hurt Emily's feelings, and that he did regret.

"I am sorry," Matt said, hoping she'd believe him. "Will you please forgive me and can I take you to dinner to make it up to you?"

Where the hell did that suggestion come from? He was supposed to be staying far away from her!

Shock crossed Emily's face, quickly followed by panic. Closing her eyes, she muttered a quiet but quite dirty curse. Not something he thought he'd hear falling from her lips. Well, well. Interesting to realize that the blonde wasn't as angelic as he thought.

Good to know.

Emily opened her eyes and when she stepped toward him, Matt sucked in a breath…was she making a move on him? All thoughts of distance and moving on evaporated and all Matt could think was that he couldn't wait to taste her, to peel that dress off her slim but curvy body, to kiss the tender skin behind her knee, to dip his tongue into her belly button, to skate his hand over her sexy butt.

They'd be good together; he just knew it. Good? Hell, they'd probably set the bed on fire.

Matt lowered his head so that she didn't have to stretch her neck to kiss him; her silver heels gave her another two inches of height but she still only came up to his shoulder. His eyelids started to lower and he held his breath, thinking that he'd waited a long, long time to do this…

But instead of his heart lurching when her mouth met his, the elevator shot upward as she slammed her open hand against the button and Matt was caught off-balance, physically and mentally.

Emily sent him an evil smile and her hand came up to pat his cheek. "Did you really think that I'd just fall into your arms because having me now works for you?"

The doors to the elevator opened and Emily sent him a smile cold enough to freeze the balls off a brass monkey.

"Six years ago, I thought you were my cup of tea, but I drink champagne now."

Matt watched her walk away, thinking she was a beguiling mixture of sexy, sensitive and savage. And, because he was obviously an idiot, she was also now a hundred times more intriguing.

And that, to a man who thought the height of commitment was an occasional sleepover and breakfast the next morning, was terrifying.

Matt felt the vibration on his wrist, looked down at his watch and saw that his phone was sending him multiple alerts. Frowning, he tapped the black screen and stared at the colorful map. It took him a moment, maybe two, to work out that the dot flying down the road leading away from the country club was his car, his brand new, stupidly powerful AMG Roadster and that someone—a certain choirboy-looking valet—was taking it on a joyride.

The little shit. Matt just prayed that the same god

of stupidity who'd protected him when he was sixteen was on duty tonight and that the kid didn't find himself wrapped around a light pole.

What else could go wrong, Matt wondered as he stepped out of the elevator.

As it turned out, quite a lot, actually.

She didn't have the time or the inclination to deal with the still-sexy Matt Velez, Emily thought as she stepped out of the elevator and headed for the ballroom, the diamond ring on her left ring finger both heavy and hot.

And why, oh why, did her body still betray her every time she and Matt shared the same air? Her heart started to sprint, her boobs tightened, her nipples ached and yep, the space between her thighs heated. Her eyes kept going to his sensual mouth; she wanted to trace his thick brows with her thumb, run her fingers over his flat stomach and over the masculine bulge in his pants.

Six years had flown by but her lust for Matt hadn't diminished. *So* annoying.

Emily glanced down at the unfamiliar ring and all thoughts of the smoldering and ripped Matteo Velez retreated as her stomach flew up to lodge in her esophagus, cutting off her air supply.

Yesterday, her life was normal, maybe even a little boring. Tonight, she was, very temporarily, engaged to a raging lunatic.

How the hell had it happened?

Unable to face the crowds within the ballroom, people she'd known since she was a child, Emily walked down the hallway and slipped inside a small, thankfully empty meeting room. Gripping the back of a chair, she dipped her head and stared down at the expensive carpet, trying to get her nausea under control.

She kept to herself, worked hard, obeyed the rules, tried her best. Why was this happening to her?

Emily heard the door open behind her and she whirled around, releasing a relieved sigh when she saw Gina closing the door after her. Gina, her oldest friend and her PA at Arnott's Wealth Management, hurried over to her and placed her hands on Emily's shoulders, her expression radiating her concern.

"I saw you stomping away from Matt Velez. Did you have words with him? Did he upset you?"

Emily snorted. She wished Matt Velez was the sum total of her problems. She could handle him with one hand behind her back. "Like I would allow Falling Brook's part-time lothario to upset me. I've been calling you and I left a bunch of messages."

"Phone died and I had company," Gina replied.

Situation normal. Not knowing where to start, Emily lifted her hand and showed Gina the solitaire diamond ring on her finger. Gina gripped her hand, confused. "What? What the hell is this?"

"I am, apparently, engaged to Nico Morris."

Gina stared at her until a smile hit her eyes. "Okay, that's funny. Like you'd allow that toad to put a ring on your finger."

Oh, how Emily wished it was a joke. And she didn't blame Gina for not believing her, as she'd told Nico on their last date a few weeks ago that they could only be friends, that she wasn't interested in a relationship with him or anyone else. She'd kept her explanation simple, not bothering to explain that she was perfectly content being on her own, that she'd witnessed the devastation love could cause and she wanted no part of it. Emily clearly remembered how emotionally eviscerated she felt when her mom left, withdrawing her love.

Marriage, children…a life intertwined with someone who might leave her swinging in the wind wasn't an option. She wasn't that brave. Or that stupid.

"Nope, it's his ring and this is what I'm doing."

Gina stared at her and when Emily didn't smile, she lifted her hand to her mouth. "Why the hell did you say yes? You told him that you weren't interested in him, didn't you?"

And that, Emily was convinced, was the catalyst for his crazy proposal. Nico wasn't a man who could deal with rejection.

Gina took her finger and tried to pull the ring off. "Take this off and tell him that you had a rush of blood to the brain and that you can't, won't marry him. What the hell is wrong with you, Emily?"

Emily curled her fingers and tugged her hand from Gina's grip.

"He's had affairs with married women, been involved in some dodgy deals and nobody can trust a word he says. He's beyond redemption," Gina muttered. She glared at Emily. "I can understand him wanting to marry you but why the hell would you say yes?"

And here came the sticky part, the part she couldn't, shouldn't, reveal. But she had to tell someone and Gina was her go-to person, the only person she could trust with this information. She couldn't run to her dad—she'd never been able to—and she hadn't had any contact with her mom since she did a runner twelve-plus years ago.

She was, as always, on her own. Well, apart from Gina…

"You can't tell anyone, Gee, not one soul, but… He's blackmailing me."

Gina frowned, obviously puzzled. "What?"

Emily repeated her statement. "Last night he came by, told me that I'm what he wants in a wife and that he loves

the idea of being married to Falling Brook's angel—"
Emily pulled a disgusted face "—and marrying me will
improve his standing in the community."

Gina frowned. "But blackmail implies that he has
something on you."

And he did. "Nico went with me to Brook Village
once, to meet Davy, and Dad was there. Dad was in the
coffee shop, sitting with another parent of a resident, a
guy we know by the name of John. He and Dad were
deep in discussion and I was thrilled because, as you
know, Dad doesn't have friends or interact with people
outside the office."

"I don't understand how this relates to you being
blackmailed," Gina complained, gesturing for her to
hurry up with her explanation.

"John, as Nico told me, is the English name for Ivan.
The man Dad was talking to was Ivan Sokolov, the head
of the Russian mob up and down the East Coast, from
Maine to Miami. Unknown to me, Nico managed to take
a series of photographs of him and Dad enjoying a cozy
chat."

Gina threw up her hands, confused. "I don't get it."

"Nico wants to marry me and if I don't agree, he's
going to start a rumor, backed up by the photographs,
that Arnott's Wealth Management is laundering money
for the Russian mob. Dad, despite being a workaholic
and a social recluse, is incredibly well respected and has
built a business on honesty and integrity and the slightest hint of being associated with the mob will destroy
our reputation."

Gina's mouth fell open. "You're joking."

Emily shook her head. She wished she was.

"Why is Nico doing this?" Gina cried, tears in her eyes.

Emily looked away, also feeling the burn of a fast-approaching crying jag. But tears wouldn't help; they never had before.

"He told me, quite openly, that he doesn't like being rejected and that he's determined to have me, one way or another. He's also quite fond of the idea of marrying the town princess, someone respectable and who is an integral part of the Falling Brook community."

Emily blew out a long breath. "I'm not, obviously, going to marry him. I'd rather die. I only agreed to wear his ring because I need time to think."

Gina dropped to sit on the edge of the chair. "God, Em, what are you going to do?"

Emily looked down at the ring, scowling. "Play along until I find a way to extricate myself from the situation and save Arnott's without putting our reputation at risk. And I will, have no doubt. I'm not marrying Nico Morris, or anyone else."

Marriage, after all, was just another word for adopting an overgrown man-child with issues. Not for her, thank you very much.

And Morris was an idiot if he thought she'd just nod and acquiesce. She was stronger and tougher than her good-girl reputation and angelic face suggested.

# Two

An hour later—after inspecting his undamaged car and tearing a strip off the kid for his unauthorized use of his expensive vehicle—Matt returned to the ballroom and handed his ticket to the bubbly blonde standing at the door to the function room, refusing her offer of a free cocktail. The hostess offered to accompany him into the room and Matt didn't miss the interested gleam in her eye. If he hadn't encountered Emily earlier, he might've considered her offer for some conversation, a couple of drinks and the silent invitation for bed-based fun later.

But, while he wouldn't object to some no-strings-attached sex, she wasn't the woman he wanted to have no-strings sex with. Matt smoothed down his tie, looking around the packed room, and scowled when he couldn't see Emily.

This was classic déjà vu: the same ballroom and the same woman on his mind.

He needed a drink so Matt headed toward the bar,

greeting people along the way. He'd grown up in this town—albeit on the wrong side of the tracks—and was a familiar face in Falling Brook. It didn't bother Matt that many of the residents of Falling Brook remembered him for being the town's bad boy, the rebel, the kid with a chip as big as a redwood on his shoulder. It did bother him that whenever he moved in circles such as these, a part of him still felt like he should perform or impress to feel valued.

He'd rather die than admit it but, here in Falling Brook, despite being known as one of the youngest CEOs in a dynamic Manhattan investment firm, he occasionally still felt like that lost kid, eclipsed by his older brother and seldom seen by his parents and teachers.

For a while he'd given up, run wild, but when he went away to college, his innate competitive streak—and not having to compete against a once-in-a-lifetime genius—shot him to the top of his class. Winning became his drug of choice and being anything less than exceptional was unacceptable. He succeeded at nearly everything he tried.

Except for love and relationships.

Matt didn't play that game at all. Love was a tool his family wielded, or in his case, never used at all.

It was better to keep his distance, to operate on the surface when it came to relationships. It was far easier to exit the shallows than fight the currents in the open ocean.

At the bar, Matt ordered a whiskey and looked around, wondering where Emily Arnott was. Matt pulled a face; the room was filled with gorgeous women but he couldn't get his mind off Emily.

She was like a particularly annoying, sexy-as-sin itch he couldn't get rid of. Maybe if he stopped avoiding her and made an active effort to get her into bed—for a night or for a weekend—he could stop fantasizing about her. He was an experienced guy and he knew that the reality was never as good as his imagination but, in Emily Arnott's case, he needed to test the theory to believe it.

But, judging by her cold and snarky attitude earlier, he had a snowball's chance in hell of that happening.

*Shit.*

"Matt."

Matt turned slowly, instantly recognizing the voice of Joshua Lowell. He'd thrown his hat in the ring as a replacement for Joshua Lowell's job, the CEO position at Black Crescent. After a few meetings with Joshua, he was waiting on his decision. An offer, so he'd heard, had been made to another top contender, but the guy had turned it down—all good news for Matt. He wasn't sure he would take the job but Matt liked to keep his options open.

"Joshua." Matt shook Joshua's hand and gestured to the bar. "Can I buy you a drink?"

Joshua nodded, ordered a whiskey and tapped a long finger on the surface of the bar. "How's it going?"

Matt shrugged. "Always good."

Matt noticed Nico Morris approaching the bar and deliberately turned his back on his one-time, incredibly annoying colleague. Ignoring Morris, which was not difficult, Matt turned his attention back to Joshua. They exchanged casual conversation about mutual acquaintances and Matt knew that Joshua was waiting for him to ask whether he'd come to a decision about the CEO position at Black Crescent. Matt never did what was expected so he just handed Joshua a cool smile.

"I'm still debating who would be best to take over from me and I hope to make a final decision soon," Joshua eventually answered Matt's unasked question.

"I gathered. But we both know that I'm the best qualified, have great instincts and have the track record to prove it." It wasn't a boast; he could fully back up any claims he made.

"Yeah, I'm fully aware that MJR Investing's profits have tripled since you became CEO."

"That's my job." One he was damn good at. Matt smiled. "I'd hire me if I was you."

One of the reasons he'd been hoping for an offer from Black Crescent was because he was about to renegotiate his contract with MJR Investing. An offer from a rival firm would make his board of directors that much more amenable to his demands of a significant salary increase, more company stock and, most important, more autonomy.

Matt decided it was a good time to change the subject. "Congratulations on your engagement."

Joshua's smile reached the eyes that immediately went to Sophie, his fiancée, standing across the room. "Thanks. We're happy."

"Have you started painting again?" Matt asked, genuinely interested.

Joshua grimaced. "I'm so out of practice."

Joshua excused himself to find his fiancée, taking another whiskey and Sophie's champagne with him. Matt was about to start working the room when a hard hand gripped his shoulder. He spun around and relaxed when Zane Patterson stepped into the space Joshua Lowell had vacated.

Matt and Zane could trace their friendship back to high school, to when they'd both attended the regional high school instead of the exclusive Falling Brook Prep.

"Still no news on the CEO offer?" Zane asked after ordering a drink from the very busy barman.

Matt shook his head, frustrated. "I'm in a holding position. I can't push for more from MJR until I have a solid offer from Black Crescent. Damn, it's frustrating."

"Yeah, patience was never your thing," Zane commented, lifting his glass in a silent toast.

Matt pushed back his suit jacket to slide his hands into his suit pockets, thinking that Zane looked happier than he did last month. Like so many other people in Falling Brook, Vernon Lowell's disappearance, along with a hefty chunk of Black Crescent's clients' money, deeply affected Zane. Although it had been fifteen years since the Black Crescent Hedge Fund collapsed, its effects still reverberated throughout the community. Matt knew that Sophie's fifteenth-anniversary article painting Josh Lowell as a superhero for rebuilding Black Crescent made Zane fume. He'd freely offered his own insights and photographs to the reporter. He'd also passed along a bombshell DNA test showing Joshua Lowell to be the father of a little girl—but that never made the article. But it didn't matter since the news had already hit the Falling Brook rumor mill.

Matt, because he wasn't the type to beat around the bush, looked Zane in the eye. "The town is speculating wildly, saying you know who sent you the DNA test but you're just being coy."

Zane sighed and shrugged. "I genuinely have no idea who sent it to me. I know *why* they did it—my hatred for the Lowells isn't exactly a secret. The person with the report knew I could be counted on to pass it along."

Matt heard the regret in Zane's voice and a touch of embarrassment. He knew Zane, happy at last and in a relationship with his best friend's sister, would like to put the Lowells and his past behind him. Matt didn't blame him. He preferred not to think of the past either.

Matt always could multitask and he continued to chat to Zane while monitoring the ebb and flow of the room. Nothing seemed out of the ordinary until Matt's eyes flicked over to the door and Zane's voice faded away as Emily Arnott stepped into the room.

And everything else in the room faded... God, she was lovely. And he wanted her more than he needed his heart to beat, his lungs to take in air.

Zane bumped Matt's shoulder with his own, pulling him out of his fantasies of a naked Emily with her legs wrapped around his hips and back into the noisy room. "I cannot believe she is going to marry Nico Morris."

It took a few seconds for his words to make sense, but when they did, Matt wanted to, but couldn't, laugh at Zane's joke. Because he had to be jesting; no way was Emily going to marry that algae-eating pond scum and his ex-colleague, the man who'd made Matt's life hell for two years until Morris left MJR Investing.

"That's not even remotely funny, Patterson."

Zane frowned. "Damn right, it's not. Nico is a slea-zeball."

Matt's heart plummeted to his toes. "You're *not* joking?"

"I never joke about Morris," Zane said, his expression grim, gesturing to Emily who now stood next to Morris, his arm around her slim waist.

None of this made sense. Why would someone like Emily marry someone like Nico Morris? Nico was one of the least-popular people in Falling Brook and for good reason. He lied, he cheated and he'd amassed a list of enemies as long as his spine. While Matt collected and acted on information he received, he never used said information as a carrot or a stick. Nico, by comparison, used every dirty trick in the book.

Their animosity went back to when Nico was still employed by MJR Investing, before he left the company to go out on his own. Matt was on the fast track while

Nico's prospects for career advancement had hit the ceiling. Nico spread rumors about him and actively tried to sabotage his career.

Morris had been a constant pain in his ass back then but Matt was, mostly, over his childish antics.

But Nico having Emily Arnott, the woman he considered to be the one who got away, was completely unacceptable.

Matt was the one with the glittering career, the fast cars and the fat bank accounts, so why was he even bothering to compete with Morris? Maybe it was because competition was in his blood and he hated feeling like he was a step behind.

But Nico and Emily marrying? Yeah, well, that wasn't going to happen.

Hours later, and after fielding what felt to be a hundred curious, surprised and shocked congratulations on her engagement, Emily walked down the hallway to the bathroom, conscious of a headache building behind her eyes. Nico, thank God, had left the club already and she could, momentarily, relax.

Oh, how she wished she could rewind her life and erase the past twenty-four hours. She wanted to go back to the person she was yesterday, to her relatively simple and uncomplicated life. And how she wished she could erase her dumb decision to go on a couple of dates with Nico Morris.

Nico could, admittedly, be charming but there was no chemistry between them and that was why she called an end to their brief, unexciting dates.

Yet, not two weeks later, she was engaged to the man!

It was time to go home. If she stayed much longer, she might end up screaming at someone. She'd go home, change into her yoga pants and slug down a glass, or three, of wine and bitch to her cat.

And when she stopped feeling sorry for herself, she'd start thinking of a way to boot Nico from her life without jeopardizing her father's and Arnott's Wealth Management's reputations.

Emily squealed as a strong hand gripped her wrist and tugged her into a small closet adjacent to the meeting room she'd visited earlier. She felt her breasts push into a solid, hard chest. Six years and Matt Velez, damn him, was still as gorgeous as ever. Close-cropped dark hair, those masculine features and a sexy, sexy mouth. Broad shouldered, slim hipped, ripped. And damn, he smelled good.

She loved his eyes; they were the color of a luxurious mahogany mink coat she'd once seen but would never wear, deep and dark and mysterious.

Matt reached behind her to shut the door and they were plunged into darkness. She should be feeling uneasy or even a little scared at Matt's high-handed treatment of her and Emily knew she should blast him but...

But, dammit, she just felt turned on and happy to be in his arms, feeling his heat, his hard body a perfect counterpoint to her soft curves.

She still wanted him.

Emily really wanted not to want him...

Matt lifted his hand off her hip and two seconds later weak light flooded the small room from the dull, bare bulb above them. Matt moved deeper into the closet and rested his elbow on a metal shelf behind him, his deep, dark eyes slamming into hers.

She would not, repeat not, give in to temptation and slam her mouth against his. But she really wanted to...

Emily turned away but then Matt took her hand and she

swiftly turned to look back at him. Emily held her breath as he brought her hand to his lips, but instead of kissing her fingers as she expected—wished?—he stopped and his eyes took in the flawless, massive diamond.

"How did I miss this earlier?" he demanded, his voice rough with annoyance.

Emily shrugged. "You were too busy trying to make a half-assed apology."

"Hey, I meant what I said. I am sorry for how I acted that night," Matt said, and Emily heard the sincerity in his tone. She saw his eyes returning to her ring finger and noticed the muscle jumping in his jaw. Matt Velez was not happy at her engagement and the knowledge made her heart tingle.

Stupid thing.

He lifted her hand again and turned the diamond to the dim light. "Boring, as I expected."

Say what? While she didn't like her fiancé, she had to admire the ring. It was a perfect example of a stone with all the four Cs—carat weight, cut, color, clarity—and Matt Velez could keep his snarky opinions to himself.

"My ring is exceptional," Emily told him, sounding haughty.

"Knowing Morris, the stone is probably a fake or, at best, manufactured in a factory. Even if it's real, and it's not, it shows his distinct lack of creativity," Matt snapped back. "He could've, at the very least, sprung for a deep blue sapphire from Sri Lanka to match your eyes or a pink diamond to match your lips."

"Do you often go around offering unsolicited advice on engagement rings?"

Matt didn't miss a beat. "Only to a woman who once…" he hesitated and Emily held her breath, dreading his next words. They'd covered this ground earlier

and he wouldn't go there, she was sure he wouldn't. "…
expressed her interest in seeing me naked."

He went there. Bastard!

"You called me a guppy," Emily shot back. His words
and supercilious tone still rankled.

"You were too damn innocent for the grown-up game
you were playing," Matt retorted.

Being called innocent because of the way her features
were arranged was the bane of her life. And if people
didn't think she was innocent then they thought she was
stupid or, more often, a combination of the two.

Few bothered to find out if any of their assumptions
were true. People tended to get stuck on her face and
couldn't imagine her having a conversation about the hu-
manitarian crisis in Darfur or the state of the economy.
People, she'd decided, rather liked the idea of her being
a bit dim; it was as if they couldn't comprehend Emily
being both beautiful and smart.

Her beauty was just a lucky combination of DNA; it
didn't mean anything. All it meant was that she'd just
won the genetic lottery.

Emily narrowed her eyes at him. "Why did you yank
me into this room, Velez? And why are we in a closet
when there's a perfectly good meeting room next door?"

"That small room is like Grand Central Station tonight
and I don't want to be interrupted," Matt retorted. "So,
are the rumors true?"

"What rumors?"

"Cut the crap, Emily," Matt snapped. "Tell me that you
aren't engaged to Morris?" His thumb tapped the stone,
his fingers still holding her captured hand.

God, she wished she could. "I am. And why are you
suddenly so interested in my life?"

Before Matt could answer, a deep voice drifted

through the thin walls of the closet. "Why are we meeting in this room instead of at the bar?"

Emily's eyes widened at the strange voice and Matt tipped his head. He dropped his mouth to speak in her ear. "That's Joshua Lowell speaking."

Emily nodded.

"I got a birthday gift in the mail yesterday."

"Oliver." Matt mimed the word. "His brother, I think."

"Bit late, isn't it? Your birthday was last month," Joshua commented.

Emily reached up to speak in Matt's ear. "We should go."

Matt's hand rested on her hip and she felt the heat of his fingers through the thin fabric of her dress. Sparks skidded up her spine and her mouth felt dry. "If we do, they'll know we're in here and it might get back to Morris. Better to wait until the room and hallway are clear. I'd hate to be the one to cause friction between you and your fiancé."

Emily narrowed her eyes at him, hearing the sarcasm in his voice. She had no doubt Matt Velez didn't give a fig for Nico's, or anybody else's, opinion.

"The gift was a fishing pole, accompanied by an ultrabrief message. One word. 'Someday.'"

Matt shrugged when Emily lifted her eyebrows. Obviously, he was equally unsure of why Oliver was making a big deal about receiving a fishing pole and a cryptic note.

"Do you remember when Dad used to take you fishing?" Oliver asked.

"Wow, that's a memory from way back when. And yes, I remember—it's not like it happened that often," Joshua replied.

"Dad promised to take me fishing not too long before

he disappeared," Oliver said, sounding hesitant. "Josh... do you think..."

"That it could be from Dad? That he's trying to let you know he's alive?" Joshua rushed his sentence and Emily felt Matt tense beside her. He mimed the word wow and Emily felt guilty for listening in on a private conversation.

"No, Oliver. I don't think it's that. I think it's someone trying to mess with your head. And if I find out who it is, I'm going to rip his head off his shoulders."

"I've been clean for a long time, Joshua. And I'm not a fragile piece of china."

Matt raised his eyebrows. "Issues?"

"Cocaine," Emily whispered.

How nice that Oliver had a big brother, someone he could rely on, Emily thought. Since the time she was fourteen, she became the "mom" of the house, shopping, cooking and trying to connect with her distant and workaholic dad.

She put on a smile, did everything right at home, pretending that she wasn't gutted that the person who was supposed to love her the most had left her to deal with a distant father and a brother with special needs. She adored Davy but she'd been so young to assume adult responsibilities and her mom, by leaving, stole her childhood, her teenage years and her confidence.

"I feel stupid," Oliver said from the other side of the wood paneling, pulling Emily's reluctant attention back to the conversation on the other side of the thin wall.

"Don't," Joshua replied. "Listen, the Lowells are always going to be targeted, thanks to what Dad did and the mess he left behind. You're not the only one who's been trolled, Ol."

Joshua hesitated before continuing and Emily had to

admit that Matt was right, this was riveting stuff. It was wrong to eavesdrop but, like anything to do with the Lowells, this was a fascinating discussion.

"Sophie came to me and told me that she had a DNA report showing me to be the father of a baby girl born four years ago. I was, naturally, stunned," Joshua explained.

"You have a baby girl?"

"No, you idiot, I don't. I was always careful and none of my previous partners even hinted at me getting them pregnant. But the report looked totally authentic so Soph and I looked into it. We found out that the report was generated by a doctor with a long and torrid history of shady practices and false results. When I heard that, I was relieved—with our family history, I didn't want to be a dad."

"I hear you on that," Oliver fervently agreed. "We didn't exactly have a great role model to emulate—we'd be terrible fathers. Well, I know I would. I don't want kids."

Joshua's voice held the hint of a smile. "I was convinced I didn't either but I think I might, want a child, that is. I figure that Sophie will keep our kid on the straight and narrow and I'll take my cues from her."

"You are a braver man than I am, big brother. It's hard enough to look after myself—I don't want or need the responsibility of parenthood."

Emily heard the click of high heels and the door to the meeting room opened. "Guys, the auction is in the ballroom. Why are you in here?"

Was that Sophie's voice? Emily heard the shuffle of big feet as the Lowell brothers left the room. When silence fell, Emily reached for the door handle and eased the door open. She peeked outside and saw that the hall-way was empty. Time for her to go.

It would take all her willpower to walk away from Matt when all she really wanted was to step into his arms, feed off his strength, taste his mouth. Strip his clothes…

Right, enough of that, Arnott.

"You take girls to all the best places, Velez," Emily said, making sure her voice was just a degree warmer than frozen nitrogen.

Matt tipped his head to the side and jammed his hands into the pockets of his suit pants. "Don't marry him, Emily. You'll regret it."

She started to tell him that she'd regret marriage, pe-riod, but just kept herself from uttering the words. Emily sucked in a calming breath and, looking him in the eye, raised her stubborn chin. "I'm sure your opinion mat-ters…to someone."

Matt had the temerity to smile. "I'm going to change your mind, princess. Someday my opinion is the only one you're going to care about."

Emily lifted her hand to her brow, pretending to scan the environment. "And there goes a flying pig dressed in a pink tutu."

Emily picked up the skirt of her floor-skimming dress and stepped into the empty hall. "Goodbye, Matteo."

"This isn't over." Matt's words, spoken in his deep voice, rumbled over her skin.

Oh God, she really hoped it was because she didn't know if she could cope with both Nico and Matt.

Damn, but she needed a stiff drink. At home, while she was cuddling her cat. She was, officially, peopled out.

# Three

The next evening, Matt rapped on the door to Emily's above-garage apartment, wondering what the hell he was doing on her doorstep on a Sunday at twilight. But since leaving the auction the previous night, he couldn't purge the image of Emily's head on Morris's shoulder, her hand tucked into his arm, his damned ring on her finger.

Was he simply envious Morris had a woman he wanted? So envious that he was prepared to, for the first time in his life, chase after a woman when his normal modus operandi was to let women chase him?

He'd lain awake for most of the night, thinking of the past and the present.

He'd been so young when he encountered Emily and yes, she'd knocked him off his feet. But he was older now and he could easily dismiss his initial thoughts of her being part of his forever as wishful, fanciful thinking. He didn't believe in love and forever.

The only reason he was here was because he wanted her…

Wanted her enough for him to make more of an effort than he normally did. He also wasn't the type who made a move on another man's woman but Morris was a dick, and honor, after all the crap Morris pulled years ago, didn't count in this situation.

And sure, he was a competitive SOB and, at the best of times—i.e. anything that didn't involve Emily Arnott—he didn't like someone else having something or someone he wanted. And he did want Emily, he'd wanted her six years ago and he wanted her now, and the thought of taking her away from Morris warmed his cold heart.

He would also be doing her a huge favor because he knew just how much of a dick Morris could be.

The snap of fingers in front of his face brought Matt back to the present and he focused on intense purple-blue eyes fringed with thick, dark lashes. Emily's straight blond hair was raked back from her forehead into a high ponytail and her face was free of makeup. She wore a baggy sweatshirt, leggings and fuzzy socks, and every inch of him craved her.

A massive black, brown and gray cat meowed, sat on her foot and lifted its enormous head, eyes on the sandwich in her hand.

Speaking of which, Matt hadn't eaten all day. He lifted the top slice of bread and frowned. "Cheese? And…" He wrinkled his nose. "Is that pineapple?"

"And jalapeño chilies and salt and pepper."

Ugh. That sounded gross. "Are you pregnant?"

He looked down at her flat stomach. Was that why she was marrying jerk-face; to give her child a father? When did women start having pregnancy cravings?

"No, I'm not pregnant," Emily replied, annoyed. "I just

happen to like weird combinations of food. Chicken-liver paté and marmalade, pickles and Oreos."

Yuck. "So, you'll know you're pregnant when you start craving peanut butter and jelly, cheese and ham?" Matt asked.

A hint of humor momentarily penetrated the frost in her eyes. "Why are you here, Velez?"

Matt waited for her to invite him in but when she didn't budge, he sighed. "Let me in, Emily. We need to talk."

Emily rolled her eyes, obviously exasperated, but she gestured him inside. Matt stepped over the massive fur-ball and placed his hands into the pockets of his pants, taking in her apartment. He immediately felt at home, thinking he could kick off his shoes and sink down into that comfortable sofa. The apartment was spacious, with wide wooden windows looking out to the forest behind her dad's house, and beyond that to the mountains. The apartment itself was a mishmash of colors and styles, in blues and greens with hints of pink, but nothing jarred.

Black-and-white prints of exotic places—he recognized the Imperial Citadel at Hanoi and Syntagma Square in Athens—covered her walls. He stepped up to them, captured by the moody atmosphere and the way the photographer played with the shadows. "These are brilliant. Who took them?"

"I did. I traveled solo for a few months after leaving college."

The cat did a figure eight between his legs and Matt bent down to scratch him between his ears. "What's his name?"

"Fatty."

Matt smiled. "Unoriginal but appropriate."

Emily placed her sandwich on the plate on the island counter, leaned her forearms on the counter and pinned him to the floor with her direct gaze. "What do you want?"

You. Naked. As soon as possible.

Too much? Too strong? Yeah, obviously.

Matt ran his hand through his hair as he turned to face her. "Why are you wearing that ridiculously big ring? Why are you really marrying Morris? And don't tell me it's because you love him."

"Maybe I do."

"BS."

When he got out of his head, pushed aside his envy and jealousy—and his need to have her—and applied logic to the situation he still, instinctively, had the feeling their engagement was a sham. He'd watched her last night and nothing in the way she acted told him that she was in love or was even excited about her engagement. She accepted good wishes and congratulations with a pained smile and her responses had been too deliberate, too thought out.

Too choreographed.

Living on the outside of his family, not being a part of that inner circle of three, had honed his observation and perception skills. He could read body language as well as he could walk and talk and something about Emily and her response to being newly engaged was off.

"Are you in trouble?" he demanded, his voice rough.

Emily's big round eyes widened in a too-practiced-to-be-real move. It instantly made her look younger and upped her innocence factor. But underneath the forced insouciance was panic and he wanted to know why.

"No, I'm not in trouble. And even if I was, why would I confide in you?" Emily asked, tipping her head to the side. "We're barely acquaintances. I'm just another girl who threw herself at you, one of the few you didn't bother to catch."

She was pissed because he didn't take her up on her drunk offer? Well, he was pissed off too. He would never tell her his reaction to her scared the crap out of him and that he'd been so tempted to throw caution to the wind and start something meaningful with her...

Thank God he hadn't. Attraction faded and love never lasted.

"You were a kid and you'd been drinking," Matt said, pushing his words through gritted teeth, using that same, probably tired, excuse. "Tipsy or not, I don't take advantage of young girls."

Her next question shocked the hell out of him. "And if I asked you that same question last night?"

He didn't hesitate. "You'd still be naked, in my bed." He gestured to the short hallway. "Or naked, in your bed. My place or here, trust me, you still wouldn't be wearing a stitch of clothing."

Matt watched as color flooded her face, entranced as her eyes darkened to a color similar to those African violets his mother had nurtured on the windowsill of their kitchen. Within those dark depths he saw passion, desire, the fight for control of both. Her eyes dropped to his mouth and Matt knew she wanted what he did—their lips fused, a taste of each other's breath.

He moved, or did she, and then her fingers were on the back of his neck and his hands were on her hips and he bent down and she rose up and then...

God. *Perfection.*

Soft lips with a hint of pineapple, a flowery scent in his nose and a soft, surprisingly curvy body in his arms. Needing more, needing everything, Matt pulled her closer and Emily released a tiny sound when her breasts pushed into his chest and moaned again when his tongue swept into her mouth.

Emily seemed to sag against him and Matt wrapped his arms around her slim back, lifting her up and into him, happily taking her weight. Her fingers came to rest on his jawline, as soft and arousing as a feather.

Matt felt Emily's foot run up the back of his calf, felt her hands on his back, on his butt. She, thank God, wanted him back. This time, he wouldn't hesitate; this time, he'd do everything to her that he couldn't do all those years ago.

He'd start by kissing her from tip to toe...

Matt pulled his mouth off hers and started the exploration of her face, nibbling the fine line of her jaw, tasting the skin on those cut-glass cheekbones. Her nose was straight and just a little haughty...

It took a minute, maybe more for him to realize that Emily was a stiff board in his arms, that her hands were on his chest, trying to push him, not very emphatically, away. Matt groaned, blinked and tried to get his eyes to focus on her face.

If she wanted to stop, he might just drop to the floor and howl.

"Velez! Stop!"

Yep, crap, she wanted to stop. Matt cursed silently and allowed her to slide down his body, swallowing his moan of frustration. He lifted his hands off her and stepped away. It nearly killed him but that's what grown men did. He might not have any honor when it came to poaching on Morris's territory but when a woman said no, he listened.

Emily made a fist, put it to her mouth and Matt caught the terror in her eyes, the waves of blue-and-purple panic.

"What the hell am I doing?" Emily whispered and,

while her words were low, he caught her fear. "This is madness."

Matt's protective instincts kicked in and he took a step toward her, cursing when she scuttled backward, her hands up to ward him off.

"Em, Jesus, what is going on with you?"

"Nothing, I keep telling you that!" Emily said, pointing to her front door. "I just need you to leave. Now. Immediately."

Matt thought about arguing but Em had not only physically retreated, she'd pulled back mentally, as well. There was nothing he could say or do to recapture the magic of their kiss, to put her back in his arms.

Matt jammed his hands into the pockets of his chinos, hoping his expression didn't reveal his frustration. Emily Arnott was less of a pushover and more stubborn—and more loyal, a quality Morris did not deserve!—than he expected.

He rather liked that.

But, under his envy and his lust, his gut instinct was screaming that there was something fishy about their engagement and he was the only one who realized it. He'd allow her to think that he was minding his own business, walking away, but he'd be back.

Sometimes, the only way to gain ground was to retreat.

The next morning, in her corner office at Arnott's Wealth Management, Emily stared at her computer screen, the numbers and letters blurring in front of her eyes. As the company's operations manager, she needed to stay sharp, but she was operating on less than three hours of sleep. She'd also spent the bulk of last night staring at her ceiling, her thoughts bouncing between how to save herself from becoming a trophy wife and how good she felt standing in Matt's arms, how wonderful it was to be kissed by him.

Why she was thinking about Matt Velez when her entire life was falling apart at the seams, God only knew.

Emily dropped her forehead to her sleek desk and banged her head against the smooth surface. So Matt kissed her, big deal. Or it would've been, two weeks or so ago. But really, since she was being blackmailed into marriage, she shouldn't be thinking about his dark eyes or his soft lips, the muscled body under those designer suits and his sexy scent.

Velez wasn't important; saving Arnott's reputation and, obviously, getting out of her engagement was.

Emily sat up and spun her chair around to face the window behind her. While it was still, technically, summer, there was a slight chill in the air and hints of fall in the changing color of the trees. Fall was her favorite season and she usually took a week's vacation after Labor Day. This year she'd planned to fly down to Grand Cayman to spend a week in a friend's cottage overlooking a private beach. She'd planned to lie in the sun, read a dozen books, catch fish and cook them over an open fire. Drink wine.

Chill.

Well, those plans had been blown out of the water.

She couldn't go anywhere, do anything until she disengaged herself and protected the company bearing her name.

Telling anybody, other than Gina, about Nico's blackmail scheme was out of the question. She couldn't even take the problem to her dad. Oh, she'd told him she was engaged, but Leonard had barely reacted—had he actually not heard her or did he simply not care? Davy wouldn't understand the implications of her actions and, as for her mom, well, she'd rather walk through a field of Christ's-thorn than tell her mom anything...

And, Lord, what was Nico thinking? This wasn't the eighteen hundreds when a man's standing was improved by marriage; these days you lived and died by your own choices. Sure, she came from a good family, and the Arnotts were one of the first families to settle in Falling Brook. And yeah, back when her dad liked people and before her mom left, Leonard was the unofficial mayor of the town, her mom one of its most popular hostesses.

But those halcyon days were gone, her dad was wrapped up in business and the little time he spent outside of work was spent either with Davy or in his home gym.

Her mom wasn't the only one who'd abandoned her. Her mom physically disappeared but while her dad was physically present—working in his office down the hallway—he was as mentally absent as her mother.

She'd finally learned to be independent and self-sufficient, to rely on herself and to trust her decisions. But Em sometimes wished she had someone to rely on, someone who she could talk to and who understood the issues around her father's emotional distance and her brother's special needs.

While she loved her independence, occasionally she got really tired of being a tribe of one. But being lonely was still better than being constantly disappointed by people for wanting and expecting more than they could give her. Still, she craved a strong father and a mother who could remember her name.

Love...why did people constantly look for it?

She'd veered off her original thought...why was Nico

so determined to have her that he'd resorted to blackmail? And, admittedly, his threat was a good one. They had some run-of-the-mill clients but they also worked in a niche market—looking after the financial needs of vulnerable adults—and Arnott's reputation meant everything to them. One whiff of scandal would have their clients running for the hills.

Nico told her that their marriage would bring him more clients, better opportunities, but Emily knew he was overestimating her importance in the small, wealthy community of Falling Brook.

And, while she desperately wanted to, she didn't believe him when he said that he wasn't in a rush to sleep with her. He touched her too frequently—a stroke down her arm, a hand low on her back, almost touching her butt—and she saw the desire in his eyes.

He was smart enough not to push her, to scare her more than she already was, but Em knew he wanted her—in his bed, as his wife, to make him look better by marrying into one of the "famous" families of Falling Brook—and he was desperate enough to blackmail her.

Emily abruptly stood up, frustrated. She had to figure out how to paralyze Nico, without endangering the company. Gina was looking for gossip, reaching out to her contacts for anything she could use but so far, she'd come up with nothing.

There had to be more she could do. Thanks to her big blue eyes and long blond hair and the stereotype associated with women who looked like her, few people realized Emily had a sharp brain behind her pretty face. What she really needed to do was to push Nico into a corner, to shut down his options. She needed information on Nico of greater or equal importance to what he had on her. It was imperative that she put him in a similar situation as he'd shoved her into, one where he was equally at risk.

But that meant pretending to be his fiancée while digging up damaging information on him. Emily leaned her shoulder into the window, scowling down at the busy road below her. Her only advantage was that Nico thought she was a little dim and naive and docile.

She wasn't. And she wasn't the type to go down without a damn good fight.

In his office in Midtown Manhattan, Matt threw his pen onto the desk and gripped the bridge of his nose between his thumb and forefinger, wishing he could squeeze a certain blonde out of his head.

He'd been up since four, checking the Asian markets, moving millions around with the touch of his mouse, the tap of his keyboard. As CEO, he wasn't expected to work the markets but he liked to keep his hand in so he still managed the portfolios of a handful of carefully selected clients. In six hours, he'd traded more than fifty million USD, making a small profit on both his own and his clients' money. On good days, trading was the best job in the world and a massive profit in one session could keep a smile on his face for hours. It could also be, on bad days, the equivalent of riding through hell, naked, sitting on the shell of a superslow snail. On days that trades went against him, resulting in a significant loss, he frequently prayed for his heart to stop so he didn't have to hear the blood rushing through his system, the taste of bile in the back of his throat, the cramping of his stomach.

This morning was a so-so day, minor profits, acceptable losses, resulting in a net profit of a couple of percent. Not his best day but also not his worst. Considering that thoughts of a violet-eyed blonde kept strolling through his brain, he'd done okay.

Luckily.

Reaching behind him, Matt snagged a bottle of water out of the bar fridge concealed behind a cupboard door and eyed his computer, thinking that he needed to review some reports and make a start on the next quarter's growth projections. Trading was fun but he needed to get down to the real work of managing MJR and, most days, he loved it.

And he would, in a minute. Matt leaned back in his chair, cracked the top to his water bottle and silently cursed when his mind went back to Emily. What was she up to today?

Before he could wander too far down that unproductive path, Matt heard the rap of knuckles on the frame of his office door and looked up when his senior trader, who also happened to be one of his best friends, strolled through the open door to his office.

Malcolm plopped himself down in the chair opposite Matt and linked his fingers on his flat stomach. "Good day?"

Matt rocked his hand from side to side. "Okay-ish. You?"

"Some losses this morning. I'm about to dive in again in twenty minutes," Mal replied.

Matt tossed Malcolm a bottle of water before lifting his own bottle to his lips. The reports could wait. "I think I'm going to take the rest of the day off."

Malcolm raised his eyebrows at Matt's statement. Matt couldn't blame him. He was well-known for working longer hours than everyone at the company and was always the first to arrive and the last to leave. "Problem?"

*Only a blonde I can't dismiss from my head.* Irritation

prickled and burned. He was always super focused and it annoyed him that Emily Arnott hovered on the edge of his thoughts for most of the morning.

Two main thoughts kept running through his mind: how good she felt in his arms and how wrong her engagement to Nico Morris was. If she was any other woman, he would've had her in his bed and out of his mind by now.

And she would've left with a smile on her face and a *please call me soon*.

And yes, maybe that did make him sound like a player, but he never made promises he had no intention of keeping. His lovers knew the score...

But Emily kept tipping his world upside down. He wanted to dismiss her, to walk away from this stupid situation, but his mind—or his ego or his pride, or all three bastards working in tandem—just wouldn't let her go. He couldn't walk, not just yet, not until he knew what it was like to make love to her.

Her hold on him pissed him off.

Matt's PA sailed into his office, looking as imperious as a Russian queen. Vee was Matt's right-hand person, someone he trusted more than most. She was also deadly efficient, irascible, abrupt and had few social skills.

Vee had a computer science degree, was a dedicated gamer and occasional hacker, and Matt had no idea why, with her skills, she worked as his PA and office manager.

Vee looked at Malcolm over the top rim of her glasses. "Don't you have work to do, Mr. King?"

Oh, and she also thought that she ran MJR Investing.

Malcolm, not in the least bit intimated, sent her a lazy grin. "Not right now, Miss Vee."

Vee turned her sharp gaze on Matt. "I see you are also slacking off, Mr. Velez."

Vee, despite only being in her late thirties, had the

disposition of a Victorian butler and the work ethic, and personality, of a fire ant. Matt adored her.

"I've been at it since four this morning, Vee. Cut me some slack," Matt replied.

Vee sniffed her disapproval. "Never. If I do, this place will fall apart."

Matt rolled his eyes at Malcolm, an action that was rewarded by a dirty look and a purse of ruby-red lips.

"Your messages." Vee slapped a pile of carefully printed slips on his desk. A heavy file landed next to his computer. "Turnover and expense reports."

Malcolm rose, shot him an amused grin and ambled to the door. As he passed through it, Vee ordered him to close it, which he did. Matt, wondering why his PA was being extra bossy, leaned back in his chair and waited for her to speak. Vee was never shy about saying what was on her mind.

"I heard you are talking to Joshua Lowell at Black Crescent."

Matt winced. His potential career move was supposed to be highly confidential but Vee had even better sources in Falling Brook than he did, was far too interested in his life and frequently knew what he was going to eat for dinner before he did. He'd tried to tell her that his personal life was just that, personal, but Vee had just ignored him and deep-dived into his life. A part of Matt rather liked how much she cared; God knew his parents didn't. Never had.

Juan got all of that attention…

"I have no plans to go anywhere, Vee, not yet anyway. I'm just using a potential move to Black Crescent as a bargaining chip with the board." Matt lifted one shoulder. "Unless Black Crescent makes me an offer I simply can't refuse."

"Wherever you go, I go," Vee stated, her tone brooking no argument.

That was a given. Vee was his right hand. And his left. "Maybe," he said, just to tease her.

Vee's bottom lip wobbled, just for a second, and Matt felt guilty. "I'm joking, Vee, of course I'd take you with me," he said, hurrying to reassure her. Vee was a cactus, prickly as hell on the outside with a squishy, easily hurt center.

Vee blinked and dipped her head in a sharp nod. "That's settled then."

"Don't give me grief but I was thinking about taking the rest of the day off," Matt said, pushing his chair back and standing up. "I have a birthday present to buy."

Vee's birthday was next week and he saw the pleasure flash in her eyes. He'd already approved her birthday bonus but he wanted to buy her something special, something that wasn't company related. Vee loved orchids, so he'd ordered a new variety via Falling Brook's nursery and had received word that it had arrived. But Vee would have to receive her birthday present early because houseplants came to him to die.

Vee placed her hand on her heart and sent him a sweet smile. It wasn't one he saw on her face very often, reminding Matt that she needed him as much as he needed her. "Have a good day, Matteo. Is there anything else you need me to do for you?"

Matt rubbed the back of his neck as Emily's gorgeous face drifted through his mind. Maybe Vee knew something he didn't about the Morris/Arnott engagement. But if he asked, his supersharp assistant would immediately sense he was thinking about a woman.

"Do we have any business ties to Arnott's in Falling

Brook?" Matt asked, wondering why the thought hadn't occurred to him before. A link between Arnott's and MJR could be exploited to get closer to Emily and what he really wanted, which was her, naked, under him.

Vee, used to his rapid changes of subject, thought for a minute. "Not that I can think of. Of course, every year Emily Arnott asks everyone and anyone who's even vaguely connected to Falling Brook for donations to Brook Village. She also asks for volunteers to join her fundraising committee for the same organization, whatever it may be."

"It's the residential home where her brother lives," Matt explained.

"From the tone of her letter, I thought it was the standard request for time and money. As far as I know, although a few of our clients come from Falling Brook, nobody from MJR has ever volunteered to sit on her committee," Vee added.

Sitting on committees wasn't something he did, but he couldn't keep rocking up unannounced on Emily's doorstep, and if joining her cause got him what he wanted—Emily—he'd suck it up. He needed an excuse to put himself in her orbit. And this was as good a one as any. "When did that request to sit on the fundraising committee come in?"

Vee sent him a what-are-you-up-to look. "Within the last few weeks. If I remember correctly, the first committee meeting is happening this evening, in the boardroom at Arnott's."

"Time?"

"Six p.m." Vee folded her arms across her chest and pursed her lips. "What's going on, Matteo?"

Matt grinned. "A little volunteering is good for the soul, Vee."

"And I'd agree if that was your primary motive," Vee replied, not buying his explanation and not, in any way, impressed with his show of altruism. "Just remember the old saying, Matt…no good deed goes unpunished."

# Four

Matt deliberately waited until the fundraising meeting was in progress before sliding into one of the many spare seats at the boardroom table. Emily, quickly covering her shock at his presence, paused in her opening statement to ask him, ever so politely, whether he was lost.

His statement that he wanted to help, in any way he could, was greeted with a small round of applause from the ten other volunteers, all women, but he knew Emily wasn't buying his particular line of BS.

Smart girl.

Forty-five minutes later, Emily called the meeting to a close and thanked her volunteers. Then her eyes clashed with his and he read her order to "sit and stay" as clearly as he read the boring agenda on the table in front of him. Though, he had to admit, Emily plowed through the points of discussion with the ruthless efficiency of a field marshal intent on a quick victory. It was clear that a) she was organized, b) she didn't like to waste time and c) she was passionate about making Brook Village an even better environment for its residents.

Emily Arnott had a sharp brain behind that gorgeous face and Matt was beginning to believe that most people, including him, underestimated her intelligence. And drive.

It was a mistake he wouldn't make again.

Matt stood up as a sleek brunette approached him and took the hand she held out. She introduced herself as Gina, Emily's PA and best friend, and spent a few minutes discussing Brook Village and thanking him for joining Emily's committee.

Behind her as-dark-as-his eyes, he caught her shrewdness and saw her cynicism. He knew she wanted to ask some hard questions, the obvious being *why are you hanging around Emily when you know she's engaged?*

What could he tell her?

That the thought of Nico being engaged to Emily made him sick to his stomach? Sure. He was envious and jealous of her fiancé? Absolutely.

That he wanted Emily more than he wanted to breathe? Triple check.

That he felt out of his depth because women flocked to him and he never overexerted himself in his pursuit of female companionship and this was a strange and unusual situation? God, yes.

"Good night, Gina," Emily stated, her volume button rising.

Gina pointed a finger at Emily and wagged it. "Play nice. We don't have that many volunteers and we can't afford to lose those we do." Gina grinned and Matt noticed the power of her smile. "And he's very nice to look at."

Gina gathered up her bag and her own set of papers

and walked out of the room, sending Matt another appreciative glance over her shoulder. He winked at her; she winked back and, with an extra swing of her hips, walked away.

Matt turned his eyes back to Emily and caught her massive eye roll. "You just can't help it, can you?"

"Help what?"

"Flirting. Whether they are old or young, it's like you are hardwired to charm."

Talking to women had never been an issue for him: he liked the species; they liked him back. Up until now, it was a win-win situation.

"She flirted first," Matt replied, keeping his tone mild.

"You are two peas in a pod," Emily muttered.

Matt rested his right buttock on the sturdy table and folded his arms across his chest. "Gina told you that you have to be nice to me," he teased, enjoying the sparks of irritation in her eyes.

"Since Gina works for me and not the other way around, I don't have to listen to her."

"I sympathize—I have a bossy PA, as well."

Emily rubbed her forehead with her fingers and Matt noticed the dark stripes under her eyes. She was exhausted and he couldn't blame her. Being engaged to Morris was enough to keep anyone awake at night.

"I seem to be asking this question a lot but...why are you here?"

Matt thought about spinning a line but decided she could handle the truth. "I want you—I've wanted you every time I've seen you. I'm shocked and confused as to why you're engaged to Morris and I'm not buying your sudden engagement. I don't believe you want to spend the rest of your life with Morris and nothing about this makes sense."

Nothing about his need for her made sense either but Matt decided to keep that to himself.

Surprise jumped in and out of her eyes before her expression turned implacable. Matt found that interesting; if he was wrong, he would've expected anger, some sort of denial of his words.

"I don't care what you think, Velez."

"Oh, I think you do. And I'm also quite curious as to why you kissed me, climbed all over me if you are so in love with your fiancé."

Emily flushed and Matt wondered if she'd blush like that if she was naked and he was admiring her beautiful body. He hauled in a deep breath, conscious that the fabric covering his groin was a fraction tighter. He'd never wanted anyone more...

And would he want her so much if she wasn't off-limits?

Man, he couldn't remember when last, if ever, he gave a woman this much headspace.

Emily opened her mouth to blast him but the words died on her lips. Instead of laying into him, she dropped into her chair and rested her forearms on her knees and stared at the floor. Matt, his attraction to her instantly forgotten as he'd caught the flash of panic in her eyes before she looked down, moved over to her and dropped to balance on his toes, his own arm on his bent knee. "Em, talk to me. Help me understand."

Emily continued to stare at the carpet and Matt kept his eyes on her face. Up close, he noticed how thick her lashes were, that she had a spray of freckles under her carefully applied makeup and that she had a tiny hole in the side of her nose. Emily had once worn a nose stud or ring and the thought intrigued him. Did a free spirit live under her Goody-Two-shoes, do-no-wrong, conservative persona?

Emily opened her mouth to speak, shook her head and slammed her lips closed. She pushed back her chair and rose to her feet.

Matt looked up at her and slowly stood. Ignoring him, she placed her papers into a fabric folder and closed the lid to her laptop.

He waited for her to face him again, knowing the moment had passed and that she wasn't going to open up. When she turned to acknowledge him, her remote expression confirmed that she'd shored up her defense. "Why are you hassling me? Is this what you do? Do you get off on pursuing women who are in committed relationships?"

The derision in her voice sliced through him and he fought the urge to hurl a couple of insults back. She was the only one who'd ever tempted him to engage and that was so out of character. Matt kept his emotional distance; if a woman refused his advances, he shrugged her off and moved on.

But Emily Arnott had crawled under his skin and stayed there. Part of it was flat-out desire; part of it was envy that Nico had something that Matt wanted—

Envy, one of the seven deadly sins. Matt was competitive and Nico was one of those guys whose face you wanted to shove into the mud. Beating guys like him was wired into Matt's DNA.

"Well?"

Matt pulled his attention back to her hot question about his motivations. There was no way he wanted her to know the devastating effect she had on him...he refused to give her that much power.

But, sometimes, the truth, quietly stated, held more power than volatile accusations. "I'm not going to lie to you, Em. I'm attracted to you. And you're angry because you're attracted to me too."

"I gave you a chance to act on that attraction years ago, Matt, and you rejected me."

Interesting that she didn't bother to deny her attraction.

"I explained my reasons so stop throwing that in my face," Matt replied. "Get over it already."

As soon as the words left his mouth, he regretted them. He waited for her response, wondering whether he'd get a mouthful, a wobbly lip or, God forbid, tears.

Shame flickered in Emily's eyes. Matt watched, impressed, as she pushed starch into her spine and shoulders and held his stare. "You're right. It's over and it's not fair of me to keep tossing that back in your face."

Matt rubbed his jaw, shocked at her admission. Emily kept surprising him and he wasn't a man who was easily knocked off his stride. Fighting the urge to kiss her mouth, to pull her into his arms, he walked to the far end of the table where he'd left his half-full glass of water and quickly drained it. Keeping the table between them, he quietly thanked her for her apology before launching another verbal grenade. "I know that there's something fishy about your engagement to Morris."

"You don't know that—you don't know me!" Emily cried, throwing her hands up in the air.

Matt knew the smile he managed to pull onto his face was grim. "Maybe I don't know you but I do know him."

Nico was incapable of love, he wasn't the type. Matt knew this because it was all he and Morris had in common.

"Please just leave it alone, Matt," she begged.

He wished he could but he'd sooner be able to stop the world from turning. Rationally, he had no sane reason for inserting himself into her life—and his attraction to her didn't count. He'd been attracted to women in relationships before but his own moral code didn't allow him to move in on another man's territory.

He felt nothing for trying to poach Em away—Morris didn't deserve that much respect from him—but something else was bubbling between them. Something…

More.

Em was different, this situation was different and his spidey sense was clanging in his head. But, if he thought Em loved Morris, that she was genuinely into him, he'd walk away, respecting her choice. But deep down he knew love wasn't her motivation for marrying Morris so he wouldn't leave her alone.

Not yet anyway.

Matt ambled back over to her, bent down and briefly rested his lips on her temple. "Can't do that. I'll see you around, Em."

Matt was pretty sure he heard her release a small growl as he walked away but he knew his control was about to snap. If he turned around, he might just haul her into his arms and try a different way to persuade her to end this sham of an engagement.

At the meeting earlier in the week, Emily had agreed to give her new Brook Village fundraising committee members, two enthusiastic ladies who were new to Falling Brook, a tour of Davy's residential home. It was Saturday morning and the tour was over so the last person she expected to see approaching their table on the veranda of the intimate coffee shop was Matt Velez, looking far too sexy in a designer pair of soft-looking jeans, expensive athletic shoes and an untucked rich brown button-down shirt—

sleeves rolled up muscled forearms—the exact color of his wonderful eyes.

Eyes that saw too much...

Emily looked down at her ripped-at-the-knees jeans, her off-the-shoulder black-and-white-striped sweater, and couldn't remember if she put on any makeup that morning. She'd been running late and was only expecting to meet Jane and Linda and not her pain-in-her-butt, make-my-heart-jump newest, and finest, committee member.

"Matt. I was *so* not expecting you." Emily said, placing her arm over the back of the chair. "And you're late so you missed the tour." Emily gestured to their empty coffee cups. "And we were all just leaving."

Matt ignored her belligerent tone and turned those soulful eyes onto her companions, his sexy mouth tipping up into a smile. "Morning, ladies, Em. Sorry I'm late."

He didn't give an excuse and Emily knew he'd deliberately timed his arrival to miss the tour. He wasn't there to find out more about Brook Village but to further his own agenda.

If only she knew what that was...

"Nico didn't join you this morning?" Matt asked, pulling out a chair and sitting down. Catching the eye of a waitress—Macy, one of the residents and Davy's good friend—he politely asked for coffee.

Macy, utterly flustered, giggled and skipped away. Emily sighed. Another conquest for Matt Velez.

After a few minutes of casual conversation, Jane and Linda rose and Matt, polite as always, shot to his feet. They said their goodbyes and Matt dropped down into his chair again, thanking Macy when she brought his cup.

"It's a good idea to have a small coffee shop on the premises, a place for the families to gather," Matt said, leaning back in his chair.

Yeah, it was great, except when her father chatted with *Russian mob bosses*! Emily looked around, saw many parents visiting the residents but couldn't see John, aka Ivan Sokolov. Come to think of it, he wasn't someone she often saw at Brook Village.

"Looking for someone?" Matt asked her.

Emily jerked her gaze back to him and shook her head. "No...*no*."

Matt frowned at her overemphatic response. She could see the curiosity in his eyes so she spoke quickly to distract him. He was here, so talking about the facility seemed a safe topic for conversation.

"The residents each have their own living rooms and, depending on their abilities, they can provide their guests with refreshments or, if they want to, a meal," Emily explained. "Some of our residents have jobs but the coffee shop gives others the chance to earn some money on-site. The cooks are residents too."

"There's food?" Matt asked, sounding excited. "Great, I haven't had breakfast yet."

"I can recommend the food," Emily said. "Order the brie-and-cranberry toasted sandwich, it's divine."

Matt pulled a face and Emily smiled. "You really aren't an adventurous eater, are you?"

"Eggs and bacon will be just fine," Matt replied, his eyes steady on her face. "I'm adventurous in other areas."

His tone wasn't lecherous or salacious but Emily knew, just knew, he was referring to the bedroom. And boy, yeah, she could believe that. Matt would be a demanding lover, wringing every last drop of pleasure and pushing his partners to explore their sexuality. She'd had just two very unsatisfactory lovers and she was curious as to whether she could, actually, orgasm.

So far, the Big *O*s had been elusive. Some women,

she'd read, never orgasmed at all and Em hoped, and prayed, that she didn't fall into that group. But, judging from the way Matt made her feel from just a few kisses—all hot and fluttery and off-balance—he might be the man to help her hit that particular target.

Damn him.

Matt's low laugh pulled her from the image of him taking her standing up, in a shower or against a wall, his hand under her thigh, pushing into her as he pinned her naked body against a hard surface. Yep, he'd make her come, she was pretty sure of it…

"I would donate a thousand dollars to Brook Village to know what you are thinking right now."

A thousand dollars? No way could she turn that sort of money down. "I was thinking of you taking me up against a wall and the orgasm that followed."

Matt stared at her and Emily smiled at his initial shock at her bold words—yeah, she wasn't such a good girl after all! Then Matt's eyes flashed with interest and his cheeks darkened with heat. And, best of all, the hand holding his cup trembled. Good to know that she could knock the very smooth Matt Velez off his game.

"You can make the check out to the Brook Village," Emily told him.

"Done." Matt placed his coffee mug down and rested his forearms on the table. He stared at her and Emily couldn't look away; she'd never seen eyes so dark, holding a thousand secrets.

"But, for the record, those are not the sort of comments a happily engaged woman makes to another man, sweetheart. And it just reinforces my opinion that you're not happily engaged, Emily Arnott."

Ah, crap. This again.

He was too sharp, far too quick. Matt's brother, Juan,

might be a genius but Matt had received more than his fair share of brains. Emily forced herself to act casual.

"I'm engaged, not dead, Matteo. And it would be disingenuous of me to deny I am attracted to you since we kissed the other night." She wiggled her fingers of her left hand, pulling her attention to her ring. "But I am engaged. To Nico."

She really had to work on sounding more enthusiastic.

Emily wanted to know why he was so against her marrying Nico. Why did he keep pushing and prying; why did he care? Oh, she knew he desired her—their lava-hot kiss earlier in the week proved that—but if sex was all he was after, then she knew there was no shortage of candidates to share his bed. Around him, women fell like pins in a bowling alley, unable to resist his bad-boy-made-good looks and cocky attitude.

"And this has got me wondering…" Emily said, tapping her index finger on the glass tabletop.

"About?" Matt asked, back to looking cool and collected.

"What's your beef with…" she couldn't push the word *fiancé* past her lips "…with Nico? And don't tell me you don't have one," she added.

No, Matt Velez had an agenda and it had more to do with her fiancé and less to do with her. Matt had a problem with Morris; that much was obvious.

But did the root cause of his hostility matter? Did she care as long as his animosity toward Nico benefited her? On one level, it would make sense to team up with him, both of them working to take Nico down—she was pretty sure Matt would be happy to trample on any and all of Nico's dreams and he might even have information on Nico she could use.

But she couldn't take the chance of letting him in on

her secret. Gina was the only person she'd told and that was because she told Gina everything. And Gina was trying to source information on Nico to help her break her engagement, desperately flipping over rocks to find something to get Nico to leave her alone. She trusted Gina with her life.

She didn't trust Matt. Nobody could know about Nico's bizarre but exceedingly effective scheme. He'd identified what was most important to her dad and to her, Arnott's reputation, and he'd pushed her between a rock and a concrete pillar.

She had to resolve this issue fast. She would not risk Arnott's: her dad lost his wife when Vernon Lowell ran away with his and his clients' money, and Arnott's was now her dad's refuge and his true love.

He wasn't a great dad, probably wasn't even a good one, but he was hers and she had to protect him, protect their name and the source of their income.

And keep Nico at a distance until she had the dirt she needed to force him to leave her alone. Because there was dirt, of this she was certain.

Matt was saved from having to respond to her question when arms encircled her neck and a masculine jaw rubbed her cheek. She recognized the scent of Davy's soap and pushed her way to her feet, turning to hug her big brother.

After a minute, maybe two—Davy was super affectionate and loved to hug—Emily pulled back and gripped his shoulders. "Davy. How was your week, honey?"

"Angel! You're here. I'm so happy to see you!" Davy responded. "And my week was good."

His curious eyes, the same purple-blue shade as hers, bounced between her and Matt.

"Who's he?" Davy whispered. "He needs a haircut but I do like his watch."

Emily saw Matt's mouth twitching and knew that Matt had heard his not-so-quiet words. Matt, to her surprise, held out his hand for Davy to shake. "I'm Matt. And you're right, I do need a haircut."

Matt released Davy's hand and gestured him to the spare seat next to Emily. "Take a seat, Davy. I'm about to have breakfast. Would you like to join me?"

Davy sat down and nodded. "I always have pancakes on Saturday."

"Are the pancakes good?" Matt asked.

Emily was impressed by Matt's easy way of talking, his open expression. So many people talked down, or slowly, to people with special needs, and more than a few were openly patronizing. Matt, bless him, just acted normally.

"So good. I like mine with bananas and peanut butter," Davy told him.

"I see you and your brother share a love for bizarre food combinations," Matt said to Emily, wincing at the thought.

Emily couldn't help her grin. "Try it—I dare you."

"And what will you reward me if I do?" Matt asked, amusement in his eyes.

Emily's eyes dropped to his mouth and she knew what he wanted. And damn, she craved that too but she couldn't go there. Not now.

Probably never. A weight settled on her heart as the thought grew bigger and bigger in her head. He wasn't the man for her, could never be the man for her. Not now because she was temporarily engaged and not later because she couldn't risk loving another person and having him leave her. Once was more than enough.

She'd never put herself in that position again.

"My reward, Em?" Matt prompted her.

Oh, right. "I'll pay for your breakfast," she said, wishing she could tell him that what she really wanted was to be in his arms, to feel the rough scrape of his stubble against her skin, feel overwhelmed by his kisses.

"That's not what you really wanted to say."

Of course it wasn't, but there was no way she'd ever admit that to him. She was already neck deep; she didn't need to hasten her drowning.

Davy clapped his hands and Emily looked at him, then smiled at his beaming face. She turned to see who'd caught her brother's attention and saw that it was Macy, who was approaching their table, intent on filling up Matt's cup. It didn't escape her attention that all of Macy's attention was directed to Matt and Emily had yet to be offered coffee.

Macy looked at Matt, blushed and rocked from foot to foot. "Do you want more coffee?" Macy asked Matt.

Matt shook his head. "Thank you, Macy, I've had enough. But I'm sure Emily would like a refill."

Emily felt a jolt of pleasure at his thoughtful gesture. "Thanks, Macy, that would be good. And could you ask the kitchen to bring us two plates of pancakes?" Emily arched her brows at Matt, openly challenging him. "Bananas and peanut butter?"

Matt pulled a face but didn't, to his credit, back down. "Yes, bananas and peanut butter."

"Brave boy," Emily murmured.

"Payback will be fun," Matt told her, his eyes suggesting that he'd like to take his revenge when she was naked and panting. Emily couldn't stop herself from blushing, wishing she didn't want that so damn much.

Because, really, life was complicated enough as it was…

Matt thanked Macy again before turning his attention back to Davy. He leaned across the table and tapped his finger against the dial of Davy's watch. "I like your watch too, Davy. It's pretty special. Where did you get it?"

Emily listened as Davy explained that his vintage Rolex was their grandfather's, how his dad passed it to him when he turned twenty-one. "It's not as fancy as yours, Matt—it doesn't have as many buttons or numbers."

Matt shook his head, not breaking eye contact with her brother. "But mine is new—it never belonged to my grandfather. That's a pretty special thing."

"Did you know your granddaddy?"

Emily saw pain flash in Matt's eyes and saw his lips tighten. She waited for his reply, half expecting him to deflect Davy's curious question. "No, I didn't."

Four words but they were infused with pain. Emily wanted to place a reassuring hand on Matt's, to squeeze his arm. But she resisted the impulse. Matt was a proud man and wouldn't appreciate the gesture. But, from the pain flashing in his eyes and the four words, she realized his relationship with his family wasn't good. She sympathized; she wasn't on any terms with her mom and knew how much it stung to be estranged from a parent.

"Do you play foosball, Matt? Angel and I always play foosball in the rec room. I kick her butt."

Emily couldn't let that falsehood go unchallenged. "Davy Arnott, you know that's not true. I beat you more often than not." Keeping her finger in the air, she pointed it in Matt's direction. "And Davy is the only person, ever, who gets to call me Angel."

"I wouldn't dream of it," Matt smoothly replied. "Besides, you're more of an imp than an angel."

Emily grinned at him. That was one of the best compliments she'd ever received.

Matt's lips curved and Emily felt her stomach flip over and wondered when the few butterflies in her stomach turned into a swarm.

Matt turned his attention to Davy. "After breakfast, I'll play foosball with you. And, if you like, I'll whip your angel's butt for you."

Matt met her annoyed glance with another of his devastating smiles. "Stand down, imp, I called you *his* angel. And here comes Macy with our pancakes. And can I just ask, what exactly is wrong with bacon and maple syrup?"

She got her butt kicked at foosball. Davy, inspired by Matt's take-no-prisoners policy, beat her by a few goals and then Matt thoroughly trounced her, much to Davy's delight.

Nico, Emily couldn't help thinking as she walked at Matt's side to their respective cars in the parking lot, hadn't even bothered to talk to Davy. A strange attitude since he was going to be the guy's brother-in-law. In fact, this whole engagement was super strange; Nico, apart from a few text messages, hadn't made contact with her since his proposal—could you call a blackmail demand a proposal?—nearly ten days ago.

She wasn't complaining but it was weird…

"Your brother is a trip."

Emily smiled at his words. "I'm sure playing foosball isn't how you spend most of your Saturday mornings."

"No, I normally spend my morning at my computer catching up on everything I didn't get to during the week. This was a nice change of pace," Matt replied. "I had as much fun as he did—it was nice to have some fun and easy company."

Emily, her bag over her shoulder, tucked her hands in the back pockets of her jeans. She'd enjoyed her morning far more than expected; it had been a nice change of pace for her too. And, let's be honest here, she never expected Matt Velez to be the type to play foosball with not only Davy, but some of the other guys in the rec room. They'd invited him to play basketball with them and he said he couldn't but that he'd be back to kick their asses.

His easy, normal ribbing delighted Davy and his friends. Of course, she didn't expect him to return to Brook Village—he was a busy guy with a demanding career—but he'd brightened their morning and for that, Emily was grateful.

"You're obviously committed to this place—how long have you been sitting on the fundraising committee?" Matt commented.

"I've been sitting as a trustee on their board for a couple of years and took over the fundraising portfolio a few years ago."

"You were about ten percent short of your fundraising goal last year—are you planning anything else to make up that shortfall?"

He really had done his homework. Matt, as she was coming to accept, wasn't only sexy, hot and ripped but he was also full of surprises.

"I'd love to do more but with my work and my—" Emily hesitated, looking for the right words"—with Nico, I haven't really given it much thought. I'm not sure I have the time to plan anything else."

And she still had to start on her quest for information on Nico. She had no idea where to start. That had to go to the top of her priority list. She'd start trawling the internet for information on her fiancé when she got home, maybe look into what a private investigator charged. If she could find one who was affordable and discreet, hiring him, or her, might be an option.

Maybe she could tell the PI that she wanted some background information on her reticent fiancé, wanted to know more about him before she committed herself to this man.

That sounded reasonable, didn't it?

Matt placed his hand on Emily's forearm, his big hand easily wrapping around it. "You keep doing that."

"Doing what?" Emily asked, trying to ignore her sizzling skin.

"You, mentally, wander off. I can easily see when you are miles away."

Emily sighed. "I have a lot on my mind, Matt."

"I know that." Matt lifted his hand and rubbed his thumb over her bottom lip and Emily wished he'd kiss her. Then she remembered that she was technically, albeit reluctantly, engaged and wasn't allowed to kiss other men.

This engagement really wasn't working for her. In a lot of ways…

"Do me a favor, imp?"

She so loved him calling her that. She shouldn't but she did. "What?"

"If and when you decide you are out of your depth, call me." Matt's hand dropped to her hip and, before she could complain, he snagged her phone from the back pocket of her jeans. Ignoring her attempt to snatch it from him, he slid his thumb across the screen and grinned when the phone opened.

"No passcode or thumbprint? You're not very security conscious, Arnott."

"It's a phone, not nuclear codes." Emily retorted. "And what are you doing with it?"

"Putting my number in your contacts." Matt tapped

the screen a few times before handing it back to her. Then his expression turned serious, and Emily saw the worry in his eyes. "Seriously, Em, call me. Call me anytime."

It was so tempting but the risk was too great. Emily snatched her phone back and held it in a tight grip. "I keep telling you—I'm *fine*, Velez."

Matt tapped her nose. "Thousands might believe you, my sexy imp, but, unfortunately for you, I don't."

Matt hit a button on his remote and a beautiful two-door Mercedes responded with a quiet whoop and the flash of pretty lights. Oh, she did like his car. It's long svelte hood and curvaceous lines made it instantly recognizable. "It's the new AMG GT C Roadster."

Matt's eyebrows rose. "It is. I only got it recently and I'm enjoying it. Do you like cars?"

"No, I *love* cars," Emily said, walking over to the gorgeous vehicle and running her hand over its smooth hood. "She's beautiful. And dangerous."

Emily felt Matt stop behind her, so close she could feel the heat radiating off him, smell his sex-and-soap scent. Why did he always have to smell so damn good?

"I like beautiful and dangerous," Matt said, his knuckles running down the center of her back, stopping at the tip of her butt. He leaned forward and when he spoke, Emily felt his breath on the shell of her ear and his words deep inside her. "Maybe that's why I like you."

The residents of Falling Brook, most of whom knew her from the time she wore pigtails, saw her as being polite and hardworking, conscientious and as somebody who tried hard not to put a foot wrong or rock the boat. She didn't do drugs, smoke or sleep around but the fact that Matt saw her differently thrilled her.

Matt stepped away from her, opened his car door and slid inside. He hit the start button and the engine turned, raucous and cheeky. The driver's window slid down silently and Matt nodded at her phone before pinning her with a hard look. "Don't hesitate to call me, imp."

Emily needed to say something, anything. "I'm very independent and I don't rely on anybody for anything."

"Then why are you getting married, Emily?"

Damn, she'd walked straight into that. Because he'd backed her into a corner, Emily went on the offensive. "If I was a guy, would you be saying the same thing?" Emily challenged him.

"No, because you're not a guy, you're a woman I want and can't have." Matt pushed both hands into his hair, obviously frustrated. "And that's wrong on so many levels."

"Not used to being thwarted?" Emily taunted him.

"I always get what I want. Eventually." Matt nodded at her phone still in her hands. "At the risk of repeating myself, call me. For anything…"

Emily raised her eyebrows, unable to stop herself from flushing. Anything? Anything at all? And, yes, she was tempted.

Not that she'd ever, ever admit that to him.

# Five

Emily pushed her salad leaves around her plate, idly thinking that time dragged when you weren't having fun. Nico had called her shortly after she returned from Brook Village and told her he was back in town and that they were going to dinner at L'Albri, a fine, French-inspired restaurant situated on the main street in town. It was a see-and-be-seen restaurant, upmarket and very snobby.

Emily hated the food, the small portions, the supercilious waiters and the sheer pretentiousness of the place. She'd far prefer to be eating a burger down the road at Al's Diner but Emily knew that Nico would rather die than be seen at the real, homey and down-to-earth eatery.

Soon after finishing his fish dish, Nico had excused himself to talk to a potential client across the room and left her alone at the table. That had been twenty-five minutes ago. He'd interrupted a private dinner and Emily could see the frustration on their trying-to-be-polite faces.

Unlike Matt, Nico had no idea about social cues.

She had to stop thinking about Matt Velez, comparing him to Nico. But she couldn't help it; they were complete opposites. Matt's hair was dark and unruly, he was olive-skinned and his dark eyes radiated intelligence.

Nico kept pushing his limp, dishwater-blond hair out of his cold, light, malicious eyes, and while he could be good looking if he smiled, he rarely did.

Like all women her age, she enjoyed a guy's good looks but she wasn't that shallow that looks were the beginning and end of everything. Nico would be nice looking if he wasn't a scum-sucking extortionist intent on blackmailing her into marriage.

Emily pushed her coffee cup away and, looking toward the front of the restaurant, smiled when she saw Gina standing at the concierge's table. Waving her over, she grinned when her friend dropped into the chair Nico vacated.

"Are you meeting someone?" Emily asked, happy to see her friend and to have some company.

"In ten minutes or so—you know that I like to get here early," Gina replied.

"To see if he's cute or not. If he isn't you send him a text message claiming stomach flu," Emily gently chided her.

Gina shrugged, unperturbed. "What's the point in spending time with someone you aren't, and could never be, attracted to?"

Then she added, sotto voce, "Unless you're being blackmailed…"

"Thanks for the reminder."

"Since you're not going to finish this, may I?" Gina asked, pointing to Emily's wineglass. When Emily nodded, Gina picked it up and took a healthy sip from her half-full glass. "How was dinner?"

"Interminable," Emily admitted. "I've spent most of the evening imagining stabbing him with my fork."

Emily tapped the table with her index finger. "Somehow Nico heard that Matt joined my fundraising committee and he warned me off him."

Gina grimaced. "Yeah, they don't like each other at all."

"Matt and Nico?"

Gina slowly nodded. "Nico worked at MJR Investing and the rumor is that he and Matt were at loggerheads all the time. Like…one said blue, the other would say pink. They were also super competitive. But that's just second-or third-hand gossip—I'm trying to find a direct source." She paused, and then asked, "So what did you tell Nico about Matt?"

"I picked my words carefully, reminding him that Matt is an influential businessman and that I'm grateful he's giving Brook Village his support. He called me naive, telling me that Matt never does anything out of the goodness of his heart."

"And do you think that's true?"

She did, actually; Gina's earlier words about Matt being competitive rang true. Matt wanted her and Emily wasn't sure that he'd want her quite as much if she wasn't engaged to Nico. Matt liked to win and Emily felt a little like a bone two dogs wanted. Sure, he was attracted to her, but she doubted he'd be pursuing her quite so ardently if Nico wasn't in the picture.

"I like Matt, far more than I like Nico but, as per Falling Brook gossip," Gina told her, keeping her voice low, "Matt got the CEO job Nico wanted and he's still bitter about it."

"That was years ago."

"Nico is also very well-known for holding a grudge. Like, it's his *thing*," Gina whispered. "And he never backs down from a challenge. So, did you piss him off or challenge him, Em?"

Emily darted a look a Nico before lifting and dropping her hands. "We went on a couple of dates—I told him I wasn't going to sleep with him and that there wasn't any chemistry. That he wasn't my type."

Gina clicked her fingers and pointed her index finger at Emily's chest. "Apparently he thinks he's everybody's type and he likes to be the one to break it off. So, there you go, a motive for the current madness. And when you add Matt to the madness…"

Emily scowled at her. "What does that mean?"

"Oh, please, the sparks fly when you two are together. I feel like I need to wear a fire-retardant suit," Gina scoffed.

"He's a good-looking guy," Emily said, keeping her tone neutral.

"Honey, that's like calling a NASA space shuttle a toy rocket. The man is superfine." Gina twisted her lips. "Though admittedly, as much as I like him, it is weird that he's back in your life as soon as you get engaged."

"Temporarily engaged," Emily corrected her. And yes, the thought about Matt's timing had occurred. Like Gina, she didn't know what to make of Matt's attention.

Emily noticed that Nico was now on his feet and she leaned back, putting a polite look on her face. She subtly gestured to Gina to end their conversation.

Gina frowned at her. "For God's sake, Em, get yourself out of this mess."

"I'm trying," Emily retorted, her voice low enough for only Gina to hear. As Nico approached, Gina stood up, draped her bag over her shoulder and sent Nico the fakest of fake smiles.

"My date has just arrived. And he's quite cute…"

Gina walked away before she had to interact with Nico. When Nico reached the table and sat down, he picked up the leather folder the waiter left earlier with the bill tucked inside and handed it to Emily. "Your turn to pay, my dear."

Emily opened her mouth to argue but caught Nico's narrow-eyed gaze. He was waiting for her to disagree, hoping she'd argue. Emily pulled a smile on her face and quickly nodded.

"Sure."

She opened the folder and winced when she saw that the bill for his potential client had been added to their bill. She picked it up and handed it to Nico. "They've charged us for their meals and drinks."

"I'm going to meet them in Chicago next week when I attend the weeklong investment conference. To say thank you, I offered to pay for their meal," Nico replied.

But why did she have to pay for it? On what planet was that fair?

"Is there a problem, Emily?" Nico asked, his voice silky smooth.

Emily opened her mouth to reply but held back the words. If she started, they'd be here all night.

Midmorning on Monday, Emily looked up at the sound of a light rap on her door and saw Matt standing in her open doorway, his shoulder against the frame, dressed in fawn-colored chinos, a sky blue shirt and a nut-brown jacket.

She loved his style; he always looked good and never

gave the impression he'd spent hours in front of a mirror planning his outfit.

Emily gave herself a moment to enjoy the view of a tall, masculine, hot guy standing in her doorway. But she knew she was playing with fire; if Nico found out that Matt was making unscheduled appearances at her office, he'd lose it.

It made her throat sting and her stomach cramp but she needed to keep Nico, for the time being at least, happy.

Fear, and the fact that Matt caused her skin to tingle and her heart rate to climb, made Emily's voice sharper and harder than she intended. "Why are you here? And I thought I employed a PA to guard my door."

Matt straightened, stepped into her office and closed the door behind him. After walking over to her desk, he placed his hands on the surface and leaned toward her, his expression intense.

"Are you okay?"

No, she was exhausted and stressed and anxiety was eating a hole in her stomach. No one but him had noticed and Emily lifted her hands in a gesture of confusion. Why did he keep seeing what she most wanted to keep hidden?

"What's wrong, imp?"

Emily desperately wished he was someone she could confide in but she couldn't afford to. She was on her own here. "Nothing is wrong—I'm just busy and you're interrupting my morning."

"Liar," Matt whipped back. "The shadows are deeper under your eyes and your fingers are trembling."

Emily looked down at her hands and yep, he was right, her fingers were bouncing up and down. And she hadn't slept or eaten much in the last thirty-six hours.

Dealing with Nico was like fighting a particularly nasty virus.

How wonderful it would be just to hand this over to Matt or even to talk through her options with him but she couldn't. Nico was too volatile and she didn't know Matt well enough to trust that he'd keep her secret. She'd trusted people before—her Mom to stay, her dad to connect with her—and they'd all, in one way or another, let her down.

The stakes were too high for her to take a gamble on Matt Velez.

No, she was on her own.

Emily gestured to the monitor on her desk. "I'm busy, Matt. What do you want?"

Matt straightened before moving around to sit on her side of the desk. He stretched out his long legs, folded his arms across his chest and his biceps strained the seams of the expensive fabric.

So hot… *Concentrate, Emily.*

Matt raked a frustrated hand through his hair and sighed. "For someone who looks like butter wouldn't melt in her mouth, you are more stubborn than a pack of mules. As for why I'm here…do you remember I gave Davy my cell number on Saturday?"

"Yeah?"

"He called me about forty minutes ago…and he's fine, Em."

Words to cool her blood. Emily shot to her feet, terror galloping through her system. "What happened? Where is he? Is he hurt?"

Matt placed both his hands on her shoulders and gently pushed her back into her chair. "He's fine. He was well enough to call me, remember?"

"What. Happened?"

"He got into a fight."

Emily shot to her feet again. "What the actual hell?"

A small smile touched Matt's face. "When I say fight, it was more of a scuffle, with minor injuries. Davy has a split lip. The other guy has a bloody nose. I think he was quite proud of his injuries and that's why he called me."

What was happening in her life? Her brother didn't get into fights, she wasn't sexually frustrated, normality didn't include being blackmailed into marriage and her brother didn't call virtual strangers when he got into trouble, he called her!

"Breathe, Em," Matt told her, pulling her to stand between his spread legs, his hands resting lightly on her waist.

Emily pulled in some air, held it for a couple of beats and pushed it out. She repeated the action a few times before her head stopped whirling. When she felt a little calmer, she placed her hands on Matt's biceps and looked up into his surprisingly gentle eyes. He grounded her, she realized. Just being next to him made her feel calmer and stronger and more resilient. He filled her up...

Pity she couldn't explore these new and strange feelings and the attraction bubbling and boiling between them.

Matt placed his hand on her cheek and swiped his thumb across her cheekbone. "Better?"

Emily nodded. "Davy got into a fight?" She couldn't believe it.

Matt nodded. "According to a staff member, some new guy was teasing another guy, Davy told him to knock it off, he wouldn't. Davy pushed him, new guy punched Davy, Davy smacked him back and the staff intervened."

Holy crap.

"He didn't want you fussing and it wasn't that big a deal. It was just a little scuffle." Matt moved his hand down her cheek to her neck and her shoulders, his strong fingers digging into the tight muscles of her shoulders. "Honey, you're so tense. You've got to learn to relax..."

"Relax? Are you kidding me? I have an absent mother, a father who is addicted to his work, a brother who is getting into fights and a fiancé who is bla—"

Emily snapped her jaw closed, horrified that she'd nearly let her secret slip. Oh God, she was so tired and so stressed and she didn't know if she could take much more. It was all too much.

Emily tried to swallow down her tears but they welled and she softly cursed when a couple rolled down her cheeks. Dammit, if she didn't manage to get herself under control, she might just throw herself on Matt's chest and weep for days.

Emily waved her hands in front of her face to dry her wet eyes. "Sorry. I'm a mess."

Matt captured a tear on his thumb. "You are."

Emily snorted. "Thanks." Leaning past him, she grabbed a tissue from the box on her desk and dabbed her eyes, hoping her mascara lived up to its claim of being waterproof. Looking like a raccoon would just be a step too far.

Emily pulled in a deep breath, then another. "Okay, better."

Stepping out from between Matt's legs, she picked up her bag and placed it on the table. Talking to herself, she pulled out her sunglasses, her car keys and tapped her keyboard to shut down her computer. "Gina can cancel my appointments for the rest of the day and I'll spend the afternoon with Davy at Brook Village."

Matt plucked her car keys out of her hand. "I'll drive you. Davy asked me to swing by so we'll go together."

It wasn't a good idea and Nico might find out. Emily

shook her head and held out her hand for her keys. She had to do this alone…

Matt kept her keys in his hand. "What's the problem, Em?"

Humiliation washed over her. "Nico…" She couldn't say more, couldn't explain. She wanted to be with Matt but she was terrified Nico would find out. She was acting like a woman having an affair and she didn't like it but what choice did she have?

"Morris left for Chicago this morning so, unless he has a GPS tracker on your phone or car, he won't be able to track your movements," Matt briskly told her. Before she could ask how he knew what Nico's movements were, he took her hand and interlinked their fingers.

"Let's go, imp, daylight's wasting."

Matt knew Morris was in Chicago because he followed him on Instagram under a fake name and the D-bag had posted a selfie of himself checking into the hotel where the conference was being held. Like Nico, Matt registered to attend, booked his room and his flight and canceled none of his arrangements.

He needed Nico to think that he was in Chicago, somewhere amongst the two thousand delegates. It gave him a little room to move, some time to persuade Emily to trust him.

Years ago he'd said she was a guppy amongst sharks, but this time around she was swimming with a great white and Matt was terrified she was going to be eaten alive.

Matt looked at Emily sitting in the passenger seat of his low-to-the-ground Roadster. He'd bundled her into his car, telling her that he'd drive and, to his surprise, she hadn't put up much of an argument, telling him exactly how stressed she was. Matt looked at her profile again, thinking that she looked younger than her years today and utterly exhausted. She needed a break and he intended to give her one.

It took another ten minutes for Emily to realize that they weren't on the right road to Brook Village. "Why are we heading toward the freeway?" she demanded. "We're supposed to be going to Brook Village."

"Not happening," Matt replied, sending her a lazy smile.

"I am going to see my brother," Emily stated, sounding pissed. "Turn this car around."

Matt patted her thigh and felt her stiffen. She didn't like being ordered about and he liked that she wasn't a pushover. He couldn't abide women who didn't push back.

And that was why he knew that something was very wrong with her engagement to Morris; he was the ultimate control freak and possessive as hell. Emily didn't like being told what to do and control was Nico's favorite thing so there had to be another reason why they were together...

Their engagement wasn't about affection or love. And, judging by the way she'd kissed him, it wasn't about passion either. Something else was making her act out of character. And he desperately wanted to know what that was but, until she opened up, he couldn't help her.

And that pissed him off.

Jealously and envy might've been his initial motivation when he'd first found out about her engagement; he couldn't tolerate the thought of Morris having someone he so desperately wanted. Matt felt a wave of shame; he wasn't proud he'd let his ego override his mind.

But, lately, he'd come to sense, to know, that something was very wrong with this scenario and he was becoming increasingly worried about Emily. He felt protective and concerned and, along with craving her constantly, was desperate for her to confide in him.

But the more he pushed, the further she retreated.

"Your brother doesn't need you rushing to check on his injuries. He's embarrassed and remorseful—he needs time to work through what he did and the implications of his actions by himself, for himself," Matt gently suggested. "Give the guy some space, Em."

"You don't understand, Matt, he's—"

"He's a *guy*, and he still has his pride. Give him some space, a little time. Later this evening, give him a call but don't harp on what happened. The staff has it in hand."

Matt knew that Emily wanted to disagree with him and that she was trying to find something to say to counter his argument. When she released a sharp huff, he knew that he'd won this round.

"So, if we're not going to Brook Village then you might as well take me back to the office."

Ding, ding, ding, there went the bell to commence round two. "Nope. You need a break and you've already canceled your appointments for the day, as have I, and we're going to play hooky. When last did you do something unexpected?"

He'd bet today's profits, and they'd been substantial, that Emily didn't take time off from her responsibilities, which were heavier than he'd imagined.

She needed some time away, a few hours of down time, and he was going to make sure she relaxed. Of course, he knew of one or two other activities that would take her mind off her problems but the chances of getting her naked were minuscule.

Less than that...

Sadly.

"Matt…"

"Em," Matt replied, humor in his voice. Approaching a traffic light, he braked as the light changed and when he brought the Roadster to a stop, he turned to look into her obstinate, adorable face.

"Imp, just let go, okay? Davy is fine—he doesn't need or want you around today. On our way back in, I'll check on him." When Emily started to speak, Matt shook his head. "It's a beautiful day so I thought we'd drive to Montauk. You can walk barefoot in the sand, listen to the waves—I won't even talk if you don't want me to."

Emily raised a skeptical eyebrow and Matt grinned.

"I'll try not to talk," Matt amended. He lifted his hand and squeezed her shoulder, her muscles tight beneath his fingertips. "You need a day to unwind, to de-stress. The world won't stop if you take some downtime."

"It might," Emily stated, sounding grumpy.

"I promise it won't." Matt noticed the light changing and accelerated away. "We're about to hit the highway—do you want to go back or should I keep driving?"

If she said she wanted to return to work he'd take her, of course he would. Unlike her fiancé, he didn't back women into corners, bully or coerce them into a course of action.

He was an alpha male, bossy as hell, but not, he hoped, a jerk.

"Drive on, Velez. I don't have the energy to argue with you."

Matt grinned, smart enough to take her grumpy statement for the capitulation it was.

# Six

Matt, returning from the bathroom at the beachfront restaurant, looked across the near empty eatery on the outskirts of Montauk to see Emily sitting at their small table outside, her chin in the palm of her hand and her eyes on a ship sitting on the horizon.

Longing whispered through him and his normally unflappable heart bounced off his ribcage. He was gut-wrenchingly, toe-curlingly attracted to Emily, on a deep and fundamental level. Sure, she was beautiful; it was hard to miss that but, strangely, her looks weren't that big a deal anymore. His attraction to her went deeper than the surface and, while her beauty still gut punched him occasionally, it was the little things about her that now intrigued him.

The three freckles in perfect alignment on the side of her neck; her preposterously long and dark eyelashes; her elegant fingers he longed to feel sliding over his skin.

He'd also started to look past her outer layer into what made Emily and he liked what he saw. She was a little sassy, smart and, occasionally, funny.

And yeah, his attraction to Emily no longer had anything to do with wanting what he thought Nico had.

No, his need and desire for Emily was a living, breathing entity.

It simply *was*. Hot, demanding, hard to ignore.

Matt resumed his walk and stepped onto the deck. When he reached their table, he placed his hand on the back of her head and dropped his lips to hers, unable to resist taking a quick taste, to hear that sharp intake of breath, to feel her lips soften under his.

What was supposed to be a brief peck turned deeper and darker. Em's arm came up to curl around his neck and she grabbed the fabric of his shirt with her other hand, twisting it in her fist as her mouth opened to his.

He couldn't resist; he didn't *want* to resist. Matt held her face in both his hands as his tongue swept into her mouth. She tasted liked strawberry-flavored lip gloss, the lemonade she was drinking, of heaven and hell. Heaven because he could stand here, at this odd angle for the rest of his life just kissing her. And hell because he knew that at any moment she'd return to her senses and push him away.

He felt her stiffen, her tongue retreating from his… three, two, one…

Yep, and she was gone.

Matt dropped a kiss on the top of her head before taking the seat opposite her, waiting for her to look at him. When she did, Emily showed him the back of her left hand and the god-awful diamond she sported on her ring finger. "Engaged, remember?"

"You don't kiss like you are," Matt retorted, frustrated.

Emily twisted her head to look inside the restaurant, to see if anyone was watching them. He caught the panic and fear in her eyes and that just pissed him off. "The only other customers are three old guys at the bar who are playing cards. Relax, for God's sake," he told her, his tone terse.

Emily faced forward again and gripped the sides of her head with both hands. "You're not helping, Matteo."

Matt tipped his face to the sun and looked at the blue sky above. He could argue with her, tell her that he knew she didn't love Morris and demand to know why she was engaged. Honestly, if he could shake the truth out of her, he would.

But it wasn't curiosity driving him, or his innate need to be the best; he just wanted to help Emily because he was damn sure she needed it.

For the first time ever, Matt wanted to take on some-one else's fight. But he couldn't, not until she opened up and let him in. Matt was coming to understand that Em was scared but she was also stubborn. He wouldn't get anywhere by pushing her.

A waitress approached them, told them about the catch of the day and reassured them that the restaurant was fa-mous for their seafood and that, over weekends, tables were hard to come by. When the waitress walked away with their orders, Matt leaned back and linked his hands over his flat stomach.

"Tell me about Arnott's."

Emily pushed a long, pale strand of hair out of her eyes but the wind just blew it back. Emily dug into her bag, pulled out a band and quickly and efficiently pulled her hair off her face and into a rough knot at the back of her head. Gorgeous.

"That's a broad question—what would you like to know?"

"Tell me how you got into looking after managing your clients with special needs," Matt clarified his question.

"Ah." Emily half turned in her chair and crossed her legs, her shoe dangling off the top of her foot. "Well, Davy is four years older than me and when he turned eighteen, he moved into Brook Village. Dad's small financial services company was doing quite well back then because, as you gathered, the residential village is not cheap."

He'd looked up their fees online, *not cheap* was an understatement.

"Davy loved it but, six months after he started living there, Dad lost most of his money when Black Crescent crashed. I was fourteen at the time."

So many people had been impacted by Vernon Lowell's actions but Matt hadn't realized the Arnotts were one of the families that had been affected. "Your dad is an investor himself—why did he put his money into Black Crescent?"

Emily stared out to sea, obviously debating how much to say. "Vernon Lowell and my dad were good friends back in the day. My dad knows the mechanics of buying and selling but he has no instinct for trading. He only ever buys safe, solid stocks, small gains over the long term. He admired Vernon's verve and willingness to take a risk and he invested a little money with him and it earned a huge return. Then he invested more and more until all his savings were tied up in Black Crescent. Then Lowell disappeared and so did all his investors' cash."

It was a story Matt had heard so many times before.

Emily's eyes fogged over with pain. "My mom left

shortly after Black Crescent crashed and my dad sank into a deep depression. Eventually, he pulled himself out of the fog and started to run the business again but Davy and I lost him to his work."

"And you felt abandoned. For the second time."

Emily nodded. "You're very astute and yes, I did. I've never felt so alone as I did for those six months. It wasn't a great time."

Matt knew what it felt like to feel alone. He'd lived that way most of his life. "I understand that more than you know. And your mom? Do you have any contact with her?" Matt asked.

"I went to see her after she left. I caught a bus, traveled for six hours. I got to her new place, rang the doorbell and she bundled me into her car and drove me straight back to the bus station. She told me that it was my job to look after my dad and Davy, that she'd done it for long enough and she deserved a normal family."

"Jesus."

"It really confirmed what I always suspected, that she didn't love me or want us. Then again, I did have a hint of what she was going to do when I was eight," Emily said, her voice flat and emotionless. "I knew she was going to leave me…leave us. God, I don't know why I'm telling you this—I don't generally rake up the past."

Matt ignored that comment, curious as to why so young a child would suspect her mother was going to leave. "How did you know that?"

Emily answered his gentle question. "We were in a shop and I needed shoes, or a jacket, something for school," Emily told him, drawing patterns on the wooden table with her thumbnail. "I wanted to look at a toy, or something, told her that I'd be right back, asked her if she'd wait for me and kept asking for reassurance that she'd be where I left her."

"And she wasn't."

Emily's eyes deepened with pain. "They found me somewhere in the store, crying. I remember looking for her but not finding her. They took me home and she was there and she told the authorities that she was on her way to the police to report me missing. I knew that to be a lie."

"Did you tell your dad?"

"She told me not to, that my dad would be mad at me and wouldn't love me anymore if I tattled on her."

Matt's mouth dropped open. "*What?* God, Em."

"I know it happened a long time ago but, to this day, I'll still do anything not to upset him." Emily tried to smile. "I sense that you didn't have a great relationship with your dad," Emily said, turning the spotlight on him.

"With either of my parents," Matt quietly answered her, wondering why he was discussing his past with Emily when he never discussed his family with anyone. Ever. But she'd opened up so he should reciprocate, just a little. His estranged relationship with his parents and brother was an open secret and, while she was the first person he'd discuss his past with, it didn't mean anything more than friendship. And telling her wouldn't hurt…

"They were all about Juan—"

"Your brilliant older brother." Emily placed her chin in the palm of her hand, her eyes steady on his face. "Is he why you became Falling Brook's greatest rebel?"

"Everything in our house revolved around Juan. I spent a lot of my childhood and teens looking for attention, the good, bad and ugly," Matt admitted. "I finally grew out of acting like an ass when I went to college."

"Do you have a relationship with them now?" Emily asked, her voice soft.

Matt shook his head. "We speak every six months, exchange awkward calls at Christmas and on birthdays. Do you talk to your mom?"

"No, she threw herself into being the mother to the daughters of the man she left my father for." Emily's mouth flattened in pain. "I never understood how she could just walk away and replace me. But she did."

Matt knew that if he offered any comfort, the spell between them would be broken and Em would clam up. So instead of offering empty platitudes, he just kept his eyes on her, his expression empathetic but holding no pity. He loathed pity and suspected that Emily did too.

A strand of that blond-white hair blew across her eyes, defied the knot and Emily tucked it behind her ear. She looked away and when she spoke again, Matt knew that the door to her soul was firmly latched. "So, I wonder if the rumors about Joshua Lowell's love child are true?"

It was a hell of a change of subject. "We overheard him telling his brother that he didn't have a daughter, remember?" Matt replied "And let's not forget that Falling Brook is a small town and rumors frequently don't have any basis in fact."

"But, hypothetically, what would happen if there is a secret love child? Will she inherit Joshua's wealth?"

"Or she could be an imposter trying to con the family out of their money," Matt suggested.

"Cynical," Emily commented.

"Very," Matt agreed. "Just like I'm cynical about your engagement to Morris."

Emily tipped her head back and released a huff of annoyance. "I was, almost, having a nice time." Emily placed her forearms on the table and lifted those big, bold eyes to meet his. They were eyes he could look into for eternity and he'd never be bored with the ever-changing shades of blue. "Can we please, please, talk about something else?"

Matt looked down at the ring on her finger and felt nausea swirl in his stomach. He so desperately wanted to rip it off her hand and toss it into the ocean.

Matt took a long sip of his beer before reluctantly nodding. "Okay. Let's not talk about jerk-face."

Wanting to go back to the easy conversation they'd been enjoying before he raised the subject of Morris— idiot!—he'd seized on the first topic to jump into his head. "We were talking about Black Crescent... I've had some discussions with Joshua Lowell about me filling the CEO position."

Surprise jumped into her eyes. "But why? I thought you were happy at MJR. And isn't MJR bigger than Black Crescent? Wouldn't that be a step down for you?"

Matt didn't hesitate to tell her his thinking behind his decision to apply for the position. "I've hit a ceiling with MJR—I've been CEO for five years and I think the shareholders have become a bit complacent about my abilities."

Emily lifted her eyebrows. "I'm trying to decide whether you're being a boastful jerk or just ridiculously honest."

"Ridiculously honest," Matt told her, his tone sincere. "I'm very competitive and I don't like to lose."

"Is that why you are here with me?" Emily asked, and her question punched him in the gut. Until recently, he would've had to answer in the affirmative, reluctantly admitting that part of his wanting to be with her had to do with his competitive nature and his dislike for Morris.

But that had faded and Matt knew that he wanted to be with Emily, any way he could. And if all that meant was talking to her in a near-empty restaurant, he'd take it.

"I'm here because there is nowhere, right now, I'd rather be."

Emily looked doubtful and he didn't blame her; he sounded cheesy but, sometimes, the truth was cheesy. Sad but true.

Needing to get into safer water, Matt reverted back to the topic of the career. "I'm damn good at my job and I am very, very good at reading the markets. I make sure my staff keeps making MJR and our clients a lot of money. I've proved my value to the company and I'm due for a significant raise but the board is hemming and hawing."

"And you are hoping that Black Crescent will make you an offer you can take to the MJR board to force their hand."

That had been the initial plan. "But I also like the idea of taking a smaller fund and growing it as I did for MJR. So, if Black Crescent's offer is good, I might move."

"That's not very loyal of you."

"That's unfair, Emily."

Emily frowned at his quick response. "Why? You've just told me you're happy to jump ship."

"That's business, and it's expected. But in personal relationships, and once I've decided someone is worthy of my loyalty, I'm as loyal as hell."

Matt held her eyes and slowly, softly, he saw her cynicism fade and embarrassment stroll in. "Sorry. You're right, it was an unfair comment."

Matt appreciated her apology. So many people would've moved on from the moment and brushed it off; Emily faced it head-on. "Accepted." He added, "When I make up my mind to stand in someone's corner, Em, nothing short of a bomb will dislodge me."

"And you're wanting to stand in my corner?" Emily asked, sounding dubious.

"You're catching on," Matt replied with an easy grin.

Emily nibbled on the inside of her lip, looking confused. And gorgeous. "I don't understand why because you should be running a million miles away from me. I am engaged, I've kissed you, I've basically cheated on my fiancé. On the surface, I don't seem very nice at all. Yet you are still here...*why*?"

"Apart from the fact that I can't stop imagining you in my bed, your body flushed with pleasure after I've taken you for the third time that night?"

Emily blushed at his honesty but she didn't drop her eyes. Matt, realizing she wouldn't be distracted, took his time answering her question. "I value loyalty and, generally, I would never mess with someone who is engaged."

"But?"

"But you're different—this entire situation is different and I can't stay away from you. I want to but I can't." Matt shrugged. "You're like an itch that just won't go away."

Instead of being offended at being called an itch, Emily, thank God, just laughed. "Smooth, Velez."

Fair comment. He'd been more erudite at fourteen, for God's sake!

"I just feel like you need someone in your corner and I'm big and mean and not afraid to fight. Though it would be easier if I knew what monster we were fighting." He waggled his eyebrows in an over-the-top gesture to spill.

Emily's lips twitched and his heart rolled over in his chest. "Nice try."

"Anyway, it's far too beautiful a day to talk about your fake fiancé."

Instead of arguing, Emily just smiled. Her lack of argument piqued Matt's interest. Maybe he was finally, finally getting through to her.

Emily's tongue swirled around the head of her ice-cream cone and Matt stifled a groan. Thankful for the table hiding his massive erection, he tried to recall the periodic table of elements in his head but couldn't remember much beyond carbon and nitrogen.

And then all the blood in his head drained lower, much lower and he dropped ten IQ points when Emily rolled her sweet potato, maple and walnut ice cream, a specialty item on the restaurant's menu, across her tongue.

"Would you like a taste?" Emily asked, touching the corner of her mouth with the tip of her tongue. "It's delicious."

Matt squirmed in his seat, uncomfortable. "That's not what I'm desperate to taste," Matt said, his voice hoarse. "And, just to be clear, the only way I'm prepared to sample that combination of flavors would be if it is smeared over your very naked, very beautiful body."

Emily almost dropped her ice cream, her eyes widening at his frank comment. "Uh… I don't know what to say to that."

"Say yes—say that you'll let me take you to bed and put me, hopefully, us out of our misery."

Emily didn't respond as ice cream dripped off her fingers to land on the table. She didn't notice and Matt didn't care. Say yes, dammit.

"Matt…" Emily whispered.

Matt placed his forearms on the table and leaned forward, entranced by her beautiful face and her bemused expression. But under the puzzlement was desire, hot and sexy, deep, dark, royal blue flashes of encouragement. She wanted him, and the thought made Matt's chest swell.

"Come home with me, Em. Let's explore whatever is bubbling between us."

Instead of replying, Emily stood up abruptly and dropped her ice-cream cone onto the side plate on the table. She walked over to the railing and then headed for the rickety stairs leading to the beach. Matt sighed. Too much, too strong, Velez, just as always. He had no experience of treading gently; he was more of a bull in a china shop.

Emily, this situation, needed gentle handling and he'd completely blown it. Matt opened his wallet and pulled out more than enough cash to settle their bill and to provide the waitress with a big tip. He picked up Emily's bag and followed her down the stairs, realizing they ended underneath the pier. On the last step, he noticed Emily's shoes and there she was, her back against a pole, watching the waves rolling over her toes and feet.

Matt dropped her bag on top of her shoes and quickly stepped out of his flat-soled boots, whipped off his socks and tucked them into his size thirteens. He rolled up the cuffs to his pants and followed Emily's footsteps to where she stood, then stopped in front of her. The beach, like the restaurant, was deserted and it felt like they were the only two people standing on this vast Atlantic Ocean coastline.

When Emily finally lifted her eyes to look at him, she lifted her hands in the air and he saw traces of ice cream on her fingers. "I'm sticky."

Matt captured her hand and gently sucked her index finger into his mouth, tasting the sweetness of maple syrup and the earthiness of sweet potato on her skin. "That's not too bad, actually."

Emily laughed. "Now you're the one being stubborn. It was delicious, *actually*."

"Then why did you dump it and walk away?" Matt asked, placing his mouth in the center of her palm, not breaking eye contact.

"Because I didn't want to give those old men a heart attack when I did this."

Emily gripped his shirt above his heart and twisted it into her fingers to tug him forward. She stood up on her toes and touched her mouth to his, sweet and responsive and oh-so-hot.

"Make me forget, Matt. Just for a few minutes, make me forget that my life is an out-of-control wildfire," Emily whispered against his mouth.

"I can do that," Matt replied before taking her in a kiss that was as hot as the water swirling around their feet was cold. He wrapped his arms around her and yanked her close, holding the back of her head to keep her mouth on his. He nipped and suckled her lips, teasing her by not allowing his tongue to slide beyond her teeth.

Emily, surprising him, pulled her mouth off his, gripped his face in both hands, and her voice was rough when she spoke. "Seriously, Velez, kiss me like you mean it."

Well, okay then.

Matt placed his hands under her thighs and boosted her up against his body, the vee of her mound dragging over his swollen erection. He settled her there, as close as he could get her and walked her backward, carrying her under the wooden deck of the restaurant and deeper into the shadows. Placing her against another pole, he leaned into her, swirling his tongue around hers, lost in her mouth, in her sweet ice-cream-and-imp taste.

Matt anchored her against the pole as he devoured her mouth, needing more, needing everything. Knowing they were deep in the shadows of both the balcony and the pier, he placed one hand on her breast, his thumb quickly finding her swollen nipple. He ran his lips over her jaw, down her neck, sucking and nipping and relishing her breathy words of encouragement. He pulled Em's shirt from her skirt and traced his hand over her flat stomach. He yanked the material of her shirt up and then his fingers slid into the cup of her bra, pulling it aside so he could see her pretty breast, her pale pink nipple puckered and demanding to be kissed.

Bending his head, he pulled her bud into his mouth and knew that it wouldn't take much to make him blow. He hadn't been this out of control since he was sixteen and in the backseat of his first car.

Emily made him lose control and, frankly, he didn't much care. Kissing her, having her in his arms was all that important. Allowing Emily's legs to drop to the sand, he sucked her nipple onto the roof of his mouth before allowing it to pop out of his mouth, wet and glistening. He blew across its surface and Emily shuddered.

Knowing he should stop but unable to, Matt tensed when Emily's hand rested on his bulging erection, holding him through the fabric of his pants.

He should stop, he really should but she was too tempting, too responsive. He wanted her, no, he craved her. Nothing was more important than kissing and touching Emily right here and right now.

Matt pulled her skirt up her leg, allowing his hand to curl around her thigh, dangerously close to the band of her panties. He could feel her heat and when he looked into her eyes, he saw only desire there.

Then she said the magic words. "Please, Matt, touch me."

He looked around, saw that they were still alone and

still concealed. It was the go-ahead he needed, the encouragement he craved. Without wasting a second, Matt took her in a searing kiss, his fingers sliding beneath the band of her lacy panties into her soft hair and down, down, down into her feminine folds. He groaned at her heat, sighed at her wet warmth on his fingers and he couldn't resist sliding his middle finger into her, his thumb finding her little bead with alacrity. Emily squealed, lifted onto her toes but Matt covered her mouth with his, not wanting to alert the patrons above as to what was happening under their feet. Not that there were any customers on the deck; he'd checked.

Matt took his kiss deeper, felt Emily respond and pushed another finger into her slick channel, knowing she was close. He wanted her to fall apart in his arms, needed this brief connection before they went back to their lives.

"Come for me, imp. But quietly," Matt told her, her lips against his mouth.

"This is madness."

Matt's lips curved into a smile. "But it's fun."

"What about you?" Emily asked, arching against his hand, trying to get closer.

"I'm good." He wasn't but there was nothing she could do about that now. Besides, only Emily and her pleasure were important; nothing else mattered. He tapped the insides of her channel with his finger and felt her body tense, moisture gushing over his fingers. Wanting her to have more, to have everything, he pressed his thumb into her clitoris and she whimpered, tensed, gushed again and gripped his biceps with strong, feminine fingers.

Then her knees buckled and Matt jerked her against him, holding her up with his free hand. He ached for release, needed it more than he needed to breathe but seeing that dazed, befuddled, satisfied-as-hell look on Emily's face made up for him not having his own happy ending.

Sort of.

Matt disengaged himself and rested his forehead against hers, his breath as ragged as hers.

"You are so incredibly beautiful."

A tiny smile touched Emily's lips and Matt watched as uneasiness strolled into her eyes and across her face. Holding her face in his hands, he forced her to look up, to meet his eyes.

"Please don't regret this." Matt saw that she was about to speak and shook his head. "This has nothing to do with…anyone else and everything to do with us."

And that was the hard truth. Right now, no one else was part of this magical moment. They were just two people who were out-of-control addicted to one another.

Emily looked like she was about to disagree but then she surprised him by nodding. She rested the back of her head against the pole and didn't object when he pulled her bra back over her breast and dropped her skirt down her thighs. Satisfied that she was tidy, he pulled her into his arms, wrapped them around her and placed his chin on top of her head.

For the first time in years he felt utterly relaxed, fully at ease. Holding her like this felt right…

And yeah, good. Holding Emily like this was, terrifyingly, something he thought he might be able to do for the rest of his life. But Matt was old enough not to pay any attention to the fuzzy feelings that rolled through one after good sex; they would fade and reality would stroll back in. Because Matt refused to allow himself to dream, need or want.

# Seven

Later that evening, in her bed at home, Emily rolled over and buried her face in her pillow. She hadn't been able to forget, not for one minute, how it felt to have Matt's hand between her legs, his mouth on her nipple, her tongue in his mouth.

How he'd effortlessly brought her to her first orgasm.

Her chest tight, Emily lifted her head, sucked in some air and flipped onto her back, kicking away her bedcovers in frustration. She turned her head to look at Nico's engagement ring sitting on the bedside table, fighting the urge to toss it out the window. She should feel guilty about what happened between her and Matt on the beach but she didn't.

She wasn't in love with Nico and she had no intention of marrying him. Ever. This was a sham engagement and she owed her blackmailing fiancé no loyalty.

But she couldn't allow him to find out that Matt had

touched her, with great skill, on an empty beach earlier in the day. If he did, her entire world, and her dad's and, to an extent, Davy's, would come crashing down around her. She had to tread carefully, be smart, keep her wits about her and the only way to do that was to avoid Matt Velez.

Easier said than done.

Emily still wanted him, here now. In her bed. Leaning over her, sliding into her, setting her on fire again and encouraging her to dance in the flames.

She'd had one or two boyfriends along the way, both of whom didn't last long nor knew their way around a woman's body. She'd slept with men just a handful of times and it had been awkward and bumbling and they'd walked away satisfied while she was left wondering why everyone made such a big deal about sex.

She now knew. God, how she knew. And she suspected that she'd just had a small taste of how satisfying and fulfilling lovemaking could be...

She'd love to explore this bright new world with Matt, have him introduce her to, well, *more* but that was dangerous thinking. She had, technically and in name only, a fiancé and he was threatening to destroy everything she'd worked for unless she gave him what he wanted.

But, even if Nico wasn't a factor, Matt was extremely dangerous to her emotional health. If she allowed herself to, she could love him and love never ended well for her. The people who loved her always left and Matt would not be the exception to the rule.

Emily had no intention of being left behind so she should be concentrating on how to find a way out of that mess and stop thinking about how else Matt Velez could make her scream.

*Be sensible, Emily. Focus on what is important and that is saving Arnott's.*

Knowing that she wouldn't be nodding off anytime soon, not with the whirling, swirling sensations sliding through her body—was this what horny felt like? How uncomfortable!—Emily left her bed, walked into her lounge and sat down behind her computer. She needed to trawl the web; if she didn't find any damaging information on Nico tonight, she would hire a PI in the morning.

Nico was making noises about wanting to marry soon and she was running out of time and choices.

Emily heard her phone chime with a message and looked at the clock on her screen; it was just past midnight. Concerned that it was Davy—she'd taken Matt's advice and given her brother some space—she hurried back into her bedroom and picked up her device, her heart lurching when she saw she had a text message from Matt.

You awake?

I am now, she typed back.

Can't stop thinking about you, what we did.

Emily tapped the front of her phone against her forehead, conscious of her heart wanting to jump out of her chest.

Em? Can I come over?

She couldn't say yes but neither could she say no. She wanted to see him but she knew that she should keep a healthy distance between them. She wanted to kiss and touch him—taking time to explore his stunning body—but she was playing with fire. The blaze she was stoking was becoming a little too big for her to handle and, if she didn't take care, it had the power to incinerate her.

And she wasn't talking about Nico finding out...

No, even if Nico wasn't a factor, Matt was dangerous. *If* this was just physical attraction, it would be easier to ignore but she *liked* Matt, she felt alive when she was in his company. She enjoyed the way he spoke and interacted with Davy, his sharp mind, the unexpected flashes of humor. She wanted to know what had put the shadows in his eyes, what forces had shaped him into being the man he was today.

She liked his broad hands and his slow smile, his dark hair and intense eyes. The way he spoke and, God, she adored the way he made her feel.

She liked him, she always had, and Em knew that if she allowed it too, that like could turn into something deeper. Something hazardous.

Love, as she knew, was dangerous; it was unpredictable and selfish and transactional. And, worst of all, it had no staying power. Love wasn't something she trusted.

So no, she would not allow herself to fall in love with any man. She didn't need affection, she just wanted to be free of Nico and for her family's reputation to remain unblemished.

That wasn't so much to ask, was it?

Fifteen minutes later, Emily heard the brisk rap and, with a wildly beating heart, opened the door to see Matt holding the top frame of it, his face reflecting the frustration she knew he was feeling.

"I'm not sleeping with you," she told him, not bothering with a standard greeting. Was she trying to convince herself or him? Did it matter?

All she knew was that if Matt made love to her, properly, she might slide deeper into like and be halfway to love. Not happening.

"Can I come in?" Matt asked, dropping those sexy arms with their big biceps and raised veins.

Emily nodded and stepped back, gesturing him inside. She didn't put on a light and they looked at each other in the moonlight, a million unsaid thoughts arcing between them.

"I won't sleep with you."

"I heard you, imp," Matt said, sounding weary. He scrubbed his hands over his face. "I just needed to see that you were okay. You were pretty quiet on the trip back to town."

That was because she was still riding a sexual high and an emotional roller coaster. "I'm fine," Em replied. She gestured to the door. "If that's all, then you can go."

"Dammit, stop trying to push me away!" Matt snapped.

"I have to! I can't do this!" Emily shouted, her frustration bubbling over.

"Why? Because you're engaged to that prick? If you love him, there is no way you would've let me do what I did to you!" Matt returned her shout but not for one second did his anger frighten her. Emily knew that Matt would never ever hurt her. Not physically anyway.

"I never said I loved him," Emily quietly replied, dropping to the edge of the nearest chair.

Matt dropped to his haunches in front of her and placed his hands on her knees. "Then why the hell are you marrying him? Explain that to me."

She wished she could. Emily could only put her elbows on her knees and bury her face in her hands.

Matt's hand landed on her head, his touch as soft as a butterfly. "I wish you'd let me help you, sweetheart."

"This is something I need to do on my own, Matteo."

"I suspect that you've been on your own for too long," Matt disagreed. "But I'm not going to argue with you about that now. You're exhausted and you need to sleep."

Em dropped her hands before managing a tired shrug. "I can't sleep. I haven't been able to sleep for more than a few hours recently."

"I bet your sleep problems coincided with His Awfulness putting that ugly rock on your finger," Matt muttered as he stood up. In one smooth movement, he slid an arm around her back and another under her thighs and lifted her against his chest.

"What the hell! Put me down."

Matt's mouth touched her temple. "Relax, imp," Matt ordered as he carried her across the room, down the hallway and into her bedroom. He carefully placed her on the bed and pulled the covers up to her waist. Emily watched, mouth agape, as he shed his clothing, his beautiful body lithe and muscled. God, he was lovely, she thought. Wide shoulders, a perfect amount of hair on his muscled chest, that rippled stomach.

And a very nice package under a tight pair of black boxer briefs.

She watched him swell under her scrutiny and she lifted her hands. "We're not making love and you need to go!"

"We're not making love but I'm staying," Matt calmly replied. He pulled back the covers, slid into bed next to her and hauled her onto his chest. He placed one hand low on her butt and gave her a reassuring pat. "The Asshat is still in Chicago so you can relax."

Matt kissed her temple, much like he did earlier, and held his lips there. "Let me hold you while you sleep, imp."

"I can't do this. I'm better off being alone." But he was so warm and with her cheek on his shoulder, she felt so comfortable and safe. In his embrace, Emily felt like nothing could hurt her and that, one day, everything would be okay.

"No, you only think you are better off," Matt replied, his voice a deep rumble. "But let's argue about that later—for now, just let me hold you while you sleep."

Emily didn't have the energy to argue; she felt her eyes closing and she snuggled closer, her thigh coming up to rest on Matt's, her knee brushing the underside of his briefs. This was so lovely, but she couldn't get used to it. This was only one night but it would be a memory she'd hold on to for the rest of her life.

"Em?"

"Mmm?" She was so close to fading away, in that delicious state on the edge of unconsciousness.

"Promise me that you'll come to me if you start considering doing something dangerous, illegal, stupid or consequential. If you ever get scared and don't know who else to turn to, turn to me."

"Mmm, promise."

And then there was just warmth and safety and the blessed relief of sleep.

Work the next day was a disaster and Matt, knowing when to quit, leaned back in his chair and glared at the complicated and detailed spreadsheet on his screen.

He'd made a mistake on a formula and couldn't figure out where he went wrong.

He knew that frustration was part of the deal when you ran a massive company but making mistakes because he couldn't concentrate was unacceptable. Not being able to concentrate because his brain kept returning to yesterday and time spent with Emily frustrated the hell out of him. He never allowed a woman to distract him…

It wasn't who he was or what he did.

Crap.

Maybe he was tired. Or horny. Or both. He hadn't slept much last night and he wanted, no, he needed sex.

Desperately. Immediately.

Matt ran a hand through his hair, knowing that he could take care of the immediate problem himself but it simply wasn't the same. He didn't want to do it solo, hell, neither did he want to find a willing partner for a little fun.

No, because life was screwing with him, he only wanted Emily.

She was the satisfaction he needed.

He was ass deep in trouble.

Matt linked his fingers behind his neck and looked across the room when his door opened. Vee, wearing a dress the color of cold custard marched into the room and stopped on the other side of his desk, hands on her hips.

"What have I done now?" Matt asked, instantly wary.

"Joshua Lowell has been trying to reach you on your cell but he says it keeps going to voice mail." Vee reached across his desk and picked up his phone, frowning at the blank screen. "Is it turned off or is the battery dead?"

"Battery." He'd taken the phone with him to Em's and it died sometime during the night. He'd left her place shortly before dawn to make the trip into the city and charging his phone had been way down on his list of priorities. "Did Joshua leave a message?"

Annoyance flashed in Vee's eyes. "He wants to see you, if it suits you, at Black Crescent at four p.m."

Matt picked up his pen and tapped the end on his desk. "Did he say why?"

"A follow-up meeting to the one you had," Vee replied. "He was being coy but, reading between the lines,

I presume he has more questions." Vee shook her head. "I'm not sure if working at Black Crescent is going to suit me, Matteo."

Matt sucked down his laughter. "I'll bear that in mind."

Vee nodded before narrowing her eyes at him. "You're very distracted at the moment. It's unlike you."

She had no idea. He was crazy in lust with an angelic blonde who was anything but angelic and was as stubborn as hell. A woman who made him act in ways he never had before. He didn't do sleepovers—they tended to give his sexual partners ideas he didn't need them to entertain—but last night he'd held a woman in his arms without the payoff of sex. And, worst of all, he'd liked it.

He liked her smell, the way she fit in his arms, her soft snuffle-snore, the way strands of her white-blond hair caught in his stubble.

Man, he was fast losing it. And he had to get it together, sooner rather than later.

Yes, he liked Emily and yes, he was fiercely attracted to her. No, he wasn't falling in love with her. He just wanted to help her because something was hinky with her engagement to Falling Brook's resident ass.

Every day his feelings for Emily became a little more intense and a great deal more complicated. Initially, he'd pursued her because of their hectic attraction and because of his competitive nature. Morris, his old rival, had someone he'd always wanted and he'd been envious and pissed that he'd succeeded where Matt'd failed.

But, recently—and finally—pride and ego had taken a backseat. Something was bubbling between him and Emily and he had to get a handle on it before it spilled over and scalded them both. If he wasn't careful, he'd resurrect those old dreams and wants—her in his bed, the mother of his children, his forever lover—and that was unacceptable.

Whatever they had would end at some point so maybe he should just listen to Emily and allow her the space to work through whatever was happening between her and Sir Scumbag.

So maybe he should give her a little time, trust her to handle Nico in her own way.

Emily had promised him that she'd come to him if she found herself in more trouble than she could handle and he could live with that.

For now.

After receiving another message from Joshua asking him to delay their meeting until after five thirty, Matt arrived at Black Crescent and stood in the waiting area outside Joshua's office. Before leaving for the day, Joshua's assistant Haley told him that Joshua was just finishing a call and would be with him in a few minutes.

Matt, not in a hurry and not having anywhere to go— and ignoring the fact that he desperately wanted to see Emily's lovely face—leaned his shoulder into the glass pane and stared down onto the wooded area behind Black Crescent's building. Emily's house was a few miles down this same road and her bedroom window had the same view of the same woods, deep and dark and mysterious.

Emily...man, he had to stop thinking about her.

Matt heard footsteps behind him and turned his head to see a younger version of Joshua Lowell striding across the room. It had been years since he'd seen Oliver Lowell but Matt recognized him instantly because his resemblance to Joshua was so strong.

Without breaking his stride, Oliver jerked his chin in a silent greeting and walked into Joshua's office without knocking. Matt glared at his disappearing back; he had an appointment with Joshua and he didn't like to be kept waiting. Oliver slammed the office door behind him but the lock didn't latch and the door eased back open.

"Are you meeting with Matt Velez to discuss the CEO position?"

"I am."

Matt debated whether to tell the Lowell brothers that the room had excellent acoustics and he could hear every word they said, or if he should walk across the room and close the door.

"Look, I understand why you are looking outside the family for a CEO," Oliver said. "I don't have the best track record."

No, Matt thought, he didn't. For most of his twenties, Oliver, so he heard, had a fondness for cocaine, but he was, apparently, clean now and had been for many years. But people had long memories and Oliver might not be the best choice to head up a company with an already tarnished reputation.

"Matt's been waiting on me for at least ten minutes, Ol. I need to talk to him," Joshua said, sounding impatient.

"I know but I really need to talk to you. It's important."

Matt heard a strange note in Oliver's voice and frowned. The guy sounded angry but under the anger he heard panic and confusion. He obviously needed to talk to Joshua and Oliver was lucky to have a big brother to turn to. Matt's big brother had never had the time, or the inclination, or been encouraged by their parents, to look after his younger sibling.

When he got scared and worried or panicked, he had to suck it up and deal because his brother always and forever came first.

Matt made a decision, walked over to the door and rapped on the frame. After pushing the door open, he looked across the large office to a frustrated looking Joshua Lowell.

"You guys talk—we can do this another time," Matt said.

Joshua shook his head and waved Matt inside. "No, you were good enough to come down so take a seat, Matt." Joshua pointed a finger at Oliver. "My brother Oliver. Ol, this is Matt Velez."

Oliver stood up to shake hands with Matt and after Joshua invited him to sit down, the older brother turned to Oliver. "Sit, stay, be quiet."

Oliver rolled his eyes. "Once a younger brother, always a younger brother."

Matt smiled at him, liking him. He might have once been the Lowell family screwup, but it seemed like he'd turned his life around. Good for him.

Joshua cleared his throat and Matt turned his attention back to the man he most needed to impress.

He and Joshua ran through most of the same questions he'd been asked before and Matt stifled his impatience; they were rehashing old ground. Matt felt like Joshua was looking for a chink in his armor and Matt, feeling antsy, cut to the chase. "Come on, Joshua, what's this all about? We've covered this ground in our previous meetings. I can do this job and I can do it well. You know it, I know it, so what's the problem?"

"Straight to the point," Oliver murmured. "I like that."

Matt and Joshua, engaged in a silent battle of wills, both ignored him. Joshua eventually broke the silence by picking up a very expensive pen and twisting it through his fingers. "You say all the right things, Matt, and your résumé is as impressive as hell."

Matt didn't react. "But?"

"But a part of me is wondering how serious you are at jumping ship," Joshua stated. "This company needs a hundred and ten percent commitment, that's why I'm stepping down, but you haven't given our discussion all your attention."

Matt internally winced. Okay, Joshua was seriously astute because once or twice, or ten or fifteen times, his thoughts had drifted to Emily, remembering the way she fell apart in his arms on the beach, the curves of her body, what trouble she was in with Morris.

He never allowed himself to be distracted, to focus on anything other than business…

Especially when he was conducting business.

Matt swallowed his heavy sigh. Up until Emily dropped back into his life, his personal life never bled into his business world.

"I apologize if you think I've haven't been attentive," Matt said smoothly, not admitting the truth. "But if it's any reassurance, I have an incredible ability to multitask. I just don't have a lot of patience for waiting around."

Joshua's expression remained unreadable but Matt saw the amusement in his eyes. Thinking he'd leave while he was ahead, Matt stood up and leaned across the table to shake Joshua's hand. "Do what's best for Black Crescent. And no hard feelings if you choose to go for another candidate." He slid a look at Oliver. "You two need to talk so I'll leave you to it."

Oliver stood up, shook Matt's hand and met his gaze straight on. No blinking, no embarrassment. This guy had fought his demons, conquered his drug addiction and it was obvious that he was trying to win at life.

Good for him. That deserved his respect.

# Eight

Nico was back from his conference in Chicago and, on getting his imperious text message telling her to meet him at L'Albri at seven on the dot, Emily felt sharp-bladed knives tap dancing in her stomach.

Emily parked her car, pulled her coat over her cocktail dress and avoided a puddle on her way to the restaurant. Standing outside the brightly lit windows, she peered inside and saw Nico sitting at the bar talking to two men she didn't recognize.

She couldn't keep up the charade; she wanted out…

Tonight, immediately.

But her choices were limited. If she handed Nico his ring back, he'd release those photographs and his false documents and the Arnott name and reputation would be ruined.

Along with the loss of their credibility, the loss of their income would mean forfeiting their house and their savings would be soon wiped out…

So, no, allowing Nico to besmirch the company was not an option.

Her only option was to blackmail Nico back but she'd yet to discover anything about him that was greater or equal to his fake information on Arnott's. She'd yet to find any dirt on her fake fiancé and the PI she'd hired hadn't found anything either. Sure, Nico wasn't a model citizen: he'd had a few dodgy girlfriends—not unexpected—and a couple of business deals that were sleazy but not illegal. She had nothing she could hold over him.

She didn't have nearly enough to make him go away.

Maybe if she got her hands on his phone or on his computer, she'd find something she could use, but Nico guarded those devices like the Secret Service guarded the president's nuclear codes.

But she had one more option… Maybe she could tell Matt about his blackmailing scheme; maybe he knew something or could think of a way to help her. He and Nico had worked together years ago; maybe he could point her in the right direction. Matt wasn't an angel, he was a hard, tough businessman and he had a reputation for thinking outside the box. And he seemed to like her…

Emily thought back to how right it felt to fall asleep in his arms, to feel his smile on her skin, to look into those intense brown eyes. She enjoyed Matt's company and she liked him more than she should.

And if her life was anything near normal, and if she believed in love, she could easily see herself falling for him. He was smart, successful, sexy. Oh, he was also impatient and demanding and occasionally bossy, but under his alphaness was a guy with a tender heart. He was a protector but could she trust him?

She thought that maybe, just maybe, she could.

But she couldn't afford to be impulsive and she needed

to give the idea of talking to Matt, asking for his help, a little thought. She couldn't take days to come to a decision, she didn't have that much time to waste, but she could take a few hours, a day or two. Emily saw Nico looking at his watch, the frown pulling his brows together, and knew that she needed to go inside, to act like the happy fiancée, to simper and smile and act excited about her upcoming wedding.

Frankly, she'd rather roll around in honey and lie on an anthill.

Emily pushed open the door to the bar, shrugged off her coat and draped it over her arm. Walking into the bar area, she managed to pull a smile on to her face as she strolled up to Nico.

"Welcome back," Emily said as he remained seated on his barstool, leaving her to stand next to him, still holding her coat and bag. "How was your conference?"

"Interesting," Nico replied. He picked up his whiskey and sipped from the rim, giving her a long up-and-down look. Dressed in a plain black, simple but classic cocktail dress, she knew that he couldn't find fault with what she was wearing. She'd pulled her hair back into a sleek ponytail, her makeup was understated and she was sure she didn't have lipstick on her teeth.

She desperately wanted to be with a man who thought she was gorgeous dressed in a baggy T-shirt, leggings and with smudged mascara. She wanted a man who made her feel like she was his world and not a means to padding his bank account...

She wanted Matt.

As what? Her lover? Partner? Husband?

Number one was, maybe, possible but option two and three? Those weren't viable. Matt wasn't the type to settle down and she didn't believe in love anyway. It was too vague, too restless an emotion.

Love was simply too risky.

Pulling her attention off Matt and what could never be, Emily smiled at the men Nico was talking to, introducing herself because Nico hadn't. She engaged in the usual getting-to-know-you chitchat and accepted an offer for a glass of white wine from the gentleman to his left.

Emily, ignoring Nico's brooding gaze, sipped her wine, furious that Nico hadn't offered her a seat, introduced her or ordered her a drink.

If this was any other man she'd be walking out the door...

Emily felt the energy in the room change and she turned around, immediately noticing Matt's tall, broad frame walking toward her, carrying a barstool in one hand. When he reached her, he placed the stool next to her and offered her his hand to help her up onto the seat. When she was seated, Matt took her bag, hung it over the back of her chair and plucked her coat from her hands.

"I'll ask one of the waitresses to hang it up," he told Emily, his words accompanied by a blistering look at Nico's now furious face.

"Hey, stop fussing over my fiancée," Nico complained. His words sounded slurred and Emily's heart sank. Yay, Nico was already drunk. This was going to be a lovely evening. Not.

"I'm just treating her with some basic respect," Matt whipped back. "You should try it sometime."

Emily caught Matt's angry eyes and shook her head, silently begging him not to antagonize Nico. There was too much at stake.

Matt narrowed his eyes at her and when he turned to their companions and introduced himself, Emily frowned. Oh God, he wasn't planning on joining them, was he? She couldn't juggle her half-drunk fiancé and her sexy lover. She wasn't that sophisticated.

"Are you really engaged to Nico?"

Emily jerked her head up at the incredulous question from the man to her right and nodded. She lifted up her left hand and wiggled her fingers, ignoring Matt's blistering scowl. "I am."

"Huh. That's quite a rock."

It was ugly and she hated it. "Thank you." What else could she say?

The other man, standing next to Matt—who'd yet to walk away, damn him!—picked up her hand to examine her ring. "Congratulations, I hope you'll be very happy." Was she imagining the doubt in his voice?

Emily tugged her fingers out of his grip, ignoring Matt's sardonic look. She needed to change the subject, and quickly, but before she could, the man next to her lobbed another question into the awkward silence.

"She's too angelic looking for you, Morris. Are you blackmailing her to marry you?" His blithe question was accompanied by a loud guffaw and a slap on Nico's back.

The words plowed through Emily, with all the force of a .45 Magnum.

*Do not react, do not react, do not...*

She felt the world whirling, then swirling, and then black dots appeared in front of her eyes. Then, from a place far, far away, she felt Matt's hand on her back, his touch light but reassuring. Within a few seconds it was gone, but the sensation of falling left her and she could breathe.

Laugh, say something, brush it off but do it now. Right now.

"You have a very overactive imagination." Emily

made herself look at Nico. Icy fingers walked up her spine as she saw the hot fury in his eyes. "Shall we head into the dining room? I'm absolutely starving."

Emily was being blackmailed.

Matt couldn't believe that he hadn't considered the possibility before this but, while he knew that Nico was a grade-A bastard, he had never considered he'd sink so low.

But Matt had seen her reaction to that casual, jokey question and while he didn't think anyone else had caught the terror in her eyes, her stiff body and her shaky breath, he had. She'd brushed off the suggestion as being ludicrous and everybody bought her wide-eyed explanation.

Except for him.

Because while she hid her distress well, he'd spent enough time with his imp to know when she was acting her ass off. And her performance tonight would've earned a goddamn Oscar.

Matt stood in the shadowed area below the stairs leading to her apartment and prayed Morris wouldn't accompany Emily home. If he did, he might be facing assault charges in the morning because there was no way he'd be able to keep his hands from rearranging that supercilious face.

Matt needed to know what dirt Morris had on Emily. There was no way he was going to allow her to be blackmailed into marriage with that scumbag.

Matt heard the rumble of a car and, thankful for the distraction from his thoughts, slid deeper into the shadows. He relaxed fractionally when he saw it was Emily's car making its way up the driveway and he waited to see who exited the car she parked in her space in the four-car garage.

He exhaled when he saw that she was alone. Matt watched as she approached him, taking in her pale face and haunted eyes. He was about to step into the light but hesitated, knowing that him jumping out of the shadows would scare her. His gut screamed for him to stay hidden and when another car sped up the driveway, he sent a prayer heavenward that he'd parked his car down the road and he stayed where he was.

Emily turned slowly and watched as Morris stopped his car next to her. He was half-plowed at the restaurant and he was driving? What an asshat.

Emily, Matt noticed, didn't move when his passenger window slid down.

"What are you doing here, Nico?" Emily demanded, her voice full of loathing. "We didn't exactly leave the restaurant on good terms."

"I'm happy with the outcome."

"Because you're holding all the cards."

"Yes, I am," Morris replied, his voice cold. "Let me come up—we can open up a glass of wine, forget about tonight's unpleasantness and start fresh."

Emily took a moment to reply but when she did, her words were coated with venom. "Are you kidding me? After the way you acted tonight? I'd rather have a glass of wine with a three-foot slug!"

Matt couldn't see the expression on Morris's face but he could feel the tension crackling between them. If Nico stepped out of the car and forced his way into Em's apartment, he'd rip his face off.

But Nico, luckily, leaned back in his seat and released a low chuckle. "At some point you are going to realize that my way is the only way, Emily."

Emily rubbed her forehead with the tips of her fingers and, in the shadows, Matt could see the fatigue and frustration on her face. For that alone, he could beat Morris to a pulp. "Just go, Nico."

"Since you are being so unreasonable, I think that's a good idea," Morris replied, his voice soft and menacing. "And I hope, by morning, your attitude will be adjusted."

Without replying, Emily turned to walk up her stairs. Matt held his breath but she didn't notice him standing below her, his dark clothes blending into the shadows.

Morris shut off his engine, opened his car door, stood up and, like an animal sensing danger, sniffed the air. Matt felt his heart rate speed up, its beat so loud he was convinced Morris could hear it.

Emily might have the survival instincts of a blind gazelle on the African plains but Morris wasn't a fool.

Matt considered his options: he could walk out now and confront him, and the urge to do exactly that was strong. But, if he remained hidden, he could find another way to attack later…and it would hurt for longer.

But if Nico found him hiding in the shadows, all bets were off. Matt didn't move, didn't breathe for ten, twenty, thirty seconds? It felt like a century.

For the rest of his life, Matt would be grateful that Morris climbed back into his car, started the engine and drove away.

Matt waited for five minutes, then another five just in case Morris decided his first instinct was right. And when his gut stopped screaming at him, he took the stairs to Emily's apartment three at a time. And when he hit the landing, he lifted his hand to tap the door to find it opened to his touch.

When he stepped into the room, Emily's soft voice drifted over to him. "It took you long enough to get your ass up here, Velez."

\* \* \*

She'd known he was there, standing under the stairs. She'd felt his presence as soon as she'd left her car but her inner voice had screamed at her not to acknowledge his nearness, to pretend she hadn't noticed him.

And thank God she'd listened because a few minutes later, Nico, doing his disgusting stalker thing, had roared up the drive to check on her. She'd been terrified he'd leave his vehicle and force his way inside but, thank the Lord and all his angels, he'd decided against following her up the stairs.

If he hadn't, Matt might be facing assault charges around about now.

Emily stared at him standing by her doorway, looking hard and tough and a little bewildered. She fought the urge to switch on a lamp because she knew that would show two silhouettes instead of one, so she left the light off and waited for her eyes to adjust. His black Henley clung to his muscles and hard body like a second skin.

His hair was messy and his eyes glowed with anger and fear and frustration.

"Emily, what the hell is going on?"

Emily wanted to lay all her troubles at his feet, to beg him to help her but she couldn't do that. This was her problem and he wasn't her Sir Galahad. That wasn't a role he had any interest in playing...

She would not throw herself at his feet, let him rescue her. She'd vowed to be self-reliant and she didn't want to renege on that promise to herself.

But damn, she was tempted. The situation between her and Nico was escalating and she had to tread softly, carefully. After tonight, she couldn't take any more chances with Matt; Nico was more dangerous than she thought and she couldn't risk Arnott's over her temporary infatuation for Matt.

She needed to force Matt out of her life, make him leave, make sure that he had no interest in coming back. And she'd do that but first she wanted one night with him. She wanted to have the memories of one explosive, thrilling night to carry her through whatever came next.

She was out of options but she could have one night.

Emily walked over to Matt and, after nudging Fatty aside with her foot—her cat seemed as enamored with Matt as she was—placed her hands on his hips and rested her forehead on his chest. "I know that you have a million questions and I can't answer any of them."

"Let me help you, imp," Matt begged, his lips in her hair. "He's blackmailing you, isn't he?"

Her shoulders sank. "Let's not do this now, okay?"

Emily tugged Matt's Henley up his chest to find his warm, hard-with-muscle skin. "Let's do something else right now."

Matt pulled back to stare down at her, doubt in his eyes. "Are you sure? You've got a lot on your mind..."

"I need this, Matt. I need *you*."

Matt lifted his hands; the pads of his fingers skimmed her lips, her cheekbones, the sweep of her jaw. His gentle touch surprised her; it wasn't something she'd expected and it was exactly what she needed. A little gentleness, some tenderness.

Matt knew what she needed and she sank against him, reveling in the knowledge that a tough man could be so tender.

Matt cradled her head in both hands and his thumbs drifted over her eyebrows, down her temples and across her cheekbones. She didn't want to rush this and while she wanted more, she somehow knew that dragging out their release would make this first night—their only night—so much more special. Emily wanted his mouth, his lips on hers, and finally, after many minutes, far too many minutes, Matt lowered his head and his mouth skimmed hers, once, twice, before his mouth fastened on hers. Emily tried to pull him closer, to force him to give her more but he kept the tempo slow, leisurely feeding her kisses.

Heat rushed through her but, strangely, she felt shivery, like she was running a fever. Em looked into his dark eyes, hot and frothing with desire, and swallowed.

Chemistry was such a tame word to describe what was fizzing between them. Matt drove her crazy, in the best way possible. She'd wanted him years ago but that tame want didn't compare to how much she craved him now. Their attraction was bigger and bolder and brighter and Em thought there was a possibility they'd set the room alight.

It was a chance she was willing to take.

They kissed, slow, long, drugging exchanges of discovery, and Em touched him wherever she could. She slid her hand up and under his shirt, exploring his back, the bumps of his spine, the curve of his ass. Needing to know every inch of him, she brushed her fingers down his sides, allowed her tips to dance across the ridges of his stomach. He was so male, intensely, indescribably, powerfully masculine. Emily traced the long length of his sexy hip muscles and ran her finger under the band of his pants, feeling strong and utterly feminine.

Needing him a little out of control, Emily stroked his erection, from base to tip and was rewarded by a low curse and garbled laugh. She undid the first button to his jeans, then popped open the ones below.

"Not playing fair, Arnott."

Emily looked up at him. "I'm not playing at all, Velez."

After she slipped her hand inside his briefs, pushed down the material and freed him, Matt turned her and placed her hands against the wall. This was what she wanted, something new, something delicious, something out of her comfort zone. Trusting Matt, she allowed him to drag her zip down, spread open the panels of her dress, and she sighed when he placed his open mouth on each bump of her spine. She felt the clasp of her bra opening and watched as her dress and the lace-covered cups dropped to the floor below her feet. His hands traced her ribs, drifted across her stomach and then he cupped her breasts in his hands, groaning as he buried his face in her neck, sucking on that spot where her neck and shoulder met.

"I want you," he muttered. "I've wanted you from the moment I first saw you."

Emily groaned as he teased her nipples, hitting an exquisite point between arousal, need and pain. "I want your lips on me. I need you to kiss me," she murmured, her voice raspy with need.

Matt spun her around and his eyes drilled into hers. "Where?"

Emily felt flattened by the desire she saw in his eyes, desire for her. It was heady, potent and made her feel like she was all woman and all powerful. "Everywhere, Matt."

Matt smiled, then bent his knees and pulled her nipple into his mouth, his tongue swirling over her nub. Emily felt the corresponding rush of heat between her legs and groaned aloud.

"Matt, I—aah, that feels so amazing," she muttered as Matt swapped his attention to her other breast.

"And we haven't even gotten to the good part yet."

Matt, impatient now, quickly kicked away her clothes

and Emily was surprised at her lack of inhibition. But how could she feel shy when Matt was looking at her like she hung the stars and moon, like he was convinced that making love to her was all that was on his mind?

Matt dropped to his knees and rested his forehead on her stomach, his hands digging into her hips. He hooked his thumbs into her lacy panties and pulled down her thong. He stared at her thin strip of hair and she gasped as he ran his finger over its softness "I can't wait to taste you. You're so hot."

Emily widened her legs and her eyes rolled back in her head when he kissed her hip bone, then the inside of her leg, his cheek brushing, ever so gently, over her mound.

Tiny flashes of bright, hot lights danced behind her eyes. "Matteo…"

"My beautiful imp," Matt murmured and finally slipped his finger between her folds and touched her… there, right there. Emily shook as a combination of emotion and sensation rushed through her system, sensitizing every inch of her skin. She could barely think, breathe and then his hot, clever finger slipped inside her, followed by another. His thumb swept over her clit and Emily felt the pressure building.

"I'm so close," she whispered, all her focus on what he was doing to her.

"Not yet," Matt told her, leaning back to look up at her, his fingers still deeply embedded in her.

"I can't wait."

"You can, you must." Matt's voice, rough and sexy, flowed across her skin. Not hesitating, he leaned forward to kiss her, curling his tongue around her sensitive bud. He sucked her, once and then again, and his fingers pumped into her and Emily felt herself falling and flying, both at the same time.

Would he catch her or would he let her fall? It didn't matter; all that mattered was the ride, a unique combination of joy, pleasure, a sexy high. It was everything she'd heard and read about but better. Em didn't want the feeling to end.

She didn't want anything to do with Matt to end...he was the only man she could imagine doing this to her, in this and in a million different ways, until the end of her life. He was what she needed, in a lover and in a man.

When the lights behind her eyelids dimmed and lost their color and the mini-earthquakes deep inside her stopped, Matt pulled his fingers from between her thighs and held her hips, tipping his head to look up at her.

Matt stood up in a graceful fluid movement and held out his hand. "I want you, Em. I want tonight. Come to bed with me?"

Saying no simply wasn't an option.

# Nine

Emily woke up slowly and turned her head to see the soft fingers of dawn sliding through the night sky. She patted the bed and found it empty and, rolling onto her back, she placed her arm over her eyes and released a couple of creative curses. Matt was gone and she was alone.

She'd heard that guys tended to withdraw after sex but she'd hadn't expected Matt to leave without a goodbye or even a thanks for a good time. Emily furiously blinked away hot tears, angry that she was even allowing herself to feel emotional.

What did she expect? That Matt, fully aware that she was engaged to another man, would pull her into his arms and promise her the moon and stars and to purchase her a pet unicorn? No, she and Matt had been building up to this night; they'd been playing with fire since their first kiss and last night they'd stepped into the flames.

They'd stoked the fire, built it up to a bonfire and tossed on some gas. But morning was here and the coals were dying, as all good fires tended to do.

"Morris is blackmailing you. With what?"

Emily shot up at his deep voice and whipped her head around to see Matt sitting in the chair in the corner, fully dressed and his expression serious. Emily sat up and, noticing she was still naked, pulled the covers up and tucked them under her arms. Needing a minute to wrap her head around the notion that Matt was still here, that he'd been watching her sleep, she pushed her hair off her face and looked out the window. The sky was turning from black to gray and he needed to go…

"Matt, you can't be here. I can't afford for anyone to know what we…" she gestured to the bed next to her, "did."

"I'm not going anywhere until we thrash this out." Matt moved from the chair and sat on the side of her bed, hoisting his thigh up onto the mattress. "We've been dancing around the subject for weeks now and last night you pretty well confirmed he was blackmailing you. Let me help you!"

Emily stared at him, so tempted to take the hand he held out and to let him in. Could she trust him? Then she remembered the blistering words Nico tossed at her last night and she shook her head. "I can't. Last night he told me to stay away from you and if I didn't, that there would be consequences, for you. I can't risk your career and reputation."

Matt snorted, not looking the least bit worried. He placed his big hand on her thigh. "I'm a big boy and I can take care of myself."

Emily saw the confidence in his eyes and the self-belief and one of the many knots in her stomach loosened. But he needed to know what he was risking. "He threatened to report you to the Securities and Exchange Commission if I didn't break off all contact with you."

Matt's dark eyebrows inched upward. "He can try but since all the trades I oversee are completely ethical and aboveboard, he can shove his complaint up his ass."

Another knot loosened at Matt's complete dismissal of Nico's threat. "Are you sure? He could make trouble for you."

Matt put his hand on the mattress behind him and leaned back. "I run a well-known and well-respected company, the company Morris left under a bit of a cloud. I'm not in the least afraid of what he'll do or say because there's nothing there."

Emily looked at him and he frowned at the doubt he saw on her face. "You don't believe me?" he asked.

Emily pushed her hand through her messy hair. "Of course I do, it's just that Nico has resources and he's not afraid to put a false spin on a situation."

"Is that what he's done to you?" Matt gently asked her.

Emily asked Matt to pass her dressing gown from the back of the chair next to her bed. After slipping into the gown, she slowly knotted the cord, sat down on the bed and faced him.

"Why is talking to me so hard for you, sweetheart?"

Emily took her time answering him. "A couple of years ago I promised myself that I would never rely on anyone ever again, that I would be independent and utterly self-reliant."

"We'll get back to Morris and his blackmail attempt in a minute, but why would you do that?" Matt asked. "Why is being self-reliant so important to you?"

This was like slowly picking the scab off a festering wound. "Because I got tired of people letting me down, of looking for the good opinion and validation of others. Because relying on people gives them importance in your life and everybody I've ever thought to be important has left me, in one way or another. My mom, my dad…"

Matt tipped his head to the side. "Your dad is, I presume, sleeping in his bed in that big house across the driveway."

Emily pulled a face. "Physically maybe, but he left me emotionally the time my mom did."

"Ah."

Emily stood and walked over to her window, looking out to the still-dark forest. "I guess that's a perfect segue into me telling you about Nico…"

After gathering her thoughts, Emily spoke again. "After my mom left, my dad sank into a deep depression. When he came out of it, he threw himself into building up Arnott's into a boutique wealth-management firm and recovering what he lost in the Black Crescent scandal. Dad became a semi-recluse and workaholic and one of the reasons I took the job at Arnott's was because I thought it was the only way I'd ever see him."

Emily felt Matt's presence behind her but, instead of touching her, he moved in front of her and mirrored her stance, shoulder pressed into the glass window.

"Go on, imp."

Emily ran her tongue over her teeth. "Because of Davy, Dad found a niche market looking after the financial interests of vulnerable, wealthy adults who are incapable of managing their own affairs. A lot of their income is tied up in trusts, sometimes not, and Dad, through Arnott's, is their financial adviser. We also pay the bills and report to the trusts or guardians on a monthly basis. Our reputation for honesty and integrity and playing by the rules is sacrosanct."

"You're dealing with other people's money but, because your clients are designated as vulnerable, it's even more important to be blemish-free," Matt stated, quickly connecting the dots.

Emily nodded, feeling miserable.

"And, correct me if I'm wrong, Nico has something on you that will tarnish that reputation."

Emily nodded again.

"What does he have on you?"

If she told him, there was no going back. It was like she was on the surgeon's table, wide-eyed and awake, about to be sliced open and not knowing if it would hurt or not.

"Em…"

"He has a picture of my dad shaking hands with the head of the Russian mob on the East Coast." Emily rushed her words, as if saying them quickly would make them less horrible.

Matt frowned. "Say again? Your dad is friends with a mobster?"

Emily was gratified to hear the disbelief in his voice. She waved his words away, agitated. "My dad doesn't have friends, not really. But he does visit Davy at Brook Village and he struck up a conversation with another father, Ivan Sokolov, who we know as John. Nico took a photo of them and he's threatened to start a rumor saying that Arnott's is laundering money for the mob and that Dad uses the residential home as cover for his meetings with John."

*"Holy crap."*

Emily jammed her hands into the pockets of her gown. "Being associated with the mob will destroy our reputation, Matt. We can't have our clients harboring even a whiff of suspicion about our integrity."

Matt rubbed his thumb over her cheekbone. "I understand that, but a photograph detailing one meeting? Are
you not giving it too much power, especially since you
say it was just that one time?"

"I can't take that chance," Emily said, placing her hand
on his chest. Just touching him made her feel stronger,
more anchored. And God, yes, she felt like Matt had
lifted a boulder off her chest.

Matt covered her hand with his and squeezed. "And
why haven't you told your dad any of this?"

Emily shrugged and dropped her eyes, then stared at
the floor. She felt Matt lift her chin and she took a long
time meeting his eyes. When she did, she saw sympathy but also a healthy dose of determination. He wasn't
going to let her off the hook.

He was going to make her admit her worst fear, the
one she'd never fully been able to think. Every time the
thought started to form, she pushed it away, not prepared
to deal with it.

"Why not, sweetheart?"

Emily's eyes burned with unshed tears. "I didn't tell
him because—"

She released a tiny sob and shook her head.

Matt pulled her against his chest, his big arms envelop-
ing and protecting her. "Because you couldn't trust him
to stand in the ring with you? Because you couldn't trust
him to put your happiness before the company reputation? Because you were afraid he would insist that you
marry Morris?"

Emily pushed her forehead into his chest and nodded
her head, just once.

"Ah, sweetheart."

Emily felt Matt's lips in her hair and allowed herself
to sag against him, knowing he wouldn't let her go. She

wound her arms around his trim waist, then flattened her palms against his back. "I've been so scared, Matt."

"And for that, I could rip Morris's spine out," Matt told her, his words low but vicious.

Emily pulled back and looked up into his frustrated face. "You can't tell anybody and you can't confront Nico."

"The hell I can't."

Emily stepped away from him, twisting the material of his shirt in her fist. "Matt, no! I told you because, well... anyway, you cannot do or say anything that will cause Nico to act hastily. Because no matter what you do or say, what I do or say, he will release the photograph and he will start a rumor. It doesn't matter whether it's true or not—it's the perception that counts and he'll spin a damn good story and while we try to fight it, our clients will leave. Nobody else knows about this, well, Gina does, but no one else. Promise me you won't be the one to let the cat out of the bag."

Matt stared at her, the muscle ticking in his jaw. Emily grabbed his biceps and tried to shake him but, because he outweighed her, didn't manage to move him an inch. "Matt! Promise me!"

Matt looked away and when his eyes finally reconnected with hers, she saw that his anger had faded and that some measure of thoughtfulness had returned. He exhaled and rubbed his hands over his face. "What are you going to do?" he eventually asked.

Emily released a long, relieved sigh. "Frankly, I need dirt on him. Something I can blackmail him with. It's not a pretty solution but it's the cleanest. I thought that maybe you would have something on him, seeing that you worked together years ago."

Matt shook his head. "He's a prick but I don't know of anything that will persuade him to back off."

Emily's heart sank to her toes. She'd been relying on Matt to give her something, anything, but it seemed she was back at square one.

Matt slid his hand around the back of her neck and rested his forehead against hers.

"Don't look like that." He brushed his lips across hers. "We'll find a way to get you out of this because, one thing is for damn sure, you are not marrying that loser."

His words were music to her ears.

"Now come back to bed," Matt told her, gently pulling the ties to her gown open. "It's a new day and I can't think of a better way to start it than by making love to you."

"Got a minute, Em?"

Emily looked from her computer monitor to the door and waved Gina in. She closed down her untouched spreadsheet and pushed her chair back from her desk, thinking that she really needed to do some work at some point. But since Matt left her bed early yesterday morning, she'd been less than useless, her thoughts jumping between horrified shock that she'd told him she was being blackmailed into marriage and shivery shock at the way he made her body vibrate with pleasure.

He'd kissed her from top to toe, and she'd loved every second being naked with him. The man had superior bedroom skills and yep, he'd had her screaming with pleasure.

And, better than that, some of her skills had Matt groaning and growling her name!

"Whoo boy, I want whatever you are having," Gina said, sitting down in the chair opposite her and crossing her shapely legs.

Emily opened her mouth to tell Gina that she'd slept with Matt but, at the last minute, she hauled the words back, thinking that she wanted to keep him to herself, just for a little while longer. He was like discovering a long-awaited gift in the back of her closet and she didn't want to share the surprise, not just yet.

Besides, if—when—their relationship blew up, because relationships always did, she wouldn't have to give Gina any explanations.

"Your father is asking for the Morales spreadsheet," Gina told her, glancing down at her notepad.

Emily winced. "It's not ready yet."

"Okay. Have you reconciled the Sheppard bank accounts?"

Emily grimaced and shook her head. Gina arched her eyebrows when Emily answered in the negative to her question. "Have you done any work the past two days?"

"Not really, no."

Gina smacked her notepad against the edge of Emily's desk. "Well, I'm not sending your dad that email. You can explain."

Emily nodded meekly, not looking forward to that confrontation. Her dad was a hard taskmaster and being his daughter wouldn't exempt her from a why-are-you-behind-in-your-work dressing-down.

Gina folded her arms and tapped her index fingers against her biceps, a sure sign that she was feeling anxious. Emily instinctively knew that she didn't want to hear what Gina had to say and pushed her spine into the back of her chair. She considered excusing herself to go to the bathroom but knew that when she returned, Gina would be waiting for her.

Hell, if Gina really needed to get her point across, she'd paint the letters in the sky if she had to.

"What is it?" Emily asked.

Gina hesitated, something she never did, and Emily's stomach dropped like a stone. "You know that I've been trying to dig up something on Nico, looking for a way to get you out of your engagement?"

Emily nodded. "Did you find something?"

"Nothing that would help you with Nico but I did hear about what he was like when he was working at MJR Investing. Unfortunately, I also heard a lot about Matt, as well."

Emily gripped her hands together, fighting the urge to get up and walk away. She wanted to hear bad news about Nico but she didn't need to hear anything negative about the man she'd given her body to, the man she might be in love with.

Might be? Nope, she was pretty sure she'd taken that fatalistic step into love already.

"Do you want to know what I heard?" Gina quietly asked her.

No, but she had to. She couldn't, as much as she wanted to, shove her head in the sand. Emily rolled her finger in a silent gesture for Gina to continue. "Nico and Matt worked together, as you know. They both started off as traders on the floor at MJR, both, apparently, quite talented."

"Where did you get this information? And is it credible?" Emily demanded.

"From a trader who worked with both of them. He gave me the name of someone else who also worked at MJR around the same time as Nico did and their stories were remarkably similar. Neither of them had a beef with either Matt or Nico."

So, it wasn't information that could be so easily dismissed. Dammit. "Go on," Emily told Gina.

"Matt and Nico were intense rivals and constantly butted heads. If Matt got a new car, Nico got one better. If Nico took a risk on a trade, Matt took an even greater risk. Everything was a competition, nothing was sacrosanct. They were obsessed with beating each other. And when Matt was promoted to CEO, Nico resigned shortly after."

Emily felt acid burning a hole in her stomach lining. "You didn't mention if they competed over women."

Gina winced. "Yeah, they did, all the time. Not over individual women, nobody mentioned that, but someone did say that if Nico dated a model then Matt would date a supermodel. There were office betting pools around who would bring the sexiest date to office functions."

"Charming," Emily said, feeling ghostly hands squeezing her throat. She stared down at her shaking hands and forced herself to ask the question. "Do you think it's coincidence that Matt came back into my life right at the time I got engaged to Nico?"

Gina grimaced. "I don't know, Em, only he can answer that. I'm just telling you what I heard so that you have all the facts."

Gina stood and picked up her notebook, tapping it against her thigh. "Look, everyone I've spoken to has told me that Matt is super competitive, he wants what he wants and he doesn't let anything get in his way. He's incredibly focused but, as I was told, when he achieves his goal he often loses interest in what he was pursuing."

"So, he's only interested in me because Nico has something he doesn't," Emily quietly stated.

Gina threw up her hands. "I don't know! I don't want to believe that but neither do I want you falling for Matt and having him discard you when he's bored. And I swear, if he does that, I'll freaking break his knees."

Emily watched Gina leave and after the door closed behind her, rested her forehead on her desk, trying to push away the emotions threatening to overwhelm her so that she could think. Taking a couple of deep breaths, she examined the facts. Matt rejected her years ago on the flimsy excuse that she was too young and drunk. He avoided her for years and, when they did cross paths, they didn't, as per normal, exchange more than a terse greeting. Then, out of the blue, and on the very same night he discovered she was engaged to Nico, Matt pushed his way into her life and into her heart.

He'd gotten her to open up about Nico and Emily couldn't understand why. Was it because of his competitive streak and he wanted what Nico had—her?—or was he genuinely concerned about her predicament?

Emily didn't know and she didn't care. All she knew for sure was that Matt would, eventually, bail out, just like everybody else did. When he got whatever he needed from her—edging Nico out, taking what he had, sex, a boost to his ego—he'd leave her swinging in the wind.

Just like her mom did physically and her dad did mentally.

God, she was such an idiot! She had told herself time and time again not to trust him, not to rely on him, not to open up to him, but she'd failed. And failed spectacularly.

She'd fallen in love with the man, something she'd promised herself she'd never do. Because love had no staying power…she *knew* this.

She had to stop seeing Matt, that was obvious. While she still had most of her heart intact, while she could still function, she had to cut the ties between them.

And hopefully in a few months, in a year, she would've forgotten how he smelled, how his eyes could switch from humorous to intense in a second, how solid and wonderful he felt under her lips and hands. In a year's time she would be laughing about this, mocking herself because she thought herself to be in love...

Twelve months, three hundred and sixty-five days.

In the future, she'd want to smack herself for being such a naive idiot but, right now, all she wanted to do was cry.

So she did, hot, acidic tears that did nothing to soothe the ache in her soul.

It was eight by the time she left the office and Emily, not having gotten much sleep last night, was beyond exhausted, and the crying jag she'd succumbed to earlier made her feel dried out and shattered.

Her soul was tired...

From the depths of her bag she heard her phone ringing but didn't bother to dig it out. She had no desire to talk to Nico and if it was Matt, well, she hadn't answered his other five calls or responded to his slew of text messages, and she didn't want to talk to him now.

She just wanted some peace, something she hadn't experienced for the longest while. Emily pulled her key from the side pocket of her bag and walked across the empty parking lot, tempted to book into a hotel for the night; neither Matt nor Nico would find her there.

She just wanted one night to herself, for herself, to gather her strength and marshal her resources. A bottle of wine, a bubble bath, watching a romantic movie on TV with Fatty and no chance of being interrupted...

"Em—"

Emily yelped and whirled around. She slapped her hand on her heart to keep it from springing from her chest and bent over to catch her breath. She felt Matt's hand on her back. "Sorry, sweetheart, I didn't mean to scare you."

"Holy crap, Velez! What the hell?" Emily yelled.

Matt grimaced and lifted his hands. "Sorry, but you really should pay better attention to your surroundings."

He was lecturing her when he snuck up on her? Taking a deep breath, Emily jerked open her car door and threw her bag over the console to the passenger seat.

Whipping around, she closed the door, leaned back against her car and folded her arms, handing Matt a furious scowl. "Why are you here?"

Matt looked puzzled at her virulent retort. "I've been calling you but you didn't answer. Are you okay?"

"What do you think? You scared the hell out of me."

Matt shook his head. "That's not it. Or it's not all of it. What's going on, imp?"

It hurt too much to hear his pet name for her on his lips. "Just go away, Matt. I can't deal with you or anything else tonight."

Matt reached past her to place his hand on her door, effectively preventing her from climbing into the car and driving off. "What is going on?"

When she didn't answer, Matt spoke again. "Do you regret what happened last night?" Matt demanded, his voice raspy.

Emily didn't immediately reply. She was being blackmailed into marriage; she didn't owe her blackmailer fidelity. But she did regret sleeping with the man who thought of her as a prize to be won and then thrown away.

Emily, hardening her heart and her attitude, tossed her head and narrowed her eyes at him. "I'm surprised to see you here. I thought, having achieved your goal last night, you would be long gone."

"What the hell are you talking about?"

"You've had what Nico wants so you can walk away. Why haven't you?"

Frustration tightened Matt's expression. "You're not making any sense."

Okay, then she'd spell it out for him. "You didn't want anything to do with me six years ago and you'd exchanged no more than a handful of words with me since then. But as soon as you heard that your archrival, your biggest competitor is engaged, to me, you're all over me like a rash?"

Emily saw emotion flicker in his eyes and, at that moment, knew that it was true. He was only with her because he wanted to beat Nico. Up until that moment she'd hoped, prayed, that she was wrong, that she was overanalyzing or projecting, but there was no denying the truth in his eyes.

When he stepped toward her, she held up her hands to warn him to keep his distance. "God, Matt."

"Let me explain."

"What's there to explain?" Emily demanded. "Just answer me this. If I break it off with Nico, will you be there for me? Do we have a chance at something more, something permanent?"

Matt rubbed the back of his neck. "You're upset and I don't think this is the right time to discuss this."

"Just answer the question!" Emily yelled.

"I don't know!" Matt yelled back. "All I know is that I don't *want* to want you, I don't want to *want* more."

Emily stared at him, completely confused. "What does that even mean?"

Matt jammed his hands into the pockets of his pants. He scowled at her, his face and eyes hard, his beautiful mouth thin with displeasure. "Can we stop arguing, please?"

Emily nodded. "Sure, if that's what you want."

"Why do I get the feeling that there's a subtext to your agreement that I'm not getting?"

"Because you aren't a stupid man," Emily haughtily informed him. "So let me spell it out for you. I don't need your help. And the only thing I needed from you, you gave me last night. I wondered what making love to you was like and now I know so…thanks."

Matt's eyes narrowed to slits at her flippancy. "Your acting skills need work."

"As do your hearing skills," Emily snapped back. "I need you to go. Just walk out of my life and keep walking. You did it all those years ago so do me a favor and do it again."

Matt shoved his hands into his hair and scowled at her.

"If I go, I'm going to keep walking. I'm done with begging you to let me in and to allow me to help you."

Emily felt her heart contract, thinking that she was at the end of her rope and it was fraying. "Fine. Just go."

"If I go, I'm not coming back," Matt told her, his words as hard as pebbles being dropped into a shallow puddle of clear water. "If I go, we're done. Do you understand that?"

A tear rolled down her cheek and Emily closed her eyes, hoping to keep the rest behind her eyelids. "I understand."

She heard the whoosh of air Matt released; he sounded like a balloon deflating. Emily turned and opened the door to her vehicle, telling herself that she couldn't turn around, wouldn't allow herself to look into his beloved face, into those deep, luscious eyes. If she did, she'd cave.

Emily heard his footsteps taking him away from her and forced herself to stay where she was, to not call him back. Tears slid down her face.

He was walking out of her life—no, she'd shoved him out of her life—but what he didn't know was that he was leaving with her ripped and shredded heart.

* * *

The next day, in his office across town, Matt tried to concentrate on work but it was a disaster from minute one.

He prided himself on being able to multitask, to juggle a hundred balls in the air, on his exceptional memory but today his normally agile brain had shut down, his entire attention on Emily's scared eyes, hunched shoulders, the tears rolling down her cheeks.

Matt pushed his shoulders back and rubbed his eyes with his thumbs. *You can't blame anyone else but yourself for this mess you're in, dude—you did everything she accused you of.*

He'd pushed himself into Em's life because he'd always wanted her and because he hated the idea of Nico having her. It wasn't nice and it wasn't pretty and it most certainly wasn't something he took pride in.

But he'd soon stopped thinking with his pride and ego and started tuning in to her, looking past the beautiful face dominated by those amazing violet-colored eyes. He'd seen her loneliness, her determination to be self-reliant and the hurt she'd pushed down deep. He liked her sharp mind and her sly sense of humor and, God, yes, he adored her body.

She was the one woman he could see himself with for the rest of his life. His first reaction, the one he'd had so long ago with images of her as his bride and the mother of his children, was right. And because he was young and stupid, he'd run as fast and as far as he could from her.

He loved her and the thought of her marrying anyone else but him was the equivalent of a tooth abscess, a knife plunged into his heart, a cancer in his stomach.

But her pride was hurt; she thought he was only with her because of his old rivalry—and it was old and so very dead—with Morris. But, because both he and Morris had been immature, arrogant pricks, their legend lived on and Emily had somehow gotten to hear about their embarrassing interactions.

Man, he'd been such an ass.

*The only thing I needed from you, you gave me last night. I wondered what making love to you was like and now I know so...thanks.*

Matt rubbed his temples with the tips of his fingers, wondering if she really meant what she'd said. Last night, while making love to her, and because he'd had enough sexual encounters to understand the difference between sex with and without love, he'd thought they had an intense connection, a real meeting of minds and bodies and emotions. He needed to wake up with her, go to sleep with her, hear her laugh, make her smile, explore her body and plumb the depths of her agile mind. He yearned for her to be at the center of the family he now so desperately longed for, to be the mother of the children he suddenly craved.

He'd thought they were on the same page but her words last night made him doubt what he thought they had.

And why hadn't he been able to answer her when she demanded to know what he wanted from her? Because the words *marriage* and *babies* and *forever* had never passed his lips before? Because he was scared? Because he was a coward?

All of the above and more.

Matt leaned back in his chair, conscious of the headache behind his eyes. He swiveled around in his seat and stared out his window at the view of the Hudson River. Emily might think that they were over, and they might be, but whatever was going on with Emily was coming to a head; he knew that like he knew his own signature.

And, he didn't care whether she wanted his help or not; he was not stepping out of the ring when she needed him the most.

After Nico was out of her life, she could tell him to go to hell but, until then, he was going to help her, whether she wanted him to or not. And that meant getting to work...

Happy to have something else to focus on besides his hurting heart, Matt turned his focus on how to end Morris.

Killing him sounded good but Matt wasn't keen on a lengthy jail sentence, so he'd have to settle for destroying his reputation. Getting Morris out of Emily's life was all that mattered. After Emily was safe, he'd walk away again because he was damned if he'd stick around where he wasn't wanted. He'd done that when he was young—he hadn't had a choice when it came to his family—but he refused to do that again.

He could patch up his aching heart later; right now he needed to take action to boot Morris out of Em's life. He could, maybe, live without her but he absolutely could not live without knowing she was safe. And, until Morris was away from her, she would never be.

But, dammit, he had no idea how to do that.

Matt looked up as Vee entered his office, holding his favorite mug in her right hand and papers in her left. Matt took his coffee with a grateful smile, sipped and closed his eyes. "Thanks, I needed this."

"You look like hell," Vee commented, placing her papers to the side of his computer.

"I feel like hell," Matt told Vee.

Vee sat down on the edge of the visitor's chair, her normally stern face reflecting her deep concern. "How can I help, Matt?"

"A friend of mine—"

"Emily Arnott—"

Of course Vee knew whom he was referring to; she was crazy intuitive. Or nosy. "—has somehow gotten herself tangled up with Nico Morris."

"The Nico Morris who worked here?" Vee asked, wrinkling her nose.

"Yep. Him."

"I never liked him and he always cut corners. Some of his trades were borderline unethical."

His interest caught, Matt sat up straight. "Really?"

Vee nodded. "At the time of his resignation, I was toying with coming to you about my suspicions, but then he resigned and he wasn't a problem anymore."

Matt grimaced. "I wish you had. I might have something to work with today."

Vee's smile reached her eyes and turned her from plain to pretty. "Well, I did do something that might be considered a little unethical myself…"

Oh, *interesting*. "What did you do?"

"On the day you were promoted to CEO, I worked late. I had a feeling he was going to leave. I was concerned he'd destroy sensitive company information so I did a backup of his desktop."

Matt pulled his keyboard toward him and quickly checked the company server, identified the files that came from Morris's machine and shook his head. "I've checked these files already. There's nothing there."

Vee stood up, walked around his desk and peered at the screen. "That's a backup done by someone from the IT department. That file is a lot smaller than the one I did two nights before he resigned."

Matt's heart started to gallop and the moisture from

his mouth disappeared. "Please, please tell me that you still have that backup."

Vee rolled her eyes. "I file everything. Of course I have it." Vee nudged him aside and Matt rolled his chair back to give Vee access to his keyboard. A minute later she was on the internet and code was rolling across his screen. And then, thirty seconds later, a folder popped up on his home screen, dated five years back.

Vee stood back, gestured to the folder and smiled. "If you find anything worthwhile can I have a raise?"

Matt rolled his chair closer to the desk. "Even if I don't, you can still have a raise," Matt told her, opening the folder and scanning the directory. There was a huge discrepancy in the size between the files he had access to and Vee's backup copy. The obvious place to start was to see what Morris deleted before the techies from IT came in to back up his system.

Matt prayed he would find something he could use.

# Ten

Pack a bag, we're heading to Vegas. You'll also need a wedding dress.

Emily read the text message from Nico again and tasted bile in the back of her throat. God, this was happening, this was *really* happening.

So, was this what all those French aristocrats felt like when they were facing the sharp blade of the guillotine? Terrified and subdued, resigned and a little dead on the inside?

Maybe that was the trick to survive the next however many years of marriage to Nico? Don't feel, don't react, don't think.

Just be…

Emily rested her aching head on her office window, feeling utterly wiped out. If she felt like a shell of the person she usually was right now, then there would be nothing left of herself when, and if, she was finally free of Nico.

She couldn't do it.

Emily turned and put her back to the window, her hands flat against the glass. Yes, she'd be taking a huge gamble with the company, with their clients, but they had the financial records to back up every transaction they'd made; their paper trail was clean. Yes, they'd take a hit reputationwise but it wasn't like they'd be going up against a choirboy or the most well-respected person in Falling Brook. Nico wasn't well liked and she and her dad were; maybe they'd have a fighting chance.

She couldn't marry Nico. And she'd rather do battle in the open than skulk in the shadows.

And maybe, just maybe, Matt would help her. Okay, she accepted that she'd never have a happy-ever-after with him but maybe his competitive streak was strong enough to want to take Nico down, to help her. Maybe, possibly, his offer of help was still on the table.

It wasn't like she had any choices left and she'd definitely run out of time. She had to put her pride aside and accept she couldn't do this on her own; she needed help. Matt's help.

Before she could talk herself out of her decision, Emily lunged for her phone and dialed Matt's number, then cursed when it went straight to voice mail. She didn't bother with a long explanation when a few words would do...

"I know you're mad at me but Nico wants us to leave for Vegas tonight to get hitched. I'm out of my depth and I need your help. Will you help me?"

How long would it take for him to listen to her message? Did she have that much time? Emily bit her lip and placed her hand on her stomach, pushing her other fist into her sternum, trying to ease the burning sensation.

While she waited for Matt to call back, she needed to do what she could to mitigate the disaster looming in her future. And the first step was to confront her father and to make him listen to her. She needed to connect with him, not as employee and boss but as father and daughter.

She needed her *dad*.

Clutching her phone to her chest, Emily walked out of her office and after passing Gina's empty desk, she walked down the hallway to her dad's office. She was going to have to tell him what was going on, inform him of the fight they were about to wade into. She needed to prepare him, to shore up his emotional defenses, to re-assure him they would, with Matt's help, be okay. That the business would survive.

That he, and his reputation, would be fine…

Emily knocked, entered and jerked to a stop when she saw Nico lounging in the visitor's chair across from her father. Her dad's eyes looked haunted. His face was the color of fresh, falling snow.

Oh, shit. He already knew.

Even from across the room, Emily could see his trembling chin and lips and the bulging cords in his too-tense neck.

"Emily…"

His voice sounded thin, as if he couldn't get enough air. "Em, what are we going to do? I can't lose the business. I can't. It's all I have."

Emily wanted to scream at him that he had her and Davy, that they were more important than the business, but the words got lodged in her throat.

Emily felt her heart sink and cursed herself for imagining, just for one second, that he'd have a plan, that he'd step up to the plate and find a solution instead of looking to her for one. That he'd put her first, that he'd risk losing his business to save her.

But that wasn't the way her family worked; she made the sacrifices for everyone else.

"I've shown your father the photograph and the press release I intend to send to the police and the press if you don't agree to marry me, in Vegas, tonight. They are pretty damning." Nico sent her a cold smile. "And don't think that Matt Velez is going to ride in on his white horse and rescue you, Emily—he's only interested in you because I have you."

He had her? Who used words like that anymore? God, she couldn't do this, she couldn't tie herself to a misogynistic narcissist. Not for her dad, not to save their reputation...

Her father cleared his throat and she turned her eyes back to him. "Emily, it's everything I've worked for, all that I have. I won't be able to rebuild the company if our clients leave—the stain on our reputation will be too damaging. I have some savings but I won't be able to keep Davy in Brook Village for more than a few months and even if we both get other jobs, we wouldn't be able to afford the fees. That's even if I manage to find a job because I'm pretty sure I'll slide back into that dark place I was in after your mother left."

Emily knew, from a place far, far away, that this was another type of blackmail but it was working, dammit. She didn't want Davy to leave Brook Village or for her dad to take to his room for months and months. A part of her wanted to scream *what about me?*

But her dad didn't care. The truth was that he didn't want the situation to change and she was the sacrificial goat. But, as much as she wanted to protest, he was right in one aspect: if she refused to marry Nico, Davy would suffer and, of all of them, he was utterly blameless.

Emily knew that she'd run out of choices so she forced the words through her tight throat. "Well, I guess I'm getting married."

Nico slowly climbed to his feet, a smile touching his thin lips. "Excellent." He leaned across Leonard's desk and picked up the photograph and copy of his press release. "Next stop, Vegas."

No, next stop...hell.

*Matt, Emily's left Falling Brook and has gone to Vegas, to get married. What the hell are you going to do about it?*

Matt exited the taxi and stepped onto the sidewalk, looking down the busy Vegas Strip, Gina's message bouncing around his head. In between hearing Em's desperate words—*will you help me?*—played over and over again, he kept recounting his less-than-wonderful confrontation with Emily's father hours before. It was a hell of way to start a relationship with your future father-in-law (if all went well) by yelling at him.

*Once I calmed down, I tried to call her back,* Leonard told him, wringing his hands, his eyes watery with tears. *I reacted badly—I was scared—and I want her to know that she mustn't marry Morris, that we'll fight this but she's not answering her phone.*

Matt climbed out of his taxi and glanced down at his phone, willing it to ring. But the only new message on his screen was one from Leonard, asking for an update. Matt frowned, feeling sick to his stomach. He didn't have an update for anyone; Emily's phone was off, as was Morris's, and he had no idea where to start looking for Emily in Vegas, heaving with tourists. Looking for her in a wedding chapel might yield some results but there were over fifty chapels in the city and he didn't know where to start.

Matt gripped the bridge of his nose between his thumb and index finger and, for the first time in forever, prayed that he would find Emily before she hitched herself to that POS. If he only found her after they were married, well, then he'd get his lawyers working on how to get the marriage annulled or a quickie divorce, but one thing he was crystal clear: Emily would not remain married to Morris.

He might not be able to save Arnott's reputation but he sure as hell could save Emily. If, after fighting back with an intense PR campaign and having one-on-one meetings with every client of Arnott's, they still lost the company and their reputation, he was wealthy enough to keep Davy in Brook Village and to support her dad.

He didn't care about the money: Emily was all that he could think about.

Matt still didn't know if she loved him—she'd asked for his help but hadn't said anything else—and, frankly, it didn't matter. He loved her; she was all that was important. Her happiness, her security, was his ultimate goal; she was his to protect. His heart was hers, whether she wanted it or not.

But to move on, he had to find her! And God, how was he going to do that in a city of more than three million, excluding the tourists?

Matt felt the vibration of his phone and had it to his ear before it could ring. "Vee, anything?"

"I went back through his expense reports from when he was at MJR, padded I'll have you know, and on them I found three payments to the same hotel. I also found more receipts from a bar within the hotel—it's all I could find."

It was, at least, a place to start. And hopefully Nico was a creature of habit and had returned to the hotel he was familiar with.

"I've sent you the address of the hotel," Vee told him and Matt heard the ping of an incoming message.

"Are there any wedding chapels close to the hotel?" Matt asked, opening her message. He quickly plugged the address into his mapping app and tried to get his bearings. He switched his phone on to loudspeaker as he squinted at the map. It wasn't, thank God, far away.

Matt heard Vee typing and held his breath, waiting for her answer. "Yeah, there's one, just around the corner from the entrance of the hotel."

Matt grinned. "Thanks, Vee, you are an angel."

"I am very much not but that description certainly fits Emily Arnott."

Matt turned around and started heading north, thinking it was quicker to walk than take a taxi in the heavily congested traffic. "She hates being called angelic and it really doesn't suit her. She's obstinate and feisty and too independent by half."

"But you still love her."

He did. "I do. And I always will."

"Then I suggest you run not walk, Matteo Velez."

That was a damn good idea. Matt tucked his phone into the back pocket of his pants and started to sprint, refusing to consider what he'd do if she wasn't in the chapel, if they weren't registered at the hotel.

He would find her because losing her wasn't an option.

Emily, dressed in a stupid white lace dress Nico insisted they buy at the hotel boutique, sat on the pew in the surprisingly pretty chapel and stared at her shaking hands. The synthetic smell wafting from the fake floral bouquets dotted around the chapel made her want to throw up and a headache threatened to split her head apart.

Could her day possibly get any worse?

Emily stared down at her hands, wishing she was carrying her phone instead of this stupid bunch of white roses. But Nico, jerk that he was, had confiscated her phone and she had no idea where it was. Besides, who should she call? She'd left a message with Matt but she doubted he'd gotten it; she assumed that he seldom checked his phone at work because he was busy running MJR Investing. Her dad? Well, he'd made it very clear that the company and its reputation, and his mental health, were more important than her happiness. Her mom? Funny.

Emily untied the ribbon wound around the stems of the bouquet, allowing the silk to flow between her fingers. It was a pretty bouquet but it represented fear, stress and anguish. Emily ran her finger over the soft petal of the center rose, before methodically stripping the rose of everything that made it luscious and lovely. With every petal that fell, Emily felt like she was losing a little bit of herself, and when the rose was denuded, she promised herself she'd never wear white again.

Ever.

God, what was she going to do? Emily allowed the last of the petals to flutter to the floor and, dropping the bouquet, wrapped her arms around her waist, gently rocking back and forth. She was so tired, emotionally whipped and, for the first time since she was fourteen, ready to give up.

Emily watched a tear plop onto the toe of her shoe, then another. She didn't bother trying to curtail her tears; she'd earned her right to bawl her eyes out.

Everything was ruined...

Emily heard the door to the chapel open and, not bothering to turn around, thought she should vacate the room; the happy couple walking in wouldn't want their marriage ceremony to be witnessed by a weepy woman with a mangled bouquet and a bleak outlook on marriage.

She wanted to leave, she did, but her legs and arms were heavy, and she was dreading the future. Emily slammed her eyes shut, thinking that she just wanted to stay here for the next few minutes, hours, maybe for the rest of her life.

"Okay, you're married. Don't panic—we can sort this out."

Emily opened her eyes to see Matt sitting down beside her on the pew, his normally olive skin pale in the subdued light of the chapel. Emily looked into his luscious eyes and read worry and concern within those dark depths.

Matt took her trembling hands and lifted both sets of knuckles to his lips. "I'll sort this out, Em, I will. You can ask for an annulment, file for divorce—I've already briefed my lawyers and they are waiting for your call."

Emily, not able to believe that he was here, stared at him, unable to get her brain to work. "Matt? How did you find me?"

"I'll explain later," Matt told her, looking around. "Where's the dipstick?"

"Uh..." Emily blinked, trying to get her brain to work, completely nonplussed by Matt's appearance. He looked a little sweaty, completely harassed and very stressed. To Emily, he'd never looked as gorgeous as he did right then.

"Em, concentrate. Where is Morris?" Matt demanded, giving her a little shake.

"Uh, up in the room," Emily replied, lifting her hand

to touch his cheek, needing to check that he wasn't a figment of her imagination. "You're really here."

"I'm really here." Matt turned his head to drop a kiss into her palm. "I know that you have had a completely shitty day, sweetheart, but we need to work out the quickest and easiest way to get you out of this marriage."

Emily blinked at him, his words not making sense. She looked down at her bare ring finger of her left hand just to check. "I didn't marry him, Matt."

Matt's mouth dropped open and he stared at her, his face reflecting his confusion. "What?"

Emily lifted her shoulders and dropped them again. "I couldn't do it. I mean, I was going to, up until the preacher started saying love and cherish and in sickness and in health and I just couldn't. I told Nico to take his chances, that I wasn't going to marry him. He lost his temper and started screaming and yelling and then the preacher person told him to leave." Emily bit her bottom lip. "He's probably up in the room, sending the photograph and his press release to news outlets."

A muscle started to tick in Matt's cheek and his eyes turned cold and hard. "How long ago did this happen?"

It felt like years had passed but it couldn't be any more than ten minutes, as Emily informed Matt. "What's the room number?" Matt demanded.

Emily told him and when Matt leaped to his feet, Emily knew that he was headed upstairs. While she appreciated his gesture, there was nothing he could do. Nico, because he was a self-serving, malicious bastard, would've already played his cards. Emily grabbed Matt's arm.

"It's too late. It's over and I have to live with the consequences. We'll be okay, if Arnott's is destroyed. I'll make a plan. I always do."

Matt stared down at her, shaking his head. "Yeah, that's the problem—it's always you trying to make it work, by yourself. I told you that I'd stand in your corner with you—when are you going to realize that you are no longer alone?"

"I'm not?" Emily asked, hope piercing holes in her despair.

Matt dropped a quick, hard kiss on her lips. "No, dammit, you're not. I'm going to go now but I want you to go back to the hotel and wait in the lobby for me—I promise I'll meet you there as soon as I can."

"But…where are you going?" Emily demanded as he started to walk away.

Matt turned and one corner of his mouth lifted. "I'm going to beat the crap out of Morris. I thought that was self-explanatory."

Emily watched Matt stride away and, after a minute of trying to make sense of the last five minutes, jumped up to follow him. She hadn't bailed out of marrying Morris, risking everything she loved to see Matt in jail on assault charges.

And if he did punch Nico, she'd punch him too because if Matt was going to jail, she'd be there beside him. She loved him and they were, apparently, a team. Where he went, so did she.

Those lawyers, she thought, hurrying to catch up to Matt, were going to be working overtime.

Nico opened the door to his room and Matt didn't hesitate, he just grabbed his shirt and flung Morris into the nearest wall. Matt watched as his head bounced off a picture frame and smiled with satisfaction. That had to have hurt.

Surprisingly, Morris came back swinging but Matt

ducked, plowed his fist into his sternum and followed
that up with another punch to his nose. Nico yelped, covered his face with his hands and Matt used the opportunity to pin Morris to the wall by placing his forearm
across his throat.

Nico's pale blue eyes bulged in fear. "What do you
want, Velez?"

"Many things, Nico, many things," Matt softly told
him, "but top of the list would be seeing your useless
ass in jail."

"That's not going to happen," Morris said, with as
much certainty as he could.

Matt pushed his arm harder into his throat. "Now, the
SEC might feel differently."

"You have no proof!"

Matt raised his eyebrows. "You wiped your desktop
before you left MJR but not before Vee did a backup. I
have a mile-long list of emails detailing your involve-
ment in insider trading."

Morris's white face turned whiter. He tried to struggle
but then he slumped and his knees gave out.

"Matt, please… Don't. Don't send me to jail."

Matt stepped away from him, disgusted by his whin-
ing.

"I haven't sent those photos yet, nobody else has seen
them but Emily and Leonard," Nico desperately added.

Matt stepped away from Nico and looked around the
room, spying Nico's laptop on the desk in the corner.

Matt hurried over to the computer, frowning when he
saw his email program. Matt quickly moved the mouse,
clicked on the Sent box and scanned the emails he'd recently sent. When he realized that Morris was telling the
truth and that nothing had been sent since last night and

specifically nothing about Emily, Matt finally pulled in a breath.

Matt glanced over at Nico, saw that he was still struggling for air, his shirt front nicely saturated with blood from his broken nose, and went back to the home screen. He looked for a program, opened it and pulled his phone from his back pocket.

"Vee, here's the number to remote access his laptop," Matt instructed, rattling off the number to give Vee complete access to Morris's computer. "Are you positive you can wipe it clean, including any cloud accounts?"

Matt heard and ignored Morris's mumbled protest and listened to his exceptional assistant instead. "Matteo, have some faith."

Matt stood back and watched as a ghost arrow floated over the screen and then the screen went black, to be replaced with code running across it. While he waited for Vee to run her magic, Matt calmly opened Nico's briefcase and went through his papers, removing anything with reference to Emily and Arnott's, including the hard copies of the photographs and the copy of the press release. He also grabbed Emily's cell phone and tucked it into the back pocket of his pants.

Matt looked over to Nico, who was leaning back against the wall. "Unless you want me to call Sokolov and tell him how you were using him to blackmail Emily, I suggest that you stand up and walk your pitiful ass out of this room. And if I ever see you in Falling Brook, if I even hear your name, I will find you and finish what I started. Got it?"

Nico nodded and stood up slowly, covering his nose with his hand. Matt walked over to him and, keeping the laptop and the papers he'd found, handed Nico his briefcase. "Get the hell out of here, Morris, you worm."

Nico walked slowly to the open door and when he reached it, Emily flew into the room, nearly knocking him over. She stopped in her tracks and grimaced. Matt caught her eye and frowned at her. "I thought I told you to wait downstairs in the lobby."

Emily narrowed her eyes at him. "I'm not good at listening to orders."

"I noticed." Matt jerked his head. "Come here, Em."

He didn't want her anywhere near Morris; the thought made him want to punch someone, preferably Morris, again. Emily inched her way around Nico and hurried across the room to him, then stepped into his open arms and snuggled in close.

"Close the door behind you, Morris," Matt said, and when the door clicked shut, Emily tipped her head up to look at him, her eyes filled with questions.

"Is it done?"

Matt looked down at the completely normal-looking screen and remembered that Vee was still on the other side of the open line. He lifted the receiver to his ear. "Are you finished?"

"Sure am," Vee replied. "I wiped out his cloud accounts. Please tell me you had the good sense to confiscate his laptop because nothing is ever completely erased."

"I did."

"Good boy," Vee replied, as if he wasn't in his thirties and she didn't work for him. "Now, sort out your personal life, Matteo."

"Yes, ma'am." Matt disconnected the call and when he looked down at his screen, he saw at least a dozen missed calls from Leonard. He showed Emily the screen and watched a frown appear between her eyes.

"He's worried sick," Matt explained. "He didn't mean to throw you to the wolves—he tried to call you back."

He saw a little of her anguish diminish but a lot of hurt remained. "I can't talk to him just yet, Matt. I need some time."

Matt nodded. "Let me quickly send him a text message so he can stop worrying."

Matt, his arms still around her, typed a quick text to her father before tossing the phone onto the sofa. Gathering her close, he held her tightly, resting his head on her bright hair, thankful to have her in his arms, safe and, yeah, unmarried.

It was over and they could relax.

Matt lifted his hands up to cradle her face and slowly lowered his mouth to hers.

So much had happened today that Emily wasn't sure whether she was coming or going, but Matt's hot kisses and his clever hands on her body she understood. Emily wound her arms around his back, holding on tight, content to follow his lead as he dropped lazy kisses on her lips and along her jaw.

Needing to feel his bare skin under her hands, to ground herself, Emily pulled his shirt out of the back of his pants and slid her hands up and under the fabric, digging her fingertips into his warm, masculine skin. Needing more, she lifted one hand, held his jaw and turned it back so that he could kiss her, giving her the long, deep and drugging kisses she so badly needed.

Nothing about today made sense but being in Matt's arms did.

"Let me love you, imp," Matt murmured the words against her lips. "Let me take you to bed and let me love you with nothing between us."

Em knew what he was saying, that this was a new start for both of them, a blank page. She wasn't Nico's fiancée and they didn't need to hide—they could be who they were, honestly and openly. She wanted that…no, she needed a new start, a fresh beginning.

Emily stepped back and held out her hand to Matt. When his fingers gripped hers, she tugged him toward the bedroom, then opened the door to a huge bed covered in white linen. Through the open drapes she had a view of downtown Las Vegas, but she wasn't interested in what lay outside her window—Matt held all her attention.

Standing next to the bed, Emily turned her back to Matt and pulled her hair off her shoulders. "Unzip me, please—I can't wait to get out of this dress."

Matt eased the zipper down and Emily released her breath when his lips kissed the bumps of her spine. She felt his hands on her shoulders, easing the dress down her arms until it pooled at her feet. Emily kicked it into the corner of the room with the toe of her white stiletto.

Emily tried to turn but his hands on her hips kept her facing forward, and he buried his face in her neck, breathing deeply. "Your scent drives me wild."

Emily smiled—his scent had always done the same to her, as she breathlessly told him.

"I should have taken you up on your offer six years ago, Em—we've wasted so much time."

This wasn't the time for talking, not yet. Right now, she just wanted to feel and to be with this amazing man. Emily spun around and placed her hands on his broad shoulders, looking up into his messy hair and still-shadowed eyes. "Later, we'll talk later. Right now I need you to love me. We need a new start, a fresh start."

Matt nodded before dropping his mouth to cover hers. Bending his knees, he wound his arms around the backs of her thighs and easily boosted her up his body, urging her to encircle his hips with her legs, allowing her shoes to drop to the floor. Emily, only dressed in her bra and panties, pushed her aching breasts into his chest. "You have too many clothes on, Matteo."

"Funny, I was just thinking the same thing about you," Matt replied, his free hand sliding behind her back, quickly unsnapping her bra. Emily leaned back in his arms and pulled the garment off, reveling in the passion in Matt's eyes as he stared down at her chest.

"You are indescribably beautiful, Emily Arnott."

Emily flushed, a little embarrassed, a lot turned on. Matt lifted one breast in his hand, testing her weight, his thumb sliding across her distended nipple. "Lean back," Matt told her and Emily didn't hesitate. She'd trusted him with her Morris situation and he, even though he'd thought they were over, had come to Vegas to help her. She trusted him implicitly, with her heart and her body.

Em leaned back and Matt dipped his head to pull her nipple into his mouth, to swipe his tongue over her, sending prickles of pleasure rocketing through her. He moved to her other breast and lathered it with love, and Emily couldn't keep her moans of encouragement to herself.

Matt lifted his head to look at her, his deep, dark eyes intense. "Don't be afraid to tell me what you like or don't like, imp."

"I really like that," Em told him.

Matt grinned and he suddenly looked ten years younger than he did in the chapel. "Good to know." Matt held her close and allowed her to slide down his body, groaning when the vee of her legs slid over his pipe-hard erection. Emily, because she could, placed the palm of her hand over the bulge in his pants, testing his length and his strength. The first time she saw him she'd noticed, as naive as she was, how masculine he was and if anything, the passing years had made him even more so. A small part of her was glad she hadn't known him at nearly twenty-one; she hadn't been enough of a woman for him then, but now she was.

Emily gently pushed Matt's hands off her and reached for the buttons of his shirt, before slowly sliding them open to reveal his chest. She pushed his shirt off his shoulders, eyeing the bulging muscles in his arms, his hard pecs and gorgeous, ridged stomach. "Love your body, Velez," Emily murmured.

"Love yours more," Matt replied, his voice hoarse. "Can I please touch you now?"

Emily shook her head, smiling. "Not just yet."

Reaching for the band of his pants, she popped open the button, worked his zipper down and pushed his pants down his hips, resting her head on his chest as she looked down at his very impressive package.

He wanted her; she could see it in his eyes, in his pants. Suddenly Emily couldn't wait any longer; she needed him, in her and now. Jerking her head up, she met Matt's eyes, hers gaze open and frank. "Can I ask you one favor?"

"Anything, imp, you know that."

"Can we just strip and can we climb onto that bed and can you drive away the bad memories and replace them with something wonderful and, well, good?"

Matt swiped his mouth across hers, once and then again. "Darling, don't you know that there's nothing I wouldn't do for you?"

Emily shimmied out of her panties and, after taking Matt's hands, placed them between her legs. He instinctively and immediately found her small bundle of pleasure, sending hot flashes through her. Hovering on the brink of orgasm, Emily felt Matt pull back and then he was lifting her onto the bed and a few seconds later, he was naked and looming over her, his shaft probing her entrance. Emily wound her legs around his hips and pushed up, sighing when he filled and then completed her.

Matt rocked once, then again and Emily shuddered, the cliff she was standing on falling away and crashing into the sea. She screamed as she plummeted, only to be lifted up again and hurtled toward the sun. Matt plunged within her, his hoarse voice urging her to come again and because he asked her to, she spasmed again as he emptied himself inside her.

As she floated back to reality, Matt heavy and damp as he lay on her, Em turned her head and smiled as a beam of sunlight hit the edge of their bed.

Everything, including sex, was better in the bright light of honesty and freedom.

# Eleven

Emily rolled over, slowly opened her eyes and blinked at the clock sitting on the bedside table. Night had fallen and she realized she'd been asleep for three, no, four hours. Rubbing her eyes, she slowly sat up and, feeling a cool breeze hit her skin, realized she was naked.

Emily pulled the bedcovers up to her chest and tucked them under her armpits. She slowly rubbed the bare skin on her ring finger, happy to be rid of the ostentatious, probably fake diamond.

She was also free of Nico; she wasn't in danger of losing Arnott's, and her life, as of this moment, was back to normal.

But what did normal mean? If it meant going back to a life without Matt in it, she'd pass, thank you very much.

She loved him…and not only because he'd broken Nico's nose. No, she loved him because, despite telling her that he wouldn't, he'd come running when she told him she needed him, when she'd asked him for his help. She loved him because he'd been there for her, because he stood in the ring with her, because he'd waded—figuratively and literally—into her fight.

But she also loved him because, well, he was Matt, and he deserved love. He was funny and caring and tough and determined and loyal and, yeah, sexy.

Matt walked into the room, sat on the bed beside her and tucked a long strand of hair behind her ear. "You're smiling," he commented, his thumb skating over her cheekbone.

Emily's lips twitched. "I was just thinking how sexy you are and how good you make me feel. You wore me out and I passed out."

"While I'm happy you think I'm a stud, I think the fact that you haven't been sleeping well for weeks might've contributed to you falling asleep on my chest." Matt pulled his thigh up on the bed and rested his hand on her knee. "How are you feeling, imp?"

Emily, losing herself in his deep, dark eyes, considered his question. "Good." The tips of her fingers drifted across the top of his hand. "Thank you for coming to help me—I'm so grateful you did."

"Sweetheart, when are you going to realize that there isn't anything I wouldn't do for you? You call and I come—that's the way it works, the way it will always work." He looked at his swollen knuckles and half smiled. "There isn't anyone I wouldn't fight, there's no limit on the amount of money I'll spend, the distance I'll travel… you can ask anything of me, Em."

Could she, really? He looked sincere, sounded genuine and if she didn't ask, she'd never know. "Can I ask you one more favor, Matteo?"

"Sure."

Emily sucked in a deep breath and with it, a blast of courage. "Do you think there's any chance of you standing in the ring with me for the rest of my life? Will you be my person, my rock, the one person I can rely on and trust?"

Matt stroked his hand down her messy hair. A smile danced across his lips. "Yes to all of the above."

Emily let out a shaky laugh. "You didn't even stop to think about that!"

Matt lifted one shoulder in a casual shrug. "I don't need to. I wanted you in my life six years ago but neither of us were ready for each other and when I saw you again, I knew I wanted you in my bed. It wasn't long before I knew I wanted you in my life, although I tried to fight that."

Matt looked down and for the first time she saw him stripped of his confidence. "There are things I've got to say to you, Em, and it's not easy…"

Emily immediately shook her head. "You don't need to. This is a new day and a new start."

Determination flooded Matt's face. "No, honey, we need to do this because if we don't, it'll always be there. We can't move forward until we address the past."

Emily took his hand and held it between her own two.

"I told you, briefly, that my parents were all about Juan. What I failed to mention was that they had absolutely no interest in me, at all."

Emily wanted to say something, anything, but knew he wouldn't appreciate pity and sympathy might cause him to shut down. So she gave him the best gift she could: silence and her complete attention.

"I tried to do everything he could, with no measure of success. No matter what I did, I couldn't be perfect and that was what Juan was, to them. My default mechanism was to compete and when I realized I couldn't, that he was way out of my league, I rebelled. My competitive streak came back when I went to college and realized I could actually win at some things. Then winning became an addiction."

"Okay…"

Matt looked down at their linked fingers. "At the same time I was trying to compete with Juan all I ever wanted was something, anything, from my parents. I gave up wishing for toys or new clothes or a bike for Christmas and started praying for the big things—a kind word, a hug, conversation, affection. But the more I wanted it, the more elusive their attention became. Eventually, I stopped hoping and decided that dreams were for fools and if I didn't want, I couldn't be disappointed."

Wow, their parents had really messed them up, in different but equally destructive ways. It was a minor miracle that both she and Matt were as normal as they were.

"With you it was the perfect storm."

Emily frowned. "Me?"

The corners of Matt's mouth lifted. "Six years ago, I saw you and I think, at the risk of sounding, cheesy, I recognized you."

"We'd never met before," Emily informed him, puzzled.

"I don't mean it like that—I recognized you as being… *mine*. For the first time since I was a kid, I wanted something, someone, so much that it scared me so I ran. Hard and fast."

Emily leaned forward and dropped a kiss on his bare shoulder and rested her forehead against his collarbone.

"Six years later and I see you again and you're engaged. Worse than that, you're engaged to a man I competed against. I told myself that I was interested in you because I wanted to take you away from him, because I was a competitive douche and I was. But, underneath the lies I was telling myself, because wanting and dreaming and being disappointed wasn't something I was prepared to feel again, I knew what I felt six years ago was still the truth."

Turning her face into Matt's neck, Emily kissed him, once, then again.

"You are what I want and what I need. You are my biggest dream, Emily. Winning has always been important to me, but, with you, I don't care if I don't get all that I want from you. I'll settle for what I can get. So yes, I'll stand in the ring with you."

Matt looked down, bit his lip and Emily was touched to see her alpha man looking vulnerable. And when he lifted his eyes back to hers, she saw the love within those depths, love he'd been needing to give someone and was prepared to offer her. "Do you think you could ever love me?" he asked.

She wouldn't make him beg; that wasn't fair. Nor would she tease him or make him wait. This was too important; he was *all* that was important. "But I do love you, Matt, intensely, crazily. You're..." Emily hesitated, looking for the words to make him understand.

"I'm what?"

"You're what I've been looking for since I was fourteen, the missing piece of my heart. Strong, steady, reliable and God knows, sexy."

The corners of Matt's mouth twitched but his eyes remained serious, as if needing more. She could give him more; there wasn't anything she'd hold back from him. "It feels like I've been on a long, lonely road and when I met you again, it felt like I'd arrived home. You're my home, Matt. You are what the rest of my life looks like."

Happiness replaced the apprehension in his eyes. Emily smoothed the wrinkles out of the sheet covering her knee. "I've been used to operating on my own—"

"And that changes today," Matt interrupted her.

Emily smiled at his very alpha-male, top-dog comment. "And it might take me a while to get used to that but I'll do everything I can to make us work."

Matt shook his head. "I'll make you happy. And I promise to protect you always. I'll make us work—I promise."

Emily slid her hand under his and pushed her fingers between his. "I don't know much about relationships but I'd like to think that, if we decide to jump in—"

"Oh, we're jumping in," Matt insisted.

Emily smiled. "—we go in knowing we're on an equal footing with both of us committed to making each other happy. We won't always both be strong at the same time, Matt—we'll take turns being strong for each other, protecting each other when the other feels weak."

Emily saw a hint of doubt on Matt's face and shook her head. "I've always been the strong one, for my dad and for Davy, but that doesn't mean that I now think that I have to be weak or want to be protected all the time. You've also been alone for a long time and the only way this can work is if we go forward as a team. Can we do that?"

Matt pushed his hand through his hair. "Yes, okay…" Matt hooked a finger in the edge of the blanket and tugged. "Can we stop talking now and can I show you how much I love you?"

"In a minute…" Emily looked out the window, wishing they didn't have to talk about Nico but knowing that they must. They needed to move, permanently, past him.

"Do you think he'll come back to Falling Brook?" Emily asked Matt.

"He'd be stupid if he does," Matt replied. "I sent a dossier to the SEC detailing some of his dodgy trades and I've no doubt that Morris will be investigated. I'm not sure if he'll face a criminal charge. You can also lay charges against him for blackmailing you. Morris is going to have a lot to deal with in the near future." He paused, then added, "And I threatened to tear him from limb to limb if he comes back."

"And the photograph of my dad and Sokolov?"

"I have the hard copies from his briefcase. I very much doubt Morris will resurrect his blackmail attempt. I think that ship has sailed."

Emily mulled over his words, agreeing he was right. "Talking about another aspect of the future, are you going to take the job offer from Black Crescent?"

Matt shook his head. "No, I'm not. I used them to twist my board's arm but also because I have this thing about winning, about wanting to be chosen. Knowing that you love me and that you have chosen me, that's all I need. Besides, Vee isn't keen to move from MJR to Black Crescent."

"And we can't upset Vee," Emily teased.

"Damn straight."

Matt leaned forward and nuzzled her cheek with his lips. "Can I propose a way forward, a plan of action?"

Emily's mouth twitched with amusement. "Certainly."

"I suggest that you drop the blankets and let me love you again. And after that, why don't we head out? I know a small, lovely restaurant and maybe, if I give you enough wine, I can talk you into marrying me, right now, here in Vegas. I can't wait to make you mine, imp," Matt added.

Emily's heart bounced off her ribcage before doing happy somersaults. She pretended to think, drawing out the anticipation. "I have another idea…why don't we make love, then eat, and then you can bring me back here and we can pretend we're on our honeymoon? Then, in a couple of months, we can make it official back home, with Davy and my dad and all our friends as witnesses." Emily wrinkled her nose. "But…"

Matt arched his eyebrows. "But?"

"But I still expect a kick-ass proposal and," she glared at the rumpled lace dress in the corner, "I absolutely refuse to wear white."

Matt grinned, his face open and full of joy. He tugged the bedcovers away and pulled her into his arms. "Now there's a deal I can't refuse. And, I didn't need to blackmail you into doing it."

Emily wound her arms around his neck and brushed his lips with hers. "And what would you have blackmailed me with, Velez?"

"I would've refused to sleep with you."

"Effective, I have to admit," Emily told him, laughing.

Matt captured her mouth in a long, sexy kiss before pulling back and looking in her eyes. "I know. Now, my delicious imp, be quiet and love me."

It was an order she was happy to obey. "I do—I will… forever."

Matt poured coffee into two mugs and looked out Emily's windows to the forest beyond her father's yard. They'd been bed hopping for three weeks—from her bed here to his bed in his house across town, and occasionally she stayed over in his apartment in Manhattan—and they were both sick of shuffling around.

Matt felt Fatty brush against his legs and leaned down to pick up Em's very rotund cat. "You weigh a ton, dude. I think we need to think about putting you on a diet."

Fatty responded to that suggestion by digging his claws into his arm. Matt rubbed his ears and head, eyeing the boxes scattered around Emily's apartment. Later on today, the movers would be coming to move all her stuff into the old farmhouse they'd purchased on the outskirts of town.

Their new property would be a fresh start, a place that was theirs as opposed to his or hers and he couldn't wait. And, best of all, Emily had finally decided on a wedding date, three months from now.

Matt, desperate to start a family, had asked her to go off the pill and she'd agreed so, with any luck, their firstborn would arrive before their first wedding anniversary. That might raise some eyebrows of the more conservative folk in town but Matt didn't care. He was, after all, the town rebel who'd corrupted their favorite good girl…

Besides, he'd just make them some more money and all sins would be forgiven. Matt grinned. If those same conservatives knew how his fiancée and the future mother of his children blew his mind last night, and this morning, they'd know exactly how bad his imp could be…

And he loved it. He loved her.

"Where's my coffee?"

Matt lowered Fatty to the floor and smiled at the grumpy words drifting down the short hallway to him. Em was not a morning person and only a cup of coffee, or a deep, drugging morning kiss, turned her grumpiness to gratitude.

God, he was lucky. He'd hit the jackpot; Emily, as beautiful on the inside as she was on the outside, loved him and never missed a chance to tell him how much. And, God, the sex just kept getting better and better. Matt glanced at his watch and decided they had enough time for shower sex before the movers arrived.

Matt picked up Em's coffee and was about to turn away when his electronic tablet beeped with a news alert. Swiping his finger across the screen, he stared down, unable to process the words…

"Vernon Lowell Lives! Black Crescent Fugitive Discovered in Remote Caribbean Location."

Well, now wasn't *that* interesting?

\* \* \* \* \*

# COMING SOON!

We really hope you enjoyed reading this book.
If you're looking for more romance, be sure to
head to the shops when new books are
available on

# Thursday 3rd
# September

To see which titles are coming soon, please visit
**millsandboon.co.uk/nextmonth**

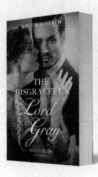

# MILLS & BOON

## THE HEART OF ROMANCE

## A ROMANCE FOR EVERY KIND OF READER

**MODERN**

Prepare to be swept off your feet by sophisticated, sexy and seductive heroes, in some of the world's most glamourous and romantic locations, where power and passion collide.
**8 stories per month.**

**HISTORICAL**

Escape with historical heroes from time gone by. Whether your passion is for wicked Regency Rakes, muscled Vikings or rugged Highlanders, awaken the romance of the past.
**6 stories per month.**

**MEDICAL**

Set your pulse racing with dedicated, delectable doctors in the high-pressure world of medicine, where emotions run high and passion, comfort and love are the best medicine.
**6 stories per month.**

**True Love**

Celebrate true love with tender stories of heartfelt romance, from the rush of falling in love to the joy a new baby can bring, and a focus on the emotional heart of a relationship.
**8 stories per month.**

**Desire**

Indulge in secrets and scandal, intense drama and plenty of sizzling hot action with powerful and passionate heroes who have it all: wealth, status, good looks…everything but the right woman.
**6 stories per month.**

**HEROES**

Experience all the excitement of a gripping thriller, with an intense romance at its heart. Resourceful, true-to-life women and strong, fearless men face danger and desire - a killer combination!
**8 stories per month.**

**DARE**

Sensual love stories featuring smart, sassy heroines you'd want as a best friend, and compelling intense heroes who are worthy of them.
**4 stories per month.**

To see which titles are coming soon, please visit

**millsandboon.co.uk/nextmonth**

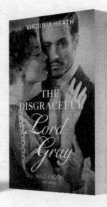

# MILLS & BOON

## MODERN

# Power and Passion

Prepare to be swept off your feet by sophisticated, sexy and seductive heroes, in some of the world's most glamourous and romantic locations, where power and passion collide.

# MILLS & BOON
*True Love*

## Romance from the Heart

Celebrate true love with tender stories of heartfelt romance, from the rush of falling in love to the joy a new baby can bring, and a focus on the emotional heart of a relationship.